W9-BWV-141

The game was up

There was no hope of storming past the guards to catch the capos by surprise. Bolan saw two gunners down, a third collapsing with his back against the wall, and he knew that it was time to make the three-way massacre a foursome.

He braced the mini-Uzi in a firm two-handed grip and held the trigger down. A mafioso crouching near the doorway took his first rounds, jerking sideways, squeezing off a last round as he went down in a heap. The dying reflex shot kneecapped a Rasta boy.

Breaking from the cover of their luggage cart, two "bellboys" raked the nearest Rasta gunners with a pair of submachine guns. They hadn't noticed Bolan yet, and that was their mistake.

Advancing with the mini-Uzi in his right hand, the Beretta 93-R in his left, Bolan riddled them with short precision bursts, dropping them in their tracks. He came down on his adversaries like the wrath of God. The surviving gunners started falling before they understood exactly what was happening. Blood fever, and the crash of doomsday thunder rang in Bolan's ears.

The Executioner was on a roll.

DON PENDLETON'S
MACK BOLAN.
VENDETTA

A GOLD EAGLE BOOK FROM
WORLDWIDE.

TORONTO • NEW YORK • LONDON
AMSTERDAM • PARIS • SYDNEY • HAMBURG
STOCKHOLM • ATHENS • TOKYO • MILAN
MADRID • WARSAW • BUDAPEST • AUCKLAND

If you purchased this book without a cover you should be aware that this book is stolen property. It was reported as "unsold and destroyed" to the publisher, and neither the author nor the publisher has received any payment for this "stripped book."

For the men and women of the FBI's National Center for Analysis of Violent Crime. Good hunting.

First edition April 1995

ISBN 0-373-61441-1

Special thanks and acknowledgment to
Mike Newton for his contribution to this work.

VENDETTA

Copyright © 1995 by Worldwide Library.

All rights reserved. Except for use in any review, the reproduction or utilization of this work in whole or in part in any form by any electronic, mechanical or other means, now known or hereafter invented, including xerography, photocopying and recording, or in any information storage or retrieval system, is forbidden without the written permission of the publisher, Worldwide Library, 225 Duncan Mill Road, Don Mills, Ontario, Canada M3B 3K9.

All characters in this book have no existence outside the imagination of the author and have no relation whatsoever to anyone bearing the same name or names. They are not even distantly inspired by any individual known or unknown to the author, and all incidents are pure invention.

® and TM are trademarks of the publisher. Trademarks indicated with ® are registered in the United States Patent and Trademark Office, the Canadian Trade Marks Office and in other countries.

Printed in U.S.A.

Big mouthfuls often choke.

—Italian proverb

This time, the savages have bitten off more than they can chew, and I mean to ram it down their throats until they choke on it. We're reserving judgment for dessert.

—Mack Bolan, "The Executioner"

The heroin, 120 pounds in all, was bagged and double-wrapped in plastic, covered by the new upholstery of a vintage Cadillac. The driver had precise instructions, knew which customs agent had been greased to let him pass without a serious inspection. No dogs around the Caddy, sniffing in the trunk and underneath the seats.

Smooth sailing.

It was normally a crapshoot, coming from Tijuana with a shipment, overland. The customs men were taught to watch for certain types—the biker look, for instance. Any kind of weird, stuck-in-the-sixties-looking hippy dinosaurs. In general, the young, black, Latin, seedy, greedy types. Of course they broke their patterns now and then, to roust a clean-cut middle-ager just for practice, stop a family on occasion, but it seldom paid.

For every shipment intercepted at the border, customs and the DEA had estimated publicly that ten slipped through. The truth was closer to a hundred, but you couldn't put those kinds of numbers on the air and still expect appropriations from the House Judiciary Committee in D.C. A ten-percent success rate in the so-called War on Drugs was standard, but a sorry one percent could get somebody canned, whole programs scuttled in the interest of economy.

Mack Bolan had the Caddy spotted when it cleared the customs checkpoint, rolling north on I-5, eight or nine miles into San Diego proper as the buzzard flies. He marked the tail car, right on time, four gunners waiting on the U.S. side to watch the driver, watch his back, watch everything.

Don Masciere did not like mistakes, especially when the price tag ran to double-digit millions. It was cheap insurance, shadowing the driver, making sure nobody ripped him off and that he did not go in business for himself.

Protection.

Bolan palmed the compact two-way radio and brought it to his lips.

"We're rolling."

His brother's voice came back from somewhere up ahead: "I'm set."

He got in line, an old van and a family sedan between his rental and the tail car. Bolan knew where they were going, so surveillance was not critical. With Johnny at the point, they had Masciere's skag and soldiers in a sandwich, ready to be toasted when the time was right.

But not just yet.

If Johnny's field intelligence was accurate, the heroin would not be stopping off in San Diego, even overnight. The mule had people waiting for him at De Anza Cove, on Mission Bay. A cabin cruiser fueled and ready for the short run north to Newport Beach. It was the kind of simple two-step that could shake a tail, confuse the narcs with footwork, if you didn't spring a leak along the way.

Unfortunately for Masciere, when his operation started leaking this time, it was not to the authorities. Indictments he could dodge, delay or beat with high-priced lawyers. But this time, he was dealing with the Executioner. No writs and no appeals.

The tail car was a Lincoln, weighted down with guns and muscle. It maintained a cautious distance from the Caddy, Bolan hanging back and giving both of them sufficient room to breathe. He left the two-way radio alone and trusted Johnny to perform the role they had rehearsed.

The kid had never let him down before.

Beside him, on the shotgun seat, a black Adidas gym bag held his hardware for the strike. An Uzi submachine gun with a folding metal stock. Spare magazines including Glaser safety slugs and armor-piercing rounds, in case it went down wrong. Two frag grenades, two smoke, and one white phosphorus, for starting fires that water would not drown.

The usual.

His backup weapon, worn in armpit leather, was a sleek Beretta 93-R autoloader featuring selective fire, a custom-fitted silencer, and an extended magazine containing twenty rounds of 9 mm parabellum hollowpoint ammunition. Johnny had selected hardware of his own, and Bolan reckoned they had arms enough between them to dispose of any challenge from the gunners in the tail car.

Still, you had to keep one eye out for the unexpected. It was only common sense.

Passing National City now, on his right, I-5 synonymous with the Montgomery Freeway, now. His targets stayed with the main flow of traffic, ignoring the cutoff for Wabash Boulevard, tracking toward San Diego International Airport and beyond, to Mission Bay.

On schedule, right.

Don Masciere was a stickler for punctuality.

It would never do for his soldiers to miss their own funeral.

JOHNNY GRAY, NÉ BOLAN, had been waiting for the Caddy three miles north of T.J., coming off Palm Avenue and running up beside his quarry, verifying face and vehicle before he pulled ahead and took the lead. A forward tail was risky if you didn't know exactly where your target planned on going. He could make an unexpected turn and throw you off, necessitate backtracking, maybe ditch you altogether if his luck was holding or he had a sense of being watched.

This time, however, it was cool. They had confirmed the *Scooby Doo,* moored at De Anza Cove and waiting for Don Masciere's shipment to arrive. Assuming that the mule was faithful, frightened of his boss, or both, they should expect no deviation in the route. The ambush site had been selected with an eye toward minimizing danger to civilians, but the young man knew enough to keep his eyes peeled.

Just in case.

One hundred and twenty pounds of skag, uncut, would net Masciere's Family close to twenty million dollars, free and clear, once it was stepped on, packaged, and delivered to the street. It was Masciere's fourth such shipment in as many months, the second Johnny Gray had been aware of since he tapped a brand-new source of information on the local Mafia. There had been no way for him to divert the first load, but a phone call to his brother put the wheels in motion for this afternoon's adventure.

It was still a spooky feeling, every time he worked with Mack this way. No problem with his conscience, but he always came back to the risks, comparing them with what he stood to gain. A combat veteran of Grenada and a practicing attorney, licensed in the states of California, Arizona and Nevada, Johnny Gray had gone for years without participating in his brother's one-man holy war. His involvement now was occasional at best, although he kept in touch with information on the local scene: street gangs and paramilitary groups, the Mafia and its competitors from China, Mexico, Colombia, Japan, Jamaica.

It was like a zoo, these days, in California and from coast to coast. The underworld bore small resemblance to the ironclad network that had dominated gambling, drugs and racketeering during Johnny's childhood years, around the time his family had been destroyed, propelling Mack into his long crusade. The old-line Mafia was still around, of course, but it was reeling from disastrous state and federal prosecutions, fighting for control of shrinking turf and markets with a growing list of black, Hispanic, Asian and Caribbean competitors. The free-for-all reminded Johnny of his reading on the Prohibition years, when ethnic gangs fought tooth and nail for bootleg territories, killing hundreds, maybe thousands, by the time a working syndicate was organized from coast to coast.

Déjà vu.

He had armed himself for the occasion with a SIG-Sauer P-229 semiauto pistol, chambered for the same .40 caliber Smith & Wesson cartridge recently adopted as standard issue for the FBI. It nestled in a holster under Johnny's left arm, extra magazines beneath his right. Beside him, covered by an open copy of the daily paper, lay a Heckler & Koch MP-5 submachine gun, compact enough to fire one-handed in a pinch, still capable of spitting out 9 mm parabellum shockers at a cyclic rate of 800 rounds per minute. Spare mags were underneath the paper, stacked three-deep.

He wondered what the gunners in the tail car would be packing. Side arms, definitely, each man with a pistol of his own. Beyond that, Johnny estimated they would lean toward shotguns, maybe something flashy in the SMG department. Rifles would be off the list, no point in stocking long-range weapons when the average urban firefight was conducted at a range of thirty feet or less. As for the mule, unless he violated his instructions from the men who hired him, he would be unarmed.

No problem, then.

Four shooters made it two for Johnny, two for Mack. Surprise and strategy should level out the odds. If nothing unexpected happened in the next ten minutes, it should be an easy strike.

Or, anyway, as easy as the killing ever got.

The government had taught him how, but it took something extra—something special—for a man to implement that training on his own home turf, without an enemy selected for him by the government. There were a few like that around, these days—his brother one of them—and Johnny Gray had taken his cue from the best.

Still, it was a peculiar way to live, habitually gearing up to fight or standing down. At least, in Johnny's case, he got a respite from the struggle in his daily life, pursuing justice through the courts and civic work, beside his covert efforts on behalf of Mack and Hal Brognola's team at Stony Man.

At least he had a life, of sorts.

As for his brother...

Skip it!

He was lapsing into territory best left unexplored, at least for now. The next step after introspection was analysis, repentance, all the crap that led a man around to wishing he could be "politically correct" and please the whole damned world at once.

No thanks.

Some problems cried out for immediate solutions, and The System had allowed itself to be co-opted by the heavies, bogged down in a bullshit blizzard that brought justice, for all intents and purposes, to a grinding halt. How many shipments would Masciere move from T.J. into California and beyond, before the courts could bring him down? Enough to flood the world, or only the United States?

Too much.

This afternoon, due process was taking a back seat to justice in the raw, with no holds barred.

He saw the warning signs for San Diego International and checked his wristwatch. Right on time. The river would be coming up, Old Town away on Johnny's right. Across the river, they would have only another two miles left to go.

And he would be there, waiting for them. Ready when the enemy arrived. Forget about the law books, for the moment.

He was rolling toward the court of last resort.

MOST PEOPLE CALLED Ignacio Saietta "Little Joe." It was a reference to his fondness—some might say obsession— with the game of craps, the double deuce that he had rolled repeatedly and run into a thousand dollars on the night he turned sixteen. That game was still remarked upon, from time to time, but lately, Little Joe was finding that he had to bring the subject up himself.

So much for glory days.

Nobody looking at Saietta would have guessed his nickname in a thousand years. He stood six-one and tipped the scale at some 280 pounds. It wasn't flab, but he was no devoted bodybuilder, either. Pumping iron, to Little Joe, was an activity reserved for wise guys when they went away on a vacation paid for by the state, and there was no young female flesh around to pump, instead.

He got his exercise in bed, and on the muscle errands that he ran for Don Masciere, keeping pimps and pushers in their rightful place. Today's job was a milk run, shadowing the mule and his consignment out of Baja. No one was supposed to know about the shipment, so it stood to reason there would be no problem. Little Joe knew they were checking on the driver, more than anything. Make sure he didn't have some kind of mental lapse and take off for the hills with Don Masciere's stash.

In that case, Little Joe would get some exercise.

He smiled at the thought, beady eyes focused on the Cadillac running four lengths ahead, already crossing the San Diego River.

"Close it up a little," he advised the driver. "We don't want to lose him."

"Think he's stupid, this one? He ain't goin' nowhere that he ain't supposed to go."

"Just close it up a little, like I said."

"Awright, already."

The mistakes began to happen when you took your work for granted. Little Joe had learned that coming up, the hard way. Getting cut so bad he nearly died, the time he let himself get cocky with a weasel half his size. It was three months before he had the strength to track the bastard down and teach him some respect.

"Here goes," the driver said as the mule got off I-5 on Clairemont, looping back around to catch East Mission Bay Drive. Another quarter mile or so, and it became North Mission Bay, the final loop around De Anza Cove, and they could ditch him there, once Little Joe was satisfied their man had made delivery to the *Scooby Doo*.

What kind of dipshit name was that to call a boat, for God's sake? Something from a kid's cartoon, the old man thinking it was funny. You could never tell about some people, what it took to put their wheels in motion. If Saietta had a boat, he would have called it—

Shit!

The year-old Buick seemed to come from nowhere, cutting right across the Caddy's path and stalling out. Some kind of fruitcake at the wheel . . . or, did he know what he was doing? Was it all a setup?

"Watch it, Tony!" Snapping at the wheelman now, Saietta reached for the stubby riot shotgun tucked beneath his seat.

Some guy unloading from the Buick on the far side, keeping it between him and the Caddy, leaning out across the hood and firing on the Caddy with a compact submachine gun.

The Lincoln shuddered to a halt, and Little Joe smelled burning rubber as he stepped out of the car. He put a live one in the shotgun's chamber with a sharp flick of his wrist, one-handed, scoping out the action from a distance, lining up his shot.

One guy, it shouldn't be so bad. The four of them could take him, easy.

Little Joe was smiling as he raised his weapon, taking aim.

MACK BOLAN CAME UP on the Lincoln's rear and cranked his steering wheel hard left, a broadside skid before he came to rest with twenty yards between his rental and Masciere's gunmen. One of them was staring at him, scrambling from the Lincoln, as he brought his Uzi out of the gym bag and left the vehicle.

So far, so good. His brother had the Caddy neutralized, and now they had the shooters in a box, nowhere for them to run. He caught the nearest of them just emerging from the Lincoln, looking angry and confused, a heavy automatic pistol in his hand. The mafioso had a glimpse of Bolan and the Uzi, blinked once in acknowledgement of death, and took a short burst in the chest to close the deal. He went down like a puppet with the strings cut, stretched out on the blacktop in a boneless sprawl.

And that left three, with everybody firing now. The mobsters knew they were surrounded, more or less, two of them pegging shots at Johnny and the Buick, while the third survivor turned on Bolan, hosing short bursts from an Ingram or a mini-Uzi. It was hard to tell, the way he waved it back and forth, as if intent on riddling the scenery, but Bolan's rental car was taking hits, along with trees and bushes and the nearby bay.

The guy was smart enough to stay inside the Lincoln, using it for cover, firing blind around the doorframe in the general direction of his target. Bolan chased him with a few rounds, knowing it was hopeless, and he finally reached back inside the car to snag his gym bag, fishing out a frag grenade.

A little something extra.

Bolan yanked the pin, wound up the pitch and let it fly. A practiced overhand delivery dropped the egg some ten or twelve feet from the Lincoln. It could roll from there, a wobbly path that put it just outside the open door as Bolan finished counting off five seconds.

The sound of an exploding hand grenade is never half as loud outdoors as in the confines of a building. Here, beneath the open sky, with water on his left, a golf course on his right, the blast seemed almost trivial.

Unless you found yourself on the receiving end.

A storm of shrapnel raked the Lincoln's flank, some of it whistling through the open doorway, rattling around inside the car. It may have found a human target, maybe not. In either case, his gunner made a hasty exit on the far side of the vehicle . . . directly into Bolan's line of fire.

A short burst from the Uzi caught him in the attitude of flight, one foot raised off the pavement, elbows cocked to run. The shooter had forgotten all about his urge to stand and fight for Don Masciere's load of poison. He was running for his life, but not quite fast enough.

Two down, and Johnny made it three a heartbeat later, triggering a burst that nailed the wheelman through the windshield, spattering the inside of the car with gray and crimson. That left one, a beefy gunner who was shouting curses, cranking hot rounds from a 12-gauge pump until the magazine ran dry.

He dropped the shotgun and broke from cover, digging underneath his jacket for a pistol. Bolan saw him coming, had him lined up in the Uzi's sights, when Johnny hit the runner with a short burst from behind. Momentum punched him into Bolan's line of fire, twin streams of parabellum manglers holding him erect for something like a second and a half, before they let it go and he slumped over on his face.

And that was all, except for scorching Don Masciere's smack.

Another trip to the Adidas bag, and Bolan had the thermite can. He walked around the Lincoln, watching fallen enemies for any sign of life, and came up on the Caddy from the driver's side. Behind the wheel, Masciere's mule was slumped against the door, stone dead. His body would not feel the flames; his soul, meanwhile, was not the Executioner's concern.

Bolan armed the grenade, fired a one-handed burst from his Uzi to clear the back window, driver's side, and dropped it on the seat. He had six seconds to retreat, felt Johnny watching as he turned back, jogging toward the rental. Not a word between them since the border. Nothing words could add to the experience.

He heard the muffled pop and whoosh of the incendiary bomb, glanced back in time to see the Cadillac erupt in white-hot flames. Johnny had the Buick rolling, safely out of range before the Caddy's gas tank blew, 120 pounds of killer smack reduced to ash.

It was a start.

The Masciere Family had not felt the last of Bolan's wrath, and they were not the only targets on his hit parade.

The Executioner was just getting started.

And it promised to be one hell of a ride.

CHAPTER ONE

It is a twenty-minute drive from Mission Bay to the Fort Rosecrans National Cemetery, on Point Loma, seven miles due south; but traffic slows you down along the way. I-5 runs to Rosecrans Avenue, past the San Diego Sports Arena, the U.S. Marine Corps recruit depot, and the U.S. Naval training center, picking up Cabrillo Memorial Drive for a run through the naval reservation that occupies most of Point Loma. Uniforms and military vehicles appear on every side, a portion of the Navy presence that makes San Diego Bay one of the largest military bases in the world.

The cemetery has an ocean view, the vast Pacific stretching off forever to the west. It is appropriate, somehow, for men who gave their lives on ships and islands stretching from Hawaii to Wake and Midway, the Gilberts and Solomons, New Guinea and the Philippines, the Mekong Delta and the South China Sea. Some of them were heroes, mostly warriors who answered the call of duty and paid with their lives resisting tyranny, defending liberty.

The cemetery is a small one, by comparison with Arlington, but there is nothing small about it when you stand among the graves and try to count the markers. Rows of crosses, Stars of David, simple headstones marching off in all directions, perfectly aligned, without the random, scattered look so common to civilian graveyards. Even in death, these men have dressed ranks and fallen in to be counted.

The Executioner felt comfortable here. He understood these martyrs, knew that most of them were less than perfect in their daily lives. There would be thieves and cowards and adulterers among them, some who let their buddies down and froze when they were needed most, but each and every one of them had paid the cover charge in blood. Through sacrifice, they had a retroactive pass to immortality, as long as anyone recalled their wars and lighted a candle to the memory of strong men armed.

The Executioner was buried in a grave resembling any one of these, back east. He had been dead for years, officially, but headlines and official records often lied. Reports of Bolan's death had been concocted to provide him with some combat stretch, a new direction in his one-man war, but he still felt a personal affinity for these men who had given up everything: their homes and loved ones, hopes and aspirations, life itself.

"He's late," said Johnny, glancing at his watch.

"He'll be here."

Bolan's tone was confident. It never crossed his mind that Leo Turrin would have flown across the continent from Washington to stand them up. In all the years that Leo and the Executioner had known each other, he had only missed a scheduled meeting when his life was on the line, and things had not progressed to that extent.

Not yet.

They kept on walking toward the ocean, Bolan reading markers, Johnny checking out the territory. Anxious.

It was understandable, of course. His call had opened up the San Diego game, and now that it was going national, the kid could feel it slipping through his fingers. How did you control a situation, when a whole new cast of players with their own agendas fell into your lap from out of nowhere?

Johnny knew the stakes were life and death before he laid his money down and drew his cards, but it was suddenly a very different game. Instead of playing on a local scale, with Don Masciere as the opposition, he was up against the syndicate at large, plus some of their most energetic and insidious competitors.

It was the kind of shift that gave a player pause, if he had any sense at all, and Bolan would have no complaints if Johnny wanted out. In fact, the more he thought about it, Bolan knew he would be tickled pink to have his brother safe at home.

He spotted Leo from a hundred yards away, a solitary figure moving toward them, one hand in a pocket, carrying a small bouquet of flowers in the other. Cover, just in case somebody spotted him and questioned his attraction to the boneyard.

"There."

"No backup," Johnny said, confirming it. "I should have waited at the car."

"It's fine," said Bolan. "We're alone."

And that was true enough, at least. A cool day on Point Loma, scudding clouds above their heads, and three men had the graveyard to themselves.

If Bolan stopped to think about it, Leo Turrin was his oldest living friend on earth. There was a moment, early in his private war against the predators, when he had almost killed this man, and Leo's wife had almost finished Bolan with a lucky pistol shot. They understood each other now, the years that Turrin had invested as an undercover agent in the Mafia, producing evidence and testimony that had sent at least a hundred men to federal prisons. They were older now, and things had changed. The world moved on.

These days, as Leonard Justice, Turrin mostly rode a desk in Washington, as Hal Brognola's number two on org-crime operations, with administrative duties in regard to Stony Man. He was legit, across the board, but Leo kept his finger on the pulse of the Italian syndicate and those outside the law who sought to cut themselves a piece of the illicit pie. Drug dealers, trigger men, white slavers, outlaw bikers who had traded in their hogs for limousines and three-piece suits.

The more things changed, the more they stayed the same.

Before he reached the brothers, Leo stooped and left his bouquet on a grave, selected totally at random. A remembrance for a stranger, as he greeted friends.

"You're looking good," he said to Bolan, offering a strong, dry handshake. "Johnny."

"Leo."

"I was checking out the P.D. band a little while ago," he told them, nodding vaguely toward the distant parking lot where he had left his car. "It sounds like Danny Dick just lost a bundle."

Daniel Masciere's nickname dated from his youth, when he was known for chasing anything in skirts and scoring with a regularity that made his homeboys envious. He barely had to try, these days—and there were rumors that the plumbing was defective, anyway—but nicknames had a way of hanging on, especially in the company of savages.

"The word was sixty keys," said Bolan. They were moving now, with Leo in the middle, shorter by a head than either one of his companions. "Four guns and a mule went down behind it, but he'll miss the money most."

"Damn right. That kind of payoff doesn't grow on trees."

"It grows in poppy fields," said Johnny, still alert for any sign of surveillance.

"Danny Dick's got all the problems he can handle, at the moment," Leo said. "His profit margin has been fading since the Triads started moving skag through Chinatown, and he's been hassling the Colombians for months to try and talk them down on wholesale prices for cocaine. They're running it behind his back, eliminating the middleman, and Danny's not amused. On top of that, he's got the FBI and IRS all over him for racketeering, tax evasion beefs, you name it. He could use a change of pace."

"That's why I'm here," said Bolan, smiling.

"Something tells me that you're not the answer to his prayers," the man from Washington replied. "On top of everything, he's got Barbados coming up. From what I hear, he can't decide which way to jump."

Barbados.

Bolan had been following the headlines, supplemented with reports he got from Stony Man. He knew the old-line Mafia was reeling after years of federal prosecutions coast to coast that had imprisoned ranking leaders, decimated Families, and left the way wide open for insurgents from left field. A recent FBI report on twenty-two Mafia fiefdoms across the United States had described half of the traditional Families as "near extinction" or "virtually nonexistent." Such former strongholds as New Orleans, Cleveland, Pittsburgh, Philadelphia, Saint Louis, San Francisco, Tucson and Tampa were all up for grabs, the time-honored underworld leadership packed off to prisons and boneyards, leaving chaos in their wake.

And chaos meant a power vacuum.

The time was ripe for a dynamic newcomer to make his play, gamble big on the national scene, with everything to win or lose. The membership of La Commissione was being whittled down by old age, homicide and prison sentences, its influence declining in direct proportion to the blows it suffered without hitting back. A change was desperately needed if the Mafia was going to survive.

Enter Julio DiBiase, forty-one, a New York up-and-comer in the old Gambino Family who had sweeping plans to remake La Cosa Nostra in his own image, establish a "new order" of organized crime in America with himself at the top of the pyramid. Based on the reports from Leo's eyes and ears inside, DiBiase's program included a complete top-to-bottom shakedown, cutting dead wood and promoting strong men with the nerve and initiative to follow his lead. He meant to consolidate surviving territories—in New York, Chicago, L.A., elsewhere—and begin to purge the ethnic gangs that had been cutting into Mafia preserves the past few years. Jamaicans, Cubans and Colombians. Vietnamese. The Chinese Triads. Yakuza from Tokyo.

The would-be Boss of Bosses clearly had his work cut out for him. Before he could begin to win back territory lost to outside enemies, he had to secure his own internal power base. Persuade the handful of surviving dons to cast their lots with him, accept his leadership—and, not so incidentally, to cut him in for a percentage of the action from their several Families, as partial payment for the miracles he promised.

It was not an easy sale, but DiBiase had been winning allies in the past eight months or so. On his home turf, in New York, Don Vincent Scarpato was firmly allied with DiBiase, while the Bronx's overlord, Don Carmine Tattaglia, was staunchly opposed. The remainder of New York's traditional five Families had been decapitated and dismembered in criminal court, troops drifting aimlessly, in search of leadership, some gravitating toward Tattaglia, while others went with DiBiase.

Chaos.

Next door, in New Jersey, Don Joseph Graziano was carefully neutral, sniffing the wind and waiting to see which way it was blowing before he committed himself to one side or the other. In spite of state and federal prosecutions, Don Graziano still had strength enough to hold his ground... unless a coalition was devised to root him out. In that case, Leo had predicted, Joe would find a tactful way to back the winning side.

Chicago's Don Ernesto Cavalcante was reported leaning toward support of DiBiase and his "new order," but Chicago would always be a wild card, unpredictable. The Windy City's Mafia had never quite decided whether it was more at home with East or West, in terms of national alliances. Its rugged independence dated back at least to Prohibition and the days of Scarface Al Capone. It would be one thing to seduce Don Cavalcante, something else entirely to invade and take his town by storm.

In Southern California, Daniel Masciere had adopted a cautious wait-and-see attitude toward DiBiase and friends, working overtime to secure his own turf before he chose sides. A man who could not deal from strength was dealt with as his enemies saw fit, and that inevitably meant that he was stripped of everything he had, reduced to puppet status, maybe dumped into a shallow, unmarked grave. Masciere meant to make the best deal that he could for San Diego, but he knew that he would have to deal with strength, and that meant fattening his war chest soon, by any means available.

Miami's Don Roman Graffia was allied with DiBiase in principle, to the extent that he had volunteered to host the first Mob summit meeting in a decade. Florida was hot at the moment, crawling with Feds, but Graffia had found a way around the problem, in his own inimitable style.

Barbados.

A short vacation in the Caribbean sunshine might be just what the doctor ordered, well away from prying eyes and U.S. jurisdiction. Graffia could book his guests with a variety of pseudonyms and supervise their routing through Miami, dodge the Feds as best he could and grease the cops in Bridgetown to insure a modicum of privacy. An independent state within the British Commonwealth, Barbados could not be manhandled by Justice or pressured to give up her guests. There was no foreign aid to be suspended, no real leverage for Washington at all.

The Executioner, however, was not bound by strictures of diplomacy.

He could pursue his enemies wherever they might try to hide, assuming he could track them down. With Leo's help and bulletins from Stony Man, he saw no problem where the tracking was concerned.

"What's new with DiBiase?" Bolan asked.

"He's hassling with Tattaglia," Leo told him, "getting ready for the summit. Calling in his markers where he can. He knows that California and New Jersey could go either way. Chicago, who knows what they're thinking? How it looks to me, he'd like to make a deal with Danny Dick and throw in with him on a move up north, to grab L.A. They're still screwed up, since Fortunato died last spring. Smart money says it wouldn't take that much for Masciere to consolidate, grab everything from Bakersfield to Baja, if he had a little help."

"And DiBiase's share?"

A shrug from Turrin. "Less than half would be an insult, right? I figure Danny Dick would need a watchdog to protect his interest. Maybe DiBiase sends him someone from the Apple. Call them partners, if you want. Masciere gets a huge shot in the arm, say half the state. He'll recognize the price tag, going in."

"It has to go both ways," said Bolan. "DiBiase won't be terribly impressed if he sees Masciere getting slapped around in public."

"Right." The man from Washington was nodding. "That's why I caught the red-eye out to have a chat before you started working east. We think that Southern California may be critical. It's still the richest market in the country—maybe in the world—and DiBiase can't afford to let it slide. If he has doubts about Masciere, that will mean dissension in the ranks before they hit Barbados. Anything that we can do to screw their summit up is money in the bank, as far as I'm concerned."

"They're scheduled to arrive in Bridgetown when?" asked Johnny.

"Saturday," said Leo. "You've got three days, free and clear."

"I'll need to make some stops along the way," said Bolan.

"That's affirmative. Hal thought you might. He's got your transport standing by. Across the water, there." As Leo spoke, he nodded to the east, toward Coronado and the North Island Naval Air Station. "Anytime you're ready, we can route you through."

"Two tickets," Johnny said. His tone was firm, and Bolan knew he was prepared to stand his ground.

"You've got a life, here," Bolan told his brother, trying anyway. "Your practice."

"Nothing that I can't postpone until next week," said Johnny. "This is where we started, Mack. I missed round one, okay? You had to do it on your own, but now I'm here. I'm ready, and I'm going."

There was no point arguing with Johnny. Short of having Leo find a way to lock him up for the duration, Bolan knew the kid would simply follow him by one means or another, maybe even stumble into danger that he might avoid if they were working as a team.

So be it.

Bolan nodded, saw relief in Johnny's face as he turned back to Leo. "We've got cleanup work to do with Masciere, first. From there, I'm looking at Chicago, New York City and Miami. Pit stops. Just enough to keep the heat on, make the natives restless going into Bridgetown."

Turrin knew what that meant, smiling ruefully. In different circumstances, he might have mustered up some sympathy for Bolan's opposition, knowing what lay in store for troops on the receiving end, but there was too much riding on the line this time. If DiBiase was allowed to make his program work, rejuvenate the wounded Mafia, it would cancel out years of effort by the federal government and various state prosecutors. It was even possible that DiBiase's version of the syndicate would come back larger, stronger than before.

"You've got carte blanche," he told the Executioner, "and that comes from the top. The A.G. wanted in—which means she had in mind to run the show—but Hal's been calling in his markers. If you pull it off, his stock goes up."

And Turrin did not have to talk about the flip side. If they blew it, dropped the ball somehow, it would be Hal Brognola taking heat from the congressional investigators, the attorney general breathing down his neck and using every trick at her disposal to retire him, maybe see him do some time, if possible.

Incentive, sure, but Turrin did not mention it, because he knew what failure meant to Bolan and his brother. An investigation was the least of Bolan's problems, if he fumbled in a play against the Mafia. In fact, if that should come to pass, the Executioner would have no problems left.

He would be dead—and Johnny with him, more than likely.

Failure had a price in combat, and the kind of struggle Bolan waged made no allowances for prisoners of war. If you were captured by the enemy, it simply meant a slow, protracted death, the kind that made a bullet through the heart or head seem merciful.

The Mafia had placed an open contract on Bolan's head years earlier, a million dollars to the fastest gun in town, and only the report of his destruction in New York, so long ago, had canceled out that threat. He had gone up against the Mob on more than one occasion, since his "death." None of those who knew that Bolan lived had managed to survive and spread the news.

So far.

This time around, his efforts would not be confined to local operations, one specific Family. With each new stop along the way, each strike against his enemies, the chances of exposure multiplied. He could disguise his hand, of course, avoid the trademark moves, but there was no denying that a move against the Mafia was personal.

And having Johnny on the team would only make it more so.

It felt like yesterday, the Bolan family slaughtered. Papa Sam besieged by debts, with brutal loan sharks on his back. A pistol in the house. The night Sam snapped, young Johnny had survived by pure, dumb luck. A message to the older son in Vietnam. Come home and put your people in the ground.

With anybody else, that would have been the end. But Mack "The Bastard" Bolan, a.k.a. The Executioner, had not been anybody else. He was a one-man army bent on vengeance, learning over time that hatred, in and of itself, was not enough to fuel a war machine. He came to recognize the broader problem of a syndicate that held the nation captive, but his understanding did not translate into paralyzing fear.

The rest, as someone said, was history.

And history, sometimes, had a way of coming full circle. When someone, anyone, refused to learn from their mistakes, they set themselves up for a fall. Sometimes, it was a gentle drop, with superficial bruises. In other cases, it was one hellacious roller coaster ride, filled with blood and pain.

On second thought, the man from Washington *did* feel a twinge of sympathy for Bolan's chosen targets. Not the capos or their trigger men, specifically. Those men had chosen a specific predatory life-style, loving the material rewards, accepting the potential risks. If they went down in flames, they had no one to blame for their dilemma but themselves.

But there were others to consider, when you thought about it. Wives and lovers, children, grandkids. Some of them were implicated in the sickness, equally corrupt, but Turrin knew from personal experience that others would be wholly ignorant of how their husbands-boyfriends-fathers earned their daily bread. A visit from the Executioner, to those, meant life turned upside down, forever changed.

But there was nothing to be done about them now.

Once war had been declared, the innocent and guilty took their lumps together. Standing back and doing nothing would not help the families of those savages intent on stealing or corrupting everything their greedy, grasping hands could reach. The broad needs of society at large outweighed the losses of a few.

"How long to wrap up here?" he asked, dismissing sympathy and concentrating on logistics.

"Three, four hours," Bolan said. A confirming nod from brother John. "We won't be going after Masciere, yet."

"Just shake him up before he flies? Okay, your call. You've got my number, when you're ready."

"Who's on tap?" asked Bolan.

"Are you kidding me? Grimaldi found out what was shaking, and we couldn't keep him out of it. Hal tried to put him on another job. I thought the guy was losing it."

Grimaldi. It was like the last piece of a puzzle falling into place.

"Okay, we'll call you," Bolan said. "It won't be long."

"Stay frosty," Leo cautioned, knowing that the words were wasted even as he spoke them. Bolan never shied away from risk, and asking him to take it easy was like trying to convince Madonna she should keep her clothes on in a public place.

"I'll see you," Bolan answered, and they shook hands all around. He stood and watched his old friend moving through the ranks of markers, back toward the cemetery parking lot.

His brother, Jack Grimaldi and the Mafia. Ingredients of an explosive recipe that never cooked the same way twice. One time, the product was delicious. Next time, it could blow up in your face.

No matter.

Bolan was committed to another taste.

For old times' sake.

CHAPTER TWO

Driving east along Balboa Avenue, toward Montgomery Field, Mack Bolan ran a short list of potential targets through his mind, examining each one in turn and ranking it according to significance, accessibility and the expense that Daniel Masciere would incur if it was damaged or destroyed.

There were enough prime targets in the San Diego area to keep him busy for a week, nonstop, but Bolan did not have a week to spare. He was not angling for a knockout punch against Masciere in his own backyard, but rather shooting for the syndicate itself, a few days down the road. His San Diego strike was calculated as an overture. The main event—his symphony of death—would build through several movements in Chicago, New York and Miami, to the ultimate crescendo in Barbados.

If he lived that long.

Survival meant he had to concentrate on one thing at a time, and right now, he was thinking skin.

Despite his rise to fame and fortune, of a sort, Masciere was, at heart, the same old Danny Dick of adolescence. Still a playboy, swinger, lady-killer—pick your tag of preference. Aside from drugs and gambling, which paid his bills, Masciere also bagged an estimated $15 million yearly out of vice: street girls and escort services, blue movies, with a side of kiddie porn and worse for certain "special" customers.

It would be early yet, for hookers, with the sun still out, but Bolan had a fix on one of Danny Dick's "movie studios." It was an old apartment complex, formally condemned, but well-placed bribes had kept the place from being leveled well beyond its demolition deadline. While it waited for the wrecking ball, some of the rooms were used as shooting sets for porno reels and videos. A sixty-minute film took maybe two, three hours to complete, with any luck. Put half a dozen crews on site, and you could grind out twenty flicks a day, assuming that your leading men could keep it up.

A hundred movies every week, on average, if they took the weekends off. Some screening publicly, from coast to coast, while others went direct to video and sold for anything from twenty-five to fifty dollars each. Big business, with a sweet fringe benefit. Masciere liked to help with the auditions, and he loved to watch.

No hope of catching Danny Dick this time, but that was not the plan. Bolan was simply rattling his cage...and planting seeds of doubt in Masciere's mind before the summit meeting in Barbados. Let him take some extra baggage on the trip: a little paranoia, something in the way of fear, suspicion toward his fellow dons.

The usual.

He spotted the apartment complex, fading stucco, Spanish tile on top, and made a drive-by, watching out for spotters. Nothing obvious. He parked downrange and walked back half a block. His jacket was unbuttoned, easy access to the sleek Beretta underneath his left arm and the Uzi riding on a swivel rig below his right. The extra magazines were tucked inside his belt. His pockets held incendiary sticks.

The Executioner was dressed to kill.

Three flats in use this afternoon, and no way for him to crash all three at once. The good news: no one watching the perimeter tried to stop him as he made his move. Apartment 7 had the blinds drawn, nowhere close to soundproof on the moans and groans.

Bolan kicked the door, went in behind his Uzi, the director asking "What the fuck?" before he glimpsed the submachine gun and went mute. The Uzi answered him, two short bursts from the hip. One dropped the camera from its tripod in a snarl of wasted film, the other stitching holes across the near end of a water bed at center stage.

Two naked women hastily dismounted from their leading man and scrambled toward the exit, no false modesty as they hit the parking lot and kept on going in their birthday suits. Crew members next, a swift kick for the cameraman that sent him sprawling on the threshold. Mr. Big was off the bed and groping for his boxers when the Executioner uncapped his first incendiary stick and let it fly.

"You're out of time," he snapped. "Haul ass."

Next door, Apartment 6, the gunshots had distracted them. Three women, this time, with assorted toys between them, sharing. Muscle waiting for him just inside the door, but this guy was a poser, used to slapping girls around. He mustered up sufficient guts to fire a curse at Bolan, instantly regretting it. The Uzi's muzzle punched incisors down his throat and left him mewling on his knees.

A stainless steel revolver on his hip, and Bolan yanked it, pumping all six rounds into the standing camera. No argument from cast and crew as he stood back and waved them toward the open door.

"Get moving. That's a wrap."

A stampede moved toward the parking lot, with Muscle Boy still groveling at Bolan's feet, blood drooling through the fingers of a hand cupped to his face. The fire stick, first, and then a strong hand gripped the slugger's jacket, hauling him outside and dumping him facedown on dusty asphalt.

Apartment 5 was empty when he got there, with the film crew and their actors—three black men, an Asian female—milling on the sidewalk, sniffing smoke and muttering among themselves. They gaped at Bolan, taking in the hardware and the way he handled Muscle Boy.

"What's going on?" the woman asked.

"Joint's closed, remodeling," the Executioner replied. He shouldered past her, edging back the others with a waggle of his SMG. Incendiary through the door and Bolan was back again to join them on the sidewalk. "Anybody wants to have a chat with cops and firemen, you should stick around. Otherwise..."

They were sprinting for cars before he could finish, leaving Bolan alone on the set. He moved along the sidewalk, finishing the ground floor. Short bursts through the windows, followed with incendiary sticks. Smoke billowed as Bolan tucked the SMG away and jogged back to his car, a half block down.

The place was cooking as he pulled out from the curb, flames licking in his rearview mirror. Cleansing fire.

It was a start.

The clock was running, but he was not finished yet.

THE UNLISTED NUMBER was a gift from one of Johnny's contacts in the local office of the DEA. Masciere's private line, screened through a houseman only when the don himself was unavailable, a hedge against important contacts falling through the cracks. If Danny Dick was home, he would be answering the call himself. A rule of thumb.

There was no reason to believe that he could trace the call, but stranger things had happened. With the new technology available, a little caution was the cheapest form of life insurance. Johnny chose a service station in the 3700 block of Clairemont Mesa Boulevard and dropped his quarter in the pay phone's slot. He attached a small disk to the mouthpiece that would frustrate any effort to produce a voiceprint from the call.

Three rings before a man answered. The voice was baritone, devoid of any noticeable accent.

"Yeah?"

"Too bad about that shipment for the *Scooby Doo,*" said Johnny.

Momentary silence on the other end, Masciere thinking fast. "Who is this?"

"Names don't matter, do they, Danny?"

"What the hell—"

"You're flying out tonight, I understand. Miami, is it?"

"Listen, I don't have the time—"

"To save your ass? Hey, that's too bad. I'll let you go, then. Maybe, if you make it back, you'll still have something left to call your own."

"Who is this?" Sounding nervous, now.

He could almost read the mafioso's thoughts, long-distance. Who would have his private number? Cops could get it, if they wanted to, no sweat. Who else? The mention of his latest shipment, up in smoke, would be the hook. Cops didn't operate that way, not even Feds. It was a shot from nowhere, costing Masciere megabucks. If he could get a line on those responsible...

"Let's say I sympathize with your position," Johnny told him. "Sitting on the fence, it's easy to get splinters in your ass."

"Is that supposed to tell me something?"

"Maybe. Is this line secure?"

More hesitation, Masciere running angles in his mind. "I should be asking you," the don replied.

"I'm not the heat," said Johnny, "but you figured that, already."

"If you say so."

"What if I should tell you I'm in town on business, from the East?"

"I guess I'd ask what kind of business you were in."

"The same as yours, Dan. This and that. I get around."

"Congratulations." The tone was sour, running into pissed.

"The last few days, I'm mostly traveling. Convention business. Ring a bell?"

"It might. Depends."

"Okay. I hear things, on the road. Some guys confide in me, you know? Some just forget I'm in the room."

"That's careless."

"What the hell, they trust me."

"Sounds like a mistake," Masciere said.

"That all depends. I'm loyal to people who deserve it."

"Meaning?"

"I was thinking, one good turn deserves another. I scratch your back, maybe someday I'll be itching. If you get my drift."

"I'm listening."

"That beef, this afternoon. I guess it crimped your action pretty good."

No answer from Masciere. He was not expecting one.

"I guess you'd like to square the books away on that," he said.

"Whatever's fair."

"Exactly. That's what I've been saying."

"You've got information for me, is that it?"

"I might. As far as what you do about it . . . well, that's up to you."

"I'd have to hear it, first."

"It could be someone thinks you're sitting on the fence too long, you know? They want to shake you up a little, get your full attention, make you think before you cast your vote, okay?"

"That doesn't tell me who," Masciere answered. Sounding hungry, now.

"Let's say New York."

"New York's a crowded town. I know a lot of people there."

"A couple, in particular?"

"Could be."

"They don't see eye to eye on certain things, these two guys. Am I right?"

"You're getting warm."

"You've got a choice to make before this weekend, one way or another."

"I've been working on it."

"Someone thinks you're taking too much time. He figures it should be an easy call. You're either for him . . . or you're not."

"I didn't catch the name," Masciere said.

"I didn't throw it. This is touchy stuff, you understand?"

"They're touching me already."

"Yeah, well, you've got insulation I don't have. I spill my guts on this, somebody else may want to spill them for me."

"You could use a friend."

"I could, at that." John smiled at his reflection in the glass.

"Ask anyone in town about how generous I am," Masciere said. "You need a reference? What?"

"I asked around already, or I never would have made this call."

"Okay then, what's the problem?"

Johnny hesitated, feigning indecision. Making Masciere wait until the mobster's tension fairly crackled on the line.

"I'll have to call you back," he said at last. "I want to double-check some things, make sure I've got it straight."

"Hang on, now—"

"I'll catch you in Miami," Johnny interrupted him. "Meantime, you want a word of sound advice, Don't trust New York."

He cradled the receiver, cutting off Masciere's protest in midsyllable. Let paranoia and his brother's rapid-fire attacks combine to do the rest. With any luck at all, before he caught his flight out to Miami, Danny Dick would be a nervous wreck.

Step one.

There was dissension in the ranks already, but it never hurt to stir things up a little, keep the pot boiling. Barbados was four days away, no telling how much damage Mack could do before the dons assembled for their summit in the sun.

It was a short walk to his car and four miles home, say twenty minutes, if he caught the lights. He was expecting news within the hour, possibly a call to help his brother out with one or two refinements on the San Diego sweep.

And after that, Chicago.

Johnny Gray was looking forward to it.

He was thinking he could use a change of scene.

THE NIGHTCLUB OCCUPIED a corner lot off Mission Boulevard, Pacific Beach. Ostensibly it was a place for dinner, drinks and dancing, with the emphasis on drinks. You needed special friends to hear about the back-room action, much less get a pass to see it for yourself.

Behind a sort of air lock, guarded by a no-neck "maîtred'" through business hours, Don Masciere had a midsize gambling casino, open to the affluent by invitation only. He was never short of customers, at that, with slot machines and craps, roulette, blackjack and poker tables, plus a sports book on the side. The gaming tables made more money for Masciere in an hour than the dining room and bar made all night long. A portion of his profits was channeled back to county vice detectives, making certain they were deaf and blind.

It was the kind of operation that police could easily ignore, victimless crime all the way, discreetly out of sight, nobody getting fleeced except the suckers who could easily afford it. Happy losers coming back for more. If Masciere comped a visiting high roller to a party girl from time to time, what of it? Once again, no one was being harmed.

The Executioner had learned to view things differently.

He knew that Masciere's profits from a "clean" pursuit like upscale gambling would be used to purchase heroin from Mexico or Thailand, cocaine from Colombia, and teenage prostitutes from anywhere young flesh was available. Another portion would be cycled through Masciere's loan sharks, using muscle to collect their vigorish when threats were not enough. Some thirty-odd percent would go for bribes—to legislators, judges and police—corrupting public servants who had sworn an oath to put Masciere and his kind away.

The well-dressed men and women who came in with cash to burn might not complain about the operation, but there would be victims, all the same. Drug addicts. Those they robbed and murdered in pursuit of cash. Young women brutally degraded and abused for the amusement of a paying customer. The debtors hounded, beaten, sometimes killed, when they could not produce Masciere's hundred-percent interest on outstanding loans. Civilians caught in the cross fire and slaughtered when contracts or drug deals went bad.

The list went on and on.

The club would not be open for another ninety minutes, but Masciere's manager was there ahead of time to supervise the kitchen staff and cleaning crew. He frowned at Bolan, following the stranger with his eyes, alarmed when Bolan passed without a word, continuing toward the rear and the back-room casino.

"Excuse me?"

Ignore it, making him run to catch up.

"Excuse me, sir?"

A glance then, heavy with disdain. "What is it?"

"May I help you?"

Bolan frowned. "I doubt it very much."

The manager was out in front of him before he reached the door. "I'm sorry, sir, but if you'd care to tell me what it is you want, perhaps . . ."

"Nobody called you?" Four parts disbelief, six parts suspicion in his tone.

"Regarding what?" The manager was baffled, hanging on to courtesy by sheer determination.

"Regarding the vice squad, you moron! Some kind of a screwup downtown, what they told me. They've laid on a raid for tonight, and we just got the word. I've got men coming out to remove the equipment, but Don Masciere sent me on ahead for the cash. Are you following this?"

He was following, sure, but belief was a whole separate thing. "I'm surprised no one called me," the manager said.

"You're surprised?" Bolan reaching for outrage. "I'm fucking *amazed* no one called you. When I report this, someone's going to *wish* he had called you, I guarantee that."

"I should check this," the manager said, glancing rapidly from Bolan to the nearest telephone and back again.

"You want to check it, be my guest. Save me the trouble of reporting Don Masciere's cousin for the fuckup. All I need from you would be the combination to the safe, before you get tied up with other things."

"The combination." Supercautious now.

"Right. As in, to open up the safe."

"I really ought to—"

"Tell Don Masciere that the cops got rich while you were thinking over what to do? Your call. I figure Cousin Vinnie gets his ass kicked, maybe sent back to his mother in New Jersey. You're not family, though, I guess."

"Well, no." Fear overriding caution, draining all the color from his face.

"Too bad."

Another heartbeat, and the crucial decision was made. "I don't want to waste any time."

"I'm with you."

He recognized the typical casino smell: cigar smoke, after-shave, perfume, an undertone of sweat and tension. Anywhere you went, from Monaco to Grand Bahama, Vegas or Atlantic City, upscale gambling houses always seemed to smell the same. It came together as a money smell, and it could jazz compulsive gamblers to the point that they lost all control.

For Bolan, there and then, it simply smelled like luck.

Good luck for him; the worst for Danny Dick.

He waited while the manager unlocked the safe and started hauling out the greenbacks, bundled by denominations. C-notes first, then fifties, twenties, tens, fives, singles. Bolan brought a king-size Hefty bag out of his pocket, whipped it open, shoveling the cash inside. When he was done, it weighed close to thirty pounds.

Around $300 to the ounce, if he was adding it correctly in his head.

Whatever, it would smart when Masciere heard the news.

"That's all of it," the manager informed him, smiling weakly as he dusted off his palms and closed the safe again.

"Appreciate your help," said Bolan, moving toward the exit with his trash bag full of treasure. "Let me put this in my car, real quick. The other boys should be here any second for the gear."

"Of course."

The manager was all accommodation, trained to serve and anxious to please. It would be some time yet before he understood how badly he had blown it. By the time he worked it out and came to grips with the catastrophe, it would be too late for the guy to save himself.

Tough luck.

You rolled the dice and took your chances, working for a man like Danny Dick Masciere. Anything could happen, when you started prowling on the wrong side of the law. Arrest, indictment, trial... or things the average flunky didn't like to think about, if he could help it. Things you saw in gangster movies.

Harsh reminders that shit always rolls downhill.

Outside, the afternoon was leaning into dusk, the shadows lengthening and taking on a deeper hue. He crossed the parking lot to reach his car, unlocked the trunk, and stowed the liberated cash inside. Whatever happened next, Masciere would be picking up at least a portion of the tab.

Poetic justice, right.

It would have pleased the Executioner to make a call, meet Jack Grimaldi at the air base, and forget about his brother's role in whatever was coming. Wednesday in Chicago. Thursday in Manhattan. Friday in Miami.

As for Saturday...

Too late.

He had agreed to Johnny coming on the sweep because the kid was smart enough to make his own decisions, sane enough to handle it, and skilled enough to be of real assistance when the chips were down. Still, Bolan knew that he would always worry where his brother was involved. The sole survivor of a family that started out with five and vanished when he wasn't looking. Vaporized.

He closed the door on memory and concentrated on his driving, working back toward Johnny's hideaway at Strongbase One. The kid had done a first-rate job at covering security, no doubt about it. None of it had come from law school, precious little from the Army Ranger training he had undergone before Grenada.

Maybe it was in the Bolan blood.

Would any of that blood be spilled, the next four days?

Perhaps, but there was no reward without some risk involved. This time around, the risks were multiplied by Johnny's presence on the firing line, but his abilities would also help to balance out the danger.

And this time, Bolan grudgingly admitted to himself, was personal.

Some missions—most, in fact—he treated as strategic exercises, calculating odds and angles of attack, assessing risk and gambling only when he saw no way around the numbers.

This time, though, he would be squaring off against the enemy who got him started on his everlasting war. The names and faces had been changed, of course, but nothing ever really changed about the Mafia. They learned a new technique from time to time—stole billions with computers, now, instead of the outmoded smash-and-grab—but they were all still savages at heart.

And he could hear those savage heartbeats echo in his dreams.

Before the week was out, he meant to remedy that situation, still as many of those hearts as he could reach.

It was a challenge he had set up for himself, and underneath the worry, having Johnny at his side felt right, somehow.

It felt like coming home.

CHAPTER THREE

The charter flight from San Diego was five minutes early, circling into its approach over Miami International Airport. In his window seat, Don Daniel Masciere watched the swamps give way to residential property, a cemetery and a golf course rubbing shoulders down below, a glimpse of Hialeah racetrack.

The Beechcraft 1900C airliner seated nineteen passengers, and every seat was filled as they approached the runway, Masciere's pilot throttling back on the twin 4,000 horsepower TBO Pratt & Whitney turboprops, reducing their speed into touchdown. Eighteen guns surrounding Masciere, and he still felt nervous, hating the fact that someone he had never seen could frighten him this way.

The major bonus of a private charter flight was relaxation of security around the airport. Passengers were boarded on the runway, well outside the terminal, without their luggage or their bodies being checked for weapons by a team of flabby rent-a-cops. Arriving in Miami, Masciere and his men would not be naked and defenseless when they hit the street. A lesser benefit of flying private was that passengers could smoke, unlike commercial airlines dominated by the pantywaists who called themselves "politically correct." No limit on the liquor, either, if you brought your own.

But, at the moment, Masciere was concerned primarily with guns.

From his recent experience in San Diego, he thought he might be needing some in Florida, perhaps across the water in Barbados. You could never tell, and one trait Danny Dick shared with the Boy Scouts was an urge to be prepared.

It had been crazy back in Dago, for the last few hours prior to takeoff. First, his brand-new load of skag from Mexico was ambushed, some two hundred yards from the delivery point, and seemingly reduced to ashes. Masciere was not positive about the last part yet, suspecting that the drugs might have been stolen, with the fire set as a ruse, but lab reports were coming from a contact at the sheriff's office that would tell him, one way or another.

Either way, it still came out that five good men were dead—well, four men and mule—with no clear leads on who had pulled the trigger. Make that plural, triggers, since a punk kid passing by had told police he saw four cars, with two men shooting up the others, one guy dropping something in the Cadillac that made the car go up in smoke.

And that had only been the start.

Another fire had blitzed his most productive porno studio, a short time later, and the witnesses his men had talked to all described one guy, a big, tough-looking bastard with an automatic weapon and some kind of flares that set the joint ablaze.

Coincidentally—or not—that gunner matched the physical description of the man who waltzed into Masciere's hottest night spot, gave the manager a line of bullshit, and walked out with close to half a million bucks from the casino safe.

The manager had gone to his reward. New job description for the careless bastard: try to count the fish in San Diego Bay, and take your time. Forever and a day.

For all Masciere knew, the raids might still be going on at home. No one had called him since the Beechcraft lifted off, but maybe they were frightened of his temper, scared that he would turn around, fly back and kick some ass among the home team if they didn't wrap things up.

Or, maybe, it was over.

No. Whatever this was all about, Masciere did not read it as a passing thing. Some suicidal cowboys might have grabbed his skag to try and sell it on their own if they lived long enough, but taking out his porno works and the casino was a different story. Someone with a hard-on for Masciere had begun to make his move in San Diego, and it was coming at the worst of all possible times.

Barbados.

He thought about the phone call he had taken from the so-called friend who wouldn't give his name. "Don't trust New York," he said, as if the guys back east were all one happy family, moving in the same direction. Masciere knew damned well that Carmine Tattaglia was bucking DiBiase and Scarpato on this whole "new order" business, and both sides had been lobbying for California's backing in the past few months. Which one of them would risk a war to put his side across the finish line?

Don't trust New York.

Well, that was easy, anyway. Considering the late events in Dago, Masciere wasn't trusting anybody but himself, his capos, and the button men he paid to risk their lives upon command.

For now, until he saw which way the wind was blowing in Miami, it would have to be enough.

The Beechcraft jolted into touchdown and began to taxi toward the terminal. Masciere tried to make himself relax as he unbuckled, soldiers moving in the aisle beside him, getting ready to deplane.

If there was trouble in Miami, it was someone else's problem...to a point. Don Graffia was in charge of preparations for the conference, but Masciere was not about to let his guard down, just because he found himself on foreign turf. He had not reached his present stage of life by being careless, and he would not live much longer, Masciere realized, if he allowed his enemies free rein to plot against him.

Stepping off the plane, he found three limos waiting for him, drivers standing by. Don Roman Graffia was stepping forward, open arms outstretched to give the boss of Southern California a tremendous bear hug. It was old-world bullshit, but Masciere took it in his stride.

"We heard about your troubles on the coast," said Graffia. "You have my word that no one's gonna bust your chops here in Miami."

"That's good news," said Masciere, putting on a smile he didn't feel. "You've got a nice town, here."

"The best," Don Graffia replied, already turning toward the second limousine in line. Masciere waved his soldiers toward the point and tail cars, following his host.

The air-conditioning inside the limo kissed his sweaty face, reminding Masciere that he was in Florida, bound for the tropics. He would have to face another kind of heat, the next few days, and that was fine. He didn't mind a little sun, as long as he was not afraid to show his face outside.

Relax, he told himself. You're here now. Let it go.

His second in command, back home, could deal with any problems he had left behind. Five days was not a lifetime, after all.

Or was it?

Listening to Roman Graffia with half his mind, a running promo for Miami and Barbados, Masciere knew that he would have to keep his guard up through the summit meeting and beyond. His fellow dons all had their eyes on San Diego and L.A. these days, hungry for a piece of the action in one of the few remaining viable territories.

But Daniel Masciere was not offering a slice to anyone outside his Family. Not today, not ever. If they wanted any part of his turf, they would have to come and take it, fight for every inch of ground and every dollar. That was final. If it meant a shooting war, then he was ready to defend himself.

And, in the meantime, he would have to watch his back.

The stranger's words came back to him again.

Don't trust New York.

JACK GRIMALDI'S CHOICE for the flight to Chicago was a Gates Learjet 24F, the custom six-seater with twin General Electric CJ610-6 turbojets, with a cruising speed in excess of 500 miles per hour at an altitude of 30,000 feet. He only had two passengers on this excursion, plus their baggage, running more toward military hardware than civilian gear.

Their liftoff from the North Island naval air station had been uneventful, covered by a need-to-know tag bounced from Washington to the commander of the post. A portion of the hardware came from Johnny Gray, the Strongbase stash, but most of it was Stony Man equipment, requisitioned by Brognola's team for situations such as this.

They were passing over Flagstaff, six miles up and streaking toward New Mexico, when Bolan left his window seat and settled in the cockpit, next to Jack.

"I didn't catch our ETA," he said.

Grimaldi checked his instruments and said, "We're scheduled into Glenview N.A.S. at 1930 hours. That's a few miles north, above Des Plaines and Skokie. We can chopper out of there or drive, whatever suits you."

"Hold the chopper," Bolan said. "We'll start on wheels."

"Okay by me."

Whenever Bolan flew this way, at twilight, he invariably felt like he was running from the darkness, chasing daylight to the edges of the earth. It never worked, of course. The darkness always found you. There was no place any man could hide for long.

"It's been a while," Grimaldi said, and Bolan knew he was not speaking strictly of their working as a team. There was a vague hint of nostalgia in the pilot's voice.

And it had been a while, indeed.

Grimaldi had been flying for the Mob when Bolan met him for the first time, commandeering Jack to fly him from Las Vegas down to the Caribbean. No reason to believe that Bolan would survive to see another day, much less that they would ever meet again, and yet, they had. A combat veteran of the Asian war that gave the Executioner his nickname, Jack was trading on his skill and his Italian heritage to turn some easy bucks when Bolan met him, and the rest was history. Grimaldi had decided on his own that it was time to change his life-style and allegiance. He had volunteered for Bolan's lonely war, and neither one of them was ever quite the same from that day forward.

Now, the specter of a resurgent Mafia brought them back together for another run against the odds. New names and faces, but the same old enemy. The same familiar stakes.

They would be playing this one out for life or death, as usual.

"I guess they briefed you at the Farm," said Bolan.

"Leo ran it down," Grimaldi said. "This DiBiase character's some piece of work."

"It sounds that way."

"You figure he can pull it off?"

"Somebody thinks so," Bolan answered, "or they wouldn't have us chasing him."

"You're going for divide and conquer, am I right?" the pilot asked.

"With all these players," Bolan told him, "it's the only way to go. They've got dissension in New York already, and the other Families have been choosing sides or trying not to, waiting for a winner."

"What's the program in Chicago?"

"Shake and bake," said Bolan. "Ernie Cavalcante's had it too damned easy for a while, and now he's leaning toward support of DiBiase. Leo tells me that Tommy La-Rocca's in town at the moment, trying to firm up support."

"Is that LaRocca, as in DiBiase's number two?"

"The very same."

"Why is it that I get this feeling Tommy won't enjoy his stay?" Grimaldi asked, a slow grin spreading on his face.

"You've always been a pessimist," said Bolan, smiling.

"I guess that's right."

"I'll need about twelve hours on the ground," said Bolan, "if we really want to shake them up."

"No problem," Jack replied. "I'm yours for the duration, and the only deadline I've heard mentioned is Barbados, Saturday."

"We'll be there," Bolan told his friend, but even as he spoke, it struck him that his words took much for granted.

Would they be there, four days down the road? No man was guaranteed a future, especially when he put himself in danger's way by force of habit. Bolan could be dead within an hour of arriving in Chicago, if he dropped his guard, and what would happen to the summit meeting then?

He knew that Jack and Johnny would proceed, with all the help available from Stony Man...but would it be enough?

If necessary, yes.

No man was truly indispensable, the Executioner decided. It was ego talking, when a soldier started thinking only he could do a certain job and keep a mission rolling on its course. Ego and wishful thinking.

Bolan did not want to lose it now, when he was up against the very enemy who got him started on his long crusade, back home in Massachusetts. He was too involved, had too much personal investment in the struggle, to let someone else take over for him now.

And that could be a danger, too, he realized. A soldier thinking with his heart too often put the brain on hold and lost it all as a result. It was a tested rule of thumb that anger kept men warm at night, but it could also get them burned in killing situations, when they needed icy logic standing in the place of rage. A warrior who subordinated strategy to raw sensation never lasted long.

Chicago was a stepping-stone, and nothing more. He had a mission in the Windy City, but his final goal lay elsewhere, days and miles away. There was a strong temptation to unleash himself on Cavalcante and the others, let his anger rip till there was nothing left, but that would doom his larger mission at the outset.

He was moving toward Barbados, and a clean sweep of the syndicate.

This time, the Executioner would not be satisfied with less than total victory.

And if he failed, what then?

Start over, if he could. If not, leave tracks for someone else to follow. Johnny. Leo Turrin. Anyone at all from Stony Man.

"I'm glad we're in on this together," Bolan said.

Grimaldi smiled at him and said, "Me, too."

"I've got some things to check with Johnny. Can I get you anything?"

Grimaldi shook his head and cocked a thumb at his thermos bottle, filled with strong, black coffee. "I'm all set," he said.

"Okay."

It was a short walk back to Johnny's seat, the younger Bolan staring into darkness from the window on his right. He glanced up as his brother took the seat across the aisle.

"I guess we're in it now," he said.

"No argument," said Bolan. "We were in it from the time you called about Masciere."

"Right."

"I meant to tell you, that was good intelligence about the Baja shipment."

Johnny shrugged. "I try to keep my sources current."

"Kurtzman tells me you've been feeding quite a bit of information to the Farm, these past few months."

"I pass on what I can. It comes and goes."

"We're in the majors, this time," Bolan told him. "Everybody and his cousin will be heading for Barbados."

Anyway, he thought, the ones who are alive come Saturday. As for the others . . .

"I can handle it," his brother said.

"I never doubted that."

"So, what's the problem?"

Bolan thought about it, finally shrugging. "Maybe it's the job," he said. "The two of us together. Jack and Leo. Hal directing, out of Wonderland."

He did not have to spell it out in any greater detail. They were launching a major blitz down memory lane.

"I'm squared away," said Johnny. "Honestly."

"Okay. We'd better talk specifics for Chicago, then. Our show is definitely on the road."

One stop behind them, four ahead, and each one a potential killer.

"What kind of weak points are we looking at with Cavalcante?"

"Pressure, paranoia," Bolan answered. "And he's power-hungry. As he goes with DiBiase, he'll be using the new order as a vehicle."

Johnny shook his head. "Whatever happened to honor among thieves?"

"It's highly overrated," Bolan said. "Assuming it exists."

"I'd hate to be the capo of Chicago, right this minute."

Confidence, thought Bolan. Fair enough. It couldn't hurt, as long as Johnny kept it on a short leash, going in.

"He's got some fight left in him yet."

"I'm counting on it," Johnny said. And smiled.

CHICAGO'S federal building fills a block between West Adams Street and Jackson Boulevard, a short walk south of Marshall Field. Grant Park is close enough to tempt employees for a lunchtime getaway on sunny days, and the Chicago River winds its way through downtown, six blocks to the west. In days gone by, a team of agents huddled there to plot the end of Scarface Al Capone. More recently, the FBI and IRS had spun their webs for thugs like Momo Giancana, Joe Aiuppa, Anthony Spilotro.

Leo Turrin knew his way around the complex from experience. His office was in Washington, D.C., but duties took him on the road from time to time. More often than his wife would like, in fact, but Leo didn't really mind. It made him feel that he was still a soldier in the trenches, rather than an officer with graying hair, deskbound and useless when the action started.

At the moment, he was running interference, serving as the pointman for a storm about to break across Chicago. Facing him across a spacious desk was George Krockover, special agent in charge of the FBI's Chicago field office. The expression on the G-man's face was grim, to say the least. His present attitude fell somewhere in the gap between suspicion and hostility.

"You're telling me that Washington is operating Cavalcante now, without assistance from the Bureau?"

"I believe I said we have a special task force covering his movement through the coming visit to Miami."

"I would have thought that something on that scale should come across my desk, through channels."

Leo wore his diplomatic smile. "The A.G. thought it might be better if we talked it over, one on one."

Krockover thought about that for a moment, visibly displeased. "Is that supposed to mean I've got a leak, for Christ's sake? Are you telling me the Outfit has been operating *me?*"

A twist, and Leo ran with it. "I wouldn't want to speculate, at this point," he replied. "My point is that we have a task force up and running. Cavalcante's movements are of interest only as they impact task force operations on a broader scale. You're with me, so far?"

Krockover was frowning, still considering the prospect of a leak. "I follow," he responded tersely.

"Very good. Now, for the next few hours—say, until this time tomorrow—I'll be supervising coverage of the local syndicate, across the board."

A flush of color stained the G-man's cheeks. "We have ongoing cases in the works," said Krockover. "Deep cover agents in the field."

"It might be wise for you to call them in," said Leo.

"Mr. Justice, I don't know how you do business back in Washington, but in Chicago—"

"You take orders from the top, like everybody else," said Leo. "Am I right, or am I right?"

"What's that supposed to mean?" asked Krockover. "I run this office. You're not even FBI, for God's sake. What's the nature of this task force?"

"That," said Leo, with another smile, "is need-to-know. You don't."

Krockover leaned across his desk, one big hand reaching for the telephone. "Is that a fact? You waltz in here and tell me that I'm sidelined in my own damned office? I think I should take this up with Washington."

"Your call," the man from Justice told him, "but before you make it, maybe you should read this."

Leo took a letter from the inside pocket of his coat and handed it across the desk. Krockover used a letter opener to slit the envelope, removed a single sheet of stationery and unfolded it. The color left his face abruptly as his eyes moved down the page.

"You recognize the signatures, I take it?"

"Yes." Almost a whisper.

"Sorry?"

"*Yes!*"

"That's the attorney general, your director and—"

"I see it!"

"Are we in agreement, then?"

"I follow orders, Mr. Justice. Always have. Agreement's something else."

"I'll settle for cooperation, then. If that's too much for you to swallow, I suggest you take a leave of absence, starting now."

"I'll do my job," Krockover said. "What is it that you want, exactly?"

"Breathing room. Withdraw surveillance on the Cavalcante operation as of now, this minute. Have your troops stand down and wait for further orders. I'll be handling the Outfit for the next few hours. If it goes to shit, I guarantee you won't get any on you."

"That's official?"

"As can be."

"In that case, I don't seem to have much choice."

"Consider it a paid vacation," Leo said. "And there's one other thing."

"Which is?"

"The substance of our conversation here today, and anything that follows from it, is entirely classified. No leaks of any kind will be permitted. Understood?"

"I hear you, Mr. Justice."

"There must be crime enough in town to keep you busy for the next twelve hours, right?"

"I wouldn't be surprised."

"Well, there you go."

"I'd hate to see this kind of thing become a habit," said Krockover.

"So would I," the man from Justice told him. "So would I."

CHAPTER FOUR

The van was federal issue, with civilian plates. The easy-off magnetic logo on its sides identified it as the property of Metzger Air-Conditioning, a nonexistent firm. The name tag on the driver's denim jumpsuit labeled him as "Jeff."

In fact, his name was Mack.

The Executioner was cruising, scoping out potential snipers' nests. The van rolled south on Oakley Boulevard, turned left on Taylor Street. At Bell and Taylor, Bolan found what he was looking for.

The block of condos rose eleven stories from the street, with balconies displaying flowerpots and stationary bicycles, a piece of abstract sculpture, dangling wind chimes. Tenants in the common hive, asserting individuality in subtle ways.

He parked behind the building, checked his watch, and estimated that most of those who lived in Bellglade Place would be at work by now. Midmorning in Chicago, with a layer of scudding clouds that cast a gray pall on the Windy City.

It had been a relatively uneventful night for Bolan and his two companions, settling in, arranging transportation south from Glenview N.A.S., and touching base with Leo Turrin at his Lake Shore Drive hotel. The Executioner had dined out on the town, picked off a Cavalcante numbers runner and a pimp to keep his hand in, but he had not felt like rushing it.

LaRocca, from Manhattan, would be meeting with Chicago's don this morning, dropping by the high-rise office block where Cavalcante rented space. West Ogden Avenue, four hundred yards and change from Bellglade Place.

The set was perfect.

Bolan locked the van and walked around in back to get his toolbox, feeling slightly awkward with the clipboard underneath his arm. The paperwork was window dressing, strictly bogus, but it looked real, and he trusted it to dazzle any opposition he encountered on his way up to the roof.

In fact, he had the service elevator to himself, got off on ten and climbed two flights of stairs to reach the roof, where air-conditioning compressors squatted in two north-south rows. A satellite dish was mounted at the southeast corner of the roof, and Bolan moved in that direction, kneeling in the shadow of the dish and opening his toolbox.

Underneath a lift-out tray of odds and ends, the Walther WA2000 sniper rifle lay in rubber-cushioned pockets, disassembled for an easy fit. It took him all of thirty seconds to complete assembly, snap the six-round magazine in place behind the pistol grip and stretch out prone behind the weapon, peering through its Schmidt & Bender telescopic sight.

The Walther was a marvel of technology, constructed in "bullpup" design, with the gas-operated bolt mechanism set behind the trigger group. The weapon's total length was thus reduced to 35.63 inches overall, the 26-inch barrel anchored fore and aft for stability, fluted longitudinally to minimize heat and vibration. A bipod braced the muzzle, letting Bolan track his target through the big ten-power scope.

Downrange, a window filled his vision. Bolan caught a secretary leaning forward, smiling at her boss and giving him a glimpse of cleavage with his morning memos. Tracking on, he left the strangers to it, stopping when he recognized Ernesto Cavalcante's profile through the scope.

The capo was alone, so far, still waiting for his scheduled visitor. The lag gave Bolan time to check out Cavalcante's office, noting photographs and plaques for "public service" on the walls. The mobster could have passed for a philanthropist, unless you know that he had been arrested twenty-seven times before the age of thirty, six of those arrests for questioning in unsolved homicides.

Don Cavalcante seldom had to answer questions from police these days, though he was constantly subjected to surveillance by the FBI and DEA, his business records studied by the IRS and ATF. His last indictment, on a charge of income tax evasion, was dismissed when two of his accountants stooped to falsifying records on their own, without Don Cavalcante's knowledge.

Right.

His visitor should be arriving anytime now, dropping by to pay respects and try to cinch the Windy City capo's personal support for Julio DiBiase's "new order" Mafia. Chicago would be critical to any national alliance, and Don Cavalcante knew that, going in. He could write his own ticket, where perqs were concerned. If Cavalcante turned against the DiBiase plan, it would be a major stumbling block, perhaps a fatal one.

He heard the numbers running in his head and dropped his sights to scan the street outside of Cavalcante's office building. He was just in time to see a white stretch limo pull up to the curb.

Show time.

"I'M THINKING this should take about an hour. Mike can take you shopping, if you want. Just get back here to pick me up by half past ten, all right?"

"Tell Mike," the foxy blonde replied. "He's driving."

"Right."

LaRocca waited for his driver to come back and get the door, delivering a set of rapid-fire instructions as he stepped out of the limo. The driver listened, nodded, filing all of it away.

To look at him, you wouldn't think that Mike could read, much less take orders and retain them in a photographic memory, but looks could be deceiving. There was muscle on him, sure, but he had brains, as well. At least enough to know which side his bread was buttered on, and what would happen if he dropped the ball with Tom La-Rocca counting on him.

Some guys believed in acting like a friend to their employees, but LaRocca took a different tack. He treated his subordinates with due respect, when they deserved it, but he also had a knack for kicking ass when they were out of line. On rare occasions, when a soldier really blew it, Tommy took the time to make a personal example for his troops.

It was a grave mistake to underestimate the power of selective terror.

"Half past ten," the driver echoed, walking Tommy to the curb.

LaRocca saw no major risk of danger in Chicago, while they were romancing Cavalcante, but defensive attitudes were only useful if you kept them up around the clock, in every situation.

It was a calculated show of trust that brought him out to meet Don Cavalcante on his own, without a bodyguard. Ernesto was the kind who liked to flex and throw his weight around, impressing visitors with his control of local politics, the unions, the police. It would have been an insult, bringing soldiers to his office, and the last thing LaRocca wanted to do, at the moment, was insult Don Ernesto.

Not when they needed his vote in Barbados so badly.

He breezed in through the lobby, past the information desk, and went directly to the elevator. Riding up to number nine, where Cavalcante had his office suite, LaRocca used the mirrored walls to check his hair, his suit, his smile.

The button men on nine were unobtrusive, but you couldn't miss them if you knew what you were looking for. Hard eyes and jackets tailored with a little extra room for hardware. Nothing that would stand out in a crowd, but if you tried to muscle past them, looking for the boss, you were inheriting a world of hurt.

LaRocca was expected, and the soldiers let him pass without a second glance, the visual I.D. enough to get him through. Ernesto's secretary was a redhead with a smile as big as all outdoors and curves that wouldn't quit. She wore a minidress that matched her bright green eyes; LaRocca wondered if she was hired for her dictation skills or as a visual aid.

She buzzed him through without a lot of chatter, strictly VIP. It was another ego stroke, like the hotel suite Cavalcante had provided free of charge, and Tommy knew enough to let it go without believing Don Ernesto was his new best friend. Respect was standard, even when the Families stood at arm's length from each other, on the verge of war. In present circumstances, Tommy thought, it could mean anything or nothing.

Cavalcante met him in the middle of a roomy office, polished hardwood on the walls, deep carpet underfoot. The giant windows faced across West Ogden Avenue, toward Western and the Eisenhower Expressway, traffic bustling in a steady stream. LaRocca knew three-quarters of the people out there would be feeding Cavalcante's bank account each day, in one way or another. If they laid out cash for hookers, drugs or bets; if they paid union dues or had their garbage picked up on the street; if they took taxi rides or played a jukebox; if they purchased any product hauled by one of half a dozen trucking firms Ernesto owned through front men, spanning half of Illinois.

Not bad.

That kind of wealth and power could be very useful, when it came to building up the syndicate. Or, it could be a fatal stumbling block, if Cavalcante sold his muscle to the other side.

LaRocca's mission was to see that didn't happen. He was authorized to promise Cavalcante damn near anything he wanted, in return for his support at the Barbados summit. After DiBiase's plan had carried by a comfortable majority, of course, there might be changes made.

"It's good to see you, Tommy." Cavalcante shook hands, retreating to a high-backed leather chair behind his massive desk. LaRocca found himself a chair and settled in.

"I hate to think how long it's been since I was in Chicago," Tommy said.

"You oughta come more often," Cavalcante said. "We'll make you feel at home."

"It's good of you to make the time for me, on such short notice."

"Hey, forget it. Friends are one thing. Business takes care of itself."

"You run a tight ship, Don Ernesto. Everybody says so."

"Ah." A little smile. It gave up nothing.

"Don Julio is looking forward to your meeting in Barbados."

"Fun and sun," Ernesto said, still smiling. "I can use a break."

"He's hoping that you haven't changed your mind about supporting his proposal."

"I've been thinking, Tommy. Maybe my support's worth more than what we talked about last time."

So, there it was. The squeeze. LaRocca nodded thoughtfully, prepared to give away the moon and stars with one hand, while the other snatched them back.

"What did you have in mind?" he asked.

THE EXECUTIONER was waiting when LaRocca entered Cavalcante's office, watching through the Schmidt & Bender telescopic sight. He had a live round in the Walther's firing chamber, five more in the magazine. A fresh clip waited at his elbow, just in case he needed more for emphasis.

The Walther WA2000 Bolan held was chambered for the .300 Winchester Magnum cartridge. His chosen loads for this mission were 150-grain Sierra GameKing bullets, with full-metal jackets to penetrate the heavy plate-glass windows of Ernesto Cavalcante's office. Departing the Walther's muzzle at a speed of 3,290 feet per second, with a muzzle energy of 3,605 foot-pounds, the Sierra boattails would still be traveling 2,068 feet per second at 400 yards, delivering 1,424 foot-pounds of destructive energy on impact.

More than ample for bringing down two-legged game.

He had to make allowances for the trajectory, at that range. With the Walther zeroed at 250 yards, his rounds would drop 15.4 inches at the 400 mark, requiring Bolan to adjust his sights accordingly. The wind was something else, six miles an hour off the lake, due east. One more adjustment as he settled in and started lining up his shot.

It would have been a relatively simple thing to kill Ernesto and his visitor, but that was not the plan. Eliminating Cavalcante now might cancel the Barbados summit, leaving DiBiase and his whole "new order" scam on hold, still viable, but waiting for a better time to strike. As for Chicago proper, clipping Ernie now would only mean promotion for his second in command, no great disruption for the Windy City syndicate at large.

Disruption was the key, this time around, and Bolan knew the rattling game by heart. A little nudge in one direction, then the other, keep the bastards guessing while they ran around in circles, chasing shadows. Make them doubt each other. Fray their nerves and keep the pressure on till something snapped. When they were at each other's throats, then it would be his time to close in for the kill.

LaRocca was a cool one, Bolan gave him that. Arriving in his chauffeured limousine, his blond companion leaning out to peck his cheek as Tommy left the vehicle. A glimpse of profile on the woman, nothing more, before LaRocca made his way inside and disappeared.

Now, Bolan had him back, sharp profile in the Schmidt & Bender's field of vision. A ten-power magnification, he might have been twenty feet away, instead of 400 yards. Bolan could not count the hairs inside his nose, but he could trim them with a bullet if he wanted.

Not yet.

Ernesto had cigars out, talking through a broad smile as he leaned across the desk and lighted LaRocca's. From a distance they were just two businessmen at work, with all the old-boy camaraderie you might expect. Nobody would have guessed, from looking at them, that their business ran toward multimillion-dollar theft, white slavery, narcotics trafficking and contract murder.

Between them, Bolan asked himself, how many addicts had they spawned? How many teenage girls and boys would sell themselves today, in New York and Chicago, with the money going back to these two men through pimps or pushers? How many families were pushed to the breaking point and beyond by debts incurred from gambling or desperate dealings with loan sharks? How many debtors would be muscled, tortured, even killed, before the sun went down again?

The bloody buck stopped here, on Cavalcante's desk . . . but not just yet.

This morning, Bolan was about to place a wake-up call.

He swept the office one more time, seeking a suitable target, and settled on Ernesto's telephone. The first round ought to do it, with allowances for windows, elevation and deflection by the glass, but Bolan would be satisfied with a near miss. He did not plan to write his name on Cavalcante's wall.

It was enough for now to make a shocking first impression on the mobster's mind.

As for LaRocca, he was sitting on a time bomb, and he didn't even know it yet. His master's dream was wobbling out of orbit, veering sharply toward the blazing sun of Bolan's wrath.

And Tommy was about to feel the heat.

The sniper took a deep breath, slowly released half of it and held the rest inside his lungs. He ignored the drop of perspiration rolling down his left cheek, toward his jawline, and tightened his index finger on the Walther's trigger.

"I'M THINKING when this deal goes through—*if* it goes through—Don Julio will be a very wealthy man." Ernesto spoke to Tommy through a blue cloud of cigar smoke, gesturing with manicured hands for emphasis. "He'll have more money coming in than he knows what to do with."

"Realignment should be good for all concerned," LaRocca answered.

"That's my point, exactly, Tommy. Here I sit, I'm nowhere near the Apple, but I've got this swing vote in my pocket. Funny how things work, you know? And I start thinking to myself, why should I vote to help New York get rich, when my reward is holding on to what I got already? That make sense to you?"

"It does," LaRocca said. "Self-interest makes the world go round. It's business, Don Ernesto."

"There you go. I knew you'd understand. So, what I'm thinking is, I'd like a healthy piece of what New York takes outa the Caribbean, once things get rolling. Big things planned down there, from what I hear."

"You heard it right," LaRocca said. "How healthy was that piece you had in mind?"

"Well, we're a modest operation here, compared to New York City. I've got—what?—300 made guys in my Family, altogether. Let's be reasonable, shall we? I'd say twenty-five percent."

"Of the Caribbean?"

"Hey, why split hairs? Say twenty-five percent of everything."

LaRocca almost laughed out loud, but he controlled it with an effort. DiBiase had been counting on some stiff demands from Cavalcante. Tommy's standing order was to pacify the capos, promise anything that nailed their votes down in Barbados. They could always deal with Don Ernesto later, take him out if necessary, and arrange for one of his more reasonable underlings to mount the throne.

"I'd have to ask Don Julio, of course..." LaRocca said.

"Of course."

"But I can tell you, on the record, that he highly values your support. I have no reason to believe he will reject your terms."

Ernesto's smile was threatening to split his skull from ear to ear, the big Havana clenched between his yellow teeth.

"You make me very happy, Tommy."

"That's what friends are for."

The crack came out of nowhere, sounding in LaRocca's left ear like the sound of ice that pings and echoes on a frozen lake in winter. He was turning toward the noise, his plastic smile already wilting, when the telephone on Cavalcante's desk exploded, flinging plastic shrapnel in his face.

Before LaRocca could react, a second crack was followed by the detonation of an ornate paperweight at Cavalcante's elbow. Don Ernesto toppled over backward in his chair, feet pointed toward the ceiling, shouting startled curses.

Tommy hit the floor and started wriggling toward the nearest filing cabinet. They were under fire, for Christ's sake, and it didn't take a mental prodigy to know the sniper had them spotted. It was dumb luck either one of them was still alive, and Tommy figured he could lose it in another heartbeat, if he did not find some solid cover.

There, behind the desk. He almost butted heads with Cavalcante, great minds with a single thought. They heard the third round strike somewhere above them, bringing down a couple of Ernesto's plaques and photographs.

LaRocca could not hear the rifle fire itself, which meant the shooter had a silencer, or he was way the hell across West Ogden Avenue, somewhere. A pro, for damned sure, shooting from that range.

But who?

The door burst open then, before LaRocca could begin to sort his mental list of enemies, much less consider who might have a grudge against Ernesto in the Windy City. Two of Cavalcante's soldiers barged into the office, waving pistols, searching for the source of all that racket.

"Boss," one of them blurted out, "are you—"

The sniper cut him off, a head shot, and LaRocca saw it happen. Right between the eyes, or close enough, and who could make that kind of shot from way the hell and gone across the avenue? He saw the gunner topple over backward, spraying crimson from a fist-size exit wound behind one ear, his buddy spattered with the leavings as he fell.

And that left one.

The second soldier lost it, firing three quick rounds in the direction of the window, as if their adversary was a window washer perching on the ledge outside. When the fifth round drilled his throat and nearly took his head off, Tommy knew that they were in the sights of a stone-cold murdering machine.

He could admire that in a man, but at the moment, his survival instinct tempered admiration with a healthy dose of fear.

Beyond the blood-flecked doorway, from the outer office, he could hear the foxy redhead screaming. She had caught a glimpse of Ernie's soldiers going down, and it was obviously more than she could handle. Angry voices, male, told Tommy reinforcements had arrived, but they were hanging back, none of them anxious to become statistics.

"Boss! Are you all right?"

"Fuck, no, I'm not all right!" Don Cavalcante answered in a raspy voice. "We're getting shot to hell in here!"

As if to prove his point, a sixth round cracked the plate-glass window, spinning another plaque to the carpet.

"Where's it coming from?" the soldier asked.

"I don't know where the fuck it's coming from," Ernesto snarled. "Across the street, somewhere. Get out there, will you? Do your fucking job!"

"Sure, boss. You bet."

A sound of running feet, retreating from the outer office. Tommy wondered how long it would take those boys to get downstairs, and what good it would do. It would require a miracle for them to spot the sniper from the sidewalk, much less run him down. He had to be at least 200 yards away, considering the angle. Maybe more. The bastard would be gone before they got a fix on his position, up in smoke.

If they were lucky.

Tommy lay behind the desk and waited, counting off the seconds since the last shot, hoping it was over. Don Ernesto lay beside him, cursing a blue streak and pounding the floor with his fist.

One minute.

Two.

"I think he's gone," LaRocca said, at last.

"Somebody fucked up bad," Ernesto muttered. "I can promise you, somebody's gonna rue the fucking day they pulled this shit on me."

I wonder, Tommy thought. And said: "I wouldn't be surprised."

CHAPTER FIVE

The multicolored flashing lights of emergency vehicles were visible from two blocks out, through traffic. Sharon Pryor leaned forward in the back seat of the limousine, confirming that the ambulance and squad cars were, in fact, lined up outside the high rise where Tommy was waiting.

Or was he?

Police cars meant trouble, of course, but it was the ambulance that concerned Sharon more. When they had closed the distance to a single block, she had no trouble making out the legend on the double doors in back: Cook County Coroner's Dept.

That was worse than trouble. It meant somebody was dead, and the police cars—nine of them, including two unmarked sedans that meant detectives on the scene—told Sharon that the death or deaths had not been natural.

She wondered whether Tommy would be coming out of Cavalcante's office on his own two feet, or on a stretcher, zipped inside a rubber body bag. The thought disturbed her, made her wonder if her time with Tommy had been wasted, after all.

The business he was in, he made new enemies without half trying. New York was teeming with competitors, inside the Family and beyond. There had not been a shooting war in some time now, but it would only take a spark, she realized, to set the whole thing off.

Of course, this was Chicago, and it stood to reason that Ernesto would have problems of his own. She had no reason to suppose that Tommy was the target, if there had been an attack, but the timing was suspicious, all the same.

"I'd better check this out," said Mike, behind the wheel. His dark eyes were reflected in the rearview mirror, pinning hers. Expecting what? Hysteria? A feminine display of anguish?

Sharon kept him waiting for it, nodding in response to his announcement. "Yes," she said, "I think you should."

The answer seemed to puzzle Mike, as if he were expecting her to scream and wail, instead of speaking normally. "I'll have to park around the corner," he informed her, turning on the blinker as he spoke.

They sat and waited for a truck to clear the intersection, followed by a van that turned the same way they were going. Mike was looking for a place against the curb on Leavitt, mouthing curses as he came up empty. Coming up immediately on his right, a high-rise public parking lot. Reluctantly he pulled in, took his ticket, and began the zigzag climb that took them to the upper level, room enough to leave the white stretch limo with a clear view of the city on all sides.

"You'd better wait here, ma'am."

"I guess that's right," she said, trying hard to keep the sarcasm out of her voice. If Mike detected any of it, he was too distracted to respond.

"I won't be long."

"Whatever. I'll be here," she said.

And it was not like Sharon Pryor had anywhere to go. Not in Chicago, where her only function was as fancy window-dressing for LaRocca on his little business trip. She was along to stroke his ego, and some other things besides, but she had no friends of her own residing in the

Windy City. Damned few in New York, when it came down to cases.

She would wait, and keep her fingers crossed that Tommy was alive. It wouldn't be so bad if he was wounded, shake him up a little, but she did not want him dead. Not yet, before the meeting in Barbados. She had worked too hard, endured too much, to see it blown away like this before the main event.

If he was dead, it meant that her part in the game was finished. She was sidelined, benched, removed from play. It galled her, even thinking of it, but she knew that there was nothing she could do to change what might have happened in her absence.

Shopping, Jesus.

It was Tommy's natural reaction. Send the little woman out to spend some money, while the boys talked business. S.O.P. for gangsters, who were basically all chauvinists at heart. She hated all that macho bullshit, one more reason why she hoped that Tommy was alive and well.

It would be fun to see his face and hear him squealing when she took him down.

She didn't see Mike coming, nearly jumped out of her skin as he slid in behind the wheel. It struck her that he must have been some kind of track star, getting there and back again in—what, two minutes flat?

And then she saw it wasn't Mike at all.

The stranger turned and smiled at Sharon from the driver's seat. She didn't recognize him from New York, the gang that hung around with Julio and Tommy.

Great.

Her snub-nosed .38 was in Manhattan, waiting for her to return. She was unarmed, but not defenseless. If he tried to come across the seat and take her, he would have his hands full, damn it.

"This is a mistake," she told him, trying to sound casual about it. "If you knew who you were dealing with—"

"LaRocca, Thomas J.," the stranger said. "That makes you Sharon Pryor."

Oh, shit.

Her real name, just like that. No reference to "Parnell," the handle she was using in New York.

"Who are you?"

"Possibly a friend," he said, and turned the key that Mike had left behind. The limo's engine came to life.

Before they pulled away, the stranger turned to her again, still smiling as he told her, "Leonard Justice says hello."

ERNESTO CAVALCANTE had no patience for police. They had harassed him through his teenage years, kept after him while he was coming up inside the Family, and now that he was paying half the goddamned force to let him have some peace and quiet, here they were again, back in his face.

Of course, he understood they had to ask about the shooting. That was business. Two men dead, their uniforms still looking for the sniper's roost, he had to figure there would be some questions. What Ernesto didn't like was sitting still and wasting time with cops, when he could just as well have been out hunting for the gunman on his own.

It was ridiculous to think the cops could track his adversary down. How many gangland murders in Chicago during Cavalcante's lifetime? Hundreds, anyway, and the police had yet to nail their first conviction on a Mob-related contract. They were simply going through the motions for the media, and that meant wasted time.

"I'm telling you, I didn't see the guy, all right? I didn't *hear* the shots. I heard the friggin' *bullets* when they came in through my window. Are we clear on that?"

The homicide detectives were a Mutt-and-Jeff team, an Italian and a Jew. Their suits were off the rack and out of style, unbuttoned jackets showing badges fastened to their belts, but there was small chance anyone might otherwise mistake them for civilians. Jesus, he could smell them coming halfway from the elevator, with that air that always seemed to follow plainclothes cops.

"It was a rifle, then," the short Italian said, as if he'd made some marvelous discovery.

"You ever seen a pistol shoots that far?" Ernesto asked him, pouring on the sarcasm.

"We'll need a list of enemies," the tall Jew chimed in.

"What enemies?" The capo feigned confusion. "I don't got an enemy on earth. I'm just a simple businessman."

"Somebody tried to shoot you, Ernie." The Italian cracking wise, insulting him with the first-name familiarity. "I'm guessing now, but that don't sound like he was being friendly."

"Hey, they teach you jokes like that in the police academy? I oughta get some money back on all the tax I pay, if you're the best the city's got to offer."

"We don't handle taxes, Ernie. That's the IRS. You've heard of them, I guess."

"It rings a bell."

"So you were sitting here, just talking business with your buddy from New York," the Jew put in, "when someone started blasting at you, out of nowhere?"

"That's exactly right," said Cavalcante, scowling at the officers.

"What kind of business would that be, exactly?"

"Mine," the capo told him, glaring daggers. "What I talk about with my associates is no concern of yours at homicide. In case you missed the job description, you're supposed to catch the piece of shit who killed my boys."

"We're working on it, Ernie," said the Italian. "I suppose your *boys* had paper for the side arms they were carrying?"

"They're licensed bodyguards. Damn right they got the permits."

"Not much good, though, were they? I don't think you got your money's worth."

"You come up here to bust my chops, or catch a killer?" Cavalcante asked.

"We're working on it, Ernie. Job like this, it takes a little time."

"I guess that's how you run up such a great solution rate?"

Both of them glared at him now, with angry color in their cheeks.

"We do all right," the Jew informed him, "when it isn't wise guys popping one another."

"Yeah? Why don't you try and sell that over at Cabrini Green? You're doin' *real* good over there, I understand. And what about that psycho who's been cutting up the girls in Douglas Park? You got a name for that bum yet, or are you *working* on it?"

"Listen, you—"

The short *paisan* was getting pissed off, going for it, but his partner held him back.

"I take it, Mr. Cavalcante, that there's nothing you can tell us that might aid in our investigation of this shooting?"

"That's what I've been telling you the past half hour."

"And you won't mind if we have a word with your associate, Mr. LaRocca, is it? From New York?"

"Hell, no. He saw the same thing I did, which was nothing."

"If you think of anything..."

"I'm thinking I should call my alderman and shake things up downtown," said Cavalcante. "Maybe put the doughnut shops off-limits till you catch this crazy bastard."

He felt better as they left him, moving on to hassle Tommy for a while. LaRocca knew exactly how to deal with cops, the same as Cavalcante did. It was a talent you developed early, on the streets. Now all he had to do was wait for the police to leave, and hope that it was not too late to trace the gunner who had tried to take him down.

Or was the bastard shooting at LaRocca?

Anything was possible, these days, and Cavalcante knew that it would be a fatal error to ignore one angle of investigation for another. He would check them all and see what he could see.

The phone was ringing on his secretary's desk when he walked out there, but she wasn't at her post. Still in the little-girl's room, he decided, throwing up her breakfast.

Cavalcante got it on the fourth ring. "Yeah?"

"Ernesto?"

"Yeah, who's that?"

"A friend, with some advice. Don't trust New York."

"Hey, what the hell—"

But he was talking to himself, the dial tone buzzing in his ear like some demented insect. Cavalcante cursed and cradled the receiver.

Christ, what next?

Don't trust New York.

Well, that was good advice, at least. From this day forward, Don Ernesto wasn't trusting anybody.

"YOU'RE WITH LEONARD?"

They were driving west on Roosevelt, approaching Ashland Avenue, when Sharon Pryor spoke. Her eyes were cautious in the rearview mirror, watching Bolan, taking stock.

"We work together, now and then. Right now we're working on Barbados."

"Really."

It was understandable that she would doubt him, in the circumstances. Giving anything away was tantamount to suicide, and Bolan knew that he would have to draw the lady out.

"He briefed me on your mission. It takes some nerve to work LaRocca. You've been feeding back some good intelligence."

The lady Fed went pale. "I don't know what you mean," she said.

"Relax. I'm not with DiBiase, Sharon. If I were, you never would have left New York alive, last night."

"Who are you, then?"

"The name's Belasko. You can call me Mike. I lend a hand sometimes when Leo has a special problem. Like Barbados."

"What about Barbados?"

"How it looks, right now, LaRocca's boss may have the votes he needs to make his program fly. I'm turning up the heat to see what happens."

Recognition in the blue eyes, now. "What happened back there, at Ernesto's office?"

"Nothing much. A couple of his button men got careless, playing with their guns."

"And Tommy?"

"He's all right," said Bolan, "but I wouldn't want to check his shorts, right now."

She laughed at that, recovering an instant later. "And Ernesto?"

"Fighting mad, would be my guess. A little less inclined to follow DiBiase's lead."

"So, you just killed a couple of his boys, like that?"

"I needed to get his attention."

"Well, murder will do that, I guess."

He registered the lady's disapproval, understanding where it came from. She had spent the past twelve years in law enforcement, following the rules and mostly playing by the book. Her present mission, with LaRocca, was a deviation from the norm, but it still stopped short of killing in cold blood.

"I thought we'd better talk," he said, "before the smoke gets any thicker."

"You've still got some shooting left to do, I take it."

"That's a fair assessment."

"I don't know what your game is," Sharon told him, "but guerrilla warfare wasn't in my job description."

"No one's trying to recruit you," Bolan said. "I just don't want you standing in the line of fire."

"Are you recalling me? Is that it?" Angry, now. "Because if that's what this is all about, I'll need to hear it from the Man himself."

"I don't do recalls," Bolan answered. "This is in the nature of a friendly warning. And I thought that since we're on the same team, maybe you could help me out."

"What did you have in mind?"

The University of Illinois was coming up on Bolan's left. He made a right-hand turn on Morgan Street. Another right on Maxwell. Right again on Miller, coming back around to Roosevelt once more.

"I'd like to leave a message for LaRocca, when I drop you off."

"That's it? You don't want me to slit his throat or something?"

"Not today."

The lady still looked troubled and suspicious, but relief was creeping into her expression.

"What's the message?"

Bolan smiled and told her, listened while she played it back verbatim.

"Perfect."

"I'm not just another pretty face." Defiant, now.

"That's obvious." He hesitated for a moment. "I was thinking, if we want to make this look right, then I shouldn't be in any rush to take you back."

"Kidnappers' protocol?"

He caught the fleeting smile, reluctant as it was, and answered with his own. "That's right."

"Okay by me," she said. And then: "You know, this business with LaRocca..."

"I'm in no position to be judging anybody," Bolan said.

"That makes you more or less unique."

He caught the underlying bitterness in Sharon's tone and understood that, whatever anyone else had to say, the lady was judging herself.

"It's war," he said, "whatever else they choose to call it. Soldiers do what they have to do."

"I never thought of myself as a soldier before."

"Maybe you should start," he said.

"Maybe that's right." A kind of resignation in her voice. Not hope, but something better than despair.

"Where to?" he asked. "We've got some time to kill."
She smiled. "Once more around the park."

JULIO DIBIASE hated bad news with a zeal most men re-
serve for their mothers-in-law. A discouraging word set his
teeth on edge, brought angry color to his cheeks, and if the
news was *really* bad, he had been known to lose it, getting
physical.

The doctors, some years back, had tagged him with an
antisocial personality disorder and psychotic tendencies,
but DiBiase had no interest in the rambling of shrinks.
Some little shit from Harvard figured he was crazy, what
the hell? As long as no one thought that he was stupid, so
that they could try and take advantage of him, everything
was fine.

A psycho reputation even worked to his advantage, now
and then. When he was dealing with subordinates, for instance, chewing someone out, and they began to see his eye
tic, note the twitching in his hands, then DiBiase knew he
had their full attention. Thinking that he might explode
right there and rip somebody's head off for the fun of it.

Of course, he did enjoy a killing now and then, but since
his elevation to the rank of capo, he had tried to keep his
hands clean, more or less. It looked bad to the soldiers, if
a don went out and did his own hits for the pleasure of it,
not to mention the attendant risks involved. With all that
he was trying to accomplish in New York and nationwide
these days, the last thing DiBiase needed was another bust
on suspicion of murder.

He was working overtime at being Mr. Diplomat, the
ever-smiling face and all. If he could hold that pose until
the meeting in Barbados was completed, he would be home
free. Once everything was set, he reckoned there would be

some ass in need of kicking, and he hoped to get a little workout in the process.

Later.

It was not smooth sailing yet. Dissension from the sticks and problems in his own backyard, from the Tattaglia Family, were keeping DiBiase on his toes. It wouldn't take much, at the moment, to destroy his dream of empire. Just a little shove could send the whole thing spinning like a jet out of control, and all his work, his scheming, would go down in flames.

It was the worst time he could think of for the problems in Chicago. LaRocca on the line, complaining of a hit and worse.

"So, let me get this straight," said DiBiase, interrupting his subordinate. "You're in the office with our friend, and some guy shoots the windows out?"

"A sniper, right." LaRocca's voice reminded Julio of taut piano wire.

"And two of Cavalcante's boys went down."

"Like they were fucking targets in a shooting gallery," LaRocca said.

"But you're all right?"

"I got behind the desk, yeah?"

"And Ernesto wasn't hit?"

"No, he's okay. Pissed off, you know, but otherwise—"

"You think this shooter could have nailed you, if he wanted to?" asked DiBiase.

Tommy thought about it for a moment, and nodded. "I'd say so, yeah. The way he took those two boys down, hell yes."

"That means he missed the two of you on purpose, Tommy."

"Well . . ."

"You ask me, I'd say someone's playing footsie with Ernesto. Tune him up a little, maybe. Keep him on his toes."

"It isn't just the hit," LaRocca said.

"I'm listening."

His teeth were clenched so hard his jaw ached. DiBiase made a conscious effort to relax and ease the pain.

"Okay, it's like I told you. Everything was cool, before the shooting started. I had Cavalcante hooked, I swear to God. You told me, promise anything he wants, and we can stiff him later, right?"

"I know exactly what I told you, Tommy."

"Right. So, anyway, he's friendly to the max before this thing went down. And afterward, of course, he's pissed, but not at me, you follow? Then the cops show up, they roust him for a while and take a turn with me. I hear Ernesto take a phone call while they're grilling me, except he doesn't say much. More like someone's talking to him, and he hasn't got an answer for them. After that, when all the cops were gone, he comes on frosty, like I told a dirty joke about his mother."

"Don't sweat it, Tommy. Some guys, getting shot at takes the shine right off their day."

"Well, then, there's Sharon."

"Sharon? What, *your* Sharon? Jesus, Tommy, if you have to take a broad on business trips—"

"Somebody snatched her, Julio."

"Say what?"

"I had her in the car, when I went up to visit Ernie. Mike, my driver, takes her shopping for an hour, and the cops are blocking off the street when they get back, okay? This bonehead leaves her at a fucking city parking lot and walked around the block to see if I'm okay. I chew him out and send his ass back for the car, but it's already gone. No limo in the lot, no Sharon. Gone."

"She didn't take off on her own?" asked DiBiase, knowing it was stupid, even as he spoke.

"And drive a stretch? No way. Mike put the arm on the attendant at the lot. Guy tells me that she had a driver, coming out. Big guy, no real description worth a shit."

"Has anybody called you?" DiBiase asked.

"You mean, like for a ransom? Nothing, yet."

"They've got some crazy people in Chicago. You know that, Tommy."

"I don't figure this is any kind of psycho deal," La-Rocca said. "On top of what went down with Ernie, that would be too much of a coincidence."

And he was right, of course. There was no arguing with logic.

"You've still got your ticket on the flight back home, this evening?"

"Sure."

"So, make the flight. You hear from Sharon in the meantime, great. If not, we've got important work to do, you follow me?"

"Sure, Julio. I hate to lose her, though."

"That's life. If someone's after you—or after *me*—you're better off at home than in Chicago. We've got too much riding on the next few days to let a broad get in the way."

"You're right."

"Damn right, I'm right. I'll see you, Tommy. Keep your head down, in the meantime."

"Fucking A."

He severed the connection, fought an urge to fling the telephone away from him against the nearest wall. Displays of rage would get him nowhere. DiBiase had to think, and that meant thinking clearly, minus any crimson haze of fury.

Trouble in Chicago could mean trouble in New York, or in Barbados. If Cavalcante had a problem, that was one thing. If LaRocca had a problem, that meant it was coming back on DiBiase, through his underlings.

And he did not need any fucking problems at the moment, thank you very much.

If someone tried to mess around with DiBiase's master plan, he meant to squash that someone like an insect.

But in the meantime, he had work to do.

He had an empire to create.

CHAPTER SIX

The warehouse occupied a strip of river frontage in the wedge-shaped block between North Clybourn, on the east, and Ashland on the west. A railroad spur provided access to the Deering yard, three-quarters of a mile due north, and semitrucks had access on North Dominick, from Webster Avenue.

In short, it was the perfect stash for a variety of stolen goods arriving or departing from Chicago, each and every piece of merchandise—from cigarettes to home appliances and furs—providing tax-free income for the Cavalcante Family. At any given time, Ernesto's warehouse stash was worth an estimated million dollars, minimum, in resale on the street. If merchandise went out of town or out of state, Don Cavalcante had to figure transportation costs, but since he owned the trucking companies as well, he always turned a tidy profit.

Checking out the warehouse, Bolan wondered if the mafioso kept his fire insurance up to date.

He parked a short block south and left his nondescript sedan with others in the lot outside a lumberyard. No one appeared to notice as he walked back toward the Cavalcante warehouse, raincoat flapping like a cape around his legs.

The sky was clear and blue, but you never knew about the weather in Chicago. Rain could blow in off the lake at any moment, without warning.

And the raincoat helped conceal the hardware he was carrying.

Specifically, the Executioner had opted for an Uzi submachine gun on a swivel rig beneath his right arm, balancing the sleek Beretta 93-R slung below his left. Spare magazines were slotted into canvas pouches on his belt, and he was packing four incendiary bombs. G.I. white phosphorous, designed to burn through damned near anything, from steel to concrete, blazing white-hot even underwater. Special foam was needed to contain a thermite fire, and Bolan guessed that Cavalcante's warehouse crew would not have any of the proper stuff on hand.

He counted three cars backed into the loading dock, no trucks in evidence so far. Deliveries were frequently nocturnal, no set schedule for authorities to note and memorize. The staff kept busy, forging bills of lading and replacing serial numbers on the heavy items, arranging for deliveries and pickups. Some of the collected merchandise was sold through discount outlets Cavalcante owned in Skokie and Des Plaines; the rest went through black-market channels, sold to honest, upright citizens who couldn't let a bargain slip away.

He went for the direct approach, up concrete steps to reach the loading dock. The giant metal doors were closed, but Bolan found a smaller door unlocked and slipped inside. He dropped his raincoat just across the threshold, brought the Uzi out of hiding, flicked the safety off. A narrow hallway led him past the shipping office, empty now, into the warehouse proper.

It was some forty feet by eighty feet in size, merchandise arranged in about a dozen rows of crates and cartons, narrow aisles between them to accommodate the forklifts. Two of these were parked on Bolan's left, beside another office space, created from partitions made of glass and plywood.

In the "office," three men stood around a desk, discussing paperwork. They didn't notice Bolan till he knocked lightly with the Uzi's muzzle on the open door frame.

"Jesus Christ!"

The tallest of the three men wore a suit that fit him like a tent, all sags and wrinkles. At his first sight of Bolan's gun, he made a move to reach for hardware of his own, an armpit holster, showing more courage than good common sense.

The Uzi stuttered, stitched a line of holes across the shooter's chest and punched him over backward, stretched across the desktop. His companions froze, both of them gaping at the Executioner, hands rising jerkily to shoulder height.

"Don't shoot, okay?"

The older of the two survivors pulled his jacket open, demonstrating that he was unarmed. His young companion followed suit, but Bolan kept them covered, just in case.

"You want to live?" he asked.

"Yes sir," they answered, more or less in unison.

"Okay, then. What I need is someone who can take a message back to Don Ernesto. Either one of you feel up to that?"

"I'll do it!"

"Me!"

They glared at one another for a heartbeat, then their eyes came back to Bolan and the Uzi, waiting.

"Maybe I could use two messengers," said Bolan. "Tell the man he's looking at a world of hurt unless he votes for DiBiase's plan. You got that?"

"DiBiase, right. A world of shit."

"That's close enough. Now, I'd suggest you both take off, before you get your asses toasted."

Bolan did not have to ask twice. The door slammed after them, and he was left alone with Cavalcante's merchandise.

"It feels a little cold in here," he told the dead man, sprawled across the desk. "You cold?"

No answer.

Bolan palmed the first white phosphorus grenade and yanked the safety pin.

"I think we need a fire to warm things up."

IT IS A COMMON FALLACY that Al Capone controlled Chicago like a modern emperor throughout the Roaring Twenties. If the truth be told, Capone's near-global notoriety was due in equal parts to his flamboyant life-style and the ceaseless wars he fought against his many rivals, from the day he landed in Chicago to the day he was imprisoned, twelve years later, on an income tax evasion charge. Chicago was a madhouse in those days, one giant shooting gallery, and Emperor Capone was forced to travel in an armored limousine, with troops around him to avoid assassination at the hands of Bugs Moran, the Genna brothers, and a lengthy list of other enemies.

In fact, the seat of power for Capone's gang was suburban Cicero, across the river, where police and politicians came with price tags on their sleeves, and Scarface made himself at home buying municipal elections, punching Cicero's police chief on the steps of City Hall if he was so inclined. In Cicero, for years on end, Capone's word was the law, no questions asked.

The Mob still rules in Cicero, to some extent, despite unending state and federal investigations, an occasional indictment, a conviction of some minor hoodlum every six or seven years. In Cicero, blood money talks, and everybody listens.

Johnny Gray came looking for a whorehouse in the heart of Cicero, that Wednesday afternoon. He knew the address, one block north of Cermak Road, and he was checking out the neighborhood. Grimaldi drove, feeling less at home behind a steering wheel than in the cockpit of an aircraft, reading numbers as they made a circuit of the block.

"Right here."

"Okay."

He had arranged the call with help from Leo Turrin. Leo had some dirt on a state senator who liked his extramarital relations on the rowdy side, and the esteemed official had provided names, the code required to book a stranger through without a detailed credit check. The madam knew her frequent fliers, and another customer was always welcome, if he paid up front in cash.

"You don't want any backup?" asked Grimaldi, for what seemed to Johnny like the sixth or seventh time.

"I'm fine."

"Okay. I'm standing by, you need some help."

"This won't take long."

The house was old, two-story Tudor, but it showed signs of remodeling, a touch-up here and there. He left Grimaldi in the car and walked along the drive, some sixty yards, to reach the spacious porch. The MP-5 submachine gun brushed against his hip with every step, and he was conscious of the squat SIG-Sauer autoloader in its shoulder rig, underneath his left arm. The fire sticks in his pocket barely registered, a few more ounces in the scheme of things.

He punched the bell and waited, putting on a cautious smile to greet the madam. She was fortysomething, shaving five or six years off the top with skillful use of makeup, but she did not fare that well in daylight.

"Mr. Jones?"

"Yes, ma'am."

The alias amused her, bringing on a smile. She ushered him inside, and Johnny followed her into a spacious parlor, where a dozen women were assembled to receive him. They were young, and came in every color of the human rainbow. Black, white, Asian, Hispanic. Short hair, long hair, pink hair. Nothing much to speak of, in the way of clothes.

A female smorgasbord.

"See anything you like?" the madam asked.

"I like it all," he told her, honestly, "but I'm afraid we won't have time to get acquainted."

"Sorry?"

"Not as much as I am," Johnny said, and let them see the little stuttergun he carried underneath his jacket.

"What the hell?"

"You need to get your ladies out of here," he said. "Right now, in fact. Smoke inhalation has a tendency to ruin everybody's day."

"What smoke? Is this some kind of fucking joke?"

He fired a short burst at the ceiling and unleashed a fall of plaster dust. "No joke," he shouted, over startled screams. "The boys downtown forgot to tell you, there's a fire sale coming."

As he spoke, his free hand fished out an incendiary stick and primed it. Johnny tossed it wide, in the direction of the rec room, where he glimpsed a billiard table through the open door. His fire stick sizzled as it landed on the deep pile carpet, catching instantly.

The madam wasted no more time on arguments. She started barking orders at the dozen lovelies, sending them in the direction of the nearest exit and the street beyond. None of them seemed especially embarrassed as they hit the porch, half-naked, scattering across the lawn.

He hoped that Jack enjoyed the show.

Another fire stick, and another, spreading them around, one looping toward the upstairs landing. Johnny was retreating toward the front door when a bullet struck the wall behind him, missing him by inches.

On the landing, weaving through a pall of smoke, he saw a gunner moving toward the staircase, lining up another shot. Johnny stroked the trigger, rattling off a burst that caught his adversary in mid-stride and dumped him over on his back, legs twitching, finally going slack.

He waited, giving it a moment, just in case Ernesto had more muscle on the premises. When no one showed, he put the place behind him, jogging down the drive. Behind him, smoke was wafting through the open doorway of the brothel, spreading rapidly.

"Somebody ought to call the fire department," Jack suggested, after Johnny settled in the shotgun seat.

"I'll make a note. What's next?"

"We've got a date," Grimaldi said.

The younger Bolan flashed a smile. "That's what I like to hear."

ERNESTO CAVALCANTE'S largest numbers bank was situated on Monroe Street, equidistant between the Leavitt Street railroad yard and Davis Square. It occupied the floor above a neighborhood tobacco shop, an outside staircase leading to a drab, anonymous door. No lookouts visible, but Bolan knew there would be guns inside to guard the cash and betting slips.

He had connected with his brother and Grimaldi at McKinley Park, a half mile north. They left one car behind, drove east on Pershing, south on Ashland, west again on Forty-fifth Street to the chosen target.

"Going up," he said. "Who wants to man the car?"

His brother and Grimaldi glanced at each other, hesitating for a beat before Jack nodded. "Sounds like me," he said.

"Okay." The warrior palmed a gold detective's shield and handed it to Johnny, kept another for himself. "We badge our way inside and play it out from there. I don't expect civilians on the premises, but you can never tell. The runners normally don't carry."

"Right."

"We bag whatever cash we find and torch the slips," said Bolan.

Johnny nodded, making an adjustment to the H&K's swivel rig. "Let's do it."

Up the stairs, Bolan led the way, Johnny on his heels. The plain door had a button set beside it on the wall. He tapped it twice, then once, with a delay, and twice again. The signal passed along by Leo Turrin from a mercenary source inside the operation.

Would it work?

The door swung open to reveal a beefy slugger with a scar above one eye. He blinked at the two strangers on his doorstep, was about to challenge them, when Bolan showed him the detective's badge and wedged the Uzi's muzzle in between his double chins.

"Step back."

The bruiser did as he was told, no further argument. If looks could kill, the Bolan brothers would have dropped dead on the spot. Once they were in, John kicked the door shut with his heel and brought the MP-5 out from underneath his jacket.

"Vice!" he shouted to the room at large, perhaps a dozen men engaged in counting money, logging slips collected from their several territories. "Let me see those hands!"

The gamblers did as they were told, with one exception. Off on Johnny's left, a swarthy shooter in a double-breasted suit thought he could beat the odds. He had one hand inside his jacket, reaching for a side arm when the younger Bolan caught the movement from the corner of his eye. The shiny automatic made it halfway into target acquisition, then a burst from Johnny's SMG ripped through the gunner's chest and dumped him over on his backside, going limp in death.

The doorman lost it, made a grab for Bolan, but he did not have the speed to make it work. The Uzi's muzzle whipped around and caught him on the temple, dropped him like a sack of dirty laundry on the floor at Bolan's feet. Out cold.

"Enough bullshit!" snapped Bolan to the men still on their feet. "I want the heroes lined up to my left, so we can shoot them now and get it over with."

Nobody moved.

"Okay, good choice. Now bag the money up and get your slips together. Pile them over here."

He pointed with the Uzi to a space between two tables, waiting as the ten survivors hastened to obey. The rumpled greenbacks, some of them uncounted, went into a leather satchel, not unlike a doctor's bag. The banker was about to load a second bag with coins when Bolan stopped him.

"Never mind the change. Just dump it with the slips."

The banker did as he was told, weighting the loose pile of betting slips with handful after handful of quarters, dimes and nickels. Bolan took the bag of currency and dropped it near the exit, for retrieval as they left.

"This bank is closed," he told the hostages. "In fact, you're just about to have a fire. Somebody wants to help that tub of lard—" he nodded toward the doorman "—be my guest."

They hesitated, frozen, no one sure exactly what to do as Bolan palmed a fire stick, crossed the room and dropped it on the pile of betting slips and coins.

"I would suggest you hit the bricks," he told them. "Now!"

They bolted for the exit, two men pausing long enough to grab the fallen doorman underneath his arms and drag him out of there. The Bolan brothers waited, heard his feet thump on the steps as he was dragged downstairs.

The fire stick popped and smoked, flame spurting. Bolan tossed a second one behind the banker's desk and left a third inside the door as they retreated toward the stairs.

Enough.

The word would get to Cavalcante, one way or another. Nothing he could put his finger on, but it would make him wonder, keep his nerves on edge. Whatever else went down that Wednesday, Don Ernesto would remember it as one of his worst days.

Grimaldi had the motor running when they reached the nondescript sedan. "How much?" he asked.

"I didn't count," said Bolan, sitting with the gladstone at his feet. "It looked like two, three hundred thousand."

"Ernie's bound to shit a brick," Grimaldi said.

Bolan smiled. "We aim to please," he replied.

CAVALCANTE'S HAND was trembling as he lit a fresh cigar. It wasn't fear, of course. He had the shakes because he was so angry he could hardly see straight, wishing he could lock his hands around somebody's throat and squeeze until the bastard's eyes bugged out, his face went purple, and he frigging died.

The problem was, Ernesto didn't know whom he should blame for all the troubles piling up on him that morning. He had mixed-up signals pouring in from every side, and it was difficult, if not impossible, to sort them out.

Tommy had come in to see him at the office, right on schedule, promising whatever Cavalcante wanted in return for his support at the Barbados meeting. That was standard, offering the moon and stars, but Cavalcante was not shy about employing pressure, when it came time to collect.

Then came the shooting, two of Don Ernesto's soldiers wasted in his private office, with detectives crawling up his ass and asking snotty questions. Bad enough, he had to suffer the embarrassment, but then he gets the phone call from a total stranger, warning him: Don't trust New York.

Ernesto wouldn't trust his sainted mother, where his business was concerned, but it disturbed him, being warned about New York ten minutes after someone tried to snipe him in his own damned office. Worse, the caller didn't tell him *who* he shouldn't trust, as if New York's five Families—really three, now, after federal prosecutions—were a single unit, under one command.

He had been skulling that one over, when the word came in from a survivor at the warehouse on North Dominick. Some crazy bastard shot up the place and tossed fire-bombs, burning up a shitload of Ernesto's merchandise. The gunman also left a message, warning Cavalcante there was worse in store, unless he went for DiBiase's great "new order" at the meeting in Barbados.

No message from the last two raids, his whorehouse out in Cicero, immediately followed by the numbers bank on South Monroe. Between the burned-out property and loss of cash, he estimated two, three million dollars down the tubes. The numbers betting slips were something else, no proof of who had backed which number for the day, and Cavalcante knew that meant all kinds of losers would be on his case by nightfall, claiming they had put their money on a winner. He would have to bluff it out, pay some of them, use muscle on the rest, and hope it didn't queer the game for weeks or months to come.

What *was* this shit?

He felt like reaching out for Tommy, at his hotel suite, and grilling him until he got some righteous answers, but a move like that would only boost the tension with New York. Before he took a step toward open warfare, Cavalcante had to scout his ground and try to pin a label on his enemies.

The way he had it figured, DiBiase had another of the New York capos, Brooklyn's Vince Scarpato, in his pocket. Over in the Bronx, Carmine Tattaglia was firm in opposition—maybe firm enough to take a shot at Tom LaRocca in Chicago, if he thought that he could pull it off.

Would DiBiase offer cash with one hand, then attack Ernesto with the other, tossing threats around? It seemed irrational, at best, but there were stories on the street about Don Julio, his mental state and all. The grapevine said he was a headcase, prone to screaming fits of rage, but you could never really tell about that kind of rumor. Cavalcante had been subject to a whispering campaign or two in his day, and he knew enough to take such stories with a grain of salt.

Still . . .

If Tattaglia or DiBiase weren't behind the recent incidents, then who was?

Ernesto had his share of enemies, no doubt about it. Any man in his position stepped on toes—or necks—as he was climbing up the ladder of success. The trick was making sure your enemies had fatal accidents along the way, but there were always some survivors lurking on the sidelines, nursing grudges that a busy man might not recall, unless somebody brought the problem forcibly to his attention.

Well, they had Ernesto's full attention now, and he was ready to hit back with everything he had . . . if only he could figure out exactly who and where to strike.

It would have pleased him to abort the whole damned meeting in Barbados, put it off until another time, but everything was in the works. If he refused to go, a one-man boycott, it would simply make other capos view him as a coward or a bumbling fool who couldn't handle business in his own backyard, much less deal from strength on a national—or international—level.

Screw that.

Ernesto Cavalcante would be in Barbados, walking tall and daring any cocky bastard with the nerve to take a shot at him to do his worst. Meanwhile he had some work to do at home, tracking down the sons of bitches who had challenged him in Chicago.

And when he found out who they were, there would be hell to pay.

They might even feel the heat in New York.

CHAPTER SEVEN

George Krockover had seen more than his share of violent crime in the years since he was elevated to the post of Special Agent in Charge for the FBI's Chicago office. The Windy City had bank robbers and kidnappers. Black militants and street gangs that dealt with Middle Eastern terrorists for high-tech hardware. Syndicate assassinations. Arson for profit. Cop killers and killer cops. Now and then, a bizarre case of serial murder.

Every day was another challenge in Chicago, and Krockover loved it. The action kept him feeling young and useful, even when he passed the big four-five. There were frustrations, sure, but on the whole, he ended each day with the feeling that he had accomplished something.

Strike that.

Krockover had not accomplished anything today, nor was he likely to.

The cuffs were on, this time, and had been since yesterday afternoon, when Leonard Justice strolled into his office, twenty minutes shy of quitting time. Chicago's SAC was not accustomed to being overruled or sidelined, much less cornered in his private office by a total stranger bearing orders out of Washington.

But he had seen the order for himself, above the signatures of his director, the attorney general, and . . .

Krockover had known there would be trouble coming, from the way his visitor had looked and spoken. Calling off surveillance on the Cavalcante Family, and for what?

His crap about a special task force didn't wash. Krockover would have known about the operation, caught some rumor at the very least, if it existed.

Bullshit.

Mr. Justice and his friends were working Cavalcante, that was obvious, but something had gone drastically awry. At least five men had died within the past few hours, three of Cavalcante's properties reduced to ashes by incendiary fires. That added up to war, in Krockover's opinion, and it meant the time was ripe for putting federal pressure on the Mob, exploiting any weakness they could find.

Except that he was under orders not to move. His very power to investigate a string of federal crimes in progress had been stripped away by orders from the top. If Krockover investigated on his own, it could be tantamount to suicide for his career.

He wondered what the hell his job was coming to.

Krockover had his twenty years, and then some, with the FBI. He could resign today, this minute, with his pension guaranteed.

And then, do what? Go fishing? Watch sports all day and think about the children he had never had? Start playing bingo with the senior citizens, in preparation for his "golden years"?

No, thanks.

He still had nine years left before mandatory retirement put him out on the street, and Krockover was not giving up on his life because some bureaucrat from Washington blew into town and started changing all the rules. As soon as Mr. Justice hit the road, Krockover and his agents would be on the case, picking up the pieces, trying to make sense from chaos.

The telephone shrilled at him, demanding Krockover's attention. He lifted the receiver, heard his secretary speak the now-familiar name.

"Yes, put him on." Brief hesitation. "Mr. Justice, I was wondering if you would call."

"You've heard the news, I take it," said the man from Washington.

"I have. Is this the way your task force covers syndicate activities?"

"Despite appearances," said Justice, "everything is well under control."

"I'd hate to see your definition of a fuckup," Krockover replied.

"I understand that you're concerned. You needn't be. Whatever's happened or may happen in the next few hours, it will not reflect on you or your command."

"Is that a fact?"

"It's guaranteed."

"So, I just watch the Cavalcante Mob go up in smoke, and when somebody asks me, 'Hey, what happened?' I can shrug and say, 'Beats me.' Is that about the size of it?"

"There won't be any questions," Justice said.

"Is that a fact? Do you control the press now, too? I don't know how it works in Washington, my friend, but in Chicago, the reporters have a way of asking questions. So do the police, from time to time. My own damn people have been asking questions since I pulled them off surveillance on the Family, so fuck your guarantees!"

"You have your orders," Justice said, a new edge on his voice. "You know the numbers, if you want a confirmation. Otherwise . . ."

He left it hanging, no need to complete the sentence. Krockover was beaten, but he didn't want to let it show.

"And how much longer should your task force be in town?" he asked.

"A few more hours," Leonard Justice told him. "Out of here by nightfall would be my best guess."

"I hope you're right," said Krockover. And with that, he cradled the receiver, cutting off whatever else the man from Washington might have to say.

Chicago's ranking federal agent had already heard enough.

HEADQUARTERS for the Department of Justice is located on Constitution Avenue, in Washington, D.C. Hal Brognola's office occupies the northeast corner of the fourth floor, with angular views of the National Archives, due east, and the FBI building, across Pennsylvania Avenue.

This Wednesday afternoon, the spectacle of Washington was not enough to capture Hal's attention. He stared out through the window, but he scarcely saw the city spread in front of him. It might have been a painted backdrop or a photograph, for all the interest he displayed.

His thoughts were elsewhere, scattered far and wide. A part of him was in Chicago, some at Stony Man, and yet another part was in Miami, looking forward to the weekend in Barbados with a sense of apprehension.

Pull yourself together, damn it.

It was coming down so quickly now, but he had known that it would be this way. You didn't unleash Striker on a target and expect some kind of leisurely progression toward the finish line. At that, four days was somewhat longer than the typical campaign, where Bolan was concerned, but he was covering a lot of ground.

Too much?

The telephone distracted Hal. He got it on the second ring, his secretary patching Leo through, from Illinois. He reached inside the top drawer of his desk and switched the hidden scrambler on before he took the call. He would assume that Leo had a similar device in place at his end of the line.

"What's up?" Brognola asked, as if the call was unexpected and he didn't have a clue.

"We're cooking," Leo told him. "Cavalcante's taking hits all over town, and Striker jazzed LaRocca up a little bit to keep it interesting. They're watching each other like a pair of junkyard dogs with one good bone between them. If they held the vote today, I don't think DiBiase would be Ernie's fair-haired boy."

"Okay. That leaves New York and Florida, before the main event."

"One local note," said Leo.

"Yeah?"

"The SAC out here is getting antsy. I can't blame him, with the fireworks going on, but it could be a problem if he starts to sniff around. I've got him covered for the moment, but it may not last."

"I'll see what I can do," Brognola said.

And that was all he needed. Running back to the director of the FBI with a request to sit on one of his top agents, in one of the Bureau's busiest field offices. All for the sake of an extralegal operation that was spreading carnage in the streets and escalating by the hour.

No problem, right. It came with the territory, and Brognola was used to running interference for the Stony Man team on Capitol Hill. It could be done, because he had the necessary muscle at the moment. But, if things should change...

"What else?' he asked, derailing the negative train of thought.

"We've got confirmation on Masciere's arrival in Miami," Leo said, "and we're expecting Graziano in sometime tomorrow morning. DiBiase and Scarpato fly down Friday. No word on Tattaglia, but I'm sure he's going."

"Right. He can't afford to miss it. What about Barbados?"

Leo cleared his throat. "We're doing what we can. The locals live on tourism, you understand, and if the money's green, they don't care where it comes from. I got nowhere with the cops in Bridgetown. Ditto with the prosecutor's office. They'll take care of any crimes committed in their jurisdictions, but they're not concerned about what tourists do at home."

"You're telling me the fix is in," Brognola said.

"I'm guessing, but it all adds up. Caribbean expansion's been the trend for years, in everything from gambling and drugs to money laundering. With the economy down there, it doesn't take a lot to turn some heads."

Brognola knew that story well enough. For over thirty years, between the Great Depression and the Eisenhower era, mobsters in the States had made a point of colonizing towns where poverty and graft went hand in hand. Casinos and distilleries meant jobs for local residents and payoffs for the men in power. Since the 1960s, there had been a growing trend toward offshore banking and casino gambling, notably in the Caribbean. As taxes rose and law enforcement in the States grew more efficient, criminals had even more incentive to invest abroad.

"Phase one of the new order," said Brognola, almost talking to himself.

"And phase two brings it home," said Leo. "DiBiase needs to prove himself across the board. It isn't getting any easier."

"Let's hope not. When is Striker heading for Manhattan?"

"Four, five hours, tops. He wants to wrap a few loose ends around Chicago, first."

Brognola knew what that meant. He had watched the soldier work, up close and personal, on more than one occasion. Those "loose ends" would wind up as a noose around somebody's neck before the day was out, and Cavalcante could begin to count his losses in double digits. By the time he rolled out for Miami and Barbados, Don Ernesto would be wondering which way was up.

"You're leaving pretty soon, I guess?" he asked.

"An hour, if the flight's on time. I have to cover some advance work in the Apple."

"Watch yourself," Brognola said. "It's getting mean out there."

"Will do."

He cradled the receiver, rocked back in his chair, and focused on the view of Washington once more. He saw the city this time, but he wasn't thrilled about the view.

Sometimes it felt like he was looking at a madhouse, with the inmates in control.

And other times, he felt like there was no one in control at all.

SHARON PRYOR HAD KILLED another ninety minutes after Mike Belasko dropped her off on Jackson Boulevard. The Institute of Art lay one block east, and she had walked directly there, allowing him a chance to ditch the limousine and get a fair head start before she thought about calling LaRocca, who was probably waiting for her in the hotel suite they shared.

Belasko.

It was not his name, of course. She knew that much from the beginning. Agents working undercover did not throw their given names around on short acquaintance, in a hostile theater of operations. She might never know his name—the odds were heavily against it—and it did not matter at the moment.

Sharon's feelings were jumbled. There was anger, jostling with frustration, curiosity, more than just a trace of fear, all jammed together, making her feel vaguely schizoid as she thought about her strange encounter with the tall, dark stranger.

It sounded like a pitiful cliché, except that he *was* tall and dark. And definitely strange.

It was the kind of close encounter that could change your life...or end it, if you dropped your guard.

She started sorting out her feelings. Anger first, at Leonard Justice for exposing her that way to someone she had never met. Of course, he had his reasons, but she should have been consulted. What if this Belasko should be captured by the Families and grilled for information? What became of Sharon Pryor when he broke and gave her up in an attempt to save himself?

She did not see that happening, in fact—he struck her as the kind of soldier who would go down shooting from the hip—but anything could happen, damn it. Justice should have warned her first, before he started leaking information to the world at large. Next time they spoke, she meant to give the man from Washington a sharp piece of her mind, and no mistake.

Frustration emanated from the feeling that she might have wasted all the time she spent with Tommy and the others, all that she had sacrificed to gather information for indictments, prosecution. What was it about, if Justice turned around behind her back and sent in some kind of hotshot mercenary to start a shooting war? What rule book were they using back in Wonderland, where wiretaps were forbidden but assassination was okay?

That brought her back to curiosity, the whole damn thing compelling her to question everything that she had learned and done since she came on the job eight years ago. What kind of game was Justice playing? Who was calling the shots upstairs?

And that left fear. If Washington was killing people now, in lieu of taking them to court, it meant the gloves were off. She had been conscious of the risks involved in her assignment when she took it, but the stakes had inevitably changed when you revised the rules of play. Instead of simply watching out for Tommy and his goombahs, now she was about to be caught in a cross fire.

There was nothing she could do, at this point, but continue playing out her role as Tommy's mistress, storing information and transmitting it to Washington. Belasko knew her face, and he presumably did not intend to harm her.

Not deliberately, at least.

If she asked Justice to relieve her, it would be a frank admission of defeat. The end of everything that she had worked for, up to now.

She checked her watch, decided it was time to make the call. The first try got her through to Tommy's hotel suite. She recognized Mike's voice when he came on the line.

"Hey, Mike, it's Sharon."

"Jesus! You okay? Where are you?"

"I'm okay. We lost the car, though. Bastard dropped me off on Jackson Boulevard. I'm at the Institute of Art. Can someone pick me up?"

"Hang on a sec."

Mike covered the receiver, but she still heard muted voices as he huddled with LaRocca. Tommy did not bother coming on the line. The little shit.

"I'm back," Mike told her, sounding nervous. "Institute of Art, you said? On Jackson?"

"Right."

"I'll be there, soon as we can get another car. You be out front, okay?"

"I'll see you, Mike."

More time to kill, and that was fine. She had a message for LaRocca, and she knew he would not like it. Not at all. He could not blame her, logically, but this was Tommy. Logic didn't always have a lot to do with his behavior, much less with the way his boss reacted to grim tidings.

She started for the exit, dawdling along the way, and cursed the impulse that had made her long to be a federal agent, all those years ago.

"HEY, DOLL, you had me worried sick."

LaRocca crossed the room and folded Sharon into his embrace. Ten seconds, fifteen—that was plenty. Stepping back a pace, he studied her and was relieved to see that she seemed unhurt. Tommy did not like to think about his private property in someone else's hands.

"They didn't rough you up at all?"

"I'm fine," she told him. "I could use a drink."

"Sure thing." LaRocca snapped his fingers, sending Mike to fix the usual, at the complimentary wet bar. "Jesus, babe, when Mike came back and said the car was gone, you with it...well, you can imagine what I thought."

"I'm fine," she said again.

And damn, she *looked* fine, thought LaRocca. Not like she had just been kidnapped, really. There she was, all spit and polish, every hair in place. A little tired, perhaps, but that could just as easily have been from shopping.

"Where's the limo?" Tommy asked, when they had drinks in hand and they were seated on the couch, a yard of empty air between them.

"How should I know? This guy drops me off on Jackson Boulevard, says 'Don't forget to tell LaRocca what we talked about,' and off he goes. I didn't try to follow him on foot, you know?"

"It doesn't matter, anyway. The agency's insured for theft." A frown was tugging down the corners of LaRocca's mouth. "What did he mean, for you to tell me what you talked about?"

"He had a message for you, Tommy. That was it, I mean. The reason that he grabbed me. So that I could tell you what he said."

"Okay, I'm listening."

"You want it word for word, or what?"

"Whatever."

"Well, he says to me, 'Barbados isn't happening. You tell LaRocca that. His boss can't sell it to the Families.'"

LaRocca waited for a moment, finally said, "That's it?"

"You got it."

"Nothing else was said, the whole two hours you were with him?"

"Well, we *talked,* of course, but there was nothing special."

"Let me be the judge of that, all right?"

"Sure, Tommy. He was asking me how did I like New York, did I like Mr. DiBiase, things like that. How was it, sleeping with . . . well, never mind."

"Go on, babe. I can take it."

"Tommy . . ."

"Go ahead, I told you."

"Fine. He asked how was it, sleeping with a weasel. Are you happy, now?"

LaRocca clenched his teeth. "That's everything?"

"Well, no. He talked about himself a little bit. No name, or anything like that, but he went on about how he was earning more for this job than he had on any contract in the last few years."

"He said a contract?"

"Yeah. Is that important?"

"Never mind. How come he asked you about Julio?"

"You're asking me to read a stranger's mind now? Jesus, Tommy, I don't know! I'd have to say he asked because he wanted me to answer him."

"And what, exactly, did you say?"

"I told him that I didn't spend much time with Mr. DiBiase—which I don't, you know? But that he seemed all right to me. A gentleman, like that. Okay?"

"This whole thing stinks," LaRocca said. "Somebody shot up Don Ernesto's office while the two of us were sitting there. A couple of his boys went down, and then this crazy fucker grabs my limo, telling you this crazy shit. What did he look like?"

"Look like?"

"His face, you know? What did he fucking *look* like, Sharon?"

"Hey, don't take it out on me, all right? He was a total stranger, Tommy. Not bad-looking, if you like the type. Dark hair. An okay face, I guess. I didn't pay that much attention, and he mostly kept his back turned, driving. He was looking at me in the mirror, mostly, if you get the picture."

"Yeah, okay. You never saw this guy before, around New York?"

"I said he was a stranger, didn't I? Last time I checked, that means we never met."

Her lip was getting on his nerves, and Tommy fought a sudden urge to slap her for the hell of it.

"You might've seen him," he replied. "Say, when we had the dinner party, three, four weeks ago, with the Don Tattaglia's people?"

Sharon thought about it for a moment, finally shook her head. "I don't remember him. He could have been there, I suppose, but if he was, it didn't register."

"Okay."

What was he thinking, anyway? Tattaglia was smart enough to send a stranger on a job where there would be survivors to recall his face. Assuming that it *was* Tattaglia at all, instead of someone else.

But who?

LaRocca did not like the implications one damned bit. What he liked even less, however, was the grim necessity of calling Julio with more bad news. The prospect of a shooting war, perhaps.

Barbados isn't happening.

Well, he would have to tone that down, for openers. If he came on to Julio with any shit like that, LaRocca might as well just go ahead and put a pistol in his mouth. But he could get the point across all right, let DiBiase know they had a major problem coming through the pipe. It only took a measure of finesse.

"I need to make a call," he said at last. "You want to get cleaned up or something, babe? You look like hell."

"Thanks much. I love you, too."

"Go on, now."

She was sulking as she left, and that was fine. LaRocca had more pressing worries on his mind than whether some dumb blonde was pissed off by his attitude.

He had to think about survival, and hope that Julio could take more bad news without deciding it was time to kill the messenger.

CHAPTER EIGHT

The South Side Cartage Company, a trucking firm owned by the Cavalcante Family, was based on Forty-third Street, near the Ashland Avenue railroad yard. At any given time, a dozen semitrailers could be found inside the chain link fence that ringed the parking lot and cinder-block garage facility, with gasoline and diesel pumps along one side. The South Side truckers picked up merchandise from trains arriving at the Ashland yard and elsewhere, running loads as far afield as Iowa and western Tennessee.

As far as Bolan knew, the bulk of merchandise conveyed by South Side Cartage was legitimate, but DEA suspected Cavalcante of secreting drugs on board his trucks from time to time, and there were doubtless shipments that included hijacked items from the former Dominick Street warehouse and similar drops.

For Bolan's purposes, it was enough to know that Cavalcante owned the company.

It had to go.

He parked his car a half block west and walked in like he owned the place. The gate was open, no guards posted, but he kept an eye on the garage, where voices and the sound of clanking tools confirmed that there were men at work. His jacket was unbuttoned, granting easy access to the Uzi in its swivel rig, and Bolan's black Adidas bag held seven blocks of C-4 plastique, each with detonators waiting to be armed.

Another moment brought him to the trucks and put him briefly out of sight from the garage. For anyone to spot him now, they had to step outside and check the grounds, perhaps approach the semis for a closer look. The chain link fence at his back, Bolan moved along the line of trailers to the farthest from the gate.

He worked methodically, no rush, and yet no movement wasted. Nine long trailers lined up side by side, with two uncoupled tractor cabs parked closer to the building and a third inside, receiving the mechanics' full attention. For maximum effect, Bolan placed his charges on alternating trailers, one through nine. No timers on the detonators—they were radio-controlled—but Bolan armed them each in turn, as he went down the line.

Four minutes and counting on the probe, as Bolan finished with the trailers, moving toward the tractor rigs. His hand was on the Uzi now, prepared for anything, the voices close enough that he could make out every word said. An ethnic joke in progress, winding up to the predictable, unfunny punch line.

Bolan placed his sixth charge on the nearest tractor's fuel tank, wedged against the driver's side, and armed the detonator. Moving on, he fixed the second rig identically and left the empty gym bag on the running board.

He walked around the second tractor to the open door of the garage and scanned the drab interior. Three men were working on another truck, one stretched out on the floor beneath, a second underneath the hood, while number three retrieved some wrenches from a nearby workbench.

Bolan captured their attention with a short burst from his Uzi, shattering one of the long fluorescent fixtures overhead. A rain of brittle glass shards clattered on the tractor's roof and hood, three sets of wide eyes focused on the Executioner.

"You've got one minute to remove yourselves, before this place goes up in smoke," he said. "I wouldn't hang around, unless you have an urge to see the world from outer space."

The three mechanics did not argue, dropping their equipment where they stood and bolting past him toward the exit. Bolan caught the last man out and held him up a moment, tickling his grizzled jawline with the Uzi's muzzle.

"How's your memory?" he asked.

"O-okay, I guess," the flunky stammered.

"When Ernesto's men start asking questions later on today, I've got a message for them."

"Message?"

"Right. You listening?"

"I hear you, mister."

"Good. The message is: It's dumb for Cavalcante to consider backing out on his arrangement with Don Julio. You got that?"

"Backing out on Don's a dumb idea."

"Don Julio," the Executioner corrected him.

"Don Julio, okay."

"Now, hit the bricks."

He watched the last of the mechanics disappear, sprinting flat out along Forty-third Street, abandoning his post without a backward glance. Bolan took his time leaving the lot, his Uzi tucked away, the compact detonator cupped in his left hand.

As Bolan reached his car, he turned and aimed the detonator back in the direction of the South Side Cartage Company. His thumb depressed the button, and he watched Ernesto's rolling stock disintegrate. The tractor rigs and trailers blew together, one terrific thunderclap that rocked the neighborhood and sent an oily fireball spinning skyward. Smoking shrapnel pattered down on all sides of ground zero: chrome and crumpled siding, insulation from refrigerated trailers, blackened engine parts. A burning tire came down some twenty yards from Bolan's vehicle, bounced twice, and took off rolling down the street.

He was seated at the wheel, one hand on the ignition key, when Bolan saw the enemy approaching in his rearview mirror. One crew wagon, then another, and a third. The lead car hesitated for an instant at the sight of smoke and flames, then charged ahead as Bolan's sedan shot away from the curb.

The chase was on.

"STRIKER CALLING Wingman. Do you read me, Wingman? Over."

Jack Grimaldi took the walkie-talkie from the seat beside him, thumbing the transmitter button. "Wingman reading. What's your twenty, Striker?"

"North on Ashland, passing Forty-second. I've got Pershing up ahead. Three bogies on my tail. Can you assist?"

Jack glanced at Johnny in the shotgun seat and made a rapid calculation.

"We're on Cermak, westbound," he replied, "approaching Loomis. We can pick you up on Ashland, if you stay the course."

"Affirmative. I'll see what I can do on that. Evasion may be necessary. Out."

A burst of static severed the connection.

"Jesus!" Johnny blurted. "How did they get on to him?"

"Could be coincidence," Grimaldi said. "It stands to reason Cavalcante would be beefing up his guards around the city. Striker may have stumbled into something."

Johnny had a map out, open on his lap, an index finger tracing. "Call it two miles, give or take," he said. "We're screwed on traffic."

"Maybe not," Grimaldi told him, swinging out to pass a station wagon on the wrong side of a double yellow line. He slipped back into his lane with a yard or so to spare, ignoring angry bleats from vehicles in the oncoming lane.

At Loomis Street, Grimaldi made a left against the light, tires screeching as a florist's van stopped inches short of a collision. South on Loomis, flanked on either side by railroad tracks, they crossed the north branch of the Chicago River on a two-lane bridge and made a squealing right on Eleanor. Two long blocks brought them to another bridge, this time across the river's south branch, and they intercepted Ashland north of Archer Avenue.

"Not bad," said Johnny, snapping back the cocking lever on his MP-5 submachine gun. He had slipped the weapon from its shoulder rig and held it in his lap now, ready.

"Getting there," said Jack. "We're not home, yet."

The southbound traffic wasn't crawling, but it wasn't setting any land speed records, either. Add the fact that Bolan might be forced to leave the main drag, trying to elude the gunmen on his tail, and it was very possible that they would miss him altogether—or arrive too late to be of any help.

Still, they could only try.

The arch of Highway 55 loomed overhead, its shadow blotting out the sun. Grimaldi jumped the light at Archer Avenue, surprised that he had not picked up a squad car in his race to beat the clock. If Bolan made good time, they should be closing with him sometime in the next half mile or so.

They had another major intersection coming up at Thirty-fifth Street, with a red light glaring in his face. Grimaldi clamped down on the horn and kept his foot on the accelerator, lunging into east-west traffic like a movie stuntman with a death wish. On his left, he saw a motorcycle going down, the driver wallowing across the pavement on his back, the Harley shooting sparks. A sports car on his right tried hard to miss him, almost made it, but the starboard fender clipped Grimaldi's bumper, slamming him off course and scorching rubber as he struggled to correct.

"Goddamn it!"

They were through the intersection now, cars piling up behind them, jolting into one another, four deep as the lights changed and the flow of traffic stalled. Grimaldi kept his pedal on the floor, past Thirty-sixth and Thirty-seventh, dodging a pedestrian who tried his luck at crossing in the middle of the block.

"Up there!"

He followed Johnny's pointing finger, spotted Bolan's car with headlights flashing into the approach. Grimaldi's foot was lifting off the gas and shifting to the brake as Bolan made a left-hand turn in front of him, westbound on Thirty-eighth. Behind him, burning rubber, three crew wagons formed the body of the train.

"Hang on!" Grimaldi snapped.

"I'm hanging," Johnny told him, as they veered hard right and fell in line behind the tail car, closing fast.

It was a Lincoln, big and bulky, but the driver knew his stuff. He hung in close behind the second tank in line, and there were windows down on both sides of the Lincoln, gunners ready to shoot at their elusive prey.

"I'm going for his blind side," said Grimaldi, speeding up and swinging out to pass the Lincoln on the right. It was a risky move, all things considered, but the lane was clear a full block down, and there might be no second chance to thin the herd.

"I'm ready," Johnny told him, leaning out the window with his submachine gun braced to fire.

Grimaldi thought to himself: I hope so, kid. I really do.

THEY CAME UP HARD and fast behind the Lincoln, riding in the big car's slipstream, on the driver's side. Two windows were down, and while the driver was concealed behind a pane of tinted glass, his passengers in back were on display, guns visible, all straining forward like a pack of hunting dogs.

They had the scent of blood, and they were hungry for the kill.

Johnny lined his target up and squeezed the trigger of his SMG, a short precision burst to open the festivities. The nearest gunner's face exploded, spewing crimson, chips of bone and shreds of mutilated flesh. The guy slumped over sideways, dead before his comrades knew exactly what was happening.

One of them turned to face the sound of gunfire, taking Johnny's second burst between his upper lip and eyebrows, spattering the others with his brains.

And everyone inside the Lincoln was reacting now, loud curses, one of them unloading with a big revolver, aimless bullets pumping through the open window on the driver's side. A slug whined close to Johnny's head, but he was firing back in spite of it, hosing the last rounds from his magazine into the crew wagon as they roared west along Thirty-eighth.

"Hang on!" Grimaldi shouted, tramping on the brake and swinging back in line, behind the Lincoln. Head-on traffic passed them on the left, horn blaring, and the tank in front of them was weaving now, fishtailing from side to side, the driver trying to prevent another strafing run.

One of the soldiers leaned out on the Lincoln's driver side and fired a stubby riot shotgun toward the chase car. Jack veered to the right as his assailant drifted toward the center line, the combination of their zigzag movements scattering the buckshot harmlessly to their left.

The snarling mafioso pumped another round into his shotgun's chamber, lining up the shot as the Lincoln came back into line. The wind rush from behind him made his hair stand up around his head like a weird halo.

"Take him, Johnny!"

As Grimaldi spoke, he swerved left, straddling the center line, to give his passenger a shot. Beside him, Johnny had the MP-5 loaded with a brand-new magazine, his head and shoulders out the window, aiming.

It only took a heartbeat, lining up the gunner in the Lincoln, knowing if he hesitated that the next blast from the 12-gauge would be guaranteed to take his head off.

Johnny stroked the trigger of his SMG, stitched half a dozen rounds through the gunman's skull and upper body. Impact knocked the shotgun from his adversary's hands, and Johnny heard it clatter underneath their tires as Jack veered back into the westbound lane.

The speeding caravan crossed Honore, Wilcott, Winchester. Ahead, he caught a glimpse of Mack's sedan, a sharp right onto Damen, running north beside McKinley Park. The lead crew wagon hung on tight, its trailers following, with Jack and Johnny bringing up the rear.

"He's going for the park," Grimaldi said. "More combat stretch."

"We need to shave these odds," said Johnny.

"Can you get in back?" Grimaldi asked.

"Damn straight."

"Okay, let's take this mother out."

Before Jack finished speaking, Johnny had completed the maneuver, scrambling between the seats and shifting to a place behind the driver, cranking down his window in a rush of wind and noise. He braced his subgun on the windowsill, prepared for anything as Jack swung to the right and came up on the outside of the bullet-punctured Lincoln.

They were short of gunners in the tail car now. One or two alive, at most, besides the driver, and for all he knew, those might be wounded. Better if they were, to shave the chances of effective counter-fire.

"I'm going for the rubber," Johnny said, already aiming as he spoke.

A long burst flayed the Lincoln's right rear tire to shreds of rubber flapping on the metal rim. He heard a screech and watched the sparks fly, metal biting asphalt, and the Lincoln swerved without assistance from the driver, shooting left across the center line to meet oncoming traffic.

Johnny saw the yellow taxi coming on at speed, a moving van behind it, both drivers looking stunned and frightened. They were past the scene of the collision in another instant, echoes of the pileup ringing in his ears.

Civilians, damn it. Nothing he could do, and yet . . .

"Turning!" snapped Grimaldi, as the lead car—Mack's—swung left on Thirty-seventh, looking for an entrance to the park. "I told you!"

Two crew wagons remained, and one of them was slowing down a fraction now, the occupants aware of what had happened in their wake. A head poked out and glared at them, took in the smoking wreckage half a block back. It was gone before Johnny had a chance to aim and fire.

"They made us," said Grimaldi. "No surprise with these guys."

Johnny saw his brother driving fast across the almost-empty parking lot. McKinley Park looked green, inviting, peaceful. It was all about to change.

"Get set," Grimaldi said. "We're going in!"

THE NEARER of the two surviving Lincolns rode up close on Bolan's tail and kissed his bumper, nudging him across the parking lot. He locked the brakes and let inertia do the rest, his sedan spinning sideways and forcing the Lincoln out of line, sliding past on his left with a loud grinding sound, paint stripping from the driver's side.

He stuck his Uzi out the open window, firing for effect, saw windows open, swarthy faces scowling at him over guns. His bullets ripped into those faces, punctured them and blew them backward, out of frame. Spent brass bounced off the inside of his windshield, rolling on the dashboard with a bright, metallic sound.

The Lincoln rolled past him, braking, as the second one came in behind. He heard more firing, glimpsed his brother leaning out the window on the driver's side of Jack's sedan and blasting with his SMG at someone in the tail car. Some of Cavalcante's men were firing back, Grimaldi's rental taking hits along the starboard side, across the windshield, up and down the hood.

Bolan bailed out of his own sedan, taking cover behind it, dragging his satchel of spare magazines and grenades to the pavement beside him. The point Lincoln had stopped a few yards to his right, doors springing open as surviving troops unloaded in a rush. Three gunmen and the driver, looking for a place to hide.

He came up firing, caught them in the open. Two of them jumped back inside the Lincoln, seeking cover there, but Bolan nailed the driver with a burst across the chest and dropped him where he stood.

The odd man out was staring back at Bolan, leveling a shiny automatic pistol, but he froze. A wasted moment, and he had no time to make it up as Bolan stroked the Uzi's trigger once more. A stream of parabellum shockers flipped the mafioso over on his back and left him twitching as his life ran out in crimson rivulets across the pavement.

Bolan reached into his grab bag, palmed a thermite bomb and yanked the pin before he lobbed it overhead. He watched it sail in through the Lincoln's open door and heard a shout from someone in the car before it detonated, gutting the interior in seconds flat. The fuel tank blew a moment later, thick smoke rolling skyward in an inky column.

Bolan turned to face the last crew wagon, found it under fire from Johnny and Grimaldi. One of Cavalcante's men was stretched out on the pavement, while another draped across the Lincoln's fender, scarlet streamers bright against the midnight paint job.

Bolan dropped the Uzi's empty magazine and snapped a fresh one into place. He moved alongside his sedan, duck-walking, following the sounds of combat emanating from the second Lincoln. He could hear the doomsday numbers running in his head and knew the sirens would be coming soon, perhaps within the next few moments.

They were running out of time.

Three men were crouched behind the Lincoln with their backs to Bolan, two more firing from inside the car itself. He could not reach the last two from his present vantage point, but that left three, and Bolan seized the opportunity.

He came up firing, strafed the Lincoln with a long burst from his Uzi, watching bullets strike the mafiosi as they ducked away from gunfire behind the vehicle. His first rounds struck the gunner on the left and slammed the man face-forward into hard, unyielding metal. Impact dropped the gunner on his backside, slumping in an awkward sprawl.

The second man in line was vaguely conscious of some danger on his flank, but he could not respond in time. The parabellum rounds sliced through him as he tried to turn and face his enemy, too late to save himself. Blood spouted from his wounds, and he went down without a word, a dazed expression on his face.

Number three, blasting buckshot rounds at Jack and Johnny with his semiautomatic shotgun, seemed deafened by the loud voice of his weapon. Death came up behind him in a rush and stitched a line of holes along his spine, the fabric of his jacket rippling on impact. Bolan watched him dance and held the Uzi's trigger down until the gunner's legs betrayed him and he went down on his knees. A moment later, he was stretched out on his side. Unmoving, lifeless.

Two gunners were left inside the Lincoln. He was reaching back behind him for the satchel of grenades when Jack and Johnny made their move.

They came from opposite directions, breaking cover in a rush and sprinting toward the Lincoln, firing as they came. The cornered mafiosi tried to handle it, one firing through the windshield of his own crew wagon, but they could not seem to get their act together.

Jack came in with pistols blazing, Johnny firing short bursts from an SMG. They had the mafiosi in a deadly cross fire, pumping rounds through tinted glass and proving that the Lincoln wasn't bulletproof. A high-pitched squeal from someone in the vehicle, and Bolan saw his brother step up to the open window, firing down into the car at point-blank range.

And it was over, just like that.

He rose and walked around to meet the others, knowing time was of the essence now. Grimaldi's car was spilling oil and water on the blacktop. He could smell the engine coolant as it drained away.

"Looks like you need a lift," said Bolan.

"Wouldn't hurt," Jack answered with a rueful smile. "I need new wheels myself, but this should get us out of here."

"Let Ernie pay for the replacements," Jack suggested.

"Now you're talking."

He heard the sirens coming, as they drove away. Still distant, but another moment would have made the difference.

It was coming up on sundown in Chicago, wrapping up the latest stop on Bolan's hit parade. Before they found themselves a used-car dealership, however, he was looking for a pay phone.

Bolan wanted to touch base with Leo, and he also had a message for Ernesto Cavalcante. Just a little something to make sure the capo passed a restless night.

All things considered, Bolan thought it was the least that he could do.

CHAPTER NINE

Times Square was cooking.

It was 10:05 p.m. when Bolan reached the "crossroads of the world" on foot and merged with the frenetic crowd that jammed the sidewalks. Pressing close around him there were representatives of every race and nationality, some of them tourists, others longtime residents. There were civilians, servicemen in uniform, rich and poor, young and old, all drawn like moths to the electric bonfire burning at the heart of old New York.

Times Square was once a magnet for the wealthy and elite in New York City, but the world had changed. Its great hotels—the Astor and the Knickerbocker—have long since vanished, replaced by soulless blocks of high-tech offices. Even the New York *Times* itself, after lending its name to the square in 1905, has moved on to new quarters on Forty-third Street.

A different breed inhabits Times Square now. Down on the street, a world away from lavish penthouse offices, a seamy underworld has grown up in the shadow of success. Peep shows and porno houses by the dozen. Massage parlors that have nothing to do with physical fitness. Prostitutes of all descriptions. Pushers serving wasted junkies at the curb, or in the passageways that New York tour guides stubbornly describe as "streets" instead of "alleys."

Progress.

Bolan knew about New York from way back. He had been here many times on business, tracking this or that appointed target in his one-man war. He knew the Apple's history and recognized its role as Mafia Central for the past three-quarters of a century.

New York was the only town big and bad enough to rate five Families of mafiosi, one for each great borough. Through the years, the shining lights of gangland graced Manhattan. Rothstein. Masseria. Maranzano. Lansky. Siegel. Luciano. Genovese. Costello. Anastasia. Gambino. Gigante. Castellano. Gotti.

Dead and gone, most of them, but the syndicate lived on. It had been battered lately by a string of federal prosecutions, but three of the city's Mafia Families were "still viable," in FBI jargon, while the other two were busily reorganizing, shooting for a comeback.

Five boroughs, and Manhattan was the plum. In normal times, New York's five Families worked Manhattan on a kind of time-share basis, knowing there was loot enough to go around. One Family occupied the island, while its neighbors colonized the Bronx and Brooklyn, Queens and Staten Island, but Manhattan was immediately recognized as too damned rich for any single Family to dominate. There were so many hookers, johns and junkies, scams and suckers.

Plenty until the Feds moved in and upset everybody's applecart. Now, one of New York's ruling dons was dead, the other doing life on racketeering charges, and their Families had gone to hell. The three surviving capos had to watch their backs around the clock, beware of microphones and fiber optics, wiretaps, traitors in the ranks.

It was a whole new ballgame, nationwide, and it demanded brand-new rules.

Enter Julio DiBiase and his "new order."

The plan was simple, on its face. Reorganize the Mob to cut dead wood, weed out the stoolies, streamline everything. Regain the strength that made adversaries cringe in terror. Punish those who came on strong against La Cosa Nostra—the Colombians, Jamaicans, Cubans, Asians, ghetto street gangs, bikers, anyone at all.

You needed leaders for a revolution, and DiBiase volunteered his services. A man of vision, courage and determination, he would turn the game around, restore the Honored Society's tarnished reputation... for a price. As payback for the miracle, he would accept a share of profits earned by each and every Family around the nation.

He would be the Boss of Bosses.

The more things changed, the more they stayed the same.

Bolan knew it would be relatively simple to eliminate Don Julio, but that was not the answer, in itself. A movement had been started in New York, with ripples spreading out across the landscape. Killing DiBiase might delay things, but it would not stop the other dons from dreaming, laying plans among themselves.

A bit more strategy was needed to eliminate the threat and shatter DiBiase's dreams.

Beginning in Times Square, at 10:15 on Wednesday night.

A teenage prostitute fell into step beside him. "Looking for a party, mister?"

Bolan smiled and shook his head. "No thanks," he said. "I brought my own."

THE BEST THING, Joey Pica thought, about a trick hotel was that you rarely had to lift a finger on the job. Say five, six times a month, a john got rowdy and you had to chill him out a little. Nine times out of ten, it was enough to whisper in his ear and flex a little muscle, maybe let him see the big Colt .45 in armpit leather.

Now and then, of course, he had to earn his money. Wax some crazy bastard who went overboard and started swinging, maybe even pulled a weapon. Even those were no great challenge for a man of Joey Pica's size and reputation. Six foot five, 280 pounds, with seven kills behind him. Two of those were johns who wouldn't listen, who wouldn't settle down when Joey gave them half a chance.

Tonight was quiet, sitting at his army-surplus desk and reading *Hustler*, watching as the bimbos came and went with johns in tow. The trick hotel was two doors down from Forty-sixth and Broadway, sandwiched in between a porno bookstore and a bar that offered ALL NUDE GIRLS! GIRLS! GIRLS! This night shift picked up street trade, horny tourists from the bars, and rejects from the peep shows. Anyone, in fact, with money in his pocket... or her purse.

Another thing he liked about the hotel duty was you got to see all kinds. A "jane" came through from time to time, and there were always chicken hawks: the would-be kiddy diddlers who preferred their ladies of the evening anorexic, dressed like ten- or twelve-year-olds. A chubby chaser, now and then, or guys that wanted threesomes.

Take your pick.

They didn't peddle boys at Joey Pica's stand, but you could wander two blocks either way and name your poison. Grade-school dropouts. She-males. Fucking tattooed acrobats, for all he knew.

Love made the world go round.

It was a nonstop sideshow on Times Square, and Joey Pica liked that, too. He was a people watcher, soaking in the sights and feeling good about himself each time a freak came into view. It helped him, having someone to look down on all the time.

And, then again, the pay was decent.

That was one thing Joey had to say about Don Julio. The guy was strict, but he was also fair. And generous. He knew that standup soldiers didn't grow on trees these days. You got what you paid for, and if a shooter blew it, once he took the fella's money...well, you had to figure he was going to get burned.

So, Joey Pica had himself an easy job, five days a week, and if he had to do a little something extra now and then— whack out a couple of Jamaicans, for example; maybe lean on one of DiBiase's customers to keep the vigorish in play—he didn't mind at all. The truth was, Joey liked his work. Hurting people, killing them, from time to time, made him feel like someone special.

Your average Wednesday night was nothing special, six or seven johns an hour till the midnight rush, and this was no exception. Joey checked his watch and went back to his magazine. The women in the glossy photos were a cut above the ones he supervised around the trick hotel. At least they came off looking cleaner in the magazine. This issue's centerfold, for instance, with the way she shaved—

A movement at the far end of the hallway caught his eye, distracting him. He glanced up from the desk and saw a tall man moving toward him, easy strides, the jacket of his suit unbuttoned. Nothing odd in that, except the guy was all alone, no bimbo leading him.

Now, what the hell . . .

The first thing Joey Pica thought was: vice cop.

They would drop by, now and then, to shoot the breeze or ask him questions, if they had a weirdo on the loose. Last year, for instance, when that freak was cutting hookers up and leaving them in Dumpsters. DiBiase told his people on the streets to help the cops, if possible, since heavy freaks were bad for business. Joey hadn't heard of anything like that around Times Square for several months, but you could never tell.

"I help you?"

"Maybe so." The stranger's voice was deep and mellow. "You in charge, here?"

"Looks that way. What's up?"

"Your number," said the tall man. "I was sent to shut you down."

"Oh yeah?" It dawned on Joey, what the guy was saying and he pushed his chair back, coming to his feet. "What kind of shit is this?"

"You want to walk out on your own, or let the paramedics handle it?"

"Hey, fuck you, man!"

And as he said it, Joey Pica was already reaching for his Colt, the same piece he had used on three of seven hits. He kept a live round in the chamber, with the safety off. You simply had to thumb the hammer back and point it. Rock and roll.

Except he never got that far. One second, he was snarling at the stranger, reaching for his piece, and then the tall man had an ugly-looking automatic in his fist. Some kind of silent job, the way it sounded, spitting out two rounds like it was nothing, slamming Joey Pica back against the wall.

A heartbeat later, he was sitting on the threadbare carpet, wondering what happened. Numb below the shoulders, even though he seemed to feel a liquid warmth collecting in his lap.

The stranger turned away and left him sitting there, a useless decoration. It was sometime later, and his consciousness was fading fast, when Joey Pica caught the first strong whiff of smoke.

THE HARLEM RIVER separates Manhattan from the Bronx. A dozen bridges span the river, from its juncture with the Hudson to First Avenue, on the south. No matter where they cross the water, though, the wise guys know that they are leaving DiBiase territory, entering Carmine Tattaglia's preserve.

The East 149th Street bridge led Johnny Gray directly into Melrose, a Bronx neighborhood sandwiched between Morrisania on the north, and Mott Haven on the south. His target was a sports book run by the Tattaglia Family, on Prospect Avenue. The kind of setup geared to working men and women, offering an outlet for frustration, nurturing the dream of instant wealth and luxury.

Something for nothing.

The American dream.

In the Bronx, though, as in every other section of the country where the Mob had put down roots, the money earned from "clean" pursuits like gambling was immediately funneled into drugs, extortion, prostitution and the like. It paid Tattaglia's contract killers, kept his pimps in flashy clothes, and stocked his cameras with film to keep those "extra special" movies rolling out to favored clientele.

The book was large, as such things go, with twenty-odd employees on the premises at any given time. They handled walk-in bettors, if the doorman knew your face, but ninety-five percent of Carmine's action came in through the bank of fourteen telephones. Some clients called directly, but the book could also handle layoff action, if a smaller bookie was afraid of getting burned by heavy betting on a certain game, fight, race—you name it.

Informants estimated that the book on Prospect Avenue earned Don Tattaglia something like $650,000 each month, free and clear. It never closed, accommodating bets on holidays, the graveyard shift. For the past six years, there had not been a hitch.

Until tonight.

The book was situated in a spacious room behind a combination bar and pool hall. When the front closed down, from 2 a.m. till half past ten, the backroom gamblers had the place all to themselves. When Johnny breezed in off the street, 10:41 p.m., the bar had twenty-five or thirty customers. Blue-collar, for the most part, with a handful sporting ties and jackets. Not a biker or apparent lowlife in the crowd, until he passed the men's room, moving toward the backroom book.

The guard was husky, average size. He had a scar across his forehead and a pistol underneath one arm.

"You lost or somethin'?"

"Nope."

The sight of Johnny's automatic got the bruiser's full attention. He gave up his piece without a fight, rapped out a coded knock and led the way inside with Johnny on his heels. The telephones were muted, flashing lights instead of auditory signals, but the place was still a beehive of activity. Before the door had fully closed behind him, Johnny counted nineteen obvious employees, seven players, and a floor boss—singled out because he was the only person present in a suit and tie.

It was a simple thing to get the crowd's attention. Johnny pointed his SIG-Sauer at the tote board, twenty feet away, and squeezed off two quick shots that echoed through the room like cannon fire. There was an instant hush, and the manager blanched white beneath a sunlamp tan.

"Hey, what the fuck is this?" he asked, when he could find his voice.

"I'm making a withdrawal from the bank," said Johnny.

"Yeah? I'll tell you what you're making, son. The fucking mistake of a lifetime."

"I'll risk it," Johnny told him, balancing a pistol in each hand. "Just bag the cash and make it snappy."

"Do you know who owns this place?"

His third shot missed the floor boss by an inch or so, and drilled into the wall. The fat man jumped, forgetting all his arguments as he began relaying orders to the troops.

"Sack up the cash, for Christ's sake! You guys deaf, or what?"

"That's better," Johnny said. "I've got a message for your goombah, while I'm here."

"You talk like that about the man, you must be crazy."

Johnny leveled the SIG-Sauer at the fat man's face. "You always argue with a crazy man?" he asked.

"Not me."

"Tell Don Tattaglia Barbados can get hot, this time of year. He ought to watch himself, make sure he doesn't soak up too much sun."

"That's it? A fucking weather bulletin?"

"That's all, for now. I wouldn't be surprised if he heard something more within the next few hours."

"Man, I wouldn't want to be in your shoes when the shit comes down."

"I'll wear my hip boots," Johnny said.

"You better get yourself a diving bell. Some life insurance wouldn't hurt, you wanna leave your family something."

Johnny watched a young man moving toward him with a paper shopping bag. Inside it, he saw stacks of currency, with fifty-dollar bills on top.

"You have another exit?" Johnny asked the manager.

"Back there," the fat man nodded to his left rear. "By the toilet."

"That's appropriate." As Johnny spoke, he tucked the hardman's pistol in his belt and reached inside his pocket for an incendiary stick. "I'll tell you what. You want to live, go on and take your people out the front way. Tell the customers you've got a fire back here. I estimate they've got five minutes, give or take."

"You're shitting me."

He primed the fire stick's fuse and pitched it overhand, in the direction of the tote board. It was sizzling by the time it hit the floor, smoke wafting upward from the carpet.

"I don't think so," Johnny told him, taking out a second fire stick.

"Jesus, guys, let's move it!"

Johnny stood aside from the stampede and watched them go. In seconds flat he was alone, except for the gorilla who had been on lookout duty at the door.

"I can't just run away," the slugger told him. "Don Tattaglia would have my ass."

Johnny saw the resignation on his adversary's face.

"You've got a point," he said, and put a bullet through the sentry's shoulder, spinning him around to wind up on all fours. He waited till the guy had scrambled clear before he tossed the second fire stick, and the third, retrieved the sack of cash, and lammed out through the back.

New York was cooking.

And they were barely getting started.

BROOKLYN is the classic home of mobsters, dating back to Al Capone and Johnny Torrio. These days, the local syndicate is more sedate, but no less powerful, a brooding presence in the borough that affects each resident, in one way or another, from his birth until the day he dies. The last five years or so, Vincent Scarpato was The Man in Brooklyn, growing fat on gambling, the drugs he moved in Bedford Stuyvesant, hijacking, stolen stocks and bonds. He was lined up with Don Julio of late, supporting Di-Biase's plan for a "new order" in the Mafia, and that would have to change.

Bolan crossed the East River by way of the Manhattan Bridge, driving south on Flatbush Avenue through Prospect Park, branching off on Parkside Avenue to pick up Hamilton Parkway. South again from there, New Utrecht Avenue, until he found himself in Bensonhurst.

It was a quarter past eleven when he parked outside the nightclub, locked his car and walked around back. The door was open, water hissing in a metal sink nearby as Bolan entered, smelling sweat, cigar smoke, fast-food kitchen orders. One guy was washing dishes, another flipping greasy burgers at the grill. They both glanced up at Bolan, recognized the Uzi in his hand and fled without an argument when Bolan nodded toward the exit.

There was a porthole in the kitchen door, and Bolan used it, counting heads. Two dozen customers, a pair of waitresses, one guy behind the bar. Nobody paid the least bit of attention as he cleared the swing door, his entrance covered by the music throbbing from a jukebox on the far side of the room.

He lined the box up in his sights and fired a short burst from the shoulder, screams mixed in with the staccato sound of gunfire. Swinging toward the bar, he triggered off another burst that cracked the mirror, shattering a row of whiskey bottles. Now, besides the other smells, the air was ripe with fumes of alcohol.

"The party's over!" Bolan shouted. "Everybody out!"

He caught the barkeep moving to obey, a gesture with the Uzi freezing him.

"Hey, man, I don't know you."

"That's right," said Bolan. "You can take a message, though, I'll bet.

"What kind of message?"

"To Scarpato."

"Jesus, man, I'm not with them. Do I look made to you? I work the bar four nights a week, that's it."

"But you report to someone, am I right?"

"Well, sure. The manager. He isn't here right now."

"So, give the word to him. He'll pass it on."

"Okay. I'm listening."

"Scarpato should think twice about his deal with Di-Biase. That's the message, plain and simple. Julio's bad news, from this day forward. Got it?"

"Sure."

"So, let me hear it."

Staring at the Uzi, Bolan's temporary prisoner gave back the message, more or less verbatim.

"Close enough. Why don't you hit the bricks?"

Alone again, the Executioner removed a thermite can from his coat pocket, dropped the safety pin and let the can roll across the bar. He was already halfway through the kitchen when it popped, the white-hot coals of phosphorous igniting fires on any surface that they touched.

Flameout.

It would be midnight soon, a new day in New York, and he was barely getting started. How long was it, since he staged his death a few miles from this very spot, in Central Park?

Too long.

The Executioner was coming back in style, against the same old enemy. He was not leaving marksman's medals as a signature these days, but it was still the same war in his heart and in his mind.

Scarpato, DiBiase, and the rest were in for some surprises.

Hell on earth, and then some.

By the time they made it to Barbados, they would need a tropical vacation, but the island sojourn would be far from restful. Bolan had already taken over as the tour guide, and he had their whole itinerary planned, with some allowances for playing it by ear along the way.

Who said a busy mobster never got to travel?

DiBiase and his friends were on their way to hell.

It was a one-way trip, this time, with all expenses paid.

CHAPTER TEN

Julio DiBiase drained his double shot of Black Bush in one swallow. It required a concentrated force of will to keep from flinging his empty glass across the room, but he restrained himself. No time for tantrums, at the moment.

He had work to do.

The conference was coming up, with trouble out in California and around Chicago. Now, mere hours after Ernie Cavalcante got his ass kicked in the Windy City, DiBiase had a problem of his own. Somebody was working overtime to get his goat.

It wasn't just the trick hotel he minded, or the fact that Joey Pica had been killed. Don Julio could always rent another fleabag for his girls to work in, find another watchdog for the kinky johns. What troubled him was the audacity of some guy walking in and pulling shit like this, as if he thought he could get away with it.

The fucking nerve!

Don Julio was big on honor and respect. He knew a man could have a thousand guns behind him, and it didn't count for shit if people still regarded him as weak, a spineless punk that anyone could push around. If DiBiase let the latest insult pass, he would be in for greater trouble, somewhere down the line.

Barbados, for example.

How could he expect to pull the Families together, make himself supreme Boss of Bosses, if he had some wild man running loose around Manhattan, shooting DiBiase's button men and starting fires?

Then again, suppose the raid was tied in with the coming meet somehow?

What did it mean? Who was responsible? How could he fix it in a hurry to prevent himself from looking bad?

Too many questions, damn it! What he needed now were answers.

Tommy had returned from the Chicago trip with more bad news. On top of the attack at Cavalcante's office, some wild man grabbed his limo from a public parking lot and took LaRocca's bimbo for a ride. She came back with a message, warning Julio to watch his ass.

This shit was getting old.

He wished that there was someone he could punish, then and there. Reach out and touch someone, his fingers tight around the stupid bastard's throat, and squeeze until his eyes popped out. Rough justice, and the word would get around. Don Julio would see to that.

But first, he had to find out who was playing suicidal games.

He had a list of possibles to choose from. At the top, Carmine Tattaglia, an enemy from way back. Carmine was opposed to DiBiase's rise and made no bones about it. If he saw the chance to fling a monkey wrench into the works, he would not hesitate. Still, reaching out to stir the pot in Cavalcante's territory, much less California, was a stretch of the imagination. Would Tattaglia go that far, just to scatter Julio's support?

Who else?

Joe Graziano, out in Jersey, was a wild card, sitting on the fence, but he was not the kind of man to start a shooting war unless he thought he had a decent chance of coming out on top. Right now, the way things stood, Don Julio was betting Joe would come up short on nerve.

So many changes in the syndicate, these past few years, and it was hard to keep a handle on the players. Paranoia was a part of life, when you had come up through the ranks by treachery and guile, like any capo worth his salt. When all was said and done, you couldn't trust your friends much further than your enemies, but that was life.

It left a whopping list of suspects, though, when anything went wrong.

The capo of Manhattan poured himself another drink and sat down in his favorite easy chair. His drapes were drawn against the night, and he had soldiers in the yard outside. You couldn't be too careful, in the circumstances, when you had an empire riding on the line.

He thought about LaRocca, wondering if Tommy had the stones to carry out the duties that would fall upon his shoulders in the next few days. He had not faltered, so far, but Chicago made him look bad, shaky and disorganized. They had to work on that, the two of them together. Maybe he would let LaRocca prove himself once more, before they took off for Miami and Barbados.

Maybe he would let his number two find out exactly who was playing games around Manhattan, bring the bastard in and drop him at his capo's feet. That just might do the trick.

And if LaRocca failed at that . . . well, anyone could be replaced.

Correction. *Almost* anyone.

Don Julio was an original, one of a kind, the real Mc-Coy. And he was in it for the long haul; you could take that to the bank.

He did not scare when things got tough, and he would never, ever weasel out.

If someone meant to challenge him, so much the better. It would keep life interesting.

He reached out for the telephone beside his chair and lifted the receiver, waiting for his houseman to respond.

"Yessir?"

"Get Tommy over here," the capo said. "We need to talk."

AT 12:13 a.m. on Thursday, Bolan parked outside a brownstone, one block north of Gun Hill Road in Williamsbridge, the Bronx. He had not met the building's owner, but he knew the man by reputation.

Sometimes, reputations were enough.

The owner, Pablo Guzman, was a front man for the Bogotá cocaine cartel. At home, by age nineteen, he was suspected of involvement in at least six murders—roughly one-fourth of the total now suspected by police and agents of the DEA. For Guzman, killing was a business proposition, and he always focused on the bottom line, intent on earning money for himself, his sponsors, the cartel at large.

Pablo Guzman had come to the States at age twenty-seven, an advance man for the latest gang of poison peddlers from Colombia. He could have easily afforded upscale quarters in Manhattan, but the Bronx locale was chosen with an eye toward ethnic roots, the notion that Latinos might be more receptive to his charm, at first. And, once the business had begun to blossom, Guzman felt at home right where he was.

The brownstone was not Pablo's home, exactly, though he often spent the evening hours there, relaxing in the company of his subordinates and women ordered from a local escort service. At the moment, Guzman was away on business, in Manhattan. Bolan had confirmed his absence with a contact in the New York office of the DEA, to make sure that he did not stumble over Pablo by mistake, ahead of schedule.

Bolan needed the Colombian alive for several hours yet, to play his part in the evolving drama. Pablo didn't know it, but he was destined to become a star.

Bolan parked in the alley beside Guzman's brownstone, a strip of grungy asphalt lined with trash cans, and littered with beer cans and bottles, scrap paper and condoms. He parked beneath the fire escape and double-checked his silenced Uzi as he left the car, closing the driver's door softly.

Going up.

The first three floors were rented out to families, Bolan understood, from talking to his contacts. Some of them were relatives of Guzman's men, but most were unaffiliated with the syndicate. The next three floors were gangland, all the way, reserved for Guzman's shooters and their party women, plus some storage space for hardware and the like.

He scaled the rusty fire escape without a second thought for whether it was safe or had been recently inspected. Life was full of risks, and Bolan knew his greatest hazard in the next few moments would not be a set of shaky metal stairs.

He counted off the floors. Passed two, three, four. On five, he paused before a darkened window, watching, listening. He pressed one ear against the glass, heard muffled voices from another room. Nobody waiting for him in the bedroom, but at least two men were close enough to hear if he smashed the glass.

Okay.

He drew a slim stiletto from his pocket and began to work the latch. Old wood was easy, yielding to the sharp, insistent blade. He beat the latch and spent another moment hoisting up the window, careful not to let it squeal on runners that had not been oiled in years.

Inside.

He left the window open, a potential exit, smelling sex and sweat inside the bedroom, cooking odors emanating from another sector of the flat. He crossed the room and opened the door a crack, saw three young men relaxing in the smallish living room, a television tuned to MTV.

Beavis and Butthead were chasing a dog with a chainsaw when Bolan stepped out of the bedroom, coming up behind his adversaries with the Uzi cocked and locked. He stood there for a moment, unobserved and savoring the moment of surprise.

"You ought to stick with PBS," he told them, ready as the three heads snapped around and everybody made a dive for hardware.

Bolan took the shooter on his far left, first. The guy was lunging toward a riot shotgun, standing in the corner near his easy chair, and Bolan caught him halfway there, a burst of parabellum shockers slamming him against the wall and pinning him before gravity brought him down.

Number two was on his feet and diving toward a pistol on the coffee table. Bolan helped him get there with a short burst from his Uzi. The young man hit the table in a belly flop that snapped two legs and dumped him facedown on the floor.

The third man reached his pistol, spun and tried to line up his target, but Bolan got there first, a rising burst that stitched the gunner from his belt line to his Adam's apple, slamming him over on his back, dead.

How much of that was audible next door, or down the hall?

He put the flat behind him, glancing left and right as he emerged into the corridor. Six doors in each direction, salsa music blasting from behind a couple of them, covering the muffled sounds of Bolan's silenced SMG.

Bolan drifted to his left, passed silent doors, until he stood before the entrance to a flat that rocked with Latin rhythm. No point knocking, and he did not bother checking if the door was locked. A snap kick, inches from the knob, and Bolan followed through, his Uzi leading him across the threshold.

In the middle of the living room, a long-haired punk in Jockey shorts was dancing with a naked girl. She might have been sixteen, but Bolan doubted it. Her eyes went wide at sight of him, and he motioned her away. It took another moment for the punk to notice something out of place, and when he turned to the open door, he lost his rhythm, cursing, breaking for a closet on his right.

It was impossible, a desperation move. The Uzi stuttered, half a dozen rounds exploding through the runner's rib cage, spinning him around and dumping him in an untidy sprawl. The girl was winding up to scream when Bolan left the flat and closed the door behind him, counting on the racket from the stereo to buy a few more seconds.

Any way you sliced it, he was stretching the advantage of surprise.

At another door, more music blared, four guys snorting coke along the breakfast bar and giggling as Bolan crashed in. They stared at him, groping for their weapons as he pitched a frag grenade across the intervening space, stepped back and slammed the door.

He made it halfway to the stairs before the blast sent shock waves rippling through the brownstone. Smoke and plaster dust. A woman screamed, voice muffled by the walls, and two doors opened simultaneously, spilling soldiers into Bolan's line of fire.

He met them with the Uzi, tracking left to right and back again, sweeping the hallway with bullets. Bodies jerked, twitching, one of Bolan's targets squeezing off three aimless pistol shots as he fell.

Reloading as he hit the stairway, Bolan chose the upper floor and started climbing. He reached the midway landing, hesitated, hearing voices on the stairs below, coming up from three. He palmed another frag grenade, released the pin and let it drop. Two seconds into free-fall, then a bounce, one more, and it was out of sight.

A shouted warning came too late. The blast sent shrapnel slicing into walls and whispering along the staircase. Bolan ducked back out of range and kept on climbing toward the top floor.

Men were on the move when he arrived, three running toward the stairs, two others standing by their open doors and checking weapons, hesitant to venture out against an unknown enemy. He met the runners with a blazing figure-eight that dropped them in a snarl of tangled arms and legs, three bodies twitching in their death throes, leaking crimson on the rug.

The hesitant survivors ducked back into their respective rooms, one squeezing off a shotgun blast before he disappeared. The buckshot never got as far as Bolan, peppering the wall a few yards to his left.

He moved to close the gap, advancing cautiously, wielding the Uzi one-handedly while he clutched his last grenade and dropped the safety pin. A few more steps, and he was lined up for a pitch, the nearest open doorway offering a shadow where the gunner crouched, just out of sight.

He tossed the frag grenade, an easy rebound off the doorjamb, and the young Colombian let out a squeal before he bolted. In his panic, he ran headlong through the doorway into the corridor, directly toward the waiting Executioner.

A short burst from the Uzi struck him in the chest and knocked him backward, staggering. Another heartbeat, and the frag grenade exploded, punching Bolan's target right across the corridor, face-first into the other wall. He struck with force enough to dent the plaster, slowly rocked back on his heels and went down in a lifeless sprawl.

And that, apparently, left one.

The lone shotgunner had his door shut. Bolan went in low and thumped a fist against the flimsy wooden panel, lying prone as buckshot ripped the door and wall, four feet above his head. Three rounds, and from his brief glimpse of the shooter's weapon, Bolan guessed that it would hold no more than six.

If he was wrong, or if the punk had managed to reload...

He wriggled past the door, acutely conscious of the voices coming to him from the stairway, still a floor below, but closing. Reaching up, he slapped the door again. Two blasts, and a third, and Bolan scrambled to his feet, propelled by pure adrenaline.

Bolan did not bother pushing through the tattered remnants of the door. His target, standing in the living room, was fumbling shotgun shells into his 12-gauge, cursing as he dropped one on the floor and bent to pick it up.

Too late.

The Uzi caught him as he straightened up, a burst across the chest that drove him backward, reeling. A sofa broke his fall, but the Colombian was far past being grateful for small favors. He was DOA and then some, crimson welling up from half a dozen mortal wounds.

And Bolan knew that he was out of time. He burst in through the shattered door, moved past his lifeless target, toward the bedroom. Found the window, with the fire escape outside. Another moment found him scrambling down the metal ladder.

He jumped the last twelve feet or so and landed in a crouch. The car was waiting for him, and he threw himself behind the wheel, one hand on the ignition key. Upstairs, he pictured his pursuers edging down the smoky hallway, checking out each room in turn.

How long before they figured out that he was gone?

No matter.

He was rolling, and he had a call to make, before he packed it in for Wednesday night.

Correction: it was Thursday, now. A brand-new day.

And some of Bolan's enemies who watched the sun come up would never see it set.

"IT'S GETTING ROUGH OUT," Hal Brognola said.

"You got that right," said Leo Turrin, speaking from New York. "And something tells me it's just getting started."

"DiBiase's going to regret Barbados pretty soon, I wouldn't be surprised."

"Not yet, though. One thing everybody says about Don Julio, he's got determination."

"Right. What kind of action are you looking at, the next few hours?"

"Striker's stirring up the Families," said Turrin. "Get them thinking twice about cooperation. And, I wouldn't be surprised if Pablo Guzman got involved."

"That's interesting."

"Another country heard from, so to speak."

"One thing with the Colombians, they don't discriminate that well on targets."

"Striker wouldn't try it, if he didn't have a handle on the situation."

"Yeah, I know. I'm wondering if anybody broke the news to Guzman."

"I'm on top of it," said Leo. "What's the feedback from Chicago?"

"Well, I wouldn't hold my breath on any love notes from the SAC, if I were you."

"He's bitching?"

"All the way to Washington. I heard from the director earlier this evening. For the record, he's 'concerned about the implications' of our plan. He won't go public with it, being a career man and a relatively new appointee. Anyway, he knows we got approval from his boss, up front. He won't buck that, but if it blows up in our faces, he'll be on the record as opposed."

"Concerned," said Leo, chuckling to himself.

"That, too."

"We should be in Miami by this time tomorrow."

"Fair enough. So far, I'm getting zip in terms of viable cooperation from the people in Barbados."

"Hey, you sound surprised."

"Not really. It's a disappointment, though. Just once, I'd like to see a government refuse to sell its soul for tourist dollars."

"Here's a tip. Don't hold your breath."

"I won't. Have you got something else?"

"Not really," Leo said. "I bypassed city hall, too many leaks. The FBI and DEA are sitting tight for twenty-four. I didn't bother with the IRS. That's book work, anyway. As far as I could tell, they don't have anybody in the field."

"Okay, let's pack it in. I'll talk to you if something breaks, or you can catch me at the office in the morning."

"Hey, it *is* the morning."

"Don't remind me, Leo."

As he broke the link with New York City, Hal reflected on the progress of their scheme, so far. From San Diego to Chicago to Manhattan, Bolan was on schedule, clocking up the miles and body count. He had convinced Dan Masciere to leave early for Miami, and the FBI had logged him in with Roman Graffia. Ernesto Cavalcante had not left the Windy City yet, but he was shaken by the near miss at his office and the losses he had suffered in the field. Manhattan would be smoking in a few more hours, if it wasn't now, and that would cast the nation's ranking Families into turmoil.

So much for a meeting of the minds when they assembled in Barbados. Gang wars had erupted over less, and Bolan knew exactly how to stir the pot in these chaotic situations. Turn the heat up to a rolling boil and see what surfaced.

The FBI's disclaimer came as no surprise. Since Waco and the fallout from the Branch Davidian disaster, G-men around the country had been walking on eggs, harking back to the motto enshrined by J. Edgar Hoover: Don't embarrass the Bureau.

The potential for embarrassment was limitless these days, and no one in the FBI, from Washington to Butte, Montana, was inclined to be the first to stretch his neck out on the chopping block. There would be more than a career at stake if Congress or the press linked Stony Man's covert, illegal operations to the FBI.

If the lid blew off on all that Striker and the rest had done the past few years, it would eclipse the Watergate fiasco in a heartbeat. Hal could almost see the headlines now, complete with former presidents subpoenaed from retirement, lining up to testify. How much of it could they suppress on grounds of national security? How long before a snitch showed up on the tube with Maury Povich or Geraldo?

Relax, for Christ's sake!

It would never come to that, and if it did, Brognola was prepared to take the heat. It was a part of his initial job description, when he got the go-ahead for Stony Man.

The buck stops here.

But even that was wrong, he knew. The buck would ultimately stop with Striker and his frontline allies, in the trenches where the game was won or lost.

Hal felt old, thinking back to the beginning of their long relationship, the changes he had gone through on the trek to reach his present state of mind. Friends and loved ones had been lost along the way. None of them could ever be replaced, but neither had they given up their lives in vain.

Not while the fight went on.

CHAPTER ELEVEN

"I don't want any shit about you don't know this or that," the dealer said. "I ask a question, I'm expecting you to tell me something I don't know."

The anger showed in Pablo Guzman's face. His pock-marked cheeks were flushed with color, and his lips drew back from small white teeth, imparting the appearance of a snarling animal. He paced the floor relentlessly, and there was murder in his eyes.

"We asked around the neighborhood, you know?" Tomas Reynoso said. "Nobody saw the guy, as far as we can tell. We also put the word out on the street, but nothing's coming back, so far."

Guzman stopped pacing, stood before Reynoso, glaring at his second in command.

"I told you what that fucker said to me."

The phone call had been worse for Pablo than the loss of nineteen soldiers to an unknown enemy. The caller used his private number, reaching out for Guzman personally, and conveyed his message in a tone that made the dealer feel like he was some kind of *pendejo,* to be pushed around and told what he must do.

"Stop fucking with the Families," the caller said. "Next time, we'll give your errand boys a pass and come for you, first thing."

And that was all.

The bastard didn't say which Families, and that could be a problem, inasmuch as Guzman had been dealing coke throughout Manhattan, Brooklyn and the Bronx. His warning could have come from DiBiase, Scarpato, Tattaglia . . . or all of them together.

No, scratch that. It was a point of common knowledge on the street that DiBiase and Tattaglia were enemies. They had not gone to war yet, but it was only a matter of time, by all accounts, until the shooting started.

In the meantime, though, someone was shooting at Guzman, and their aim was too damned good for comfort.

Back at home, in Bogotá, such problems were inevitably handled with dispatch. An insult, much less an attempted murder, was sufficient grounds for the annihilation of the man responsible, his family, his friends. There was no quarter asked or granted in affairs of honor, much less business, with a fortune riding on the line.

"How many left?" asked Guzman.

Tomas blinked, confused. "How many what?"

"How many fucking soldiers do we have?"

"Oh, well . . ." Reynoso did the calculation in his head, while Guzman waited, fuming. "Twenty-seven. I make twenty-eight."

It wasn't much, but he could always call the reinforcements from Colombia, if necessary. In the meantime, Guzman felt like hitting back with everything he had.

"You have that list of targets?"

"*Sí.*" Reynoso was smiling now. "Our life insurance."

"Time to cash it in," said Guzman. "You make the assignments. Hit these fuckers where it hurts the most."

"Which Family?" Reynoso asked.

And it came back to that, again. Without a clear fix on the enemy's identity, they could be wasting time and ammunition, stirring up another hornet's nest with powerful opponents who presently meant them no harm. If Guzman let his anger run away with him . . .

"All three," he said. "I never like Italians, anyway."

"All three," said Guzman's number two, confirming it. If he had any doubts about the plan, Reynoso kept them to himself.

It was a simple thing, declaring war on strangers. Guzman knew his enemies by sight, from various surveillance photographs and pictures in the paper, but there had been no direct communication in the past. He understood the rules and knew that dealing coke in the Sicilians' territory was essentially a hostile act, but he had managed to escape the retribution of La Cosa Nostra up to now. A part of him had known that it would come to this eventually, and he didn't mind.

In Bogotá, throughout his homeland, violence was the rule. It had been quiet too damned long in New York City, for his taste. His one regret, thought Guzman, was that he had not been first to strike. The loss of nineteen men would surely slow him down, as well as focusing the spotlight of publicity upon him.

What did the reporters say, on television?

If it bleeds, it leads.

Guzman was bleeding, at the moment, but he planned to even up the score before another day was out. The Families were strong, but they were also vulnerable in a down-and-dirty war, with no holds barred. The kind of war that Pablo Guzman knew by heart.

Soon, he told himself, there would be blood enough to go around.

DRIVING THROUGH the garment center, Bolan made a left-hand turn from Thirty-eighth Street onto Seventh Avenue, proceeding south for two blocks, then a right-hand turn on Thirty-sixth. The curbside parking was a hopeless case, so he drove one block past his target, found a seven-story public garage and walked back through the morning crush of men and women headed for their jobs.

He did not spot a single "supermodel" in the crowd.

His latest target was a furrier's that mostly dealt in stolen coats and stoles, forged labels covering for hijacked merchandise. Carmine Tattaglia owned the place, and it was time to jerk his chain again, in Bolan's estimation. Keep the capo guessing as the deadline for Barbados rapidly approached.

The shop was relatively small, refrigerated storage space in back, three pickets on the sidewalk marking time with cardboard signs proclaiming FUR IS MURDER. Bolan was not absolutely sure that he agreed, but it would serve his purposes to help the activists, this time, by putting Don Tattaglia's operation out of business.

Yukon Furs was sandwiched between a stylish dress shop and a place that seemed to specialize in lavender tuxedos, with a loft upstairs. He hit the dress shop first, flashed bogus paperwork, and asked to see the manager. A bleached blonde in her waning thirties listened to his story of a leaking gas main and reluctantly agreed to clear the premises.

He got a hassle at the tux shop, from a greasy-looking character more interested in money than the safety of his staff or customers. They had been arguing for something like a minute and a half when Bolan crumpled his lapel in one strong hand and jerked the weasel up on tiptoes.

"No more bullshit, now." His best official voice. "You want to bust my chops on this, I'll make one call and jerk your business license, for a start. If anything goes wrong because of the delay you're causing, it voids your fire insurance automatically. Are we communicating, now?"

"Yes, sir!"

He thought about the loft, but could not find an outside staircase, finally deciding it was accessed through the furrier's. One of the pickets offered him a pamphlet. Bolan stuffed it in a pocket.

"Fur's murder, man. Don't do it."

"Sorry," Bolan said. "I can't resist."

Inside the shop, a well-dressed, white-haired man came forward, greeting Bolan with a smile. "Good morning, sir. How may I help you?"

"It's the other way around," the Executioner replied. "I'm helping you."

"Excuse me?"

"No excuses," Bolan said. "I've got a message for your boss."

"My boss? There must be some misunderstanding, sir. I own—"

"Carmine Tattaglia."

The man stopped in midsentence, frowning. "Oh, I see."

"Not yet, you don't. The message comes from Julio, *capisce?*"

"From Julio. I understand."

"Tell Carmine he should think about Barbados, long and hard. He doesn't want to go down there and make a serious mistake. It could have fatal consequences."

As he spoke, he watched the old man's face lose color, till the demarcation line below his snowy hair and forehead almost disappeared.

"I have it, sir."

"You're sure about that?"

"Quite."

"One thing, before I go," said Bolan. "Just to make sure Tattaglia gets the point."

"And what would that be, sir?"

"I need to have a look at your refrigerator."

"Yes, sir. This way, please."

They passed a couple of employees on the way, young women. Bolan paused to tell them they should step outside, the manager providing confirmation at a glance. The old man's grim expression and his slouching shoulders told the Executioner he thought his time was running out.

"Back here," he said, and led the way between two racks of empty wooden hangers, to a large walk-in refrigerator.

In the cold room hung full-length coats and shorty jackets, capes and stoles, all draped in see-through plastic. Bolan picked out fox, mink, ermine, leopard, wondering where they had come from, which insurance company had shelled out thousands off the top and boosted rates to compensate for losses due to theft.

"Not bad," said Bolan. "Is there anyone upstairs?"

"No."

"You can go, now."

"Go, sir?"

"Right. Unless you want to stay and watch the fire."

The old man turned away without another word and left the shop. As he pushed through the outer doorway to the street, the pickets started chanting: "Don't kill for fashion! Fur is murder!"

Bolan unclipped the small incendiary grenade from his belt in the small of his back and brought a metal folding chair to prop open the door of the refrigerator. When he had the flow of oxygen secured, he pulled the safety pin and dropped it, took a long step back and tossed the thermite can into the cold room, underhand. The empty hangers rattled as he passed, a heavy curtain swishing into place behind him as he reached the front room of the shop.

He stood and waited for the pop-whooosh of the thermite bomb, flicked back the curtain, watching smoke waft out of the refrigerator, spreading through the shop at large.

The pickets saw him coming, startled as a puff of smoke came out behind him, through the open door.

"What's happening?" one of them asked.

"Fire sale," the Executioner replied, and moved off down the sidewalk, putting Yukon Furs behind him. When he glanced back from the corner, he could see the pickets dancing in a swirl of smoke.

He left them to it, moving toward the next appointment on his hit parade.

WEST NEW YORK is actually located in New Jersey, on the west bank of the Hudson River, opposite Manhattan. Jack Grimaldi had a road map open on the seat beside him as he cleared the Lincoln Tunnel, cursing the morning traffic that had slowed his progress to a crawl.

Each time he used the tunnel, maybe twice a year, he was impressed by the apparent lack of maintenance. The ceiling tiles were missing in an ugly checkerboard design, and thick electric cables dangled through a number of the openings, reminding Jack of giant worms...or gangrenous intestines from a mutilated corpse. The tunnel walls showed cracks that seemed a little larger every visit, and the overall effect could keep you guessing, wondering if— or when—the whole thing would collapse and drown the occupants of several hundred vehicles.

Of course, it wasn't really *that* bad...was it?

Somewhere in the middle of the river, Jack had passed from New York State into New Jersey, where the rackets were controlled—at least, in theory—by Don Joseph Graziano. Fifty-seven on his birthday six weeks earlier, Don Graziano had been calling all the shots in Jersey for the past nine years. His reign had been a relatively stable period, but there were youngbloods in the Jersey ranks who quarreled over where their Family should be standing in relation to New York.

Dissension made the world go round.

Grimaldi picked up Parkview Avenue and followed it through Weehawken, the river and a maze of railroad tracks immediately on his right. Memorial Park went by on his left, two blocks over, Grimaldi taking off on Hillside Road and keeping to his right, heading down to the waterfront.

Hudson Hauling occupied one of the several dozen piers that reach out toward Manhattan from the riverfront of West New York. Its fleet consisted of a tug and two flat barges, used primarily for hauling waste. In theory, it was all "clean" garbage, bound for sanitary landfills further south in Ocean County, but the company was also known to handle toxic cargo. Anything from AIDS-infected blood and needles to radioactive material and obsolete cathode tubes might be found on Hudson Hauling barges when they made their midnight runs into the dark Atlantic. No one was the wiser when they came back empty and were hosed down at the dock.

Grimaldi parked outside the chain link fence and walked back through a drizzling rain. With its folding stock collapsed, the Colt Commando fit beneath his raincoat nicely, on a shoulder sling, spare magazines tucked in his pockets. A fedora kept the rain out of Grimaldi's eyes and helped give him the "gangster look" he needed for the job at hand.

It was the kind of place where Graziano posted sentries, day and night, to keep the curious away. A number of inspectors had been bribed, from City Hall to the state capital, but you could never tell about reporters or environmentalists, the kind who stick their noses into other people's private business and expose all kinds of shady deals.

One button man was waiting for him on the loading dock, examining Grimaldi with a scowl as he approached the warehouse. Checking left and right, Grimaldi saw a second man emerge and take his place beside the first. Jack had his right hand in the outside pocket of his raincoat, with the lining slit to let him reach the Colt Commando's pistol grip. He flicked the safety off and let his index finger curl around the trigger, counting off the paces in his mind.

"That's far enough," the taller of the sentries said. "What do you want?"

"I need to have a look inside," Grimaldi said. "Official business."

On the dock, both men had right hands tucked inside their jackets.

"Nobody said we had inspectors coming."

"That's the point. We like surprises at the EPA."

"You'll need a warrant, even so."

"A warrant, right. I'll see what I can do."

He let them see the automatic carbine then, the gunners peeling off in opposite directions, dragging pistols into daylight. On Grimaldi's left, the spokesman for the duo held a shiny automatic in a firm two-handed grip, but he ran out of time before he had a chance to fire.

A burst of 5.56 mm tumblers from Grimaldi's weapon stitched across the mafioso's chest and slammed him back against the wall of cinder blocks behind him. Gravity took over and pulled him down from there, crimson streaks marking his passing.

Number two, breaking for the doorway he had passed through moments earlier, fired a wild shot in Jack's direction, winging high and wide. Grimaldi chased him with a burst that cut the gunman's legs from under him and dropped him squirming on his side. Another pistol shot, no closer than the first, and Jack unleashed a second burst that left his adversary limp and lifeless on the loading dock.

He took the stairs three at a time, hurdled the gunner's body on the threshold, charging through the doorway in a combat crouch. The sound of gunfire had alerted those inside, but they were sluggish off the mark, three men just retreating to cover as Grimaldi cleared the entrance. One of them turned back to level a revolver, and Grimaldi hit him with a rising burst that flipped him over on his back, legs thrashing as he fell.

And that left two.

They went to ground behind a pyramid of fifty-gallon metal drums, all painted black, while Jack ducked down behind a forklift, using it for cover. Both of his opponents carried handguns, popping out on either side of their defensive barrier and snapping shots off at Grimaldi with a minimal concern for accuracy.

Time to think.

Grimaldi reached inside the right-hand pocket of his raincoat, came out with a frag grenade and armed it, winding up the pitch. Instead of lobbing overhand, he had a sudden brainstorm, rolling it across the concrete floor so that it came to rest against the bottom row of fifty-gallon drums.

Three seconds.

Two.

One.

The explosion brought their house down, more or less, the pyramid of drums collapsing backward, several of the fat containers ruptured, spewing waves of gray-green slime. Before the echo of the blast had died away, Grimaldi caught a whiff of noxious fumes, a cross between formaldehyde and pepper gas.

Too much.

One of the gunners came out shooting, but a racking cough destroyed his aim. The toxic goop was spattered on his clothes and scalp, his free hand slapping at the back of his neck.

Grimaldi met him with a short burst from the Colt Command, spinning him around and dropping him some thirty feet from the forklift. His target went down in a heap, the pistol spinning from his grasp and clattering across the floor.

One left.

Grimaldi heard the final gunner screaming, rose and walked around to check it out. He had to hold his breath this close to the ungodly spill, and he was careful not to step in anything he did not recognize.

The guy was pinned beneath three fallen drums, two covering his twisted legs, another weighting down one arm. A couple of the drums had ruptured, spattering the punk from head to toe. The slime was in his eyes, dark smears across his cheeks, more of it soaking through his shirt and slacks. It seemed to be corrosive on the skin, and Jack was not about to test it for himself.

Instead he backed off several paces, fired a mercy burst and cut the screams off midwarble.

Now his lungs were burning, and Grimaldi double-timed for daylight, fairly gasping by the time he reached the loading dock. His clothing smelled of chemicals, and it was a relief to feel the rain beat down upon his upturned face.

The cleanup would be someone else's job, but he would make a phone call on his way back to the Lincoln Tunnel and Manhattan, warn the local fire department of a toxic spill in progress. He would also find a number for the nearest TV station and remind them who owned Hudson Hauling, just in case they felt like whipping up some bad publicity for Joseph Graziano.

"Anything that I can do to help," Grimaldi told the dead men on the loading dock, before he walked back to his car.

The game was heating up, no doubt about it. By the time they reached Miami, half a dozen Families would be watching one another with suspicion, licking bloody wounds. Don Julio would have his hands full keeping peace, much less convincing anyone to buy his long-range scheme for personal advancement.

After Florida . . . well, DiBiase would be lucky if he had a friend outside his own Manhattan Family by the time the formal summit was convened.

Grimaldi thought of one more call to make before he left New Jersey. Graziano, right. It would not do for him to leave the Garden State without enlightening Don Joseph to the source of his misfortune.

Something in the nature of a gentle warning, and if Graziano came away believing DiBiase was responsible for the attack in West New York, it would be something for the two of them to talk about, next time they sat down face-to-face.

In Vietnam, the army called it PsyWar. Short for psychological warfare. The fine art of deceiving and disrupting a selected enemy by feeding him false information, half-truths, anything at all to spread dissension in the ranks, reduce effectiveness by tying up the opposition with internal squabbling and security precautions while you wound up for the knockout punch.

Grimaldi drove off with his window open, less concerned about the rain than the pervasive stench of fumes he carried with him. It was getting better after two blocks, when he saw the Mobil station coming up. He pulled into the lot and parked beside the phone booth.

He had Graziano's private number memorized, and he would get the others from the fat directory that hung suspended from a chain inside the booth. Simple. All he had to do was make the calls and drive back underneath the Hudson to Manhattan.

How much had the brothers managed to accomplish in his absence? He would soon find out. Experience told Jack that neither one of them was sitting on his hands, with so many inviting targets readily available.

New York had lured Bolan more than once, when he was on his own against the Mafia. It was a hopeless case, of course. No one could ever hope to sweep the Apple clean. Too many generations of corruption had been piled on top of one another there. It would require a fundamental change in human nature, for a start, and even then the battle would be fought uphill, against oppressive odds.

Still, they could take a shot, and maybe do some good along the way.

Eliminating DiBiase and his major playmates should be good enough, for now. If anybody wanted to pick up where Bolan's team left off, more power to them.

Jingling quarters in his hand, Grimaldi stepped out of his car, into the gentle rain.

CHAPTER TWELVE

Tomas Reynoso knew what was expected of him when his *jefe* sent him out to seek revenge against the Families. If Pablo was subjected to Sicilian insults and he let it pass, the next attack would be more devastating than the first. No man of honor could allow himself to be insulted and abused in public. He must act, at any cost, in order to preserve his self-respect.

Because the first assault on Guzman's soldiers took place in the Bronx, Carmine Tattaglia's territory, Pablo had decided that the first stroke of revenge should be delivered there, as well. Beyond the Bronx, he had a list of targets for Reynoso and the other hit teams to pursue. Before they finished, none of the Sicilians would feel safe again, until they made their peace with Guzman.

Or, Reynoso thought, it just might go the other way. The Mafia was strong in New York City, even following the recent prosecutions. He and Pablo, on the other hand, had less than thirty soldiers standing by. A call for reinforcements had been faxed to Bogotá, but it would take some time for new men to arrive, more time to arm them and deploy the troops, much less achieve results.

Would they arrive before it was too late?

Reynoso understood the concept of defeatist thinking, and he made a point of concentrating on the job at hand. He was riding shotgun in a sleek Mercedes-Benz, an Uzi submachine gun in his lap, two gunmen in the seat behind him. Hanging back a few yards, in a navy BMW, three more shooters kept the second wheelman company.

Two other teams of equal size were on the streets of Manhattan that very moment, but Reynoso's would be first to strike. Their target, two blocks over from Van Cortlandt Park, was an Italian social club where members of Tattaglia's Family could be found at almost any time of day or night. They gathered for a game of cards or dominoes, ate pasta there, sipped wine and coffee between meals. The place was swept for bugs twice daily so the regulars were able to discuss their business dealings with some security.

Except today.

Reynoso was not planting bugs this morning, but he had a grim surprise in store for the Sicilians. They were going to discover what it meant to take Colombians for granted, treating them like peasant trash, unworthy of respect.

The BMW peeled off at the intersection, circling around the block to drop three soldiers at the back door of the social club. Reynoso and his men would take the front. A pincer movement, sealing off the enemy's retreat.

They parked out front, old women passing on the sidewalk, no one visibly acknowledging the Benz or its four occupants. His driver left the motor running, and Reynoso made no effort to conceal his weapons as he stepped from the car. Besides the Uzi in his right hand, he was carrying a Ruger Mark II target pistol in his left, the barrel lengthened by a silencer. His two companions carried Ingram MAC-10 submachine guns, smaller than the Uzi, with an awesome cyclic rate of fire. The members of his rearguard team were similarly armed.

The social club was members only, with a bouncer on the door. The bouncer took one look at Two-Gun Tom Reynoso and went apeshit, groping for a sidearm under-

neath his coat. The Ruger .22 spit twice, drilled silent key-
holes in his forehead, and the goon went down.

Their way was clear.

Reynoso shoved the pistol in his waistband, took a firm
grip on the Uzi with both hands and led the way inside. A
burst of laughter greeted his appearance on the threshold,
three men at a table to his left, one of them winding up a
joke. Around the room, perhaps two dozen others occupied tables, several seated at the bar. Reynoso did not
speak Italian, and he did not care about the subjects of
their conversations. At the moment, he only needed to
observe the stunned reaction on their faces as they
glimpsed his weapon and the guns behind him.

Recognizing doom.

He wasted no time talking to the enemy, his Uzi stuttering and pouring hollowpoints into the jokers on his left.
Reynoso watched them twitching, going over backward in
their chairs, blood spouting from their wounds, and suddenly the air was full of thunder, three guns going off at
once, his backup soldiers crashing in the back door, firing
as they came.

Reynoso loved the power that he felt each time he pulled
the trigger on a human being. There was nothing to com-
pare with life-or-death authority. He understood why rev-
olutionaries risked their lives for worthless causes, tyrants
subjugated millions, maniacs went out to stalk the streets
by night.

Because it felt so good.

Reynoso found that he was smiling as he held the Uzi's
trigger down and swept the murky room. The smile became a full-blown laugh, Tomas exulting in his power
rush.

He let the smell of blood and cordite carry him away.

CARMINE TATTAGLIA was not expecting visitors at this ungodly hour of the morning. Granted, he had not been sleeping. Who could lie in bed with all that had been happening around the city in the past few hours? Maybe someone with a brain disorder, but there were no holes in Tattaglia's head.

Not yet.

"Who is it?" he demanded of his houseman, glowering across a mug of coffee.

"Says his name's Omega, boss."

"What kind of fucking name is that?"

"He gave me this," the houseman said, as if it answered everything. He handed Don Tattaglia a laminated playing card. On one side, there was nothing but the single word: OMEGA. When he turned it over Carmine found that he was staring at an ace of spades.

Impossible!

Those guys were all extinct, like dinosaurs. Tattaglia knew it for a fact. He could remember when the stony-eyed Black Aces were the Mafia elite, a hand-picked gestapo working directly for La Commissione. The only button men with the authority to hit a capo without advance permission from the syndicate's board of directors, as long as they could offer a reasonable explanation after the fact.

"What's this guy look like?" asked Tattaglia.

"Six feet, about two hundred pounds. Dark hair, you know. He looks like anybody else, except he's got an edge."

"Okay." Tattaglia made his choice. "I'll see him, but I want you and a couple of the boys outside there, got it? If I buzz you, or you hear the least suspicious thing, I want you in here on the double, kicking ass."

"Sure, boss."

Tattaglia left his window seat and moved around behind his spacious desk. It was the centerpiece of a very masculine study, its bulk hand-carved from mahogany and reinforced with hidden plates of high-tensile steel. Beneath the desk, mere inches from Tattaglia's knee, a holster had been mounted, with a big Glock 21—the .45-caliber model with thirteen-shot magazine—ready at hand. He barely had to move to reach the gun, and he could tap the secret panic button without even shifting in his seat.

All things considered, Carmine thought it was the best he could do.

Another moment passed before his houseman came back with the new arrival. From his seat, Tattaglia saw a couple of his soldiers loitering outside the study door with hands inside their jackets. Perfect. Let the bastard know, right off, that he could try whatever shit he wanted, but the move would cost his life.

Tattaglia did not rise or shake the stranger's hand. Instead he waved Omega to a seat directly opposite the desk, positioned so that if the shooting started, he would be caught in a cross fire, from the desk and study door.

Don Carmine held the ace of spades up to the light and frowned.

"I haven't seen one of these in a while," he said.

"They're hard to come by," said Omega.

"I imagine so. Word I got was, they were abolished."

"That's what you were meant to think." The stranger's eyes were cold, his small half smile a disconcerting presence in the room.

"How's that?"

"You know how these things work. Somebody wants insurance, they don't noise it all around."

"Insurance."

"Right. In case they need to take some action, down the line."

"Assume that's true." Tattaglia's fingertips made contact with the Glock. "What brings you here?"

"I see things," said Omega. "Sometimes, if I catch an opportunity to help somebody out and help myself at the same time, I go for it."

"You're here to help me out, is that the story?"

"More or less."

"Okay, I'm listening."

"You're looking at a big deal in Barbados," said Omega. "Either way you vote, somebody's bound to be upset."

"Shit happens," Carmine said.

"It mostly happens to the guy who walks in unprepared."

"Go on."

"Don Julio's been known to hold a grudge for years," Omega said. "He likes to think his payback through and get it right, you know? Thing is, he can't afford to wait on this one, when he needs support up front."

"So what?"

"So everybody and his dog knows you're the leading opposition. If he takes you out, some other people just might fall in line."

Tattaglia stared into the stranger's graveyard eyes. "He sent you here to try and scare me off?"

"Not even close. If he knew I was talking to you, I'd be in deep shit."

"Oh, yeah?"

"Let's put it this way. When he points the finger, in Miami or Barbados, I'm supposed to make the tag. He's got it rigged to look like you were setting up a move against his men on the commission. Take them out, and grab the marbles for yourself, that kind of thing.''

''That's bullshit.''

''Sure it is, but he's got people standing by to say it's gospel. Some of them aren't far away, you get my drift.''

Tattaglia understood, all right. If all of this was true, he had some traitors in his Family that needed object lessons in fidelity. Well, stranger things had happened. Still . . .

''You know,'' he said, ''I've been around the block with Julio, but I don't know your ass from Adam. Why should I believe all this?''

''Because you've been around the block with Julio,'' Omega said, ''and you don't trust him. That's experience talking. If you thought he was straight, you'd be backing his plan, I suppose.''

''Assuming that's correct, what's your suggestion?''

''Watch and wait,'' Omega said. ''Don't change your schedule, nothing that would make him hinky. When I get the word to take you out, I pass it on. We turn the game around and put the move on Julio, instead.''

''And what do you get out of it?'' Tattaglia asked.

Omega shrugged. ''You'll have to do some cleaning up around the house,'' he said. ''I'm good at that. The way I see it, you'll be needing a replacement for your number two, before much longer.''

Rossi! Christ, if Carmine's underboss had sold him out to DiBiase, he would have to clean it up, and soon.

''That's pretty serious.''

''Yes sir, I'd say you're right.''

It was a gamble, but Tattaglia was not inclined to shrug the warning off. At worst, if this Omega was a plant or just mistaken, Carmine could refrain from taking any action of his own. And if the guy rubbed out Don Julio while he was at it, that would not be such a loss.

In fact, it might be a relief.

"I guess we ought to stay in touch," Tattaglia said at last. "If it turns out you're right about this thing, we've got a deal."

Omega rose, and this time Carmine stood to shake his hand. The ace retrieved his calling card and stowed it in a pocket, moving toward the doorway.

"I'll be seeing you," he said.

And Carmine thought: I wouldn't be surprised.

Alone once more, he gave the visitor some time to clear the house, then punched a button on his intercom.

"Yeah, boss?"

"I want to talk to Rossi. Get him out here."

QUEENS HAD more or less been up for grabs the past two years, since capo Richard Valentino went away for sixty years to life on federal racketeering charges. He had been so confident of victory at trial or on appeal that he refused to name an heir, intent on running things from prison while he waited for release. The end result, when he was stabbed to death by unknown persons in the shower, was that no one had authority to run the Family. A three-way civil war erupted in the ranks, no faction strong enough to win the day, and finally, the Mafia commission had decreed that New York's three surviving Families could share the borough, if they promised to absorb Don Richard's troops and keep them on the payroll.

Thus had Queens become an "open" territory for the local Mob. That history was fresh in Johnny's mind as he drove east on Roosevelt, toward Flushing and his next appointment with the enemy.

The avenue stopped dead at Main Street. Johnny made a right-hand turn and drove south toward Kissena Park, a winding course through residential streets, until he reached the home of Jacob Weiss. It was a fair-size house, but nothing huge. The lawyer's money—or a major share of it, at any rate—went to the Cayman Islands every month, like clockwork, edging out the tax man.

Weiss was first among the dozen-odd attorneys who had kept Don DiBiase out of jail the past few years, defeating various indictments in a kind of circus atmosphere that left the prosecution fuming, filing motions to prevent Weiss from appearing, fishing for an impropriety that would eliminate Julio's most effective defender.

So far, they had failed. Johnny Gray was prepared to try a different approach.

He parked and walked up to the door, broad daylight, leaning on the bell. A black maid answered, asking Johnny if he'd called ahead for an appointment. She stepped back to let him enter when he flashed a set of phony FBI credentials. Let the Bureau work it out if there was a complaint, when he was done.

He waited in the living room and listened to the sounds of family upstairs. At least two children. Girls. That adolescent sound. An argument about the bathroom.

Johnny hoped he would not have to kill their father on the spot, but he would have to wait and see.

The lawyer was a slender man. He wore a wispy beard, as if to compensate for thinning hair on top. His eyes were narrowed by suspicion, piggy-small behind his wire-rimmed glasses.

"I assume you have a warrant, Officer?"

"No warrant," Johnny told him. "Just a message for your client."

"Oh? Which client would that be?"

"The only one who matters, counselor."

"If this is meant to be some kind of threat—"

The sight of the Beretta stopped him. It was leveled at his face, the hammer clicking backward under Johnny's thumb.

"No threat. A message, like I said. The manner of delivery depends on you."

Weiss licked his lips, attempting to retrieve some vestige of his poise. "You're in a world of trouble, Officer."

"I'd say it was the other way around."

"This is a flagrant violation of—"

"Your rights, I know. The rights you need to be concerned about are your last rites, Counselor."

"My wife and children are upstairs. Don't do this. Please."

"I came to talk, but I don't have the time to wade through bullshit. Can you keep your mouth shut, or does Julio read your obituary in the morning paper?"

"No. I wouldn't think of interrupting you."

"All right, then. When I leave, you call your client. Tell him you had company. You're going on vacation right away, this afternoon. The wife and kiddies, too. Before you split, you've got a message for him. Are you following me, so far?"

"Yes."

"The message is, he shouldn't bet his last dime on smooth sailing in Barbados. Certain people don't like being pushed around, okay? They're sick and tired of taking orders from a lunatic."

"I can't say that."

"You want to dress it up, that's your choice. Just make sure he gets the gist. If DiBiase tries to throw his weight around the meeting in Barbados, he could wind up going for a one-way swim. You understand?"

"I do."

"That's it, then. You've got calls to make and bags to pack."

Weiss did not seem to understand, at first, and then his mask of fright began to melt, replaced by an expression of relief.

"I'll pass the word, don't worry."

"I don't have to worry, Counselor. That's *your* job, if you let me down."

Outside, the sun had broken through a scattered layer of clouds, and birds were singing in the nearby trees. It had the makings of a perfect day.

THE DRIVE OUT to Connecticut was Julio's idea. They started at the crack of dawn, a four-car caravan, with gunners on the point and bringing up the rear. Due north on Highway 87 through the Bronx, to Yonkers, picking up the Cross County Expressway through Mount Vernon, to Highway 678. They cut through New Rochelle, White Plains, across Westchester County to the border. Highway 684 to the Danbury crossing, rolling on from there past Newton, Sandy Hook, across the Housatonic River to Berkshire Estates.

Sanctuary.

DiBiase had it figured out that anybody looking for him in Manhattan would find ample targets there to keep them occupied. His troops were on alert, along with soldiers from the other Families, and there was nothing he could do on-site that could not be accomplished by a phone call. It was more important, at the moment, for the would-be Boss of Bosses to protect himself, look forward to the meeting in Barbados that he hoped would be his coronation.

When the time came, he could fly to Miami from Hartford, just as well as from Manhattan. Better, when he thought about it, since there would not be the crowds to deal with, or the problems with security.

LaRocca sat beside him in the back seat of the second car. His lady, Sharon Something, had been relegated to the third vehicle, traveling with some of DiBiase's men to keep her company. At times, he envied Tommy, being single in the modern world, but business took up most of DiBiase's time, and he was seldom troubled by his wife. She knew enough, by now, to speak when she was spoken to and keep her mouth shut otherwise.

The panic call from Jacob Weiss had come as they were leaving, DiBiase looking for a change of scene before his mouthpiece passed the cryptic message on. It didn't take a genius to decide the guy in Weiss's living room had been a phony G-man. Flashing badges at the staff was nothing new. If he remembered right, the Lepke Mob had used that trick to take out old man Maranzano, back in '31.

Some things would never change.

"I can't see everybody getting hit like this," LaRocca said. It was the first time he had spoken in the past half hour.

"So?"

"I mean, if Carmine had it in his mind to take a shot at you, he might go for Scarpato, too. I follow that. But Graziano? That's just stupid, Julio. And what about Chicago?"

"No one said it was Tattaglia."

LaRocca frowned. "Who else? He's been against us from the start, you know that. Anybody stands to benefit from blowing the Barbados meet, it's Carmine."

"Maybe."

"You got someone else in mind?"

"Right now," Don Julio replied, "I don't trust anybody. We've got too much on the table. Guys get greedy, they start thinking they can have it all."

"You mean like Cavalcante?"

"I mean anybody. Who's to say a couple of them haven't made a deal? Mobbed up, you know? Chicago and the Bronx, for instance. Maybe California."

"If you're right, who made the hits on Cavalcante? Danny Dick was taking hits out west before we started seeing any action, and the word I get, he's thinking someone in New York's responsible."

"He may be right," said DiBiase.

"Yeah?"

"Divide and conquer, Tommy. It's the oldest game around. What better way to swing the California troops against us, than to make Masciere think I tried to take him out?"

"We're back to Carmine, then."

"Could be."

"But he got hit last night, and then again this morning."

"That was the Colombians, the second deal," said DiBiase. "Hey, for all I know, they could have pulled some shit last night, on top of everything. They're crazy. Everybody knows that."

"We should put some paper out on Carmine right away, before the meeting. Take him down and get it squared away before he ruins everything."

"That's not the way to do it, Tommy." Julio was smiling, happy to display his self-control. "If Carmine wants to tip his hand, I'd rather have him do it on the island, there in front of everybody. We'll be ready for him, and I won't expect a lot of arguments when we retaliate."

It was LaRocca's turn to smile. "Not bad," he said. "Not bad at all."

Don Julio relaxed and said, "It's getting better all the time."

CHAPTER THIRTEEN

The tip on DiBiase's end run to Connecticut had come from Sharon Pryor, via Leo Turrin. Bolan got the signal on his pager, checked in with the man from Justice and decided it was worth a run across the line to rattle Di-Biase's cage. He spoke to Jack and Johnny, prior to taking off, and left them to their separate tasks in the Big Apple.

DiBiase's head start did not bother Bolan. He was not required to overtake the hoodlum caravan or keep their cars in sight. He knew where they were going, thanks to Sharon's tip. The Fairfield County hideaway was perfect—or, it would have been, if DiBiase could have kept it from the Executioner.

He trailed the enemy through Danbury, aware that DiBiase's people had a forty-minute lead. No problem. They would go to ground at the retreat, outside Berkshire Estates, and wait for a flight from Hartford to Miami in the morning. They were in no rush to get away.

Not yet.

But Bolan meant to change that in dramatic style. He meant to keep Don Julio in motion, looking back across one shoulder, worried all the time.

Across the Housatonic, Bolan drove through tiny Oakdale Manor, following the river westward. He had checked out detailed maps of the terrain and knew where he was going, more or less. The access road came at him on his right, but Bolan did not turn. It was a private drive, and he had not come looking for an open clash with Julio's defenders.

Not if he could do the job another way.

A quarter mile beyond the entrance to the private road, he found a rest stop. There was no one to observe him as he swiftly changed from shirt and slacks to camouflage fatigues, slipped into military webbing and retrieved his hardware from the trunk.

The Walther WA2000 was too delicate for hiking through the woods. His chosen weapon for the strike, not counting side arms, was a Ruger Model 77 Mark II Magnum, chambered for the .458 Winchester Magnum cartridge and fitted with a big twelve-power Leupold scope. The rifle's magazine held three rounds, and he carried half a dozen spares. At 500 yards, the 500-grain copper-jacketed bullets would be traveling at 1,161 feet per second, delivering a crushing 1,469 foot-pounds of energy to the selected target.

It was plenty, and then some.

Bolan hiked for fifteen minutes through the woods, using a compass and his natural sense of direction to keep on course. There was no wall or fence around the hideaway, his quarry trusting in the woods and sentries posted on the open grounds to keep him safe. In fact, as Bolan found his place some 450 yards from the house, he had a clear view of the property on two sides, south and west, with a partial view of the east.

Enough to get it done.

He took up position between two blackgum trees, concealed by mallows and vervain. Once Bolan started shooting, he would be on borrowed time, but at the moment he was free to scan the house and grounds, selecting targets, checking out the enemy.

Two Lincolns were visible behind the house, and Bolan reckoned there were other cars he couldn't see. The vehicles did not concern him, since he planned on DiBiase coming out alive. It did not suit his plans to keep Don Julio from flying to Miami, but he meant to send the capo off with fear perched on his shoulder, whispering dire threats along the way.

It startled him when Sharon Pryor turned up in the scope, although he knew that she was somewhere on the grounds. He found her sitting by the pool, a magazine spread open on her lap. She was not reading at the moment, turned back toward the house as if expecting someone to emerge at any moment.

There he was. LaRocca in his shirtsleeves, crossing the patio with easy strides, bending down to give Sharon a kiss. The mafioso did not find himself a chair, but stood above her with his back to Bolan, talking while the lady watched his face and nodded.

It would be an easy shot. One gentle squeeze to take his head off at the shoulders. Cancel Sharon's contract on the spot and leave her free to ditch the Mob, get back to Washington and find herself a new assignment. Something clean, that left her self-respect intact.

He caught himself and frowned. The lady had no cause for shame. She did her job and nothing more, a warrior like himself. Still, there was something in her face that made him wish he could protect her from the ugliness of living, working undercover, rubbing elbows with the scum.

Not yet.

If Bolan played his cards right, it would all be over soon, but not today.

He kept on tracking, seeking DiBiase.

Found him.

Settled back to wait.

"WE LEAVE tomorrow morning," said LaRocca, standing over Sharon, blotting out her sunlight. "Eight o'clock or something."

"Fine."

"Are you okay, baby?"

"Sure. Why not?"

He shrugged. "That business in Chicago, maybe. I don't know. You haven't seemed the same."

She forced a smile and took his hand. "I guess it shook me up a little," she admitted, faking it. "I know it took me by surprise."

"Somebody's gonna be surprised, I find out who that joker was." LaRocca puffed his chest out, acting macho for her benefit. The stupid ass. "I'll make him wish his mama kept her legs crossed."

"Tommy, you're my hero."

"Bet your ass." He grinned. "On second thought, don't do that. I prefer it where it's at."

He stooped to kiss her once more, lingering, before he turned back to the house. "I have to talk to Julio right now. You wanna take a dip, I'll join you in a little while."

"Okay."

She wished that he would drop dead where he stood, but Sharon held her plastic smile in place and watched him go. Slick bastard. She could hardly wait to see the look on Tommy's face when the indictments came down. Better yet, when she stood up to testify in court.

It could be rocky, with the issue of entrapment, sex and all, but Sharon was prepared to take the heat. LaRocca had been dirty years before she came along and caught his eye. If he was dumb enough to spill his guts in pillow talk, so be it. Let the shysters bitch and moan till doomsday, if they wanted to. She had recordings. Photographs. The works.

She thought of Mike Belasko, wondering if he had been alerted to the morning's change of scene. What was he up to, in the city, while she sat out here and listened to the soft sounds of the forest? Killing someone, more than likely. Running up his score.

There was no reason to believe that he would follow them, and yet...

She glanced off toward the trees, responding to a sudden sense that she was being watched. It was ridiculous, of course. If anyone was spying on her at the moment, it would probably be one of DiBiase's goons. He had them stationed all around the house to watch for anyone who might try sneaking through the trees.

Good luck.

If Julio had trouble with security in New York City, where he damn near owned the streets, how would he manage in the sticks? Of course, the enemy could not hide in a crowd out here, but something told her that would not slow Belasko down. Not in the least.

She had mixed feelings where the dark man was concerned. He frightened her, in one sense, with his air of ruthless violence, but she knew that they were working toward a common goal. If Leo and the brass above him sent Belasko out to hunt, it was not Sharon's place to argue. There was nothing she could do, unless she threw her job away, went public, blew the whistle.

And for what?

To save LaRocca and his boss from getting what she knew they both deserved? To guarantee her day in court, with the embarrassment that would inevitably follow? Sidelong glances at the Bureau office, when she checked in for her next assignment. Whispers when her back was turned. The knowing smiles from every macho agent she encountered for the next few years.

No, thank you.

If Belasko cut her job short, it would not have been in vain. The field intelligence she gathered would be used against surviving members of the DiBiase Family and others, putting them away. She still had work to do, and she was not deserting under fire.

She tried to read her magazine and found she could not concentrate. Too many pressing matters on her mind. Miami and Barbados, for a start. They would be flying out tomorrow, early, and she knew that sometime in the next two days, the shit would definitely hit the fan. Belasko would be part of it, but DiBiase had been making enemies within the mob, as well, the past few months. If gunners came for him—correction, *when* they came—it would require some thought to figure out where they were coming from.

It was a miracle that Julio had lasted this long, with his psycho temperament. The fear helped, certainly, but it could only reach so far and last so long. His plan to dominate the Mob from coast to coast was stretching it. Too many obstacles and would-be leaders in the way.

Unless he pulled it off.

She closed the magazine and dropped it on the deck beside her chair, leaned back and closed her eyes against the sunlight. DiBiase had a few surprises waiting for him down the road, and Belasko would be one of them.

Another would be Sharon Pryor, if he lived that long.

The sense of being watched was back, but she ignored it. Let the bastards get an eyeful, if they paused on their patrols to check her out. One thing she didn't have to think about was any of the hired help moving in on her. La-Rocca would have hit the roof, and everybody knew it.

Great. Her knight in tarnished armor.

Sharon almost laughed aloud, the image was so ludicrous. She was relaxing, almost dozing, when her hazy thoughts were shattered by the sound of rifle fire.

BOLAN SPOTTED DiBiase on his second scan, a profile in a downstairs window, near the southwest corner of the house. He had LaRocca with him, both men standing, DiBiase pacing back and forth while Tommy stood and watched him, hands stuffed in his pockets. The full-length windows opened on a little flagstone patio of sorts, from which a gravel path curved off around the near side of the house, through banks of cultivated roses.

Bolan had no eye for landscaping or architecture at the moment, though. He finished checking out the grounds, locating sentries, filing the positions of the nearest gunners. They would be a problem, once he started firing, but with any luck, he had the first ten seconds to himself.

He had a live round in the Ruger's chamber, ready. Bolan took a deep breath, filled his lungs, releasing part of it, and held the rest. His hands and eye were steady as he sighted through the Leupold scope.

At this range, he expected the heavy slug to drop an estimated seven feet six inches on its flight toward impact with the target. He had made corrections on his scope, for elevation, and he called the wind dead calm, with the surrounding trees. As for deflection of his bullet by the flimsy pane of window glass, he saw no reason for concern.

Bolan took his time, lined up his shot. As in Chicago, he reminded himself that the immediate death of his target was not desired. This probe was meant to rattle DiBiase and LaRocca, fray their nerves and leave them jumping at shadows.

As for their flunkies . . .

Bolan's index finger curled around the rifle's trigger, taking up the slack. He was accustomed to the weapon's massive recoil and had practiced long enough at Stony Man that he could nail three targets out of three in something that approximated rapid fire.

The tricky part would be correcting for a different range once sentries started rushing his position. Normally the Ruger "elephant gun" would not have been his choice of weapons for a running battle in the woods, but he would do with what he had.

He cleared his mind, confirmed the target, squeezing off. The Ruger slammed against his shoulder, bruising even with the custom recoil pad. He worked the bolt, ejected brass and had the second shot lined up and away before the echo of the first came back from the forest.

The window shattered, bright glass raining down. He had a glimpse of DiBiase and LaRocca diving for the carpet as he worked the bolt again, his third round sliding easily into the Ruger's chamber.

For a change of pace, he swung his weapon to the right, along the west side of the house, and found another window with the drapes pulled back. He caught a round face gaping at him—searching, rather, for the source of all that sudden thunder. Now the guy was turning from the window, thick lips moving. Shouting to his comrades?

Bolan dropped the gunner with his third round, crimson bursting from the dead man's skull on impact. Down and out before he knew what hit him, and the Executioner reloaded swiftly, opening the Ruger's hinged floor plate, replacing the spent magazine with a fresh one.

Off across the lawn, he caught a glimpse of Sharon Pryor stretched out near the pool, beside her deck chair, motionless. She kept her head down, knowing there was no place she could run to, in the circumstances. Did she understand that it was "Mike Belasko" firing at the house? Would it make any difference, if she did?

He spotted two goons running toward him, from 150 yards away, and made a quick correction to the Leupold scope. The big-game piece was zeroed at that range, no rise or drop in the trajectory. He sighted on the left-hand runner first, broad chest and shoulders, with a riot shotgun in his hands.

The Ruger spoke, another heavy-metal thunderclap, and Bolan's target vaulted over on his back, blood spouting from a mortal chest wound. His companion hesitated, breaking stride and glancing backward, clearly wishing he was somewhere else.

Too late.

The Executioner's fifth shot went in on target, ripping through the gunner's jaw with all the delicacy of a meat ax. Impact spun him through a wild 180, spewing teeth and shattered bone before he lost his footing on the grass and went down in a lifeless heap. His heart kept pumping for another minute, give or take, but the traumatic shock to brain and spinal cord had finished him before he hit the ground.

One round remained in the Ruger's magazine, and Bolan knew he had to make it count. He swung back toward the north end of the house, where half a dozen gunmen had collected, jabbering and pointing toward the woods. They might not have him sighted yet, but they were getting close, and they would rush him once they found the nerve.

Unless he stopped them, first.

Four hundred yards, and then some. Back to the adjustment for his first three rounds. He chose the tall man in the center of the group, who seemed to be in charge. A head shot splashed blood and brains around his circle of acquaintances.

It seemed to do the trick. The other goons retreated in a rush, while Bolan backed away. He was running when he hit the game trail, with the Ruger slung across his back to leave his hands free. All he had to do was run three-quarters of a mile to reach his car, change clothes and stow his hardware, drive away like it was another Thursday afternoon.

And while Don Julio was cleaning house, the Executioner had several things to tidy up around New York. Before Jack took them to Miami, he had work to do.

Some final touches.

Like any artist, Bolan took pride in the details of his work.

IT WAS DÉJÀ VU, all over again.

Tommy LaRocca lay on his belly with shattered glass all around, listening to bullets smack the walls and furniture above his head. They sounded bigger, louder, this time, but he reckoned part of that was being in the countryside, without the city noises to compete.

And who cared, when you thought about it, what the bullets sounded like? One hit, and you were dog meat, just like Ernie's soldiers in Chicago.

Like those boys outside.

It took a moment, but LaRocca figured out that only two rounds had been fired into the study. One had knocked some kind of antique copper kettle off the mantelpiece; the other punched a fist-size hole in DiBiase's ornate desk and spilled the contents of a drawer.

Round three had been directed somewhere else. La-Rocca heard the sound of smashing glass, then voices, several of them jabbering at once. Beside him, Julio was wriggling across the carpet like a kid in boot camp, moving toward the window, cursing as he picked up jagged slivers in his palms and knees.

"God *damn* it!"

Tommy knew exactly how he felt, but fear immobilized him. It was galling, when he thought about it, but survival was his first priority. Right now, he had some partial cover from the desk, and moving meant that he would be exposed.

No thanks.

"Get out there!" Julio was shouting through the blasted window. "Nail that bastard!"

Tommy could not see the yard from where he lay, and that was fine. He heard a couple of the lookouts shouting back and forth, reacting to their orders. Seconds later, when the next shots came, they seemed to have a different quality, and Tommy knew the rifleman was dropping bodies in the yard.

Sweet Jesus!

Would they get him? Was it possible to run a sniper down when he had cover, range and accuracy on his side? The military did it all the time, of course, and the police, but they had tanks and helicopters, body armor, all that shit. Don Julio and Tommy had a dozen shooters from the city, more at home in pool rooms and saloons than in the forest.

LaRocca wished that he could run and hide, but where would he be safe? It was the second time he had been under fire in...what, one day and change? Both times by snipers.

Or...

He stopped and thought about it, swallowing the panic, forcing his mind to function with a semblance of normality. Two snipers, in two different states? Did that make sense? When was the last time he had heard of any made guys using big-game rifles on a contract killing?

The alternative was even worse, though. If it wasn't two marksmen, then it meant the same guy had followed LaRocca from Chi to New York, and on to Connecticut. How could that be?

The implications were disturbing. First, at Cavalcante's office in the Windy City, now at Julio's retreat, presumably at a safe distance from Manhattan. That meant planning, inside information, spies.

It meant they had all kinds of problems Tommy hadn't even thought of, yet.

Or, worse: suppose the problem was LaRocca's, and the rest was merely window dressing, a coincidence? Did anyone hate Tommy bad enough to go through all this shit, provoking Cavalcante's wrath, and now Don Julio's, to make the hit?

No way.

From grim experience, he figured that the sniper—if it was one man—had skill enough to make his tag the first time out. He could have wasted Tommy in Chicago, and again just now, if that was really his intention. Better yet, he could have done it any time at all, without involving anybody higher up.

It had to be about Barbados, then. Somebody working overtime to sabotage the meet and DiBiase's dream.

But, who?

Belatedly he heard some other weapons firing on the lawn outside. A shotgun and some pistols, sounding lame and ineffectual beside the big-game piece. It took another moment for LaRocca's mind to register that the defensive fire was drawing no response.

The guy was gone.

He rose on shaky legs and went to join his capo, standing by the shattered window. In the yard, some distance from the house, he saw two bodies lying on the grass. One seemed to have no face; the other wore a shirt that had been white before his chest exploded.

Two men down, and Tommy wasn't taking any bets that that would be the final body count. How far away were DiBiase's neighbors? Had the sounds of gunfire sent them running to the telephone? Were sheriff's deputies en route to check out the disturbance, even now?

"We oughta split," he told Don Julio.

"I want this fucker, Tommy." Julio was speaking through clenched teeth. "He's mine, you understand? I want his fucking head!"

"Sure thing. We need to clear out, though, before the heat shows up."

"We take this lying down, I may as well forget about Barbados," DiBiase said. "Nobody sleeps or takes a shit until I have some information on this guy. You hear me, Tommy?"

"Sure, I hear you, Julio."

Tommy had a hunch that none of them would do much sleeping in the next two days.

CHAPTER FOURTEEN

It was an honor, Rico Abbandando realized, to draw the contract on a major target. When the chips were down, and everyone was sweating, special orders went to those the capo trusted most among his soldiers. Some would wait a lifetime for the chance to prove themselves that way, and it would always pass them by.

In Rico's case, the target was a whopper. Pablo Guzman had been giving Don Carmine fits for some two years now, cutting into drug sales in the Bronx and dodging every trap the Family set for him, but he had never risked an open war until that very morning. His Colombians were on a rampage now, across the city, and the man who nailed his ass would be a hero, marked for bigger, better things.

While others sat around and waited for the rat to come out of hiding, Rico had been busy working street informants, paying some and muscling others, getting what he wanted after seven hours on the job. He knew where Guzman's hideout was, and he had passed the word to Don Carmine like a good boy, waiting for the go-ahead, when others might have blundered in and fucked it up.

At thirty-seven, Abbandando knew that it would take a miracle to move him up the Family ladder, and his miracle was waiting for him now, this minute, in a house on White Plains Road, near Woodlawn Cemetery. Once he got the clearance and the troops he needed, he was rolling, with the old man's blessing, to eliminate the bastard who had killed some of his friends and thrown the city into turmoil.

Four cars moved in, with four men each, plus Rico. As the leader of the team, he could have bagged himself a ringside seat and let the others do the dirty work, but how would that look to the don? Not afraid to pull the trigger, he had three kills behind him, and the odds were on his side.

Moreover, Rico had a plan.

He sent four men around in back, with Molotovs and shotguns, coming in behind their target. Two guns staked out the north and south sides of the house, respectively. That left an eight-man firing squad out front, with Rico in the middle of his handpicked soldiers, sighting down the barrel of his Ruger Mini-14 rifle with folding metal stock.

It felt strange, working in the daylight, in the middle of a residential neighborhood, but there was no way they could root the greasy bastard out without attracting some attention to themselves. Cold license plates, of course, and they could always ditch the cars if necessary, afterward. It was the Bronx, though, and he had a hunch that Don Carmine's reputation would be all the cover they required, when it was done.

As if the cops would break their backs investigating Guzman's death.

We ought to get a fucking medal, Rico thought. No chance of that, but he would trust his capo to supply a suitable reward.

He checked his watch and saw that it was almost time. Another moment now, and his advance team would be lighting up their Molotovs, unloading them against the backside of the house. There were no exits on the north or south, which left the front door as the only escape route for Guzman and his cronies.

"Come on, now," Rico muttered. "Come and get it."

Abbandando heard the Molotovs exploding, saw the black smoke rising behind the house. A heartbeat later, there was gunfire. Automatic weapons chattering, the shotguns woofing back. Between the flames and buckshot, he did not believe that Guzman's people had a chance to exit through the rear.

No way.

As if in answer to his silent thought, the front door opened, two men charging down the concrete steps toward the street. At first, they seemed to think they had it made, until they saw the welcoming committee lined up to receive them. Both had weapons in their hands, but neither had a chance to use the guns, as nine converging streams of fire ripped through them, blowing them away.

And neither one of them was Pablo Guzman, damn it!

Rico waited, knowing there were still more men inside. One of them, then another, started blasting the windows facing the street, the bullets snapping over Rico's head. A third piece joined the symphony, and in another moment everyone was firing, Rico joining in with his companions, pumping rounds at first one window, then another.

This was not what he had had in mind, at all. An ambush was the ticket, quick and clean, with Guzman and his people dying in the street. A siege was something else entirely, hanging out and trading shots until the cops came rolling in and everybody went to jail. Still, Abbandando had a job to do, and he did not feel much like running with his tail between his legs.

It was the fire that saved him, in the end. A breeze came up from out of nowhere, and the house went up like tinder. Later, there would be reports of chemicals inside, some shit about the cocaine trade, but Rico was content to watch it burn, flames dancing on the roofline, gobbling the shingles up. He knew that Guzman's people must be catching hell in there, between the heat and smoke, so Rico kept his gunners firing, covering the door and windows with a screen of lead.

The house looked like a bonfire, by the time he heard the sirens. Anyone inside was baked or fried, no doubt about it. Make that *refried,* yeah. A little ethnic humor wouldn't hurt, when he reported back to Don Carmine.

Abbandando played their conversation over in his mind.

Why don't you call me Carmine, son?

Hell, yes. Why not?

EIGHTEEN MONTHS had passed since Leo Turrin last set foot inside One Police Plaza, on New York's Avenue of the Finest, but little or nothing had changed. The place still reeked of politics, and anyone who rated office space seemed more concerned with watching his or her back, than with stamping out crime.

It was bureaucracy in action, tax dollars at work.

The deputy police commissioner was Fabius Devine, a 43-year-old survivor of the Harlem Ghetto who had walked a beat in Bedford Stuyvesant for seven years, before advancing to administration. He had earned his master's degree on the side, and helped write guidelines for improved community relations. At the moment, he was the police commissioner's right hand in charge of matters where publicity was both a detriment and unavoidable.

Across the desk from Fabius Devine, and facing Leo at an angle, sat the FBI's assistant SAC for criminal investigations in New York. His name was Paul Marquette, age thirty-eight, with thirteen years federal harness.

Leo did not miss the fact that he had been detailed to meet with deputies. Despite his weight in Washington, he had been handed over to the second string. The men in charge of New York City were adept survivors. Both the FBI and NYPD would be cautious, neither agency endorsing Leo's plan. If anything went wrong—which meant, if anything leaked to the press—there would be swift denials, and the men who shared the office with him might be sacrificed.

No wonder they looked less than thrilled to see him.

"So, you're telling us that all this shit we've seen the last few hours is controlled?" The voice of Fabius Devine was frankly skeptical.

"I said we were on top of it, and Washington is very anxious that the players not be interrupted at the moment."

"By the players, Mr. Justice, you refer to those who have been killing one another in the streets?"

"I mean the local Families of La Cosa Nostra," Leo answered.

"What's the game?" Marquette inquired.

"Surveillance, for the moment."

"That's the Bureau's job."

"And ours," Devine put in. "Feds aren't the only game in town."

"As I explained, I represent a special task force, lately formed. We have one mission, at the moment, limited in time and space. We should be out of New York City by this evening at the latest. Eighteen hours, give or take, and most of that's already gone."

"The problem is, you're leaving us a mess to clean up when you're done. I can't remember when we had this many people killed on any given day. You say you're watching the Italians, but we've got Colombians unloading from Manhattan to the Bronx. The homeboys get a whiff of that, we're really in deep shit."

"It shouldn't come to that."

"As far as I can see," Devine shot back, "it never should have come to *this*. I'm not a federal officer, you understand. Now, I'll agree you've got some damned impressive signatures on this—" he raised the letter, shook it, set it down again "—but I don't take my orders from the District of Columbia."

"Perhaps, if you could speak with the commissioner again..."

"I spoke to the commissioner when he assigned me to conduct this interview. He didn't like the smell of it, and I don't blame him. I should probably have people grilling you, instead of sitting here and chatting over coffee. If I had my druthers, Mr. Justice—"

He was interrupted by the intercom.

"What is it, Sandy?"

"The commissioner, line one, sir."

"Thanks."

Devine picked up the telephone receiver, punched a flashing button.

"Yes, sir?" Listening, a pinched expression on his chubby face. "I'm with him now." Another pause. "Oh, yes?" And yet another. "Sir, I really think—" The caller cut him off, and Leo fought to keep from grinning at the black man's obvious discomfiture. "Yes, sir," Devine said finally. "I understand, sir."

After he had cradled the receiver, Fabius Devine leaned back and made a steeple of his fingers, covering an ample gut. A frown carved furrows in his face.

"You must have pull, my friend."

"From time to time."

"Okay, you've got your eighteen hours, counting back to midnight. Is that satisfactory?"

"It should be fine."

"We're finished, then...unless the Bureau wants to throw a little something in the pot?"

Marquette pretended to consider it, then shook his head, a wary negative.

"I don't think so. Gentlemen, this meeting is adjourned."

GREAT KILLS.

You had to smile at that one, Johnny thought, as he was motoring across the Verrazano-Narrows Bridge to Staten Island. Every now and then, he struck a note of irony that made him smile, or sometimes laugh out loud.

You wouldn't think a mafioso with a couple hundred murders on his head would choose an area called Great Kills for his home away from home, but perhaps Carmine Tattaglia had a sense of humor he had managed to conceal throughout the years.

Or, maybe, he just liked the neighborhood.

Staten Island, the fifth borough of New York City, is still relatively rural, except for its capital at St. George. Long Island homes were more expensive, overall, but Staten Island held its own, and there was something to be said for avoiding the old moneyed crowd. Carmine would enjoy picking their pockets, given half a chance, but he was not the sort to fit in with the social whirl.

It was a four-mile drive on Hylan Boulevard, through Dongan Hills and New Dorp, to his destination. Johnny was prepared for anything, a scrub if the security was too intense, but it appeared that Tattaglia's house had almost been forgotten as the other boroughs went to hell.

The younger Bolan found a narrow, winding access road that put him on a rise of ground behind the house—due north—and offered him a bird's-eye view of Tattaglia's swimming pool. He parked the car, got out and walked around to claim his hardware from the trunk.

Three stubby tubes of fiberglass, all olive drab. When Johnny pulled the safety pins and gave a yank, the tubes extended to a length of three feet overall, with calibrated folding sights and firing levers on the top. The LAWs— light antitank weapons—were disposable bazookas, lightweight throwaways invented for the war in Vietnam, complete with armor-piercing rockets that could stop the Russian ZSUs and Shilkas in their tracks.

Or play hell with a house on Staten Island.

When all three launching tubes were primed and ready, lined up on the hood of Johnny's car, he raised the first one to his shoulder, peering through the sight and checking out the scene below. He saw one sentry near the pool, beyond a steep embankment overgrown with ice plants, partly screened by trees. The guy would spot him, certainly, and take his best shot from the yard, but Johnny did not plan to hang around and give him any kind of decent mark.

He chose the second story, first, lined up his shot, and squeezed the firing lever. There was no recoil to speak of, just a shudder as the back-blast flamed across his shoulder and the armor-piercing rocket whistled off toward impact. By the time it struck Carmine's roof and burrowed through the shingles, detonating with a crack of thunder, Johnny had returned the first tube to his open trunk and braced the second on his shoulder.

The startled sentry spotted him once the second rocket was away, and ducked as the rocket sizzled past him, crashed a set of tall glass doors and turned the capo's living room into a blazing furnace. Downrange, Johnny heard the *pop-pop-pop* of a revolver, pointedly ignoring it as he replaced the second empty launcher with the third and last.

He could have let it go at that. The house was burning, probably a total loss, but Johnny had not driven all this way to leave a job half-done. Lining up the final shot took only a moment. When the rocket left his launcher, Johnny felt it almost as a shudder of relief.

It struck the northwest corner of the house and plowed through fifty-year-old masonry, brick shrapnel added to the general chaos at ground zero. Johnny stowed the empty tube and closed his trunk, circling around to the driver's side to take his place behind the wheel.

Their time in old New York was winding down, and he would not be sad to leave.

He put his car in gear and drove away.

Turning on the radio, he found an oldies channel, and cranked up the volume on a song that always made him happy: "Let the Good Times Roll."

THE HIGH-RISE office complex was supposed to be a landmark. "Everybody" said so, from the *Times* and television's talking heads to politicians on the stump. When it was finished, it would tower eighty floors above the antlike men and women swarming on the avenue below.

How many offices on eighty floors? How much rent per month, per office?

Millions.

The property was DiBiase's latest foray into real estate development, his ownership disguised by holding companies and fronts. Aside from whatever legitimate income the building would generate, large-scale construction was a perfect money laundry, with millions of illicit dollars recycled through payrolls, supply requisitions and so forth. DiBiase got a break on labor through the machinations of the unions he controlled by proxy, and a bit of research had revealed some sleight-of-hand with the insurance on the property.

Enough to leave him in the hole, perhaps, if anything went wrong before the building was completed.

Bolan showed a set of fake credentials to the foreman on the site, along with several sheets of legalese that added substance to his bluff.

"I'll have to call the boss on this," the foreman said.

"I don't care who you call," said Bolan, "but you'll have to clear the site right now. We can't take any chances with a major leak."

"Nobody's mentioned smelling gas." The foreman was suspicious.

"Most of them are working on the top floors, right?"

"I guess."

"They wouldn't smell a thing, up there, but I can guarantee they'll notice if it blows."

"All right, for Christ's sake, let me bring 'em down."

It took a while, but Bolan waited, standing underneath his hard hat, with the heavy satchel filled with his equipment draped across one shoulder.

"Done," the foreman said at last. "You need some help?"

"I've got it covered," Bolan said. "You want to make that call, you've got some time."

"Okay."

"Just keep your men across the street there."

"Yeah."

It took him most of fifteen minutes, poking into corners, leaving blocks of C-4 plastique in his wake. The placement was critical, each charge precisely measured, fitted with radio-remote detonators. The tricky part was working in downtown Manhattan, with its countless two-way radios, but Bolan had to take the chance or let his chosen target slide.

The foreman saw him coming out and moved to intercept him on the sidewalk. "So?" he asked. "What's happening? Can we go back to work, or what?"

"Not yet," the Executioner informed him. "I got readings out of three distinct and separate locations. This may take some time."

"Well, shit."

"The way things work, I doubt if you'll be getting back to it this afternoon."

"My boss is on the way," the foreman said. "He didn't sound real happy on the phone."

"What can I say? You think he'd like it any better if your crew got blown to bits?"

Bolan left the foreman, moving toward the car where Jack and Johnny waited, with the motor idling. Bolan took his helmet off and slid into the shotgun seat, turned toward his brother in the back.

"You want to do the honors?"

"I'd be tickled pink."

They watched as Johnny palmed the black remote control, no larger than a pack of cigarettes, and flicked a switch to arm it. Half a block away, the red lights on the several detonators would be winking, ready to receive their doomsday signal.

Johnny thumbed the button, bridged the gap, and Bolan felt the earth shudder.

"Go!" he told Grimaldi, and the drab sedan surged forward, running north.

Behind them, Bolan saw the high-rise skeleton begin to crumble, plummeting toward the earth. A mushroom cloud of smoke and dust boiled up around the site of the explosion, fanning out across the avenue, obscuring traffic and pedestrians. He had a quick glimpse of the project foreman, gaping at the sight, before the cloud swept over him and blotted out the view.

"We finished here?" Grimaldi asked.

"I'd say."

Both knew they could have lingered in New York for days or weeks, selecting targets from the thousands of facilities and businesses controlled by dirty money from the Mob. A man could spend his life there, barely scratch the surface, but the present game was moving on.

Next stop, Miami.

Bolan would be glad to put New York behind him, with its ghosts and memories. Another time, perhaps, when he could walk the streets alone and linger if he wanted to, without a deadline.

First things, first.

His enemies had either gone to Florida, or they were on their way. The Families would be gathering, preparing for their summit meeting in Barbados, anxious for some peace and quiet in the wake of three tumultuous days.

Fat chance.

The Executioner was not about to let them rest. He had a job to do, and it would not be finished till the last of them was either dead or on the run.

CHAPTER FIFTEEN

The flight from New York down to Homestead AFB, Florida, took three hours, putting Bolan on the ground by 9:15 p.m. The drive from Homestead to Miami proper, fifteen miles due north on Highway 1 took half an hour, fighting traffic all the way, but he was still ahead of schedule.

Everything was cool.

So far.

For years, Miami had been deemed an "open city" in the parlance of the syndicate, fair game for any Family to operate within a set of guidelines that insured a modicum of peace and quiet. Local operations had been run from Tampa under Santos Trafficante, but his death and the changing times had heralded a change for mafiosi in the Sunshine State. A flood of drug-war "refugees" from the Caribbean had drastically revised the status quo in recent years, uprooting Mafia control of the narcotics trade as Haitians, Cubans and Jamaicans fought for their respective slices of the pie.

In order to restore a semblance of control, Don Roman Graffia had moved his Family to Miami in the early 1980s, clamping down as best he could on "cocaine cowboys," trying to assert control on behalf of the Cosa Nostra. He had never been tremendously successful, but his tribe had prospered, even in the absence of a workable monopoly. His turf extended from the northern suburbs of Miami and Miami Beach along the Gold Coast to Fort Lauderdale, with outposts in Palm Beach, Daytona Beach and Jacksonville. The Tampa enclave was secure, and Graffia had friends in Tallahassee, at the capital, who watched out for his interests in the legislature.

Still, Don Roman was a man with enemies, and none of them had been more active in the past twelve months than the Jamaican "posse" led by Jason Frost. A ruthless band of ganja-smoking killers, steeped in blood and their devotion to obeah, Frost and company had carved themselves a thick share of the narco traffic in Dade County, dealing with Colombian suppliers, alternately underselling Graffia and gunning down his pushers on the street.

The DEA and Metro-Dade had been expecting open war for months now, but Don Roman was a man of patience. He absorbed the body blows and waited, striking back at isolated targets now and then, avoiding any large-scale confrontation with the posse. No one doubted that he had a contract out on Frost, but neither were his shooters in a hurry to collect.

The pot was simmering, but Bolan understood that it would take a bit more heat to generate a rolling boil. A little spice to give the recipe that extra kick.

Jamaican cooking, right.

The problem, as far as Bolan could determine, was that Jason Frost—for all his ruthlessness—had hesitated to provoke a full-scale shooting war between his posse and the local Mafia. Perhaps he had misgivings in respect to who would win. The motives hardly mattered.

It was time for someone to give the war machine a little shove.

For all his skill at camouflage, it was beyond the Executioner's ability to make himself appear convincing in the role of a Jamaican Rastafarian. With that in mind, he opted for the next best thing, deciding he would take the war to Jason Frost and make the posse leader think that Roman Graffia had launched a new offensive in Miami.

Simple, unless it blew up in his face.

Frost's current base of operations was the large Jamaican enclave sandwiched between West Flagler Street and Highway 41, the Tamiami Trail. In local terms, the trail was Eighth Street—Calle Ocho to the Cuban immigrants who colonized it farther east. There were no Spanish street signs in the neighborhood where Jason Frost had put down roots. White faces came in squad cars, for the most part, and they seldom brought good news.

It was a tricky proposition, all the way around. While Bolan had no interest in provoking racial turmoil, any clash between Jamaicans and the homegrown syndicate would certainly be viewed in black-white terms by the combatants, by the press, by the community at large. He hoped to keep the game in context and avoid a major ghetto conflagration, but the Executioner would take what he could get.

Beginning now.

The target was a Rasta hangout on Fifth Terrace, west of Cortez Avenue. Frost's men had taken over, edging out the normal clientele, until the club—called Java Man—was recognized by locals and police alike as a de facto adjunct of the posse.

Fair enough.

Bolan had no way of guessing just how many Rastas would be waiting for him at the club, but he was determined to proceed. Surprise and sheer audacity should be enough to see him through, with some assistance from his stock of military hardware and Grimaldi's driving.

He was ready.

Any stall, from this point on, would be a waste of precious time.

PERCY GLASS WAS FLYING when the clock struck ten. The ganja had been sweet tonight, better than usual in Percy's opinion, and he had indulged himself in classic Rasta style. It was a sacrament, of course, and what was worship for, if not to fill the mind and body with a sense of overwhelming peace?

He often thought about Jamaica at a time like this, his squalid home in Kingston, with the rats and roaches. Never mind that he was living in a section of Miami that the local blacks referred to as a ghetto. It was paradise, compared to Kingston, and the business he was doing with the posse would allow him to move on one day and occupy a mansion in the white man's part of town.

The U.S. immigration system was a marvel to behold. Instead of slamming doors in people's faces, the Americans encouraged everyone to come and bring their families along, find work and settle down. Of course, they did not have the posse's kind of work in mind, but there was still a market for the product, both in Florida and nationwide.

It was a motto with Americans that money made the world go round, but Percy Glass had questioned that, of late. If nothing else, he thought there should be an amendment to the slogan. Money made the world go round, but drugs helped people tolerate the pace.

It constantly amazed him that Americans decried the use of ganja in religious ceremonies, while they gobbled, snorted, smoked or mainlined any drug available for purposes of recreation.

The posse turned a profit on America's hypocrisy, and that was fine with Percy Glass. He worried, sometimes, thinking it was all too easy, but their leader reassured him, showing strength and courage in the presence of their enemies. Each day, they had more customers, more cash in hand. Each week brought new arrivals from the island, anxious to participate and spread the posse's influence from sea to shining sea.

Their time was coming. Percy knew because his leader told him so.

It all began to fall apart when Percy went to take a leak. The men's room was in back, a narrow hallway leading past the back door to the claustrophobic cubicle with urinals and toilets, smelling like it hadn't seen a mop in weeks. The ganja helped with that, of course. It still smelled bad, but Percy didn't care.

He did not see the white man, going in. His business at the urinal was urgent, and he failed to check the toilet stalls. There was no reason for concern at Java Man, in any case. What ofay bastard would be fool enough to trespass on the posse's turf and throw his life away?

The first hint Percy had of trouble coming was the kiss of steel against his skull, behind one ear. No virgin, he could recognize the barrel of a gun on contact, and he froze, the stream of urine from his bladder drying up without a conscious order from his brain.

"You want to live?" the gunman asked, almost whispering. A white man's voice.

For a moment, he wondered if he could reach the automatic in his shoulder holster.

"Sure, mon."

"Are you positive?"

"You gonna shoot, mon, I can't stop you." Showing that he still had nerve, in spite of his present position.

"Sure you can."

"How's that, mon?"

"What I need, right now, is someone with a decent memory. A messenger."

"You oughta try the Federal Express."

"That's cute," the stranger said. "I like a dead man with a sense of humor."

"Hey, mon, nothing personal. Don't get excited, now."

"I'm cool. You haven't answered me."

"What was the question, mon?"

The pistol bored in harder at the base of Percy's skull. Frightened, he prayed the door would open on another Rasta brother.

"I want to know if you can take a message back to Jason Frost," the stranger said.

"Hell, yes, mon. We good friends."

"That's fine. Now, put your hands behind your back."

"You mind I zip up, first?"

"I mind."

That worried Percy, but he let it go. No sooner were his hands behind his back, than he felt handcuffs snap in place. They held him fast, no slack. His captor steered him toward the nearest toilet stall and sat him down.

He had his first glimpse of the gunman. Tall and dark, athletic-looking, with an automatic in his hand. The bulge beneath his jacket, on the right, suggested larger weaponry.

"So, what's the message, mon?"

"Tell Frost that Roman Graffia is tired of playing games, okay? He cut your crowd some slack in the beginning, but it's over now. He's taking in the welcome mat, you follow me?"

"I hear you, mon."

"How many of your friends out front?"

Glass saw no point in lying. "Ten, twelve brothas, I believe."

The white man put his hand in Percy's jacket, took the pistol from his shoulder rig and stepped next door to drop it in the other toilet bowl. When he came back, his own side arm had been supplanted by an Uzi with a folding metal stock.

"One other thing, before I go," he said.

"What's that, mon?"

The words had barely left Percy's lips before the white man stepped in close and swung the Uzi in a short arc, at his head.

Pain burst behind the Rasta's eyes in brilliant colors, fading swiftly into silent darkness as he toppled off the toilet seat and hit the tile facedown.

A GLANCE around the corner showed eleven Rastas in the main room of the club. Five sat around a table, playing cards, while three more occupied a booth on Bolan's left, and three were perched on bar stools to his right.

It was impossible to cover all of them at once, but he would do his best. Surprise was on his side, so far, and he would milk that edge for all he could.

The Uzi's cyclic rate of fire, 950 rounds per minute, gobbled up a standard 32-round magazine in some two seconds flat. It took a practiced hand to keep from wasting ammunition, much less deal with several human targets in a row, and Bolan had the touch.

He came around the corner firing, going for the Rastas at the center table first, since they had greater flexibility of movement than their comrades on the flanks. He swept the table with a stream of parabellum manglers, nothing in the way of warning for his targets as he ended their game forever.

Two of them were facing Bolan as he came around the corner, but it didn't help. Death caught them with their hands full, gaping at the stranger and his weapon, momentarily immobilized by shock. His bullets did the rest, and they were down, all tangled arms and legs, before the others knew exactly what was happening.

They recognized the sound of gunfire, though, and they were seeking cover, groping for their weapons as he finished off the five cardplayers. Bolan saw his adversaries in the booth jammed up and cursing, hampered by restricted space, the table bucking under impact from their knees. He left them to it, swinging toward the bar, where three more Rastas were dismounting from their stools.

And Bolan took them one by one.

The first guy caught a three-round burst and staggered, going over backward, dreadlocks whipping as he hit the wooden floor. A final tremor racked his body, but the Executioner had already dismissed him from consideration, moving on.

The second Rasta at the bar was brandishing a Llama large-frame automatic when the Uzi brought him under fire. He managed one quick shot before he died, but it was wasted on the ceiling, bursting one of the fluorescent tubes and raining shattered glass. The Rasta's face exploded under impact of the parabellum rounds, and he went down in a bloody heap.

The last man at the bar was running, any thought of heroism banished by the grim fate of his friends. He made a beeline for the exit, but he never got there, Bolan's Uzi stuttering a burst that cut his legs from under him and dumped him on his face, a broken, sprawling mannequin. He might have survived, depending on the speed and quality of medical response, but he was finished as a star of track and field.

A bullet hissed past Bolan, struck the bar and ricocheted, rum bottles shattering, their contents adding heady fragrance to the smell of weed and cordite. Bolan spun to face his final adversaries, who were attempting to escape from the booth.

Too late.

A short burst from the Uzi stopped one of the Rastas in his tracks and punched him back into the vinyl coffin, short legs churning in their death throes. Gravity took over in another heartbeat, and the dead man slithered from the bench seat to the floor, another obstacle to his companions in their rush to fight or flee.

The Uzi's magazine was running low, and Bolan used it all to pin the last two Rastas in their booth, unloading from a range of twenty feet, full-auto, shredding them with hollowpoints. They slumped together, leaking crimson, dribbling on the floor.

The bartender stood gaping at his lifeless customers as Bolan ditched the empty magazine and snapped a fresh one into place. It took some nerve to keep from running, Bolan thought . . . or maybe he was frozen by fear.

"Are you with them?" asked Bolan.

"No, suh. They my customers, is all. I mean, they *was*."

"You need to find a better class of clientele."

"Yes, suh. I'm thinkin' that, myself."

"Somebody asked you what went down tonight, you tell them Roman Graffia was settling old accounts. You got that?"

"I should tell that to the heat?"

"Whoever asks."

"Okay by me."

"I left a live one in the crapper," Bolan said. "You want to help him out, I'm sure he wouldn't mind."

"No hurry," said the barkeep. "He's not goin' anywhere."

The warrior smiled. Two gofers for the price of one, and Jason Frost was sure to get the message, one way or another. Would he buy it? That was something else again, but Bolan saw no reason why the posse leader would suspect a ruse. Frost had been pushing Roman Graffia since the Jamaican first set foot in Florida, and he would not expect Don Roman to keep sitting on his hands forever.

A retaliatory strike was logical.

If anything, the move was overdue.

"How goes it?" asked Grimaldi, as he put the car in motion.

Bolan smiled. "We're on our way."

"I WANT YOU TO TELL ME, brudda, why it is you still alive."

The voice was calm, apparently relaxed, but Jason Frost was seething as he stood in front of Percy Glass and stared into the frightened Rasta's eyes. Ten soldiers dead, and one in hospital with shattered legs, while number twelve got off with just a light tap on the head.

"I told you, mon, this ofay wanted me to bring a message back."

"For these Sicilians."

"Right, mon."

"So, he cuff you hands and sets you on the toilet with you dangle droopin', then he knock you in the head."

"But first, he give the message, Jason. Don't you be forgettin' that."

"The message, sure. You wanna give me that again, one time?"

"He tells me the Italians, they be tired of playin' games, mon. They be takin' in the welcome mat, he says. You know the way them crazy fuckers like to talk."

"And then he knocks you on you head."

"That's it, mon."

"And you wake up after, when the others all be dead."

"That Joey, from the bar, came back and got me, Jason."

"Joe, from the bar."

"That's right."

"You never saw this white man's face before?"

"No way, mon."

"Did he look like one of Graffia's Eye-talians?"

Percy thought about it for a moment, chewing on his lower lip before he shrugged. "I dunno, mon. He wore a suit, the way they do. Dark hair, he had. And guns."

"What kind of shoes?"

"Shoes, mon?"

"They all wear fancy shoes, Eye-talians. Did you check them out?"

"I didn't see his shoes, mon. First, he was behind me, then he had a fucking weapon in my face. No way I thought about shoes."

"Too bad."

"You think he was a ringer?"

It was Jason's turn to think, now. He could list a hundred reasons for the Mafia to want his people dead, and none at all for anyone to try and frame the Mob. In fact, it made no sense at all.

"I think," said Frost, "that we be comin' up on payback time."

"I want that ofay bastard knocked me out," said Percy Glass. "He shamed me, killed my bruddas."

"Somethin' tell me there be plenty guys to go around," Frost told him, smiling thinly. "You just follow orders like a good, loyal Rasta man."

"You know I do that thing," Glass answered, realizing he had stepped across the line. "It piss me off, is all."

"I see that, Percy. Recollect where pissin' got you in the first place, though."

Who said a black man couldn't blush?

"I want the bruddas armed and ready," Frost proclaimed, his chief lieutenants nodding on the sidelines as he turned to face them. "No excuses. Everybody plays. It bad enough that the Eye-talians got more men than we, and now we lose eleven off the top."

"More comin' through the Keys tomorrow," one of his lieutenants offered.

"That's tomorrow, mon. We got a problem on we hands tonight."

"We gonna hit 'em hard?" asked Percy Glass.

"You know another way to hit 'em, brudda? Anything worth doin' should be done the right way, first time."

"That's what I say, mon."

"I thought so."

Roman Graffia had made a grave mistake in going for a body blow against the posse, when he should have taken out the head. Of course, it was no easy proposition, killing Jason Frost. A dozen men had tried in recent years, and all of them were dead. His luck had been a legend in Jamaica, where assassins missed him three times in as many weeks, before he came to the United States.

The change of scene had spelled no end to danger, though. It was a rough game in the States, more lethal adversaries than he had ever had in Kingston, with a fortune on the table. In Jamaica, there were people dying every day, but it was worth more when you risked your life here on the mainland. Make a million dollars for your trouble, letting no man stand between you and the prize.

Obeah taught that any man could tap into the power of the spirit world, if he would only follow certain rules. A failure meant that your belief was not yet strong enough, or else the other fellow had a stronger brand of magic up his sleeve.

But the Italians, now, Frost reckoned they were fat and overconfident from running things so long. It made them cocky, and they had a tendency to think about each move before they acted.

When they should have killed him, Jason knew, was when he first set foot in Florida. They should have seen the trouble coming and removed him from the scene without a second thought.

But it was too late now. They had missed their chance.

It was the posse's turn to strike, and Jason would not hesitate. He had his targets marked and memorized, against the day when war would come. That day, he knew, had been inevitable from the time he left Jamaica. Now it had arrived, and he was ready.

When the smoke cleared, Jason Frost would be the new king of Miami. He would hold the reins of power, use them as a whip to scourge his enemies and drive them from the state. With time and patience, he would forge allegiances with other posses on the Eastern Seaboard, moving inland. The Italians and their cronies would become extinct.

CHAPTER SIXTEEN

The warrior followed Biscayne Boulevard due north, past Bay Front Park, to reach the cutoff for the causeway leading to the Port of Miami terminals, offshore. Instead of driving out across the water, though, he made another right-hand turn and doubled back along the shore, in search of pleasure craft.

They called the private docking point Miamarina. Sonny Crockett kept his boat and alligator there, according to the legend of *Miami Vice,* and so-called normal citizens were welcome to do likewise if they had stylish vessels, could pay the going monthly rate, and the managers would allow them berthing privileges.

Roman Graffia easily met all three criteria, with cash and style to spare. His forty-footer, the *Calabria,* was named in honor of the village that his grandfather deserted in the latter nineteenth century to try his luck in the United States. There had been rumors, through the years, of burials at sea and rendezvous with cigarette boats up from the Bahamas, bearing drugs to shore, but nothing could be documented, and the more outlandish stories smacked of myth to Bolan.

Graffia had reached the pinnacle of his profession, and it would be doubly risky—even stupid—for him to get involved in contract murders, smuggling and the like. Some capos, Bolan understood, retained a taste for action, never quite ridding themselves of the street-punk mentality that got them started in the first place, but Roman Graffia did not appear to fit that mold. By most accounts, he was an armchair general, more than happy to rule from a distance, protected by multiple buffer layers while his soldiers did the dirty work.

It made no real difference to Bolan if the *Calabria* had ever hauled bodies or contraband. In fact, it was enough for him to know Don Roman owned the yacht and cherished it as if it were a member of his family. He went out sailing once a week, on average, and in spring he had been known to disappear for two or three weeks at a time, cruising the islands, out to Bermuda and back, sometimes a trip to Mexico, Honduras, Venezuela.

Losing something hurts more when you love it, and the Executioner was looking for a pressure point, emotional or otherwise. It might not be a major score, in terms of business lost, but it would get the don's attention, shake him up a little, offer him a preview of coming attractions.

It was 11:20 when he parked his car and left it, strolling out along the breakwater that angled northeast toward the causeway, sheltering the boats in the marina. It would not protect them from a hurricane, of course, but that was just a risk that came with living in Miami, like the prospect of an earthquake in L.A.

There seemed to be no lookouts on the yacht. He was surprised at first, but then decided the "neighborhood," together with the owner's reputation, would suffice to keep most thieves and vandals at a distance. Bolan went aboard to double-check, found no one, and retreated to the dock before he opened up his black gym bag, lifting out a matched pair of incendiary bombs.

Too bad. He would have liked to take the boat out for a cruise, but there was nothing in the way of leisure time for frontline soldiers in an everlasting war. Nice things were liabilities, a weakness, something that the other guy could crush or take away.

The door to the companionway and cabins had been double-locked. No need to force it, when he had a thermite can in either hand. The polished oak would char and melt away like balsa wood, in seconds flat. One bomb would do it, but he used them both.

Anything worth doing . . .

Bolan stood and watched as the *Calabria* began to burn, flames leaping in the dark, reflecting on the shifting surface of the water. It was a beacon glowing in the night, a signal to Miami that the Executioner had come to town.

They would not know his name, of course. Not this time. If his strategy worked out, the targets of his wrath would turn on one another like the savages they were, and no one outside Hal Brognola's net would ever know that Bolan was in town.

And if it blew up in his face, well, there were ways to cope with that. Disposal teams and press liaison officers, selective leverage with Metro-Dade, the FBI, at Justice. He could simply disappear—or be identified in press reports as an associate of Roman Graffia, if it came down to that.

Covering his tracks was not the issue, Bolan knew, as he turned back toward his car.

The problem in Miami and Barbados would be coming out of it alive.

THE HONOR of retaliation fell to Eddie Crane. They drew lots, standing up in front of Jason Frost, and Eddie got the short straw first time out. He didn't mind. The ganja took away his worries for the moment, and he knew that a successful strike against the local Mafia would lead to his promotion in the posse. Frost was always looking for a few good men to do his special jobs, and Eddie Crane was looking out for number one.

Selection of the target was a puzzler, given all they had to choose from in Miami and environs. There was gambling, prostitution and pornography, drug outlets, plus a list of several hundred legal businesses controlled in part or absolutely by Don Roman Graffia.

So many targets and so little time.

The first mark, they had finally agreed, should be symbolic. Something that would let the proud Italians know exactly what was happening, why they were being punished. Any affront to the posse must be expunged in blood.

And it was Eddie Crane's idea to hit the Marsala Social Club, on Seventh Street, three blocks from the central headquarters of the Miami Police Department. The Marsala was to Roman Graffia what Java Man had been to members of the posse: someplace for the troops to let their hair down and relax, where privacy was guaranteed. A raid against the club was simple tit for tat, and it would also send a message to the cops whom Graffia had bribed for years on end to look the other way and help him run the competition out of town.

He chose a dozen shooters for the raid and split them up among three cars. The vehicles were stolen, fitted out with license plates removed from other stolen cars, effectively removing any chance of being spotted by a sharp-eyed traffic cop. The raid would not take long, and when his men were finished, they would drop the cars off at a nearby shopping mall with keys in the ignition.

Eddie armed his soldiers to the teeth with sawed-off shotguns, AK-47s, Uzis, Ingram MAC-10 submachine guns. For himself, he chose a Tec-9 automatic pistol with a 32-round magazine, two spares for luck. He also took along a U.S. Army frag grenade, part of a shipment sto-

len six months earlier from Elgin Air Force Base, in Oka-
loosa County.

Fireworks for the celebration of a brand-new day.

The three-car caravan drove east on Flagler Street, past
Lummus Park and under Highway 95, turned north on
Second Avenue and held that course to Seventh Street. A
left-hand turn, and they were headed west, back toward
the highway, passing under it a second time. On Eddie's
right, he saw the plain facade of the Marsala Social Club
approaching, two men lounging out in front.

He did not have to point the sentries out. His men would
recognize them at a glance, and he could picture weapons
being readied in the cars behind him, heard the sound of
safety switches disengaging in the back seat of his own vehicle. Eddie clenched the Tec-9 pistol in his fist and wished
he had another hit of ganja, now that they were on the
verge of mortal combat.

They had the windows down as they approached the
social club, black faces staring at the two Italian lookouts, dreadlocks clearly out of place on Seventh Street at
this time of night. One of the sentries turned and ducked
inside the club, warning the men inside, while his companion reached inside his jacket for a gun.

Too late.

All hell broke loose as Eddie's raiders opened up in unison, their weapons laying down a solid screen of fire. The
solitary mafioso did a jerky little dance as bullets riddled
him, his body twitching, finally toppling facedown on the
sidewalk.

Eddie's driver stopped outside the social club and kept
the engine running. Following their leader, eight men lined
up on the curb, the drivers staying with their vehicles and
watching out for witnesses, police, whatever. The Marsala's broad front windows had been painted over, but they

were not bulletproof, and Eddie's Rastas made the most of all that glass, unloading on the club at point-blank range.

It was impossible to tell if they were scoring on the occupants, and Eddie didn't really care. For now, it was enough to just be firing, paying back a measure of the insult the Italians had inflicted on his friends at Java Man. The Tec-9 bucked and blazed in Eddie's hand until the magazine was empty, spent brass littering the pavement at his feet.

A number of his soldiers were reloading, getting ready for a second fusillade, as Eddie fished the frag grenade out of his pocket, stepping forward. There was something almost godlike in the feeling, as he pulled the pin and dropped it on the sidewalk, winding up the pitch.

He let fly through the nearest shattered window, seeing furtive movement in the club, a sound of angry, frightened voices coming to his ears. Someone was still alive in there, but Eddie could not place the sound well enough to guarantee a kill with the grenade.

No matter.

"Heads up!" Eddie shouted to his soldiers, mentally counting off the seconds. He noticed several of them raising arms or ducking just before the blast went off, and that was fine. No shame in covering your ass when there was every chance of being maimed or killed.

He had expected more of an explosion, something like the movies, but he reckoned it was bad enough on the receiving end. Smoke started drifting from the shattered windows. The angry voices were replaced by groans and whimpers now, and they were music to his ears.

"We're finished here," he told the others, and he turned back toward his car. A couple of the Rasta brothers squeezed off parting shots into the smoky darkness of the club, but Eddie did not snap at them for breaking discipline. Their blood was up, and it was good for soldiers when they learned to hate their enemy.

That hate would come in handy, later on.

The war was only getting started, Eddie knew. Before it ended, they would need all the committed killers they could find.

WHEN ROMAN GRAFFIA moved down from Tampa, he had settled in Miami Beach, a wealthy island enclave separated from Miami proper by the width of Biscayne Bay. Five causeways linked the island to the mainland, much as bridges bound Manhattan to the Jersey shore, but there was still a pleasant sense of living out at sea, between the bay and the Atlantic Ocean on the east. It could get rough in stormy weather, but you always got a fair head start on hurricanes, and it was simple to evacuate before the killer winds arrived, then come back later and pick up the pieces when it was calm again.

With other storms—the human kind—Don Roman normally felt safer on his island. Theoretically, he never had to set foot on the mainland. There were four golf courses in Miami Beach, along with shopping malls and supermarkets, theaters, you name it. He could sit behind his desk, complete with telephone and fax machine, communicating with the world at large, while soldiers cordoned off his property and kept that world at bay.

Unfortunately circumstances altered cases, and he had New York to thank for feeling vulnerable in his own damned home that Thursday night. If it were not for DiBiase and his precious summit meeting in Barbados, Graffia would be at liberty to deal with the Jamaican problem in his normal style. A sit-down, maybe, to discover what the problem was. And if they couldn't talk about it, he would take whatever steps seemed necessary.

Now, though, he was saddled with responsibility for setting up the conference, playing host to capos from around the country. Danny Dick was there already, bitching over problems out in California, and the calls were pouring in from Cavalcante in Chicago, DiBiase and Tattaglia in New York, Don Graziano in New Jersey.

There was truth in that old saying that it doesn't rain, it pours. Right now, it felt like it was pouring shit on Don Roman, and he was scrambling around to find his damned umbrella. What he really needed was a break, but there was no way he could hope for one, the next few days.

No way at all.

"You're sure it was the coconuts?" he asked Pete Andolini, frowning at his underboss across the desk.

"No doubt about it," Andolini said. "I got it straight from Tommy Falco. He was on the door with Benny Copa, rest his soul. He saw the fuckers coming, and he stepped inside to warn the boys. Next thing he knows, they're getting hit with everything except the fucking atom bomb."

"I shoulda taken out that fucking Frost a year ago," said Graffia.

"You couldn't know he would pull this kinda shit."

"Tell that to Benny and the other boys. They figure it's my job to know."

"I've got the eyes out, Roman. Give this thing a few more hours, I can tell you where these coconuts are at and what they had for supper."

"Do that, will you, Pete? And soon. The longer this drags on, the worse we look in front of all the other Families."

"I'm on it, swear to God."

I hope so, Roman thought, and kept it to himself. He saw no point in ragging Pete about the coconuts, when it was *his* responsibility, as capo of the Family, to see that everything ran smoothly. Anyway you tried to break it down, the buck stopped here.

He had a choice to make, some hard decisions coming up. If he could not find Jason Frost and neutralize the threat by noon Friday, Graffia would have to concentrate on mounting guards around his fellow dons as they arrived in preparation for the short hop to Barbados. The Louisiana outfit would be flying straight down to the island from New Orleans, which was fine, but that left Graffia to watch out for his brothers from New York, New Jersey, California and Chicago.

Okay, so that was it. He had to find the suicidal idiots responsible for shooting up his boys at the Marsala, and he had to rain on their parade. Teach them a lesson none of them would soon forget, assuming they survived.

On second thought, scratch that. He wanted them for gator bait. The lesson could be handed down to future generations, by example. Jason Frost had crossed the line, and there was no point in pretending he could still be saved.

The crazy bastard was as good as dead.

He simply didn't know it, yet.

CORAL GABLES IS A CITY geared toward recreation for the well-to-do. In five square miles, the suburb's planners have incorporated three golf courses, three parks, a marina, two museums, and the Fairchild Tropical Gardens. Coral Gables residents are proud of their expensive homes and cars, their wardrobes, contributions to the latest stylish charity. They do not like to think about Miami's brooding ghetto, lying just across the Tamiami Trail, due north. It never seems to cross their minds that trouble has two legs, and it can walk across the street.

In fact, Coral Gables has some trouble of its own, although the residents are not inclined to view a little quiet gambling as either sinful or a blight on the community. The days of grand, wide-open carpet joints are gone, perhaps forever, but the games of chance live on, and all of them are controlled by the syndicate.

Bolita is the Latin version of the classic numbers racket, played by thousands of compulsive fans in southern Florida. Instead of using Wall Street or the nearest racetrack to select a winning number, the bolita masters take their cue from bingo, using numbered Ping-Pong balls, much like the several state-run lotteries. In the old days, they were tossed around in burlap bags, a "catcher" grabbing one ball through the sacking, while the rest were dumped out to reveal the daily winner. New technology had made the burlap bag a piece of history, except in certain barrios where players clung to the traditional approach, but the result was similar in any case.

Bolita was alive and well in Coral Gables, operating from the back room of a small shop on Sevilla Avenue, not far from the Venetian Pool. The shop was closed to patrons at 11:45 on Thursday night, but there were human counters in the back, dividing up the take and making notes on who had payoffs coming in the morning.

Johnny came in from the back, parked in the alley, flicking off the safety of his MP-5 submachine gun as he left the rental car. No lookout at the door, and it was open when he tried the knob, defying any rumors of the war that had erupted less than one mile distant, on the other side of Calle Ocho.

Half a dozen pairs of eyes were locked on Johnny as he crossed the threshold, letting everybody see his SMG. He had a view of money stacked up on the counting table, two guys wrapping bundles, while a third was tapping numbers on a calculator. Two more no-neck types were sorting out the betting slips, while number six—the muscle—occupied a folding chair on Johnny's left.

The shooter had to know that it was hopeless, but he went with guts instead of logic, bolting off his chair and groping for the pistol on his hip. He never made it, Johnny's stuttergun erupting with a short burst to the chest that slammed him backward, flattening the chair as he went down.

And that was all.

The other guys were showing him their hands and sweating in defiance of the air conditioner, the color draining from their faces till they could have passed for ugly mannequins. They stared at Johnny as he made his pass along the counting table, checking out the cash, but no one spoke.

"You've had a busy night," he said at last to break the silence. "All this loot for Don Roman."

No answer from the sweating statues.

"What I'm thinking," Johnny told them, "is that he can spare a little for his friends, you know? Somebody get a bag."

None of them moved, each man afraid to be the first and thereby look too eager to comply. The younger Bolan made it easy, pointing to the last guy on the left.

"You, Shorty. Get a bag and put that money in it. Leave the ones for last."

The short guy did as he was told, reluctantly. He used a green garbage bag and shoveled money in until the table had an empty space between the calculator and the pile of betting slips. All gone.

"That's good. I think that makes a decent contribution to the cause, don't you?"

No answer from the captive audience.

"If anybody asks, you tell them Don Cavalcante appreciates the kind donation, right? It bothered him at first, these rumors that Roman was backing DiBiase's half-assed plan, but I can see we got it wrong, up in Chicago. That's the thing about mobility, these days. You get a chance to visit other folks and find out what they're really thinking."

It was soaking in, but no one said a word as Johnny took the bag and started backing toward the door. He didn't have a clue how much the total came to, but the money seemed to weigh a ton. He held the SMG one-handed, crouching as he swung the garbage bag across his shoulder, feeling like a strange, demented Santa Claus.

"You want to call your capo," Johnny told them from the doorway, "be my guest. I know he won't mind Don Ernesto picking up a little extra change, this way. We're all together in this thing, the way I see it, watching out against New York."

He kicked the door shut, ran back to his car and dumped the bag into the trunk. No one was in a hurry to give chase, and Johnny took his time on the withdrawal, watching posted limits, nothing to provoke a late-night traffic stop.

It would be pure, dumb luck if Graffia believed his rap about Cavalcante, but he didn't care. Confusion was the goal, and each new doubt that he could plant among his enemies was money in the bank.

Or, in the bag.

How much did that make, since the razzle-dazzle started in California on Tuesday? He would not have been surprised to learn that they were sitting on a million bucks and change, but the amount was less important than the impact on their enemies.

To hurt a thief, you hit him where he lives. And that
meant in the pocket book. It was a grim, ironic fact of life
that criminals apparently begrudged the loss of stolen
property as much, or more, than most honest citizens re-
gretted losing money they have earned through honest labor. It was something in the outlaw psyche, Johnny
thought. The notion that the world owed them a living,
that everything they coveted was theirs by right.

So much for gangland economics.

Things were heating up around Miami, racing toward
the flash point.

Johnny meant to be there when his brother struck the
spark.

CHAPTER SEVENTEEN

The cutting plant in Hialeah operated day and night, around the clock. Nobody seemed to notice, with the setup stacked above a pawnshop east of Okeechobee Road, three-quarters of a mile from touchdown at Miami International. The cocaine did not have to travel far before the lab rats took it over, testing, weighing, sifting, stretching it with additives to boost the retail price a hundred times or more.

It was a relatively simple job, but there were risks involved. You could O.D. just breathing in the lab, so everyone wore special masks and goggles to protect themselves, along with smocks and rubber gloves. They looked like something from a science-fiction movie in their costumes, but it was the only way to go.

Another threat, although implicit, emanated from the guards on duty at the cutting plant. They were assigned to watch the stash and theoretically protect the lab rats, but there had been incidents where members of the crew were apprehended stealing samples from the plant. The punishment in such a case was swift and permanent. No bargains, no probation, no parole.

Tonight, though, they would have a very different problem on their hands.

The DEA had fingered Bolan's target for him, passed the word along through Leo Turrin while the team was airborne from New York. He parked on Seventh Avenue, behind a service station that had shut down for the night, and shed his street clothes to reveal a jet black skinsuit underneath. From the trunk he took his military webbing, lightweight gas mask and the Uzi submachine gun with a silencer that he had chosen for his lead piece on the strike.

It was a short hike through the muggy darkness, back to Bolan's destination. The entrance to the cutting plant was served by steep, unlit stairs, but Bolan opted for the fire escape around back. He scrambled up the rusty metal steps to reach a window that was painted over as a hedge against the kind of Peeping Toms who came with warrants. Nothing visible to give a raiding party legal cause for search and seizure.

Bolan, on the other hand, required no warrant. Everything and everybody on the premises was fair game for the Executioner.

He snugged the gas mask into place and spent a moment breathing through it, making sure the filter functioned properly. When he was satisfied, he palmed a stun grenade and yanked the safety pin, backed off three steps and pitched it through the painted window.

Even as he made the toss, he was retreating, dropping to the landing halfway down the fire escape. The dicey part of taking out a cutting plant, aside from posted sentries, was the prevalence of chemicals like ether, with a flash point that could land you in the middle of a fire storm if you didn't watch your step.

The stun grenade exploded with a blinding flash and noise designed to deafen anyone within a radius of thirty feet. It rocked the building, blew the windows out, but Bolan was protected by intervening walls. No sooner had the thunderclap erupted than he sprinted up the fire escape and went in through the smoking window in a combat crouch.

The lights were on, fluorescent ceiling tubes, but it was difficult to see with so much smoke and drifting powder in the air. It seemed that Bolan's stun grenade had detonated on or underneath the table where Colombian cocaine was heaped for cutting by the lab rats. The explosion had converted several uncut kilos into drifting air pollution, and the dazed employees were surrounded by a swirling cloud of poison.

One of them had lost his mask or ripped it off, his gasping face converted to a clown mask, crystal white. The guy was choking on it, minutes left to live, and Bolan left him to it, savoring poetic justice.

On his left, another lab rat was limping through the haze, groping blindly for an exit. Bolan's Uzi stuttered, muffled to a sound like ripping canvas, and the guy's white smock was splashed with crimson as he fell.

More figures writhed in the dope cloud, one of them a gunner in a shiny suit. He lurched across the floor on hands and knees, a stubby riot shotgun trailing on a shoulder strap, its muzzle scraping on the floor. Another burst from Bolan's Uzi rolled him up and dumped him in a corner near the door.

That left another shooter and a third technician. Finding them huddled close together across the room, Bolan stitched them with a single burst that left them stretched out lifeless, side by side.

Case closed.

He looked around the place, deciding it would be a waste of time and energy to torch it. It would be more embarrassing for Roman Graffia if Bolan left the lab intact, for the police and Feds. For all he knew, there might be paperwork—a lease or deed—that could be traced back to the don. Not likely, but if nothing else, the wreckage would confirm that Roman's Family was facing a determined enemy.

Now, all the capo had to figure out was who and why.

He went out through the front door, left it standing open to the night and jogged back to his waiting car. The night was winding down, but Bolan still had work to do before another sunrise lit Miami.

They were closing on the home stretch now, and he could almost see the finish line.

THE BEST THING about Florida right now, in Daniel Masciere's view, was that it lay 1,200 miles from California, give or take. He had relaxed a little since arriving on the Wednesday flight from San Diego, and from his calls back home, it seemed that there had been no more attacks upon the Family.

Danny Dick was not prepared to let it go, by any means, but he could well afford to put the problem out of mind while he was in Barbados, trying to concentrate on one thing at a time and get it right. Once he got home, there would be ample time to sort things out and find the men responsible for his extreme discomfiture. He would enjoy dissecting them at leisure, once he had the chance.

Still, he could not erase the echo of that phone call, coming on the heels of so much violence in his own backyard.

Don't trust New York.

It had been on his mind since Tuesday night, a warning he could neither disregard nor properly evaluate. It would be with him in Barbados, Masciere knew, for all the good it did.

He was enjoying Roman Graffia's hospitality, up to a point. Miami Beach was warmer than his own preserve in San Diego, and he liked a change of scene from time to time. Still, he could not escape the obvious security precautions, constantly aware that there was danger on the streets.

And what the hell was going on with Graffia, these days? Some kind of shooting war with the Jamaicans, if he had it right. It seemed like all the Families were catching hell, from California to Chicago and New York, as if the summit meeting in Barbados had some kind of voodoo curse attached.

The smart thing, for Masciere's money, would have been to scrub the meet entirely, or postpone it to another time, but everybody else was hot to trot, and he could not afford to be the one who came off looking yellow, calling for delays. At times like this, a show of strength was mandatory, even if he felt like crawling in a hole somewhere and hiding from the world.

The last thing Masciere was expecting right now was a phone call in the middle of the night. He was alone on Roman's patio, a glass of brandy in his hand, blue light reflecting upward from the nearby swimming pool, when someone came up on his blind side. It was Roman's house man, with a cordless telephone and a bemused expression on his face.

"You got a call, Mr. Masciere."

"Who is it?"

"Didn't say. One of your guys back home, I guess."

"Okay."

He took the telephone and waited for the houseman to retreat. The sliding doors edged shut behind him, leaving Danny Dick alone.

"Hello?"

It didn't sound like a long-distance call, that airy whisper on the line, but maybe cordless phones were different.

"Do you recognize my voice?"

Hell yes, he did. The guy from San Diego, calling back. *Don't trust New York.*

"I think so," Masciere told him, hedging.

"Yeah, I thought you might. How's Florida been treating you?"

"I'm working on my tan," the capo answered testily. "You call to ask about my health, or what?"

"You might say that. I hope you're taking my advice about New York."

"You were a little vague on that," said Masciere. "There's a couple different angles there, you know? Besides, I don't know who I'm talking to. I don't like doing business with a total stranger."

"Are we doing business, Dan? I thought that I was giving you some good advice. Don't trust New York."

"See, that's the thing. I don't know what you mean by that, okay? If you could pin it down a little . . ."

"Hey, Dan, you know what Kipling said about the east and west. They only meet on Judgment Day."

He didn't have a clue who Kipling was, but Masciere thought that he was picking up the caller's message well enough.

"You figure someone's got it in for me, back east?"

"I wouldn't be surprised. Would you, Dan?"

"I'd have less trouble with it if I knew where you were coming from, all right?"

"Let's just say I'm a friend."

"My friends have names and faces."

"All in time," the caller said. "I'm in Miami, now. I just might see you in Barbados, if you make it."

"If I make it? What the hell is that supposed to mean?"

"Your host is having problems, right? It could get sticky for you in the next few hours."

"I can take care of myself," said Masciere, hoping it was true.

"You say so, Dan, I'll have to take your word on that. Remember who your friends are."

"I suppose you have some tips on that?"

"I might, another time."

"That doesn't help me much."

"I'm doing what I can. Stay frosty, Dan. I'll be in touch."

The line went dead, a dial tone humming in his ear, and Masciere switched off the phone with an angry gesture, laying it aside. He drained his brandy, staring at the lit swimming pool and wishing he could grab the phantom caller by his neck, shove one hand in his skull and rip his secret knowledge out, examine it up close.

More innuendo, rumors, leading nowhere. How was he supposed to base a strategy on shit like that?

He felt a sudden chill, despite the muggy warmth outside. Somebody walking on my grave, he thought, and rudely pushed the peasant superstition out of mind.

And yet . . .

It felt like someone was watching him, improbable as that might sound.

The California capo left his empty glass behind and stalked into the house.

MIAMI SHORES and yet another golf course.

Bolan had begun to think that Florida must have more golf courses, per capita, than any other place on earth. The climate played a part in it, of course, together with the age and affluence of residents devoted to the game. Not many young, poor black men or Hispanics on the links, these days, but that was life.

The Gold Coast did not earn its name from charity.

And neither did the Dade Collection Agency.

Up front, the place seemed straight enough. They had an office in Miami Shores, a short block north of Biscayne Boulevard, and big ads in the Yellow Pages. If you called to have an auto repossessed or deadbeats hassled on outstanding debts, the Dade Collection Agency would handle it, within the limits of the law. The repo men worked on commission, twenty-five percent, plus their expenses, and the paying client stood for bond if anything went wrong.

But there was more to Dade Collections than immediately met the eye.

Behind the front, so squeaky clean, there lay a shylock operation, run by Peter Girardelli on behalf of Roman Graffia. Don Roman's loan sharks put his money on the street at interest rates of twenty-five percent per day and up, depending on the risk involved. Some clients had their interest compounded hourly, and rates were known to double, even triple, if a debtor fell behind.

The staff at Dade Collections never asked about collateral when they were passing out the cash. It made no difference to them if the client had jewelry, flashy cars or real estate. His body and the bodies of his loved ones were collateral enough. The first missed payment meant a lecture, with a little rough-and-tumble on the side. If things went badly after that, the cost of doing business escalated. Beatings. Broken bones. A late-night visit to the client's girlfriend, wife or daughter.

Normally the Dade Collections staff avoided killing customers, since corpses rarely paid their debts, but an example was demanded now and then, to keep the herd in line. If eating one debt meant that fifty others paid on time without a whimper, it was worth it sometimes. Showing they meant business. Keeping up their reputation on the streets.

The loan shark racket struck a special nerve with Bolan, harking back to the destruction of his family in Massachusetts. He was not expecting any members of the Dade Collections team to be on hand that Friday morning when he parked behind their shop in predawn darkness, but he did not need an audience for what he had in mind.

The back door lock was easy, and a single bullet from his Beretta 93-R side arm silenced the alarm. It might be ringing at the local sheriff's station, loud and clear, but Bolan did not plan to stick around and meet the night shift. He was working on a simple in-and-out, no sweat, no strain.

He breezed in past the toilets, following a narrow hallway to the outer office, where he primed a thermite can and rolled it underneath the secretary's desk. Retreating toward the exit, Bolan paused to check the honcho's inner sanctum, found it locked, and snapped the door back with a well-placed kick.

The filing cabinets were locked, as well. No problem. Bolan took his second thermite bomb, released the safety pin, and dropped it down between the filing cabinets and the wall. The files might be computerized, the disks stored somewhere else, but he could only deal with stock on hand.

And he was out of there, before the first white flash erupted in the outer office, smoke and flames erupting in a conflagration water would not quench. As he was rolling down the alley, the second bomb went off, melting cabinets, furniture and all into a seething mass of superheated scrap.

It was impossible to say if any debtors would escape the shylock's clutches through his action, but it felt good at the time, and Bolan guessed that Roman Graffia would have a few things on his mind, the next two days, besides collecting from his victims on the street. Survival would be Roman's first priority, both for himself and the accumulated wealth of empire.

They were counting down the hours now, until Barbados and the final confrontation. Bolan focused on the battle yet to come, and knew that it would call for every bit of strength and ingenuity that he possessed.

He would be walking on a tightrope all the way, and one false step would send him plunging to his doom. No safety net to catch him, this time, if he got it wrong.

No net for Jack or Johnny, either, when it came to that.

Old friends, old enemies, familiar risks.

The Executioner was blitzing on.

BROGNOLA CRADLED the receiver of his private line and stared out through the window of his den at early-morning darkness. A few more hours, and they would be looking for him at the office. Hal knew he should get some sleep, but it seemed pointless.

Two brief calls, to Stony Man and Leo in Miami, had brought him up to speed on late events around the country. He was current on the action in Dade County and the aftermath of Bolan's visits to Chicago and New York. He had itineraries for the capos heading south on Friday, and the schedule of arrivals in Barbados.

Hal had everything, in fact, except a guarantee that Bolan's plan would work.

And that, he realized from long experience, would only come with time.

There were no guarantees in war, and Hal had long since come to recognize that he was locked in combat with the men he hunted for a living. Justice, in the abstract sense they talked about in law school, was as far removed from the reality of Hal Brognola's world as the canals of Mars.

In real life, crime paid handsomely, the bad guys often won, and the exalted "justice" system came complete with heavy bias in favor of the criminal, while victims got the short end of a very dirty stick.

The Phoenix project, based at Stony Man, had been designed—at least in part—to remedy that situation. It was not a vigilante outfit, in the strictest sense. Brognola did not send his warriors out to punish muggers, sneak thieves, rapists and the like. His operations were most frequently conceived and executed in the name of national security, but it was all the same to Hal.

Somebody had to tip the scales for justice, now and then.

In a demented world where cops were sued by criminals they wounded in the line of duty, and a brutal rapist was discharged because the prosecution witness showed up fifteen minutes late for court, somebody had to take a stand against the savages.

Brognola knew he couldn't save the country or the world. If he worked twenty-four hour days for fifty years, his troops would barely scratch the surface, but at least he knew that they were doing *something*. When the sun went down on any given day, he knew that certain predators were out of circulation, and that knowledge was enough to get him through the night.

Barbados was a different story, though. They were not mopping up a spy ring or a band of terrorists intent on touching off a holy war. The Mafia had been around for centuries, a greedy parasite within the democratic system, working to corrupt that system on its own behalf. The latest move by DiBiase to consolidate the Families was simply one more effort to perpetuate the syndicate and bleed another generation.

In Barbados, Striker had a chance to stop the bastards cold and scatter them in disarray. The question would be whether he could pull it off and still come out the other side alive.

Brognola took a moment to recap the odds. There would be seven capos at the meet, that he was sure of. Tony Argiento, from New Orleans, had not made his mind up yet, and no one seemed inclined to push him, with the various indictments that were pending both in state and federal court. Another six months, give or take, might see him jailed for life.

That made it seven dons, with ten or fifteen soldiers each. Say thirty men with Roman Graffia, at least, since he was acting as the host and thus responsible for the security of visitors. At least a hundred guns, no matter how you broke it down, and Bolan would be going in with two men on his side.

Brognola made it thirty, thirty-five to one, at that rate. Not the best odds in the world, by any means, but Bolan had emerged victorious from worse.

A second question: could he pull it off again?

How many times could one man charge the gates of hell before he stumbled and the flames consumed him?

Jack and Johnny were a bonus, able warriors, both of them. They tripled Bolan's combat stretch and firepower, but how much could they really do against a force some thirty times their number?

In another setting, Hal might have been able to enlist official help, but the authorities in Bridgetown made it clear that they intended to protect their wealthy guests, as long as no one violated any local laws. And if 100 or 150 mafiosi ran amok, what could the small police force in Barbados do to stop them, realistically?

Brognola longed for one of the cigars that he had given up more than a year ago, on doctor's orders, but he settled for a stick of gum instead. Life was a lot like that, sometimes: you settled for the practical and never really tried for all the marbles. What it came down to, in human terms, was compromise.

But sometimes, compromise cost lives.

And that was why the Executioner charged flat out toward his chosen target, every time. No quarter asked or offered in the hellgrounds, when a life seemed cheap enough, if it was sacrificed to help a worthy cause.

Barbados, for example.

They were coming to the wire, and any way you sliced it, the results would not be pretty when the smoke cleared.

Hal gave up on sleep and started dressing for the office. It was going to be one hellacious weekend, and he did not plan to miss a minute of it. If he could not help his soldiers in the field, the very least that he could do was watch and wait.

CHAPTER EIGHTEEN

On Friday morning, driving to O'Hare, Ernesto Caval-cante wondered what had happened to his world. There had been no reprise of Wednesday's violence, but he found himself no closer to solutions, either. He had something like a hundred people on the street, all asking questions, using muscle when they had to, and the end result was nothing.

He should have been relieved, all things considered, but it looked bad for a capo to be kicked around that way and not retaliate. But he could not punish anyone until he knew who was responsible for his embarrassment.

And at the moment, he was getting nowhere fast.

Well, that was not exactly true. Ernesto had his tickets booked through to Miami, where his old friend Roman Graffia was playing host to the assembled delegates, before they took off to Barbados. Cavalcante had been looking forward to the weekend conference as a chance to scope things out, see how the power lines were being drawn around the country. But he had misgivings now.

Too much had happened in the past three days, from California to the Windy City to New York. The reports about the violence in the Apple, slopping over to New Jersey, made him nervous. Cavalcante had been leaning toward the DiBiase wing at first, before the shooting started, and he was inclined to blame Carmine Tattaglia for the trouble in Chicago, off the bat. But there were problems with the theory, now that Carmine had also been taking hits.

And what was happening in Florida, for Christ's sake?

Here he was, about to travel south, and Roman Graffia was suddenly besieged by enemies on every side. Jamaicans, if you could believe it! Cavalcante pictured leaky boats, jam-packed with peasants from the islands, floating off Miami Beach and working up the nerve to storm ashore.

Terrific.

Cavalcante had a dozen gunners with him for security. It wasn't much, but any more would look like an invasion, and he did not want to come off seeming too aggressive. Twelve could cover him in shifts and do it right. If things went sour in Barbados, he would have enough firepower to effect a safe retreat.

Their charter aircraft was a Beech 1900C, with seating for nineteen. Powered by twin 4,000hr TBO Pratt & Whitney 6A-65B turboprops, the 58-foot aircraft cruised at some 250 miles per hour at an altitude of 14,000 feet. Ernesto knew all this because he did his homework in advance, and he was counting on five uneventful hours in the air, between Chicago and Miami.

Once they touched down at Miami International, he realized, it could be something else again.

Could the Jamaicans tell one mafioso from another? Did they even care? Ernesto knew from dealing with the restless natives in his own backyard that provocation was irrelevant, in many cases. Sometimes, it was like the moon and stars took over, maybe something in the water, and they simply went berserk. The only thing they understood, at times like that, was force.

It was a hard thing, doing business in the modern world. This civil rights crapola had too many people thinking everyone was equal and entitled to a moment in the sun. Worse yet, some of the clowns who took it seriously liked to challenge the presiding Families sometimes. Hispanics, blacks, the Asians. It was bad enough La Cosa Nostra had to deal with different ethnic groups around the States, now frigging immigrants were pouring in from every corner of the globe, pretending that the Constitution had been written just for them.

One benefit of DiBiase's master plan, the whole "new order" thing, had seemed to be that it would slap the restless natives down and keep them down where they belonged. Ernesto was prepared to compromise, of course. They did all right as numbers runners, pimps and pushers, but they could forget about the management positions, anything approximating independence from the greater syndicate at large.

A part of Cavalcante still hoped DiBiase had a chance to pull it off, but he was going in with major reservations, waiting to be sold. It would take more than Tom LaRocca's sunshine promises to close the deal this time, when they were obviously on the verge of several different shooting wars from California to the Keys.

Or, were they different wars?

Cavalcante hoped to answer that question in Barbados, but he could not deal with it right now.

The capo hated flying, and it suddenly occurred to him that he had failed to pack his Dramamine.

Five hours, Jesus.

He could hardly wait.

SOMETIMES, in spite of everything, Pablo Guzman believed that he led a charmed life. Just yesterday, he had been marked for death, but he had managed to escape with only minor cuts and burns, and a hacking cough from smoke inhalation while fleeing from his safehouse in the Bronx.

Tattaglia's gunners almost had him, but they failed to make allowances for Pablo's ingenuity. It made him laugh to see the *Post* and the *Times*, with headlines speculating on his death, grim photographs of blackened corpses. Which was Pablo Guzman? How, exactly had he died?

It would be hours—maybe days—before the stupid bastards found his tunnel. Three weeks in the digging, with a team of spademen working day and night, removing dirt in plastic trash bags for disposal in a vacant lot somewhere. The trick was buying two adjacent houses, renting one to white-bread types, and paying them to look the other way while Pablo's moles went on about their business. In the end, they had a tunnel running from the basement of the safehouse to the yard next door, due south, the trapdoor covered by a layer of dirt and AstroTurf.

A thing like that, you never knew when it would come in handy. The police come knocking with a warrant some fine morning, or Tattaglia's people storm the house with Molotovs and automatic weapons. Either way, it all plays out the same.

The one thing Guzman's *pistoleros* knew from childhood was the motto: No surrender. They would fight until they died, because they knew their enemies would take no prisoners. Surrender was the same as suicide, and it was better to die fighting, take a few down with you if you had to go.

Their sacrifice enabled Pablo to escape.

He had been dozing when the firebombs struck, awakened by the voices of his soldiers and the sound of gunfire in the alley, bullets ripping through the backside of the house. He waited long enough to brace his soldiers with a pep talk, then he raced downstairs and slithered through the tunnel, crawling on his belly with a flashlight in his left hand, automatic pistol in the right.

And it was like a miracle the way he felt, emerging from the soft earth of the flowerbed, like some dark elemental born of earth and fire. Behind him, he could see the safe-house burning, bright flames leaping underneath a pall of smoke. The battle raged, not quite one-sided, but he knew Tattaglia's troops were bound to win. They had surprise and numbers on their side.

Once he had cleared the tunnel, it had been a simple thing for Guzman to escape. He scrambled over one fence, then another and another, making for the far end of the block. When he had put five houses in between himself and the assassins, Guzman stole a car and got the hell away from there, proceeding to another hideout. Only then, when he was safe, did he begin to think in terms of vengeance.

He was running out of soldiers in New York, but that was not a problem. Morning brought word that Don Tattaglia was on his way to visit with some cronies in Barbados. Guzman didn't know exactly what they had in mind, nor did he care. It was enough to know where he could find his prey.

The rest of it came down to phone calls, dropping names and calling in old favors. He had contacts in Miami, countrymen with common roots and interests in the cocaine trade. They sympathized with Guzman's plight and saw an opportunity to gain some ground against the Mafia while helping him repay his debt. There would be men and guns available when he arrived.

He did not bother checking in with Medellín before he made those plans. It was beyond the scope of his authority to launch a shooting war against the Mafia, but Guzman was not the aggressor, here. His sponsors could have no objection if he struck back at his enemies in self-defense. And if pursuit of that most worthy goal should take him from New York to the Caribbean, so what?

When Pablo had a moment to himself, he thought about how he would rule the Bronx, once he had finally removed Tattaglia. From there, it was a short step into Brooklyn, Queens, Manhattan. He could not expect to dominate the whole damned city, but there was certainly room for expansion. The police, conditioned to accept Tattaglia's money, would undoubtedly receive his overtures with open palms. His time was coming. He could feel it.

Don Carmine would be waiting for him with the others. DiBiase and Scarpato, Graziano from New Jersey. All of them together, lined up like the targets in a shooting gallery.

Who said that Pablo Guzman could not rule New York?

The brass ring lay before him, waiting to be taken.

In Barbados.

IT FELT GOOD to Carmine Tattaglia, knowing that his beef with the Colombians had been resolved in record time. The swift conclusion would not bring his soldiers back, of course, but that was war. You took some losses now and then, but victory was gauged on who was standing when the smoke cleared.

Now, all Carmine had to think about was his appointment with the other capos, to debate Don Julio's proposed "new order" for La Cosa Nostra.

New, my ass, Tattaglia thought. It sounded like the same old shit their grandfathers had fought a war to bury in the 1930s, one guy grabbing all the power he could lay his hands on and demanding tribute from the rest. No matter how you dressed it up, it was a power play, and anyone who thought Don Julio was thinking of the syndicate at large should have his head examined.

There would be a hot time in Barbados, you could count on that. Tattaglia had selected fifteen soldiers to accompany him. No insult to Don Roman in Miami, but the recent clash with Guzman had reminded Carmine of the need for tight security. He would not put it past Don Julio to pull some sneaky shit while they were all assembled on the island, but he would not get away with it.

One of the men selected for the trip was David Rossi, Tattaglia's underboss. In other circumstances, Rossi would have stayed behind to watch the store, but Tattaglia could not shake the substance of his conversation with the Ace who called himself Omega. If the guy was right, and Rossi had some kind of bargain rigged with Julio, it would not do to leave him in the Bronx. Carmine wanted Rossi at his side, where he could be observed—and dealt with harshly— if and when he tipped his hand.

It hurt to think that Rossi would betray him, but Carmine recognized the facts of life. He had been known to stab a trusting brother in the back from time to time, if it would help him win advancement in the Family.

Was Rossi trustworthy?

There would be time and opportunity, while they were in Barbados, to observe his underboss and lay some traps, see whether Rossi took the bait. Carmine didn't need the kind of evidence they filed in court to make his case. He recognized betrayal when he saw it, but he needed more than some glib stranger's unsupported word.

On that score, he had tried to track Omega, but it was a hopeless case. Those Aces, in the old days, changed their names and faces like most people change their underwear. They moved around like drifters, no allegiance to a single

Family, and you could never tell where they would surface next.

Forget it.

Rossi was the problem, at the moment, and it did not matter where the accusations came from. They could still be checked for accuracy, and if verified, Carmine knew exactly what to do.

In fact, if it came down to that, he planned to do the job himself.

At least he had disposed of Pablo Guzman and the ragtag army of Colombians who had been raising hell around the Bronx. If nothing else, that swift response would earn respect for Tattaglia from his fellow dons. The next time anybody started thinking he was weak and ready to be nudged aside, they would be forced to reconsider.

Five hours in the air, between La Guardia and touchdown at Miami International. Sometimes, Carmine wished they had some kind of space-age transport system, like you saw on television, that could zap a body here and there in seconds flat. Five hours was a long time, when you thought about it. Anything could happen in the Bronx while he was airborne, out of touch with all his people on the ground.

The thought that he was going to Barbados outnumbered by supporters of the DiBiase plan put Tattaglia's nerves on edge. But that could change. Don Julio had taken several hits himself, the past few hours, and while Tattaglia would have liked to take the credit, he was troubled by the fact that he had no idea exactly what was going on. Some of it might have been the damned Colombians, but he had also heard about the shooting in Connecticut, at DiBiase's hideaway, and that was something else entirely.

Tattaglia wondered if he should be grateful for Don Julio's distraction. Anything that slowed the bastard down was good news, at the moment, but he also recognized the risks of all-out shooting war, if he was blamed for the attacks around Manhattan and Connecticut.

So be it.

He thought about Omega, wondering if the Black Ace had anything to do with the aggressive moves against Don Julio, deciding that it didn't matter, either way. If DiBiase started pushing, Tattaglia was prepared to make his stand and push right back. Let Vince Scarpato jump in, if he wanted to. Carmine didn't bluff, he didn't scare, and he never backed down.

Miami was coming up, and by the time he left Barbados, Don Carmine Tattaglia would be riding high. He felt it in his bones.

And anyone who tried to stop him would regret it till his dying day.

WHEN THEY WERE safely airborne out of Hartford, Sharon Pryor started to relax. The past few hours had been hectic, even grueling, and she was relieved to have the last leg of her journey underway at last.

The last attack, at DiBiase's home away from home, had shattered any vestige of control that Julio retained. It had been frightening and funny all at once to watch him pacing, cursing, throwing punches at thin air. She half expected froth around his mouth at any moment, but the seizure never went that far.

When DiBiase blew his top, LaRocca and the others stood aside and waited for the storm to pass. He was beyond their physical control in such a case, unless they chose to shoot him, and no one was openly thinking of mutiny yet.

Or were they?

She had doubts about LaRocca, now and then, but Tommy kept his personal dissatisfaction to himself. No pillow talk about Don Julio, beyond the usual—big plans and big rewards, big money waiting down the line, when they had brought the other Families into line.

From what she saw, the grand "new order" was on shaky ground, and much of that apparently came down to one man's efforts.

There was no doubt in her mind about who pulled the trigger in Connecticut. She had not seen Belasko, had not even glimpsed the shooter from a distance, but the raid had been a quasi-military operation down the line. Belasko had impressed her as a soldier—not in active service, necessarily, but someone with a heavy military background. Rangers, Delta Force, the CIA... that kind of thing.

It had been hopeless, trying to reach Leonard Justice from Connecticut, when Julio was raging and his men were covering the telephones. Belasko would check in with his control, at least in theory, but her own report would have to wait until they reached Miami.

She recalled her sense of being watched at DiBiase's place. Had Belasko been peering through the sniper scope? It was an eerie feeling, sudden death so close that it could reach across the manicured lawn and tap you on the shoulder, far enough removed that you would never see it coming.

What kind of man could do that in cold blood?

She knew about the military use of snipers, and the SWAT teams with their riflemen on tap to take a suspect down if all negotiations failed, but that was combat, even on the streets. Invariably, when the cops used snipers, they were coping with some kind of hostage situation or a shooter on a rampage. They were in the headlines all the time, it seemed . . . but the attack on DiBiase in Connecticut was something else.

Okay, she understood that it was like a war these days, between the cops and crooks, but there were still some rules, however strained or ill-defined they might seem. She had been taught that law-enforcement officers used deadly force in self-defense, or to prevent a felony in progress, when their other options were exhausted. Sniping bad guys from a distance while they strolled around Connecticut did not appear to qualify.

And, yet . . .

There was a certain rush involved, she had to grant Belasko that. For all the chances she had taken, all the shit she went through with LaRocca, Sharon Pryor had never felt the same excitement—hell, the feeling of accomplishment, admit it—that she had experienced when Belasko started kicking ass and taking names.

The downside was that Julio had doubled his security. Instead of taking ten guns to Miami, he had phoned for reinforcements from Manhattan. Nineteen men in all, plus Tommy. It required a change of planes at Hartford, spending extra money for a Saab SF 340, seating thirty-five. Commercial flights were definitely out, with all the hardware they were carrying, and the necessity of breaking up his group if Don Julio had opted for last-minute scheduled flights.

It had been touch and go there, for a while, as to her own inclusion on the trip. Don Julio had gone along with Tommy's whim before the shooting, but his mood was altered by the strike against his safehouse. Sharon feared that he would slash her from the roster, maybe even blame her for the raid, but at the final moment, Julio decided it would be more dangerous to leave her in Connecticut, a witness to his late embarrassment.

So, she was on her way.

She did not have to ask if Belasko would be traveling to Florida, and on from there to Barbados. Sharon knew that much, but she could not predict what action he would take, or how it would affect her own assignment.

One thing she was trying to accept, in preparation for the worst—or best, depending on your point of view—was that Belasko might decide to kill LaRocca. If that occurred, she was determined not to crack or throw a tantrum, thinking of the months she had invested in the case. She would consult with Leonard Justice, do her best to toe the party line, unless she found her own neck on the chopping block. In that case...

What?

Was she prepared to blow the whistle against Belasko? Would she be allowed to? Could she even make the allegations stick, with nothing but her word to back them up?

The lady Fed decided she would have to watch and wait. She was a bit surprised to hear no ringing protests from her conscience when she thought about the men killed by Belasko in Chicago, New York and Connecticut. More startling than the sniper raids was her reaction, edging toward acceptance in what felt like record time.

If this was war, then she was in the vanguard, and she might be called upon to fight. When that time came, she hoped she would be ready, equal to the task at hand.

If not...

She closed her mind to that eventuality and turned back to her window, concentrating on the clouds below. The shadow of their aircraft raced along below them. It would be there waiting for them when they touched down in Miami.

Like Belasko.

Like the war.

CHAPTER NINETEEN

"We're almost there," said Jack Grimaldi, driving into Hollywood.

The Florida edition bore no great resemblance to its namesake out in California. You could look in vain for movie studios, but you could spot a star from time to time, if you were hanging out at one of the four country clubs in town. The streets were mostly named for presidents, though none had lived within 600 miles since Richard Nixon took a hike, back in the Seventies.

It was the last place anyone would think to look for a Jamaican posse hangout—which, according to intelligence from Metro-Dade, made it the perfect place for Rasta men to hide.

Their safehouse occupied a weedy acre and a half on Johnson Street, not far from West Lake's outlet to the intracoastal waterway. The cost of real estate was high, but Jason Frost was never short of cash these days. It was suspected that his people used the intracoastal waterway to bring in loads of dope from time to time, from Biscayne Bay or through Port Everglades. No one had caught them at it yet, and Metro-Dade was glad to pass the address on to Leo Turrin and the Feds, for what it might be worth.

"How many did they say, again?" asked Johnny Gray.

"They're guessing half a dozen, but they could be wrong."

Fair odds, if they could bring the sweep off by surprise.

"That's close enough."

Grimaldi pulled onto a narrow access road and killed the motor. They were screened by live oak and palmetto from the highway, safe from prying eyes. It took only a moment, slipping on the military webbing over denim shirts and jeans, collecting hardware from the trunk.

Jack chose a Colt Commando, backed it up with his Beretta and some frag grenades, while Johnny took the H&K submachine gun and his favorite SIG-Sauer automatic. There would not be any distance work involved, and if they had to fight an army, they were out of luck.

They hiked a quarter mile through chicory and sneeze-weeds, partridgeberries and wild geraniums, with sycamores and hackberry for cover going in. The house was nothing special. Peeling paint, four bedrooms, a detached garage and boathouse on the water. From the yard's condition, it was obvious the tenants didn't own a mower and were not concerned about appearances. A Cougar and a Chrysler minivan were parked in tandem on the west side of the house.

"I'll take the front," Grimaldi said.

"Suits me."

"Two minutes."

"Right."

They separated at the tree line, breaking off in opposite directions, Johnny running in a crouch until he reached the cover of the minivan. From there, he worked his way around behind the house, the grass up to his ankles whispering at every step.

He scuttled toward the small garage and hunkered in its shadow, covering the back door and a pair of grimy windows with his SMG. No cry of warning from the house to tell him he was spotted. Maybe they were in there smoking ganja, stoned out of their minds. An easy probe, for once.

With fifteen seconds left, he started moving out of cover, racing toward the house. Three wooden steps, and then he stood before the back door, raised a foot and kicked it, barging through behind his weapon.

Murky light inside the kitchen, with a pot of something bubbling on the stove to Johnny's right. He heard Grimaldi coming in the front, his carbine stuttering. That was all he had a chance to register before a target angled into view.

The Rasta man was lean, bare-chested, with a stainless steel revolver tucked into the waistband of his baggy trousers. Dreadlocks hung around his face like rats' tails, swinging as he turned to face the stranger in his kitchen. Hauling on the pistol, almost making it.

Almost.

The MP-5 thrummed in Johnny's hands, a burst of parabellum slugs stitching holes across the lean Jamaican's naked chest. He staggered backward, gasping, and rebounded from an old refrigerator, toppling forward on his face.

More firing from the front room of the house, and Johnny moved in that direction, ducked through the connecting doorway to a hall that served the bath and bedrooms. Turning left, he checked the bathroom and found it empty. Took the nearest bedroom next, in time to find a gunner struggling into jeans, his side arm out of reach by several inches.

Modesty can be a killer.

Johnny hit the Rasta with a rising burst that slammed him over backward on the bed. The rumpled sheets and sagging mattress were turning crimson as he left the room, continuing his hunt.

Nobody in the second bedroom, and he doubled back along the hall. A wounded gunman suddenly appeared before him, one arm limp against his side, the other braced against the nearest wall, a pistol in his hand.

They faced each other for a heartbeat, each man knowing one of them must die. The Rasta had a bullet in his side, another in his shoulder, and the pain played hell with his reaction time. He tried to get the pistol up and into target acquisition, but he never had a prayer.

The SMG spit half a dozen rounds and took the Rasta down. Blood smeared the wall where he had leaned against it, leaving tracks. His weapon bounced once on the carpet, came to rest beyond the reach of lifeless fingers.

Sudden silence in the living room, and Johnny edged in that direction. "Coming through," he called.

"It's clear," Grimaldi answered.

Johnny found him standing in the middle of the room, reloading. Three dead men were sprawled around him, one reclining on a swaybacked couch, two others on the floor. They had been watching television when he entered. Some rap video, with raghead "gangstas" spewing hate at women and police.

"No messenger," Grimaldi said. "They didn't want to play."

"I passed a phone back here," said Johnny. "Do you still remember Jason's number?"

Jack was smiling. "Tip him off, you mean?"

Johnny smiled right back at him and said, "What are friends for?"

MIAMI SPRINGS is for the birds. Its streets boast names like Ibis, Heron, Bluebird, Falcon, Plover, Oriole, Albatross, Nightingale, and Meadowlark. A whole community, thought Percy Glass, prepared to spread its wings and fly away.

No matter.

He was not concerned with birds on Friday morning. He was hunting rats, of the Sicilian pedigree, and Percy knew exactly where to find the rodent he was looking for. A block west of the golf course, on Palmetto Drive, near Pine Crest.

George Turturo was—or had been—a *consigliere* for the local Mafia. He was supposed to be retired, but everybody knew that there was no such thing as a retirement from the Mob. If you were old and senile, they might put you out to pasture, but Turturo was a youthful sixty-two, still vigorous, and played nine holes a day, eighteen on Sundays. Percy Glass supposed there was an outside chance that Georgie had removed himself from active syndicate affairs, but that was not the issue. He was a Sicilian and a member of the Mafia. As such, he was fair game.

And, it should be a relatively easy hit, Turturo puttering around his house like Mr. Senior Citizen. You want to play that, Percy thought, it's fine by me. Just don't expect white hair to cut you any slack.

They parked out front and walked up to the door, as bold as brass. One man around in back to keep Turturo from slipping off once he saw it wasn't Avon calling. Ring the bell, like coming out to kill him was a thing that happened every day.

The old man should have used his peephole, but he didn't. Getting sloppy in his golden years. He cracked the door and was about to ask their business, when he got a look at all that hardware pointed at his face and tried to slam the door again.

No good.

The first shove did it, Percy with the other three behind him, pulling through. Turturo hit the carpet on his backside, bleating anger and surprise before the fear took over, leeching color from his flabby cheeks.

"What is this shit? Who are you guys?"

"You don't know who we are, mon?" Percy flashed a smile that mirrored disbelief.

"I wouldn't ask you if I did."

"We jus' dropped in to see if you could help us with a problem we been havin', mon."

"What kind of problem? What the hell is this?"

"A problem with your good friend, Roman Graffia," said Percy Glass.

"I don't know what—"

The shotgun barrel cracked across his almost-hairless skull and knocked him flat. A worm of blood crawled lazily across his scalp.

"You don't know what, mon?"

"Jesus Christ, all right! You wanna talk to Roman, he ain't here."

"I bet you got his number though. That right, mon?"

"For the telephone, you mean?" Turturo seemed confused. His fingers came back crimson from an exploration of his scalp.

"The very thing."

"I know his number, sure."

"So, call him, mon. We'll wait."

Turturo staggered to his feet and Percy trailed him to the living room. A cordless telephone lay on the coffee table, close beside the zapper for his twenty-six inch Sony Trinitron. Turturo picked it up, tapped out a number, waited while it rang. After identifying himself, he asked for Roman Graffia.

"What should I say?" he asked, while they were waiting for the capo to respond.

"I'll tell you in a minute, mon."

"For Christ's sake...Roman? Jesus, Roman, I got people here—"

Glass waved the shotgun underneath his nose, to silence him. "Say this, mon. You got Rasta devils in your living room."

"I'm s'posed to tell you I've got rusty devils in the room, here."

"*Rasta* devils, you old eunuch!"

"Rasta devils, Roman. It's the damned Jamaicans."

"That is it, mon. Say goodbye now."

"Huh?"

"Goodbye."

"Goodbye?"

The shotgun bellowed once, and George Turturo's headless body vaulted over backward, flattening the coffee table as it fell. Blood spouted from the ragged stub of his neck in a bright arterial spray, staining carpet and walls.

An angry voice was shouting from the cordless telephone when Percy scooped it up.

"Hello, mon?"

"Who the fuck is this?" snarled Roman Graffia. "Where's George?"

"He's lyin' down right now, mon. Gots a headache, Georgie does. And I'm your true-blue nightmare, mon. You're next."

He dropped the telephone before the capo could reply, and crushed it underneath his heel.

Let the Sicilians play their little games.

The Rasta posse would be coming out on top this time.

IT WAS A TRICKY SHOT, all things considered. Once he did the job, withdrawing from Miami Beach could be a problem, with the access limited to certain causeways spanning Biscayne Bay. His target was a waterfront estate on North

Meridian, but that was inland, facing onto a canal that looped around to make its exit under Alton Road, beside the Julia Tuttle Causeway. He could either drive and try to find a vantage point on land, or he could take a boat.

Mack Bolan took the boat.

A shot from water made for problems of its own, primarily the fact that you were never really still, but he had done this kind of work before. He knew the means of compensation, firing at the crest, before you dropped and lost your line of sight. It was a challenge.

He made good time across the bay, around the Sunset Isles, and ran in with the causeway on his left, the bulk of Alton Road above him. Following the sweep of the canal, he slipped past Arthur Godfrey Road and started watching for his target, summoning the memories of FBI surveillance photographs.

There could be no mistake. He made it at a glance, the big house with its sloping lawn and tennis court. He throttled back, the motor barely idling as he lost momentum, drifting almost to a halt. He put the motor in reverse to keep from riding with the current, and the slightest tremor rocked the deck beneath his feet.

He knelt and took the rifle from its case, the Remington Model 700 adopted by the U.S. Marines as their official sniper's weapon with the designation M40 A-1. Chambered in 7.62 mm with a five-round magazine, the rifle had been fitted with a Leupold ten-power scope. Less powerful than the Ruger Model 77 Mark II, less delicate than the Walther WA2000, the Remington was perfect for his present needs.

He sat and braced his elbows on his knees, the rifle snug against his cheek and shoulder, covering the house. A tall, familiar-looking man was seated on the patio, between the house and tennis courts, as Bolan brought his weapon into line. The last time he had seen that face, it had been staring back at him from one of Hal Brognola's files.

Dan Masciere, late of San Diego, soaking up the sun.

As Bolan sat there watching, Masciere's host exploded from the house, arms waving, anger blazing in his cheeks. It was impossible to guess what he was saying, but Masciere seemed unsettled by Graffia's news and his resultant outburst.

Perfect.

It was time to raise the ante.

Bolan flicked the rifle's safety off and let his index finger curl around the trigger, taking up the slack. He made it something close to ninety yards, and he was zeroed at a hundred, which meant the bullet would be rising slightly when it reached the target. Match that rise against the motion of his floating platform, and he would have to compensate significantly for a killing shot.

He set the cross hairs of his scope on Masciere's collarbone and waited. Up and down, the motion of the current.

Up.

He stroked the trigger, lost the target in a momentary blur, and reacquired it as the capo's head exploded— melon-ripe and bursting at the seams. One instant, Roman Graffia was standing there and speaking to his guest; the next, remains of what had been a living man were spattered on his face and shirt and slacks.

That was Danny Dick, all over.

Bolan set the rifle down and took the helm, a smooth shift into forward, powering away from there. He had a glimpse of Graffia responding to the engine noise, a sharp turn toward the water, but the distance ruined any chance the mobster had of making out a face, identifying numbers and the like. He stood and shook a fist at Bolan, mouthing curses that were smothered by the sound of engines racing, prop blades digging into water.

Masciere's death would put a new twist on the game for all concerned, increasing paranoia in the ranks, depriving DiBiase of a vote he had been counting on. Where would suspicion fall for the attack? It hardly mattered, just so long as the assembled mafiosi were on edge, regarding one another with a more jaundiced eye.

When he was halfway back to shore, he stopped and stowed the rifle in its case. The piece had served him well, and might again before the game was finished.

It was nearly sundown in Miami, and the other capos would be in by now, or on their way. Tomorrow they would make the short hop to Barbados, and the Executioner would be there waiting for them with his merry men.

The sun was turning bloody red.

It would probably be that color by sundown in Barbados, as well.

"WHAT DO YOU MEAN, he's dead?" Don Julio was livid, standing nose-to-nose with Roman Graffia. "Somebody shot him on your fucking lawn?"

"Slick bastard in a boat," said Graffia. "I never saw it coming. He was in and out like that—" a finger snap "—while I was telling Danny Dick about the damned Jamaicans."

"Was he black?"

The capo of Miami thought about it, shook his head. "No way. He was a white guy, that I'm sure of."

"But you couldn't recognize him if he walked in here right now."

"That far away, who could, for Christ's sake?"

"What are we arguing?" Ernesto Cavalcante asked. He turned to Julio. "You think somebody in this room's responsible for what went down?"

"I wouldn't know," the capo of Manhattan answered. "That's my point."

"From what I hear," Carmine Tattaglia said, "poor Danny had some problems on his plate out west. A lot of us have had those kind of problems lately."

DiBiase turned and glared at his old rival from the Bronx. "What's that supposed to mean, exactly?"

"Facts are facts, eh, Julio? Since Tuesday afternoon, one Family or another has been getting hit from coast to coast. I look around this room, I don't see anybody who's immune."

"And you connect that with our business in Barbados? Are you saying it's my fault?"

"You sound a little paranoid, there, Julio. Did you forget your medication?"

DiBiase took the first step toward Tattaglia, with angry color blazing in his cheeks, but caught himself before he went too far. The mocking smile on Carmine's face was calculated to provoke him, but he understood the tactic and was strong enough to hold himself in check.

For now.

"You ever hear of a coincidence?" asked DiBiase, turning to include the other capos as he spoke. "We all have problems, off and on. Nobody thinks about it twice, what's happening in someone else's territory, but this meeting brings it out. Coincidence, that's all."

"Coincidence," said Vince Scarpato, echoing the sentiment like what he was—a parrot. Carmine looked at him with frank contempt, while Don Ernesto settled for a frown of open skepticism.

"What I hear," said Roman Graffia, addressing Julio, "you took some hits, yourself."

"That's right."

"You find out who was doing it?"

"Not yet," said DiBiase, "but I'm working on it." As he spoke, he cast a sharp glance at Tattaglia.

"Just coincidence, I guess," the capo of the Bronx replied.

He hoped the shrug looked casual. "You had your beef with the Colombians, I understand. I've got some people out there, don't exactly wish me well. Same thing. I'll find out who they are when this is over, clean it up myself."

"You didn't hear about the phone calls, then?" asked Roman Graffia.

"What phone calls?" DiBiase was confused.

"To Danny Dick. He told me all about it when he flew in here ahead of schedule. Back on Tuesday, when the shit went down in San Diego, someone called him up and left a message. Then, last night real late, the same guy called him here."

"You want to share the message, Roman, or is it some kind of secret?"

"'Don't trust New York,' is what he told me," Graffia replied. "Some guy he doesn't know calls up and says, 'Don't trust New York.' If there was more to it than that, he didn't say."

"Don't trust New York."

"That's it."

Ernesto Cavalcante had a strange look on his face, just listening to Graffia, but he kept any questions to himself. A glance across the study at Tattaglia showed he was frowning, too, as if in thought. It worried DiBiase, these two possibly collaborating, when he needed the Chicago vote to put his dream across.

"You think about a call like that, it could be anybody," DiBiase said at last. "We've got three Families up and running in New York, and everybody knows a couple of us don't agree on much of anything." He smiled at that, to minimize the sting. "So, tell me this. If someone calls and says 'Don't trust New York,' what's that supposed to mean, exactly?"

"Some people," Cavalcante said, "they get outside New York, it's hard to tell the players if you haven't got a program. In Chicago, now, we got our Family, and everybody else is on the outside looking in, *capisce?* No competition in the ranks."

"That's something we should talk about in Barbados," said DiBiase. "Right now, it's important not to let some joker spook us. Anyone can make a phone call, am I right?"

"Hell, yes," the Brooklyn parrot echoed. "Anybody."

"Doesn't mean that he was giving bad advice, though," Cavalcante said.

"What's that supposed to mean?" asked DiBiase. "Have you been getting calls there, Ernesto?"

There was just the slightest beat of hesitation, while Chicago's boss considered a response. "Not me," he said at last. "I think out loud sometimes is all."

"Well, anyhow," said Roman Graffia, "we fly out in the morning, and you're under my protection in the meantime."

"Just like Danny Dick?" It was the first time Joseph Graziano had intruded on the conversation, but he made his point, and Graffia was blushing as he answered.

"I've got people on the grounds," he said, "*and* on the water. Anybody wants to take another shot, they'll have to drop in from the sky. But just the same, I'd recommend you all stay in the house until we take off for the airport in the morning."

"House arrest," Tattaglia said. "I love it."

CHAPTER TWENTY

He had to take it easy, flying out of Kingston's Palisadoes International Airport, but Jason Frost knew all the angles by heart. In theory, the police were looking for him, but they did not put much effort in the hunt these days. They understood that he was off to the United States and doing well, one less concern for them to deal with on the killing streets.

He could be nabbed by accident, of course, but that would be a total fluke. To keep it clean, he flew commercial from Miami into Kingston, Percy Glass and several other members of his posse on the same flight going down. Most of his living soldiers stayed behind, since it was easier to pick up shooters on the island than attempt to slip a regiment past Immigration in Jamaica.

Driving from the airport into Kingston, Frost was wary, checking out the rearview mirror every mile or so, to make sure he had not acquired a tail. He started to relax a little when he met his Rasta brothers in the Trench Town suburb and explained his business, how the Mafia had come out and provoked a shooting war for no good reason, killing men they all knew well as friends and allies. There was no real argument when he described the meeting scheduled for Barbados and relayed exactly what he had in mind.

It was a fluke that he found out about the meeting, really. Under normal circumstances, Frost would not have known that Roman Graffia was leaving town, much less that other capos would be going with him for a sit-down in the sun. By sheer dumb luck, one of the mobster's top lieutenants had a maid who was Jamaican, and she heard things, passed them on to someone in the family, and so the word came back to Jason Frost.

He still had time to overtake his enemies and punish them, but he would have to act decisively, and soon. There was some truth to that old saying: He who hesitates is lost.

He did not have a clue as to the subject of the meeting on Barbados, and he didn't care. Whenever mafiosi got together, they were talking business. That meant bleeding brothers in the ghetto for their last dime, spent on gambling, drugs or women riddled with disease that killed you in your prime. Did the Sicilians care if a Jamaican boy went hungry, lost his roof or died of AIDS?

Hell, no.

Frost wasn't clear on numbers, just how many mafiosi would be flying to Barbados, but he estimated fifty, added ten percent for error, and was satisfied to handpick eighteen gunmen of his own. One of his Rasta brothers owned an Embraer EMB-110 P-2, a prop plane manufactured in Brazil that seated twenty-one, and never mind that it had been around for almost nineteen years. The plane was small enough to touch down at a smuggler's strip outside of Christ Church, where they would collect four cars and make the drive to Bridgetown, eight miles west. Four hours in the air and twenty minutes on the ground to reach their destination.

Fair enough.

Frost wished that he could see the look on Roman Graffia's fat face when the Sicilian realized that he had been outsmarted by a Rasta man. It might be difficult to reach the don himself, but there was still a chance.

On days like this, Frost reckoned anything was possible.

With Frost and Percy Glass, they would be taking twenty guns against the enemy, with the advantage of surprise behind them. It would have to be enough.

Frost's leadership and honor were at stake this time, and the alternative to victory was death.

Frost did not plan to die this weekend; he was looking forward to a long and wealthy life. But if he had to go, the posse leader thought, at least he would not go alone.

There would be plenty of Sicilians on their way to hell to keep him company.

THEY HAD BOOKED a Boeing 737 for the flight down to Barbados, seating for 119 passengers, with capos and their underbosses riding in first class, the troops in coach. It was too late to find a smaller plane when Masciere bought the farm and California's delegation packed it in, refusing to proceed. They flew with twenty-seven empty seats and some misgivings all around, but they were on their way.

It felt good, stepping from the aircraft into sunshine on Barbados. DiBiase looked around and saw the minifleet of limos waiting on the tarmac. Immigration was a mere formality, the men at Customs greased up front with heavy bribes to pass the luggage on, and everything went smoothly at the terminal.

Don Julio was pleased to take it as an omen, something going right for once, this fucked-up week.

It was incredible, the way all kinds of problems blew up out of nowhere, threatening the plan that he had nursed from infancy to reach its present state. So close that he could taste success, and still he had to watch his back.

He had been counting on a favorable vote from Danny Dick, but losing California for the moment cost him nothing. It was canceled out, this way, and he could always strike a separate bargain with the new boss later on, once he had settled up with La Commissione. The Boss of Bosses could do anything he wanted to.

At least, this way, there would be no surprises coming out of California when they took the final vote. With all the problems Masciere had been having on the coast, no one could say exactly what was on his mind. He had become a wild card, therefore dangerous, and DiBiase had begun to think his death was providential.

Clearing out the dead wood, making way for a dynamic new regime.

New Orleans was a no-show at the Bridgetown Hilton, leaving six men to decide the fate of the United States for years to come. Once they had voted, after DiBiase took command, there would be time enough to gather in the broken Families from Queens and Staten Island, Buffalo and Pittsburgh, Cleveland and Detroit, Saint Louis, Tucson, California. Let the prosecutors in Louisiana take their time and do it right, eliminating clumsy dinosaurs and making DiBiase's job a little easier.

One nation under Julio.

It would be rocky at the start, of course. Tattaglia would never go along with DiBiase's plan, and Cavalcante had a shifty look about him, but the two of them with all their troops could never stand against the other Families, once Julio united them into a monolithic war machine. If Carmine and Ernesto had to die, so be it.

That was life.

His suite was spacious, with a good view of the beach, LaRocca and his woman right next door, their gunners sharing rooms on either side and just across the hall. It would be difficult, if not impossible, for anyone to take him by surprise. A gunship, maybe, on the ocean, but he wasn't sweating that one out.

The conference room downstairs had been checked out by security experts, who would sweep the place again before the capos and their underlings sat down to talk. No bugs, no unfamiliar faces and no windows to facilitate eavesdropping with directional microphones.

Don Julio had thought of everything.

This was his moment in the sun, and he was not about to have it ruined by the Feds or anybody else. Not Carmine from the Bronx. Not Ernie from Chicago.

No one.

He was on a roll, and anyone who tried to stop him now was in for major grief.

It was a shame, thought Julio, that he would not be able to go swimming in the ocean on this visit to Barbados, maybe lie out on the beach and get a better tan. Next time, perhaps, when he returned in triumph, as the Boss of Bosses, for a well-deserved vacation in the sun.

For the moment, he had work to do, potential enemies to cover, nothing left to chance. If DiBiase let his guard down now, it could be fatal.

Julio knew all about the kind of critical mistakes that led to death, disaster and the like. He had been seizing opportunities like that since he was twelve years old, taking advantage of others when they were careless or overconfident.

With DiBiase in the game, you always had to watch your back.

It was the only way to play.

ONE PLACE TO GET AWAY from Tommy was the beach, but Sharon Pryor could not risk it at the moment. Things were happening too quickly now, and if she missed a portion of the program, she might never get around to catching up.

Of course, she was not officially in the loop, as far as subject matter for the conference, the debate between respective capos. DiBiase and their host, Don Roman, were obsessive on the subject of security, and any bugs would have to be laid down by someone else. As far as overhearing conversations, she had done her best and would continue, but the big men had grown leery of discussing business with a stranger in the room.

Her leak was Tommy, and she worked him several different ways, depending on the circumstances. There was always pillow talk, when she could get him in the proper mood, but lately he was prone to angry mutterings about bad luck, the other capos pushing Julio, a litany of woes without much detail. Now and then, she caught one-sided conversations on the telephone, deducing what she could from Tommy's questions, cryptic answers and the like. And finally, on rare occasions, she could plant herself in the vicinity when Tommy spoke to Julio or issued orders to subordinates.

Unfortunately none of those techniques had yielded much since the explosion in Chicago. Tommy still had time and energy enough for sex, the greasy bastard, but he did not feel like talking business when they finished. The phone calls, always cryptic, had become almost impossible to understand, and Julio refused to speak in Sharon's presence lately, fully trusting no one but himself.

She couldn't blame him, there. Between the scheming of his rival capos and the violence that had started in California spreading eastward, DiBiase had a world of problems to contend with. He was gambling on a dream to make himself the Boss of Bosses, and a failure, at the very least, would relegate him to the low end of the totem pole.

Most likely it would cost his life.

She thought of Leonard Justice, knew he was supposed to be in Bridgetown, but she had no way of making contact. He would know that she was under scrutiny, of course, unable to make regular reports. Still, it was galling to be trapped this way, immobilized.

Whatever happened, Sharon had decided this would be her last time undercover. She had sacrificed too much, in terms of self-respect, for limited returns. It made her long for Mike Belasko's kind of freedom, the ability to run amok, wreak havoc on her enemies instead of kissing up to them and acting like a brainless Kewpie doll.

She had begun to clench her teeth, a childhood habit, but she stopped herself before her jaw began to ache. Relax and have a drink, she thought. You're in the islands now. Sun, surf and sand. Bikinis on the shore, and lifeguards showing off their muscles. Perfect.

There was danger in the ocean—shark and barracuda, stingrays, moray eels—but all the predators that Sharon was concerned with lived on land, wore thousand-dollar suits, and had their hair trimmed once a week at some outrageous price.

If Sharon had a choice of company, she would go swimming with the eels and barracuda every time. At least with fish and other predators in nature, there was never any doubt that you were on the menu.

It would be lunchtime soon, but she would not be joining Tommy and the others for their midday meal. It was supposed to be a working lunch, the first of several sessions that would hammer out the brave "new order" of the Mafia, if DiBiase had his way.

And if he failed? What then?

There would be trouble, that was certain, but she had no way of knowing whether it would mean a shooting war.

Don Julio was rash enough to gamble on a blitz, but Sharon doubted that he had the troops to pull it off. Scarpato might assist him, and she estimated that they had four hundred men between them. With the recent troubles in New York, that left perhaps 200 free for traveling around the country, tracking targets Julio selected for his hit parade.

It was a strange scenario, but anything was possible. The single biggest stumbling block for DiBiase's plan, in Sharon's estimation, would be Mike Belasko.

If she read the soldier right, Don Julio and his associates were looking at a war right here in Bridgetown, at the very time when they were sitting down and playing diplomat. The latest round of shooting had not started yet, but something told her it was only a matter of time.

The lady was surprised to find that she could hardly wait.

THE GRASSY LANDING STRIP near Lazaretto was a little rough for Pablo Guzman's taste, but he had lived through worse when he was guarding shipments from Colombia to the United States. A simple touchdown, with the cars on standby, and a few more minutes saw him on his way to Bridgetown, five miles south.

His enemies were staying at the Bridgetown Hilton. Guzman had been able to discover that much with a phone call from Miami, posing as a business partner of Tattaglia's. No message, thank you very much but he would call again when Carmine had checked in.

No need to tell the operator that he planned to call in person, with a weapon in his hand.

Surprise was everything.

His first step, in the capital, would be to take a look at the hotel. Leave spotters on the street to mark his adversaries as they came and went. If Pablo was correct, the mafiosi would be spending most or all of their time in Barbados talking business, probably confined to the hotel. He could not count on Carmine or the others offering themselves as handy targets on the street or public beaches. There was still an outside chance, of course, but Guzman reckoned he would have to hunt them down in the hotel.

Okay.

He had no problem with a public show of mayhem, if there was a viable escape hatch somewhere in the bargain. In his younger days, when Pablo was a brash young trigger man in Medellín, he used to think that he was bulletproof. And that, if he died, it would be no great loss, considering the peasant life he came from and the squalor of the barrio in which he lived.

But life was better now, for all its daily hazards. He was rich, or getting there, and the reality of death was driven home each time he pulled a trigger, issued orders for a killing or attended funerals for murdered friends. If it could happen to his soldiers, his lieutenants, it could happen to the man in charge.

Still, the reality of living in a violent world had not emasculated Guzman. He was not a coward. Rather, he was cautious, planning out his moves in detail, where a younger Pablo would have charged ahead without a second thought. He still wished death upon his enemies and acted out his wish at every opportunity, but these days, Pablo thought about his own survival first.

It came to him that if he wanted to strike his enemies inside the Bridgetown Hilton, he would have to find an angle for his commandos to get in and pass unnoticed. After several moments, driving down the coastal highway with the water on his right, thick forest on his left, it came to Pablo that he would need uniforms. His men could pass as waiters, bellboys, anything at all. They only needed time enough to get in striking range and mark their targets. After that, it would be each man for himself.

The raid itself would not take long, in Pablo's estimation. Once the shooting started, it would all fall into place. He knew that he would lose some soldiers in the process; that was understood. The fate of pawns was insignificant, if their expenditure secured a telling victory.

But Guzman's honor made it necessary for him to observe the massacre firsthand. He could not delegate the task to others, while he idled at the beach or in a shady bar somewhere. His courage had been challenged by Tattaglia, in New York, and he had so far failed to pay the old man back in kind. The best way to secure his reputation, Guzman knew, was to assert himself and lead the push that finally destroyed his enemies.

And word would get around Manhattan, Medellín, wherever the heroic deeds were talked about, enshrined as legend. He would be remembered as the man who brought the Mafia to bay and thinned its ranks, beginning at the top.

Who else could make that claim?

But first, he needed uniforms.

It should be relatively simple. Send a couple of his soldiers in to scout the Hilton, check out what the staff was wearing, maybe find a bellhop who would talk for money. Get directions to the storeroom where the extra uniforms were kept—or, failing that, to the supplier where the Hilton bought its stock. Whatever Guzman had to do to get his men inside the hotel, he would do, and not be delayed by minor obstacles.

Tattaglia and the other capos didn't know it yet, but they were all on borrowed time. Each moment ticked off on the clock was gone forever, lost. That very afternoon—or evening, at the latest—they were going to be called upon to pay their dues.

In blood.

MACK BOLAN DIALED the Bridgetown Hilton from a pay phone two blocks down and asked the switchboard operator for Carmine Tattaglia's room. An unfamiliar voice came on the line and asked his business with the don.

"It's personal," said Bolan. "Tell him it's Omega calling. If he doesn't want to talk, no problem."

"Wait a sec."

It worked out more like thirty seconds, but the Executioner was not concerned about a trace. The next voice on the line was Carmine's, sounding cautious.

"Yeah?"

"You like the island, Carmine?"

"Well, I haven't seen too much of it, so far. What's up?"

"I wondered if you've had the time to think about the problem we discussed."

"I spent some time on that," Tattaglia answered, meaning David Rossi. "I'd be interested to find out where you get your information."

"Here and there. I keep my eyes and ears wide open. You might be surprised what comes across."

"I guess that's right. Are you in Bridgetown?"

"Just got in," said Bolan, stretching it. "I thought the Hilton was a little crowded."

"I can see your point. What's new about that other thing?"

"Don Julio, you mean?"

"Exactly."

"Word I get, he had a hand in stirring up the Guzman outfit. Pretty simple, when you think about it. First, he drops a couple of their soldiers in the Bronx, and then he lets it get around that you're responsible. A guy like Guzman, he won't bother asking questions.''

"Jesus Christ! I knew it had to be some kind of runaround.''

"I understand LaRocca made the actual arrangements, left it to a couple of his shooters, with a wheelman from Scarpato's Family.''

"The fucking bastards!''

"Nothing that would pass the test in court, you understand.''

"I didn't plan on suing anybody,'' Carmine told him.

"Then there's Danny Dick.''

"Oh, yeah?''

"My sources on the coast say he was getting tired of empty promises from Julio. The more he checked it out, the more it seemed like he was being set up for a shaft job, down the line. He was a 'no' vote, coming in, but someone leaked the word back to New York. Before you know it, San Diego's going up in smoke, and Danny Dick flies out ahead of schedule. Funny thing, his sitting out on Roman's patio that way, without a guard around to cover him.''

"You figure Roman's in on this?'' Tattaglia asked.

"I couldn't say for sure,'' the Executioner replied. "But when you throw a party, you're in charge of the security arrangements, right? It looks bad when a ranking guest of honor gets his head blown off in broad daylight, in your own backyard.''

"That's right, it does.''

"So, who's in charge of the security in Bridgetown?''

"Roman is.''

"I see.''

"You're saying I should watch my back, down here?''

"Nobody has to tell you that."

"Okay. I got some people with me, as it is."

"I hope they know their business, Carmine."

"Bet your ass, they do."

"Masciere had some people in Miami, didn't he?"

The capo thought about that for a moment, finally came back with a question of his own. "So, where are you in all of this?" he asked.

"I've only got one job—to watch out for this thing of ours and see that no one, I mean no one, blows it with a one-man power play."

"Have you got paper out on Julio?"

"It doesn't work that way," said Bolan. "I'm assigned to watch and wait, you know? I check things out, see how they're going. If it looks like intervention is required, I use my own best judgment at the time."

"Suppose the guys who sent you don't approve?" Tattaglia asked.

"Then I'm shit out of luck."

"I don't know who your sponsors are—"

"That's right, you don't."

"But I was thinking, maybe you could use a little health insurance."

"Oh?"

"What I was thinking, when the time comes up for you to make that judgment call, you shouldn't have to sweat about some Monday-morning quarterback, wherever."

"So?"

"So, it might put your mind at ease to know you've got a friend with muscle, that's all. Someone who could take you in, reward you for a job well done."

"It might, at that."

"Just call it food for thought," Tattaglia said. "If something happens in the next few hours...well, a friend like that could really help you out."

"I'll make a note."

"And keep in touch?"

The Executioner was smiling now. "I guarantee it, Carmine. You'll be hearing from me soon."

CHAPTER TWENTY-ONE

Bolan made another call to the Bridgetown Hilton. This one was a long shot, but he took the chance and had the switchboard operator buzz LaRocca's room. Three rings before a woman's voice came on the line.

"Hello?"

He got right to it. "Can you talk?"

She thought about it for a heartbeat, making sure she recognized the voice before she answered. "Yes," she said at last.

"What's happening?"

"I should be asking you that question," Sharon Pryor replied.

"Let's go with first things first."

"They've got a meeting underway," she said. "Preliminary business, I suppose. Some kind of break this afternoon and then they get back to it in the evening. Working late, I wouldn't be surprised. I don't know what's on for tomorrow."

Bolan had a sudden flash of someone at the switchboard, listening. He had no reason to believe that it was true, but you could never tell. One thing the Mob had learned through years of trial and error was security.

"We need to meet," he said. "Is that a possibility?"

"When?" There was surprise in Sharon's voice.

"What's wrong with now?"

She took another moment, thinking. "I could use some sun," she told him. "Tommy wondered why I didn't make a beeline for the beach. Where are you?"

"Close enough," the Executioner replied.

"You know the beach straight out from the hotel?"

"I'm looking at it."

"Give me twenty minutes. Should I wear a red carnation?"

"Won't be necessary," Bolan said. "I'm good with faces."

"I'll bet you are."

The line went dead, and Bolan started counting off the minutes, strolling slowly toward the nearby beach. His dress was casual, a sport shirt open at the neck, short sleeves, the tails out to conceal the 93-R autoloader in his waistband. Denim jeans and jogging shoes. A jacket would have made him too conspicuous, with all that sun and bronzing flesh. He felt a trifle dowdy, as it was, but he would pass.

Another tourist, checking out the perqs in paradise.

The meet was stretching it, a calculated risk, but Bolan felt a need to speak with Sharon Pryor about her mission, find out what was happening inside the Hilton, and he did not trust the telephone for anything beyond the bare essentials. Maybe he was being paranoid, but anyone could grease the hotel switchboard operator with a C-note, flag the phone calls in and out of certain rooms.

He might have blown the game already, calling Sharon in the first place, but it seemed less dangerous than dropping by her room. It was lucky that LaRocca had been out.

They were getting down to business right away, but there was plenty to discuss. He had no fear of DiBiase wrapping up the meet ahead of schedule. Rooms were booked through Sunday night, according to the reservations clerk, accessed by Leo Turrin, but the delegates would not be staying quite that long, if Bolan had his way.

Too bad about the Hilton, but he knew the place was heavily insured. The major problem would be innocent civilians blundering across the line of fire. Whatever happened with the Mafia, he could not let the strike become a general bloodbath. More than simple nerve and firepower was called for, going in.

He moved along the sidewalk, crossing toward the beach a block short of the Hilton, islanders and sunburned tourists brushing past him on both sides. His secret business made the Executioner feel alien, like an impostor, wearing the facade of mirth and relaxation while he laid his plans for war.

How many other secrets were there in the bustling crowd that pressed around him? Lovers on the way to some adulterous liaison. Sneak thieves looking for a purse to grab, a pocket waiting to be picked. Perhaps a would-be suicide, enjoying one last fling at life. A fugitive from justice, basking in the sun and looking forward to a life of leisure with a suitcase full of pilfered stocks and bonds. A junkie seeking his or her connection. Possibly a madman, ticking like a human time bomb, ready to explode.

Or, maybe Bolan was the only person on the beach with an agenda that transcended fun and frolic. Maybe this dark mood encouraged him to think the worst of others and impute all sorts of guilty motives to the innocent.

Perhaps.

He reached the sand and started walking slowly, aimlessly. He still had time to kill. Five minutes, give or take. It would not be much longer, now.

With any luck at all, the lady Fed would have some of the answers he required to make his sanitary blitz succeed.

SHARON PRYOR LEFT A NOTE for LaRocca by the telephone. He had been after her to go and "catch some rays" while he was tied up in his business meeting and the note conveyed that she had taken his suggestion.

Getting out of the hotel was relatively simple. Each of the attending capos had a retinue of bodyguards on hand, some staking out their suites, while others roamed around the Hilton on patrol. The men from DiBiase's entourage knew Sharon's face, but they were not programmed to follow her or keep her penned inside the room. When she slipped out, in sandals, wearing a bikini underneath her terry robe, they watched her go without apparent qualms.

The sun was bright and hot outside, the tropical humidity relieved to some extent by a delicious breeze that wafted from the ocean, moving inland. Sharon thought it would have been a perfect day for lying in the sun without a care, except that she was not on a vacation in Barbados. She was working, and the job had left her feeling filthy to her very soul.

She hesitated on the sidewalk, double-checked to see if she was being followed. When she could not spot a tail, she crossed the four-lane blacktop, waiting on the center island for a break in traffic, stepping off before the next rush could arrive.

The beach was dazzling white. It would have hurt her eyes without the shades she wore. She felt the hot sand through her sandals, as she stood and scanned the ranks of tourists baking in the sun. They came in every shade, from white to lobster red to deep mahogany, depending on their length of stay and personal devotion to the perfect tan. How many tankers full of lotion would be used out here this afternoon? How many of tomorrow's cancer patients would get their start on this beach?

She was looking for Belasko, checking faces and physiques, when it occurred to Sharon that the search would be a futile exercise. If he was close to the hotel, as he had claimed, he could have gotten to the beach ahead of her, or close behind, but that did not mean she would find him lolling on a blanket, soaking up the sun.

The meet was his idea, and he would want to see if she was followed, check it out himself before he blundered into something. She could almost feel him watching, but it wasn't like Connecticut. She could not picture rifles crashing here, or bodies sprawling on the sand.

She chose her spot and settled in, threw off her robe and started smearing sunscreen on her arms and shoulders, working toward her breasts. She had one leg half-finished when a shadow fell across her, and she glanced up toward a looming, faceless silhouette.

"Is this spot taken?" Belasko asked.

"Not at all."

He sat beside her, slacks and sport shirt slightly out of place among the sun-worshippers who thronged the beach. A pair of mirrored aviator's glasses hid his eyes, and perspiration glimmered at his hairline and darkened the armpits of his shirt.

"You almost gave me cardiac arrest," she said, "back in Connecticut."

"I doubt that very much."

"You'd be surprised."

He let it go. "What's shaking with our visitors?"

"They're in and out of meetings all day, like I told you. No one got around to printing an agenda, or I would have bagged a copy."

"Are they using the convention center?"

"Right."

A copy of the hotel's floor plan, left in every room, revealed the Hilton's large convention center as a combination banquet room and conference hall, with folding walls that could divide the space in half or into thirds. From what she understood, the capos had the whole place to themselves, preferring to pay extra for wasted space rather than someone next door eavesdropping.

"I'll need room numbers," said Belasko.

"That's a problem. I'm in 814 with Tommy. Julio's next door, and he's got soldiers on both sides of us, with more across the hall. I'm pretty sure Tattaglia's on nine, but I don't have specific numbers. If the other delegations are on different floors, the placement is anybody's guess."

"The desk would know," Belasko said.

"Of course, for all the good that does. I counted heads before we took off from Miami. With the soldiers, there are ninety-two on board. Assume they've got the hard-guys doubling up, there must be fifty rooms involved. I can't roll into registration and demand a list."

"Okay." Belasko seemed about to offer some suggestion, when he froze.

"What is it?" Sharon asked him, feeling sudden chills despite the sun.

"Unless I miss my guess, we've got some company," he said.

She turned in the direction he was facing, and the chill broke through as goose bumps on her back and arms.

Three gunmen whom she recognized from DiBiase's entourage were moving down the white beach, three abreast. They had her spotted now, and they were closing on a straight collision course.

"COME ON," said Bolan. "Time to go."

He reached for Sharon, hauled her to her feet. She just had time to grab her terry robe and take it with her, shrugging into it as they retreated toward the highway.

Going back to the hotel was suicide. The lady Fed was burned, whatever happened next. Their three pursuers didn't know who Bolan was, nor would they care. If he had paused and thought about it, there might still have been a chance to bluff it out before they ran, pretend that Bolan was a horny tourist trying for a pickup—but he didn't think so.

There was something in the attitude of those three gunmen that precluded small talk. Something had gone wrong, perhaps a vague suspicion on LaRocca's part, and he would not send Sharon back to face the mafioso's wrath on any count. If Tommy lost it, started grilling her or turned her over to his men, the underboss might well discover something other than a secret tryst.

And any way you sliced it, it would be the end for Sharon.

Side by side, they crossed the four-lane highway at an angle, dodging traffic, veering off from the hotel. He led the gunners south, past shops, a stylish restaurant, another large hotel. The three men were not running, but they closed the gap a bit with long, determined strides. All three had slipped the buttons on their jackets, putting holstered side arms easily within their reach.

A public parking lot came up on Bolan's left, and he pulled Sharon in among the cars. "This way," he said.

"Have you got wheels in here?"

"Not quite."

His car, in fact, was in the opposite direction, parked north of the Hilton. What he wanted now was cover and a little combat stretch, away from innocent civilians on the street.

They moved through ranks of vehicles, reflected sunlight lancing at their eyes, heat radiating from the slabs of polished steel. When they were well into the lot, a backward glance found Bolan's adversaries stepping off the sidewalk, in among the cars.

"Get down," he ordered Sharon, leaving her crouched down between a station wagon and a minivan. "Stay here."

She did not ask where he was going, did not speak at all as Bolan left her, moving in a crouch along the line of cars until he was some twenty yards from Sharon's hiding place. He showed himself then, standing tall, the sleek Beretta 93-R out of sight, against his thigh.

The gunmen hesitated, seeking Sharon, but they could not let an easy target pass. They closed on Bolan, opting for a rough encirclement, their progress hampered somewhat by the cars.

He stood and waited for them, letting them approach to killing range. The gunner on his left was closest, having found an opening between the cars, his comrades forced to lag a bit. At thirty feet, the mafioso had a pistol in his hand. Not aimed, exactly, but he had the general direction down.

"Stand easy, man," he said. "We need to have a little talk."

With lightning speed, Bolan raised the Beretta in a firm two-handed grip, the fire-selector switch positioned for an automatic three-round burst. He stroked the trigger, held the silenced weapon steady as the parabellum manglers whispered on their way.

Downrange, his target took all three dead center in the chest, his dress shirt rippling from the impact, crimson spurting from the wounds. The gunner staggered backward, lost his weapon, rubber legs betraying him. He went down on his backside, arms and legs outflung, a final tremor rippling through his body as the spark of life winked out.

The dead man's two companions were groping for their weapons as the black Beretta swung around to find another target. Number two was standing with his shoulders hunched, behind a Honda Prelude, but his upper body was exposed, and Bolan took the shot. Another three-round burst, a little over thirty feet this time, with barely time to aim.

The first round struck his target underneath the chin and snapped his head back, just in time for the next two rounds to drill his cheek and forehead. In a heartbeat, he had tumbled back and out of sight, a muffled sound of impact reaching Bolan's ears as flesh and bone met asphalt.

That left one, and he was firing as the Executioner swung the 93-R into target acquisition, squeezing off before he had the fix. Their bullets passed each other in midair, a hot round whispering past Bolan's ear before his own burst shattered windshield glass, the last round gouging paint and whining into open air.

The gunman ducked, dodged sideways, but he kept on firing. However, he soon discovered that he could not use his weapon while crouched behind the car that gave him partial cover. So the gunman decided to run to another car. Before the moving target covered three full strides, Bolan's autoloader chugged out another burst, scoring this time, blood and bone chips in the breeze.

Three up, three down.

Along the sidewalk, pedestrians were rubbernecking, craning for a glimpse of what was going on. The sound of shots had stopped them in their tracks, but they would have missed the action if they blinked. A few of them were pointing across the rows of cars toward Bolan, but none of them were close enough to make a positive I.D.

He jogged back to the spot where Sharon Pryor was waiting, huddled between two vehicles. "It's done," he said. "Let's go."

"For Christ's sake, what was that about?"

"You just came out from under cover," Bolan said. "We have to find a telephone, right now."

THE CALL BROUGHT Leo Turrin racing to a rendezvous outside of Bridgetown. Bolan had the meeting place staked out, concealed within a roadside stand of trees, and he stepped out to flag the Justice agent's car as it approached.

"What's happening?" asked Leo, when they stood together in the shade. He listened quietly as Bolan ran the story down, face blank, a thoughtful nod from time to time.

"Well, that's a wrap," he said at last, and turned to Sharon. "Any thoughts on what went wrong?"

The lady's shrug was eloquent. "Search me. LaRocca has been after me to hit the beach since we arrived. I finally took him up on the idea. Nobody followed me from the hotel, I'm positive."

"Agreed," said Bolan. "There was no apparent tail."

"Okay, so Tommy finds you gone, whatever, and he sends the cavalry."

"I left a note," said Sharon. "He was tied up in a meeting when I left, and I expected to get back before he did. I couldn't guess what made him send the watchdogs out."

"Concern?" suggested Leo. "Maybe he was worried, after everything that's happened the past four days."

"It's possible," she said. "I guess we'll never know."

"I thought about a bluff," said Bolan, "but it didn't scan. They came in looking angry. We had too much riding on the line."

"Agreed. We need to think about what happens next. Will this abort the summit?"

"Not a chance," said Sharon. "It will tighten up security, of course, but that's a given. Tommy will be curious, pissed off. He may suspect a replay of Chicago."

"Will he look for you?" asked Leo.

Sharon thought about it briefly, shook her head in an emphatic negative. "He wouldn't bother. Maybe in New York, but he's got too much going on right now. He'll have enough heat coming down from the authorities, with three men dead on Main Street. If he mentions me at all, my guess would be he'll leave it to the uniforms."

"So, we're still on," said Turrin.

"Right." No hesitation from the Executioner.

"I've got a few more wild cards for you," Leo said reluctantly. "They may change things."

"I'm listening," said Bolan.

"Well, we thought that Carmine rolled up Pablo Guzman in the Bronx, on Thursday, but our sources in Miami say that Guzman is alive and well. In fact, he's in Barbados at the moment, with a hit team."

"Party time."

"And then some. Jason Frost is on the island, too, with muscle from his posse."

"Perfect."

"That's good news?" The man from Justice frowned and shook his head.

"It makes things dicey for civilians at the Hilton," Bolan answered. "But it helps us, going in. With eighty-nine potential targets, I'll let Frost and Guzman have their share."

"At least they'll help us with the press," said Leo, thinking of the battle's aftermath. He caught himself, remembering that it was far from over. Anything could happen in the next few hours.

"What about Yours Truly?" Sharon asked.

"You're out of it," said Leo. "Call it premature retirement, if you like. We'll get you back to D.C. when the smoke clears, work on testimony, if we've still got anyone to try. I'll have to think about a new approach for next time."

"If there is a next time," Sharon said.

"Your call. I know the weight you carry, working undercover."

Sharon did not have to brief him on the pent-up anger and frustration a deep-cover agent felt, the shame that went along with watching crimes in progress—or, in Sharon's case, consorting with the enemy—to put your act across and make it seem legitimate. He knew where she was coming from, all right, and what the job had cost her.

When Sharon made no comment, Leo forged ahead. "I've got a spare room at the Hyatt, three doors up. You take it, and I'll see what I can do about the locals. They refused to talk before the meeting, but they may have found a new perspective."

It was Bolan's turn to frown. "I'd hate to see them out in force," he said. "With so much hardware, Frost and Guzman in the action, someone's bound to tag a uniform."

"I wouldn't be surprised," said Leo, "but they don't like taking orders from a stranger. Pride, whatever. Maybe Julio can satisfy their curiosity before the main event."

"Let's keep our fingers crossed," said Bolan.

But he knew he could not count on any kind of luck, from that point on. The action would be down and dirty, when it started, and the "wild cards"—Frost and Guzman—made it that much harder to control the flow of play. He had no way of knowing when or where the rival hit teams would attack, but both of them had reputations for ferocity. They each took pride in overkill, a kind of education by example. Neither one of them would hesitate if it came down to killing innocent civilians with their chosen prey.

Bad news, but they could also play a role, if Bolan found a way to limit their involvement, square them off against the Mafia instead of hapless tourists.

Bolan visualized a basketful of cobras, dumped out on the ground. One man—himself—endeavoring to grab each snake in turn, while others twined around his legs or slithered off to menace bystanders. The trick was making sure the cobras only bit each other.

Easy, if you were a magician. As for Bolan, he could call on his experience and instinct, but it still might fall apart.

Whatever happened, he would be there in the middle of the action when it all went down, and he would never fail from lack of trying.

If the Executioner went down, he would not go alone.

CHAPTER TWENTY-TWO

"There's still no goddamn word on what went down?"

The tone of DiBiase's voice was tense. LaRocca recognized the symptoms, knew that Julio could snap if too much pressure was applied. He tried to keep it simple, as he shook his head and frowned.

"No word at all," he said. "Whoever grabbed her hasn't called it in, this time."

"So, what about the rest of it?"

"Well, we had clearance in advance for armed security. It cost a bundle, you remember, but it's paying off. Without it, we'd be up shit creek, explaining why our men were carrying."

"The cops are satisfied?"

"I wouldn't go that far," LaRocca said, "but they're not breathing down our necks. I told them victims can't be held accountable for getting shot down on the street, you know? A little extra grease on top of that, and they're out looking for the shooters."

"So am I," said DiBiase. "What's your take on this?"

LaRocca thought about it, shook his head. "We haven't got enough to go on, Julio. If we were in New York, I'd say it was Tattaglia, or maybe the Colombians. Thing is, our boys are watching Carmine's boys. They're watching everybody."

"Everybody but your fucking bimbo," DiBiase sneered.

"She went to catch some rays," LaRocca said, defensively. "I got the note she left, right here. There's nothing weird in that."

"So, why'd you send three boys to find her, Tommy?"

"Let's say I got nervous, thinking of Chicago."

"Let's say you got horny on the lunch break, and you couldn't wait to get your ashes hauled."

"Hey, Julio—"

"Hey, nothing, Tommy. I got three dead soldiers, and your bimbo's out there, God knows where. I'm telling you up front, no ransom. Do you hear me, Tommy? Someone wants to waste her, it's okay with me. The meeting's all that matters."

"Sure, I hear you, Julio."

"We won't be sending anybody out to find her, got it? If the cops can turn her up, okay. But I want answers, if and when she shows her face again."

"No problem."

"That's what you think, Tommy." DiBiase checked his Rolex, scowling at the time. "In less than thirty minutes, I'll be winding up my pitch. We lost a major vote when Danny Dick went down, and all this other shit has strained relations down the line. Scarpato's in our pocket, but the rest of them are up for grabs. It could go either way."

"You always were a salesman, Julio."

"You'd better hope I make a sale tonight," said DiBiase, "or the two of us go home with nothing. That won't make me happy, Tommy. Are we clear on that?"

LaRocca knew the flip side of a failure to succeed through diplomatic channels. They had talked about the prospects of a shooting war for months on end, debating tactics, plotting strategy. It was impossible for DiBiase's force to overwhelm the other Families en masse, but if you took it piecemeal, one step at a time, acquiring strength and territory in the process . . . well, they just might have a shot.

And if they failed, no sweat.

When you were dead, your problems went away.

The best solution, Tommy knew, would be for Roman Graffia and Ernie Cavalcante to accept the plan that Julio was offering, four Families against Tattaglia's crew if Carmine started acting tough. When that was settled, they could put some feelers out to California, find out who was standing in for Danny Dick, and nail down the alliance in the West.

The easy way.

But something told him there were hard times coming.

He thought of Sharon, wondering if she was still alive. It wasn't love, by any means, although he liked her in the sack, and she was nice to look at. Women were for entertainment, and they never took the place of paying business opportunities.

LaRocca hoped she would not suffer much, but his concern was strictly practical. If someone started squeezing Sharon, she would spill whatever information she had picked up from him in their time together. Anything at all would be embarrassing, and if the word got back to Di-Biase, it could get LaRocca whacked.

So, Tommy kept his fingers crossed and wished the foxy blonde a quick, clean death.

THE ROOM ASSIGNMENTS had been Jack Grimaldi's chore. He took one of the registration clerks aside, produced a wad of cash, and came away ten minutes later with a list of names and numbers.

Bolan reckoned that with eighty-nine made men inside the Bridgetown Hilton, say a dozen of them dons and underbosses, that left lots of surplus muscle on the premises. Deploying seventy-odd guns to guard the Hilton's conference center would be much too obvious, intimidating to the other guests and to the staff. It simply wouldn't fly.

Which meant, in Bolan's estimation, that a number of the button men—perhaps as many as half—would be engaged elsewhere, drinking in the bar or lolling in their rooms, perhaps with female company to help them pass the time. He had their numbers now, and while the names were doubtless phony, Bolan did not care.

The time had come for him to thin the herd.

The delegates were spread around four floors of the hotel, from six through nine. He waited for the capos and lieutenants to proceed downstairs, begin their final meeting of the day, before he started making rounds. With forty rooms to visit, Bolan made a list and broke it down, assigning Jack and Johnny to a portion of the job.

It would be grunt work, killing in cold blood, but there was no way to refine the business. Every shooter left alive when Bolan made his final move would multiply the odds against survival.

Do it, then, he told himself, and don't look back.

He rode the elevator up to nine, beginning at the top. The rooms assigned to capos and lieutenants, he ignored. As for the rest . . .

He had the sleek Beretta 93-R in his hand as he approached the first room on his mental list. The hammer eased back under Bolan's thumb. He knocked and waited.

The door eased open just a crack, revealing half a swarthy face.

"Yeah, what?"

He pumped a hot round through the soldier's left eye socket, and watched as the man toppled over backwards, dead. Number two was sitting on the bed, T-shirt and Jockey shorts, a cable skin flick on the tube. He turned to gape at Bolan, lunging for his weapon on the nightstand, almost reaching it before a parabellum round punched through his temple and the wall was streaked with crimson.

Two down, and Bolan closed the door behind him, moving three strides down the corridor. Another knock, another wait. A cautious gunner, this time, speaking to him through the door.

"Who's that?"

"Room service."

Hesitation, then: "We didn't order nothin'."

"Cocktails, compliments of Mr. DiBiase."

"Hey, all right."

The guy was smiling as the door swung open, but he lost it in a hurry, staring down the bore of Bolan's autoloader.

"Holy shi—"

The bullet went in through one nostril, taking out a fist-sized chunk of bone and brain behind the gunner's ear. He staggered, losing balance, going down like so much useless garbage on the rug.

And his companion was emerging from the bathroom, talking to the dead. "They must have closed the deal, if Julio—"

He did a double take and tried to save himself, reversing his direction, but the move was much too late. A double tap from Bolan's weapon, and the guy collided with the bathroom doorjamb, slithered down into a kneeling posture, where he stuck. An attitude of prayer, almost, with no response anticipated.

Out of there, along the hallway to another door. Knock twice and wait, a slow hand on the knob. He heard the latch release, had the Beretta up and ready as the round face filled his gun sights. Thick lips trying hard to form a word while there was time. A dying shudder as the bullet cored through bone and brain, the fallen body almost blocking Bolan's access to the room beyond.

Almost.

Another startled soldier, turning from the small refrigerator stocked with beer and snacks. He stared into the eye of death and could not find the strength to move, before a parabellum round released his inhibitions.

Bolan closed another door behind him and continued on his way.

THE UNIFORMS WERE PERFECT, Guzman thought. Of course, a few of them were baggy in the ass or skimpy in the sleeves, but they would serve. No one looked twice at bellboys in a large hotel, as long as they were pushing luggage carts or fetching trays of food up from the kitchen. If they weren't invisible, at least they were the next best thing: ignored.

The luggage racks were easy. Grab one from the service area and tack a couple of valises on the other bags. Inside the leather cases, automatic weapons fitted out with silencers, extended magazines and folding stocks. No nonsense, when you needed stopping power in a crunch. They favored Uzis, Ingrams, and the stylish little MP-5 models manufactured by Heckler & Koch. Nine-millimeters, each and every one of them, with cyclic rates of fire that would reduce a man to hamburger in record time.

The guns had come in from Miami on the charter flight, and Guzman's people got their uniforms from a supplier who did business with the Hilton. There had been some questions, going in, but money talked and bullshit walked. The dealer was a businessman, and that was all that mattered.

Strategy was part of a successful raid, as well. It did not take a brainiac to figure out that fifteen extra bellhops turning up at once, all clumped together in the Hilton's lobby, would produce some questions from the management. So, Pablo sent them in by ones and twos, at intervals of ten or fifteen minutes, going with the flow and hiding out as best they could, avoiding supervisors and the like to keep from getting burned before the play went down.

Each man had his instructions from the outset. Where to go and what to do, how long he ought to wait before he made his move. They had examined floor plans of the Hilton, knew exactly where to find the spacious conference room. The rest of it came down to nerve and accuracy.

It was a kick for Guzman, dressing like a lowly peon in his bellhop's uniform and marching with the troops to battle. Here he was, a millionaire, pretending that he had to carry luggage for a living, all to get a clear shot at the man or men responsible for killing off his soldiers in New York.

And it was funny, when you thought about it, how things happened in the world.

He had to trust his soldiers for the last phase of the operation, closing on the conference area from different sides in a coordinated movement. Pablo could not watch them all, but it was relatively simple, going behind their carts and trays, anonymous as furniture in hotel uniforms. Cut loose when they were close enough to nail the outer guards without a hitch, and bust on through from there to take the capos at their table, maybe sucking on cigars or carving juicy steaks.

A fucking massacre.

It was the kind of plan that Pablo Guzman favored, floors awash in blood, his enemies destroyed—dismembered, if they had the time to do it right. But this would be a simple in-and-out job, firing for effect and killing anything that moved. Not just Tattaglia and his soldiers, but the whole damned crew.

It would mean war with the Sicilians, but so what? At one stroke, Pablo would have stripped their leadership away. Subordinates back in the States would be confused at first, then terrified by details of the bloodbath. By the time they got their act together, it would be too late to salvage much.

Still, Pablo had it in him to be generous. He was not interested in whores or gambling, except as forms of entertainment. It was only on the subject of cocaine that he became an expert, from experience. In that field, Pablo was preeminent—or would be, once the mafiosi learned their lesson and retired from competition in the trade.

His masterstroke would be remembered where it counted, in New York, in Cali, Medellín, wherever men of wealth and power met to lay their plans for gaining more wealth, more authority.

He would become a legend in his lifetime, just like Pablo Escobar, Meyer Lansky, Al Capone.

The very thought made Pablo smile.

THE MUSICAL INSTRUMENTS were Jason Frost's idea. A dozen Rastas trooping through the Bridgetown Hilton might not cause security to pop out of the woodwork, but it would provoke raised eyebrows, and perhaps some questions he was not prepared to answer. Certainly, his men did not need any more distractions than they had already, working in a strange environment, targeting a group of well-armed mafiosi.

It could blow up in their faces, Jason realized, but only cowards thought of safety when their honor had been sullied, trampled in the dust. His gut cried out for action, and the men were with him, eager to proceed.

Of course, the ganja helped in that regard.

They carried drums and cases meant for musical instruments, their guns and clips packed in with wadded towels to keep from rattling around. Twelve men in grungy-looking Rasta clothes, and if they should be questioned briefly, Jason was prepared to bluff it out. A party thrown by the Americans, his group hired on to keep it jumping.

A dozen men. Two AK-47s in the cases, half a dozen shotguns, four small submachine guns. Each man carrying a hidden pistol, just in case. They were outnumbered, possibly by killer odds, but a surprise could help them pull it off.

His troops were handpicked killers, each of them a proven warrior. None of them would flinch or hesitate when it was time to pull the trigger. Each had known some of the Rasta brothers slaughtered in Miami, and they hungered for revenge. If they could also turn a profit on the deal, increase their hold on traffic in Miami, why, so much the better.

Percy Glass had scouted out the service entrance at the back of the hotel. No one to challenge them as they came in, although some members of the kitchen staff looked curious. There should have been a guard on that door, if the hotel was sincere about security, but they were in, and that was all Frost cared about.

A handy map was painted on the wall, not far from where they entered. Jason traced the hallway to its terminus and read the words CONVENTION CENTER with a broad smile on his face. It might as well have said, "Happy Hunting Ground."

"Let's do it, bruddas."

Jason led the way, as if he knew the route by heart. If they got turned around or lost, no problem. There were signs and arrows everywhere, for stupid tourists who could not locate their rooms, the restaurant, whatever.

Frost wondered, sometimes, how the white man ever came to rule the world. It must be luck, he thought, combined with pure brute force. Technology helped out, of course, when you were using guns on barefoot natives in the jungle somewhere. Rifles matched against their slings and spears.

That worked all right, but only for a while. The world had turned, and subjected people had been kicking ass for decades now, in Africa, Asia, the Latin countries. Soon, they would be kicking righteous ass in the United States, and Jason would be lining up to kick his share.

By that time, though, he would be wearing some expensive shoes, a sweet fringe benefit of selling poison to his poor, dumb bruddas in the ghetto.

Black was beautiful, at least in theory, but the posse operated on a great truth: A fool and his money are soon parted.

Tonight, they were taking their cue from James Bond: Live and let die.

Frost hoped that he would get a shot at Roman Graffia himself, but it was not essential. He would be in on the killing, one way or another, and it made no difference who took Graffia, as long as he was taken. Nailed. Obliterated.

Jason Frost had no beef with the other capos at the meeting, but they represented power, and that power had been concentrated in the white man's hands. It was his duty as a man of color and a Rasta warrior to damage them any way he could.

What better way to pass an evening than destroying men who wished him dead?

He owed it to himself, and if he saw an opportunity to mix a little pleasure with his business, all the better.

Fun was where you found it, and for Jason Frost, the greatest time he ever had was pissing on an adversary's grave.

At times like that, he knew that it was great to be alive.

THE RASTA BOYS were trouble. Johnny knew it going in, but he had been expecting something of the sort. Their presence in the hallway leading to the conference room required that he delay his own approach, hang back and find out what was happening before he blundered in and found himself surrounded.

It had been a bloody slaughterhouse upstairs. Combat was one thing, but the systematic execution of your enemies took more—or less, perhaps—than most men normally possessed. It was a grueling business, deadening to heart and soul, but necessary all the same.

He had begun on seven, working down, with Mack on nine and Jack on eight, above him. Don Graziano's troops were here, the bottom of the heap. With Families from Chicago, New York and Miami stacked above them. Not that anybody minded, from the looks of things, as Johnny checked their rooms. Some wanted sex and liquor, others would have settled for a nap.

The sleep that Johnny brought them would be long and restful, undisturbed by passing time.

By the third room, he gave up counting the naked women. One of his intended had a double-header going, designated roommate absent, and he sent one of the girls to answer Johnny's knock. She didn't bother dressing, but she wore her nicest smile...until she saw the silencer-equipped SIG-Sauer automatic in his hand.

He had the hardguy covered as he told the lovelies, "Go into the bathroom, close the door and sit down in the tub. Stay there until I call you."

Johnny watched them go, not wasting time to take their clothes along. When he was solo with the shooter, Johnny's target started talking rapidly.

"This isn't necessary, man. You want the money, I can tell you where it is. You want the broads, hell, that's okay. Go on and have yourself a jump. No skin off me. One of 'em beefs, I'll hold her for you."

Johnny shot him in the forehead, silencing his filthy mouth forever. Going on, he did not call the women. Let them sit awhile, until they started getting restless and discovered he was gone.

Lead time.

And now he was downstairs. The clock was running on the final act, and he was getting close to target acquisition.

But the Rasta boys were in his way.

He hung back, watching as the party of Jamaicans with their drums and instrument cases proceeded down the hall toward the convention center. They were strangely silent, none of the cross talk and laughter one normally associates with musicians on their way to a gig. In fact, they seemed so grim and businesslike that Johnny knew, without a single mug shot to confirm it, that he had encountered members of the posse led by Jason Frost.

And they were right on time.

His brother had predicted the Jamaicans would drop in, but there had been no way of knowing where or when the Rasta boys would make their play. Now, watching them, he wondered if their timing should be seen as serendipitous or tragic. Would it help or hinder the approach Mack had designed?

They were about to reach one entrance to the conference center now, and Johnny spotted half a dozen button men outside the door, on station, checking out the "band" with cold, suspicious eyes. The bulges underneath their coats were plainly hardware of the military kind, and it was safe to say that none of them were gun-shy.

Johnny braced himself, picked up his pace a little, checking left and right for recessed doorways that could offer cover in a pinch. He slipped the button on his jacket, granting instant access to the autoloader slung beneath his left arm and the compact submachine gun that he wore beneath his right, in fast-draw leather.

He was almost ready, when it happened.

Coming from the opposite direction, closing on a hard collision course with the Jamaicans, Johnny saw four bellboys, pushing two brass luggage carts. They were Latinos to a man, the first that he had noticed on the Hilton staff, and that alarm was chiming softly in his brain while Johnny asked himself what they were doing here, so far from registration and the guest rooms, with their load of bags.

He had his answer in another moment, as the bellboys and Jamaicans passed within a few feet of each other, crossing paths outside the entrance to the meeting room. As Johnny watched, amazed, the Rasta boys worked magic with their instruments, abandoning the cases in a flash and swinging automatic weapons toward the sentries on the door.

But they had competition now.

The bellboys were unloading, too, as if oblivious to the Jamaicans and their guns. They stopped dead center in the hallway, made a grab for bags that had been sitting on the top in each brass cart, and coming out with weapons of their own.

The mafiosi were already dodging, reaching under jackets for their hardware, and he caught a glimpse of one Latino gunner, blinking in surprise at the Jamaicans. His expression would have been amusing, under other circumstances, but the shit was coming down right now, and it was not a laughing matter.

Johnny whipped his submachine gun out and ducked into a shallow doorway on his left.

And then all hell broke loose.

CHAPTER TWENTY-THREE

He saw the flash point coming, knew that there was nothing he could do to head it off, so Bolan waited for ignition, let the three-way scramble for position run its course. The Rastas and Colombians had their Sicilian adversaries covered, two-to-one, but they were also thrown off by the unexpected presence of a strange assault force. Add to that the fact that every capo at the summit meeting had handpicked his best, most ruthless soldiers for the trip, and Bolan knew the outcome was too close to call.

The mini-Uzi he was packing had no silencer attached. He would not need one, here and now. In seconds flat, the quiet hotel corridor had been transformed into a raging battleground.

The bogus bellhops were a little faster on the draw than Frost's Jamaicans or the mafiosi standing watch outside the conference room, but it was close. They had their weapons clear and swinging into target acquisition by the time the Rasta boys began unloading hardware from their instrument cases, but it was a matter of microseconds, everybody startled by the sudden show of weaponry.

And then it broke, a rush of sound like fireworks going off at a fiesta, warriors cursing bitterly in different languages as they unloaded on their enemies with automatic fire. Each team of gunmen was surprised, off balance in the three-way firefight, no time to reflect on what was happening or try to work it out. When guns go off at point-blank range, the only thing to do is fire and keep on firing while your ammunition lasts, until your enemies are down or bullets find you and the darkness swallows you alive.

It was a madhouse, total chaos in the hallway. Muzzle-flashes. Spent brass bouncing off the walls and carpet. Soldiers dodging as they fired on moving targets. Bodies jerking with the impact of repeated hits. Harsh voices raised in fear and anger, shouting curses, questions, bleats of mortal agony.

The Executioner had seen it all before, on other battle-fields, but never quite this way. There were no lines, no cover, though a couple of the bellboys tried to duck behind their luggage carts, suitcases taking hits. The three groups of belligerents, though total strangers, were identifiable by race and clothing. Even so, at such close range, with panic setting in, it was a challenge not to waste your own.

The game was up, in any case, no hope of storming past the guards to catch the capos by surprise. He saw two gunners down, a third collapsing with his back against the wall, and Bolan knew that it was time to make the three-way massacre a foursome.

He braced the mini-Uzi in a firm two-handed grip and held the trigger down, his weapon tracking left to right across the narrow killing ground. A mafioso crouching near the doorway took his first rounds, jerking sideways, squeezing off a last round from his semiauto pistol as he went down in a heap. The dying reflex shot kneecapped a Rasta boy and forced a scream out through the hedge of yellow teeth.

Next up, the limping Rasta, four rounds punching through his chest and spinning him around before the leg wound dropped him, dreadlocks whipping frantically around his head. A fifth round from the mini-Uzi caught him in the back, and he collapsed facedown, leaking blood on the carpet.

Breaking from the cover of their luggage cart two bell-boys raked the nearest Rasta gunners with a pair of sub-machine guns, one man grinning, while the other seemed to snarl. They hadn't noticed Bolan yet, and that was their mistake.

The last one they would ever make.

Advancing with the mini-Uzi in his right hand, the Beretta 93-R in his left, Bolan riddled them with short, precision bursts, dropping them in their tracks. He came down on his adversaries like the wrath of God. The surviving gunners started falling before they understood exactly what was happening. Blood fever, and the crash of doomsday thunder rang in Bolan's ears.

The Executioner was on a roll.

THE FIRST REPORTS of gunfire interrupted DiBiase's speech. He shot a glance at the nearest door, where guards were on full alert, weapons drawn. His audience exploded into babble, frightened capos and lieutenants on their feet, and DiBiase left them to it, checking out the other exits.

All secure, for now.

At once, the sounds of battle seemed to come from every side. Staccato bursts from automatic weapons, shotgun blasts, the popping sound of pistols going off in rapid fire. A glance back at the other capos showed him various expressions of surprise and fear, none among them appearing to take the combat sounds for granted.

What the hell was happening?

No time for speculation or delay. No better time for him to demonstrate the qualities of leadership that he had been discussing since they first sat down at noon to hammer out preliminary details of his bold new order.

"Listen up, goddamn it! I don't know what's happening out there, but we've got one way out. You need to follow me."

"Like hell!" Carmine Tattaglia answered, leaning on the conference table with his big fists clenched. "For all we know, you set this whole thing up."

"You feel that way, Carmine, why don't you just wait here and see who's coming through the door? I'll get the message to your next of kin."

"You piece of shit!"

"We don't have time for this!" said Cavalcante, breaking in. "If Julio can get us out of here, I'm for it."

"Damn right," said Scarpato.

"Do it!" Roman Graffia put in.

"All right, let's go!"

Of the eighteen guards in the large room, six came from DiBiase's Family, six from Graffia's and six from the Tattaglia clan. As DiBiase led the capos from the conference table, his men and Don Roman's fell in, with weapons on display. Tattaglia's gunmen hung back with their capo and his underboss, to watch the others go.

The exit DiBiase chose had been selected in advance, with an emergency in mind. The door did not open on the corridors outside, but granted access to a smaller room, next door. The room was dark and empty, but the light spilling from the conference room behind them showed another door directly opposite. Another room beyond that, and another, ultimately leading to the hotel kitchen and a service entrance.

In moments, they could either reach the parking lot or grab the elevators, scatter to their separate floors and suites where reinforcements waited, ready to defend the leaders of La Cosa Nostra. DiBiase's preference lay upstairs, with the remainder of his hardforce. They could seal the floor and make a stand, repulse an army long enough for the police to come and scatter the attackers.

Perfect.

If the other capos chose to follow his example, that was fine. Don Julio would set the standard for survival under fire, and they would have to recognize his leadership when it was over. If they tried to split, though, it was each man for himself. Some might escape, or they might all be killed.

And that was fine with DiBiase, too.

It would not damage his ambitions in the least to have a sudden power vacuum at the top of every leading Family in the United States. Far from it. He would open up negotiations with the heirs apparent, win them over by whatever means brought swift results and get them in the bag.

For just a moment, DiBiase thought of ordering his men to turn their weapons on the other capos, but he could not take the chance. A sudden firefight in close quarters put his own life on the line, along with everybody else's. It was not a wise career move, when he thought about it, and he let the notion go.

For now, he would provide advice, then let nature take its course. Survival of the fittest, and anyone who fell along the way could always be replaced by someone friendly to his master plan.

But first, Don Julio would have to save himself.

A BURST from Johnny's subgun hit the nearest Rasta and knocked him sprawling. As he fell, the dying gunner squeezed the trigger on his sawed-off shotgun, triggering a blast that swept two other posse gunmen off their feet. Blood spattered on the wall behind them, sketching abstract patterns as they fell.

He chose another target, one of the surviving bellboys, crouched behind a luggage cart, reloading what appeared to be an Ingram MAC-10 SMG. The shooter fumbled, dropped his magazine, and was about to pick it up when Johnny fired.

Five parabellum shockers stitched the short Colombian from throat to navel, punched him over on his back, legs folded awkwardly beneath him. For an instant, Johnny thought that he was struggling to rise, despite the mortal wounds, but it was only a reflexive tremor of his dying muscles, fading into stillness as his heart gave up the ghost.

How many shooters left?

Two mafiosi huddled in the doorway they were stationed to defend, one wounded in the side and shoulder, the uninjured hardman with a stubby shotgun in his hands. One of the Rastas was crawling, gut-shot, in the middle of the hallway, trying to escape the line of fire. Another posse member lay behind the body of a fallen comrade, sighting down the barrel of a shiny automatic pistol, toward the two Sicilians. Peering underneath the luggage cart, he saw one pair of feet that shifted nervously, the hidden gunman waiting for a chance to fire or run away.

The rest of them were dead or dying, sprawled in awkward postures on the blood-soaked carpet, one dead Rasta sitting upright with his back against the wall. The hallway reeked of blood and cordite, the reports of gunfire echoing in Johnny's ears.

He calculated less than ninety seconds had elapsed, so far, between the first display of weapons and the momentary standoff. Even so, he realized that time was critical. His targets in the conference room would not be waiting for an all-clear from the outer guards, before they broke and ran. Grimaldi had been stationed on the only exit open to them at the moment, but he could not close the trap alone.

He needed help, and that meant it was time for Johnny Gray to move.

He fed a fresh mag into the receiver of his little SMG and cocked it, came up firing for effect. The mafiosi first, because he had a clear shot down the hallway, and the sawed-off 12-gauge multiplied their odds of getting lucky with hasty shot.

He raked the two of them together, rattling off a quarter magazine to finish it. The wounded gunner stopped four rounds, his body twitching with the impact, going limp against his partner as the bullets snuffed his life. Beside him, pivoting to face the newest enemy, the soldier with the 12-gauge found himself encumbered by a corpse that pinned his gun arm to his side.

Too late to fix it, as the rounds from Johnny's SMG ripped through his face and neck. The gunner's head snapped back and hit the wall with a resounding thud. A blood splotch like a giant thumbprint marked the point of impact as he toppled, slumping to the floor.

Sweeping on, he skipped the wounded Rasta, zeroed on his comrade with the shiny automatic at his fist. The lean Jamaican saw death coming, turned to face it, cranking off a quick round from his pistol that went high and wide. His cover had been adequate to fend off bullets coming from the front, but he was open from the side, and that was

Johnny's vantage point, unloading with the SMG from thirty feet away.

The Rasta man was twitching, writhing as the bullets ripped his baggy shirt and found the flesh within. Bright, floral fabric stained with crimson now and sticking to his ribs. The guy rolled over on his back and stayed there, muscles going slack in death.

That left the bellboy crouched behind his cart. Reloading swiftly, Johnny checked and saw the gunner's feet shift to the left. A frag grenade would be the ticket here, but Mack had ruled against them for the hotel probe, too many innocent civilians on the premises.

Okay.

He stretched out prone and drew his semiauto pistol, aiming at the pointy shoes, his only glimpse of the enemy. If he could do this right, he had it made. If not...

The younger Bolan squeezed off two shots from his pistol, heard a yelp of pain, and then the bogus bellboy blundered out of cover, hopping on his one good foot and firing blindly with an Ingram submachine gun.

Johnny's MP-5 answered with a measured burst that sat him down and punched him over on his back. A coup de grace from the SIG-Sauer finished it.

Step one.

The door to the convention center was unguarded now, at least on Johnny's side, but had he wasted too much time already? Were the capos gone?

One way to satisfy his curiosity.

He tried the door. It opened at his touch.

TATTAGLIA WAITED long enough to register defiance, show his men and all the other capos that he wasn't running after Julio, but then he realized that there was no more time to waste. The sound of firing from the corridor outside had slackened off, and in the absence of an all-clear signal from the posted sentries, Carmine had to guess that they were dead or wounded. Either way, incapable of putting up a fight.

Which meant that he was suddenly at risk. His unknown enemies could barge in through any doorway, hit his little party with the kitchen sink.

Unless...

"We're getting out of here!" he snapped. "Let's go!"

"Which way?" asked David Rossi, playing stupid.

"Through the kitchen."

"That's the same way—"

"Don't you think I know that, David?" Cold eyes stopped Rossi short of challenging his order.

"You're the boss."

"Remember that."

Once the decision had been made, they wasted no time moving out. Eight men, but only six were armed. Tattaglia did not like the odds, but he had men upstairs, a couple in the lobby. He wasn't finished yet.

Carmine led the way, a couple of his soldiers catching up and moving near the exit DiBiase and the other dons had used. The smaller room next door was empty, and they reached another door in seconds flat, his soldiers covering the exit to the outer corridor. There was still no sound of pursuit.

Tattaglia wondered if the outer guards had pulled it off somehow and stopped the unknown enemy before they were cut down. He could not rule it out, of course, but neither would he gamble on that kind of long shot when the stakes were life and death—his own. Escape was not a mark of cowardice in this case; it was simply prudent.

Another empty room, and Carmine rushed across to the exit, counting on his rearguard soldiers to alert him if they picked up any indication of pursuit. How far to reach the kitchen? He was guessing, but he estimated two more rooms like this, at least, before they made it to the service area, the elevators, and safely back upstairs.

Police should be converging on the Hilton. No way the management could miss the sounds of gunfire echoing from the convention center. Someone must have made the call by now, and the response would not take long in Bridgetown, even with the tourist traffic.

It was funny, Carmine thought, for him to wish for help from the police. A whole life dodging cops or bribing them, occasionally putting contracts out when all else failed, and it came down to this.

"Somebody coming, Don Tattaglia."

It was Tony, on the rear guard, hanging back and covering the last door they had passed through with a submachine gun.

"Are you sure?"

"I hear 'em talking," Tony said.

"Okay. Do what you can to slow them down. Stay with me, Eddie."

"Right." From the expression on his face, young Eddie wasn't thrilled with the assignment.

"Hurry up, you guys! Come on!"

Another room, no different from the others, as far as Tattaglia could see. Pastel color scheme and functional furniture, nothing elaborate. They had almost reached the exit when he heard the sharp, staccato sound of automatic weapons. Silently he beamed the thought back to his rearguard soldiers: Hold them! Slow the bastards down!

The last door opened on a hallway, startled kitchen workers on his right, the elevators several paces to his left. No time to lose.

They still might make it, Carmine thought. It wasn't over yet.

And if he had the chance, before the smoke cleared and the cops arrived, he just might have a private message for Don Julio.

Tattaglia thought it would be very pleasant to deliver that one on his own.

THE HILTON'S conference center had four entrances, one door on each side of the room. When Pablo Guzman chose the northern door for his approach, he had no way of knowing that the choice would add a few more minutes to his life. He missed the Bolan brothers, going in, and while the clash with armed Jamaicans was a rude surprise, his *pistoleros* won the day with two men wounded, only one of whom had to stay behind.

The soldiers were expendable, paid to take risks and to sacrifice their lives, if necessary, for the task at hand. It would not trouble him if all of them were killed, as long as Guzman managed to survive and revel in the ultimate annihilation of his enemies.

So, he was shaken when they crashed into the spacious meeting hall and found it empty. There were bottles on the conference table, beer and wine, with coffee cups and water glasses, a cigar still smoking in an ashtray near the table's head.

Too late, goddamn it!

Three doors left to choose from, but Guzman knew the Sicilians would not choose either of the doors where gunfire had been heard within the past two minutes. No, they would have gone out through the southern door, directly opposite, that opened on another, smaller meeting room.

"With me!" snapped Guzman, racing toward the exit, hesitating only when he reached the threshold.

Would Tattaglia have left a guard behind? Did he have men and guns enough to barricade each door he passed through in his flight?

One way to check it, Guzman thought. He stepped back from the doorway, picked one of his men at random, urged the *pistolero* forward. Fleeting hesitation, then the gunner made his move. No gunfire as he cleared the doorway, entering the room next door.

"Come on!"

They forged ahead, repeating the procedure with a different man at each door they encountered. Pablo's troops were getting cocky now, convinced the mafiosi were running scared, cracking jokes back and forth as they picked up the pace.

He should have stopped them, shut them up, but Guzman felt the same excitement. Hunting humans was a pleasure, most especially when the intended prey was guilty of some grievous insult to his honor. He meant to teach Carmine Tattaglia a lesson, and his one regret was that the capo would not have a chance to suffer. They were in a crunch now, short of time before police arrived, and Pablo knew that he would have to settle for a quick, clean kill.

A couple of his men were laughing as they approached the next door. One of them stepped forward, reaching for the handle, but he never got that far. The door flew open, submachine guns stuttering, and Guzman saw his *pistolero* stagger backward, falling, hit at least a dozen times.

The others started firing then, at point-blank range. At least two gunmen staked out the exit, firing blind around the doorjamb, ducking back. Guzman was ready when the taller of them showed himself, the third time, barely visible. He squeezed off a long burst from his own MAC-10.

He saw a splash of crimson, the Sicilian staggering, exposed, more bullets smacking into him as he fell. The second gunner panicked, broke and ran to save himself.

A fatal error.

Two of Guzman's soldiers hit the doorway running, firing from the hip. They brought the mafioso down and nailed him to the carpet with converging streams of automatic fire. The bullets kept him twitching after he was dead, until their magazines were empty and a pall of gun smoke fouled the air.

"We're getting close," said Guzman, knowing that Tattaglia had sacrificed two men to give himself a running start, and could not be far away.

How far?

The only way to answer that was to continue the pursuit.

Another room, another door. No gunfire, this time, as they burst through in a rush and found themselves confronted with a group of men and women dressed in white. The kitchen staff. At sight of Pablo's guns, they scattered, running for their lives.

He had a choice to make: the parking lot or the elevators? Would his quarry leave the building?

No.

He glimpsed a dark man in a suit, just stepping into the elevator. Was that a pistol in his hand?

Guzman rushed him, ducking as a bullet whispered past his head, returning fire with his MAC-10.

Too late.

He reached the elevator just in time to have the door close in his face.

CHAPTER TWENTY-FOUR

The killing on the seventh floor slowed Jack Grimaldi down. A hotel maid was working late, and Jack was forced to send her on her way, flashing a fake badge at first, then showing her a gun when that failed to work. She might go straight downstairs and tip off the manager, but he would have to take that risk. Whatever happened, once the action started in the conference room, their secret would be out the window, literally shot to hell.

The wet work took him fifteen minutes, going door to door. One room was empty, or the troops weren't answering, but Jack came up with doubles, two doors down. They had gone visiting, perhaps, a bottle being passed around as Jack took out the doorman, barging in with his Beretta covering the other three.

No giveaways on this one. They had seen the way he dealt with their companion on the threshold, and they went for hardware, scattering to make it harder on him, one guy dropping out of sight behind the bed. Grimaldi nailed the other two before they had a chance to draw, though one was close, then he circled toward the bed.

His target came up like a jumping jack, squeezed off three rounds in rapid fire, one of them close enough to pluck Grimaldi's sleeve. He answered with a double tap that drilled the mafioso high and low, bullets through his forehead and chest. The impact drove him over backward, but the dying man still had enough strength to fire a final shot through the ceiling.

Jack imagined guests reporting gunfire to the management, perhaps a tourist wounded in the room above. He had no time to run upstairs and check, so he dismissed the problem from his mind.

They had allowed for some confusion in the first part of their strike, the possibility that someone might return fire and alert the staff or guests, and now that it had happened, Jack was out of time. A phone call to the desk would bring security upstairs, but that did nothing for the capos in their basement conference room.

He fed a fresh mag into the Beretta, left the suite and closed the door, moving toward the elevator. Finished here, he was probably needed elsewhere, and decided to set up a watch downstairs.

On the way down, the elevator stopped on six, and three hard types got on. They looked Jack over and dismissed him, waited for the door to close.

"I'm tellin' you," one of them said, "smart money has it Carmine won't roll over for this thing of DiBiase's."

"Yeah? Whose money?" asked another thug.

"My money, smartass. How's a C-note sound?"

"You're covered, man."

It was a golden opportunity too good to miss. Grimaldi was behind them when he drew his pistol, pumping one round into each man's head at skin-touch range. The third man tried to turn and face him, reaching for his side arm. A parabellum round bored through his temple, and he went down in a heap.

Grimaldi stowed his pistol, pressed a button for the next floor coming up, and prayed that he would not be met by tourists when the door slid open. As it was, he had the hallway to himself, with time enough to drag the three men out and leave them stacked outside the elevator.

Going down.

Twelve rounds in the Beretta, thirty in the MP-5 SD-3 submachine gun that he carried on a swivel rig beneath his jacket. It was set for three-round bursts, but Jack could change that quickly if he needed more. Some instinct made him keep the pistol in his hand, instead of putting it away.

And they were waiting for him in the lobby, half a dozen mafiosi kicking back in easy chairs, two standing at the streetside window, smoking. Jack was conscious of the time as he emerged, knew Mack and Johnny would be closing on the conference room by now, expecting him to cut off the retreat of their intended prey.

But he could not do anything with eight guns at his back.

The soldiers had to go.

A couple of them looked him over as he stepped out of the elevator, the Beretta tucked away behind his thigh. And it was now or never, while he still had the advantage of surprise.

"What's happening?" he asked the nearest gunner, putting on a smile.

And he was smiling as he lifted the Beretta, sighting down the slide, and shot his adversary in the face.

THE CONFERENCE ROOM was empty by the time Mack Bolan made his way inside. Another moment, and his brother charged in through the eastern door, directly opposite, his submachine gun sweeping as he looked for targets.

"That way?" Johnny nodded toward the door on the south that led into another conference room. They had expected DiBiase and his fellow dons to flee in that direction, toward the kitchen, if they managed to escape the conference hall.

"Must be," said Bolan.

"Are you coming?"

Bolan thought about it, shook his head. "I'm going back the way I came. Jack's got the kitchen exit covered."

"If he made it."

There was always that, but Bolan did not sell Grimaldi short. "You want to go that way," he said, "it couldn't hurt. I'll circle back and meet you."

"Right."

They parted company, the Executioner refusing to believe that anything might happen to his brother. It was always possible, of course, but in the infantry, if you thought about it, superstition decreed you made a hit more likely.

That was nonsense, Bolan realized, but there was no spare time for dwelling on the obvious. His brother knew the risks, and he could take care of himself.

The corridor was full of dead men, sprawled in awkward attitudes, and Bolan met a stranger halfway to the lobby. With a name tag on his jacket and a dazed expression on his face, he had to be a staffer, sent out to investigate the racket of the firefight. One look at the SMG in Bolan's hands, and any color that remained was flushed out of his face. He backed against the wall and closed his eyes, lips moving in a silent prayer as Bolan passed.

The lobby was in chaos, bodies sprawled across the furniture and on the floor. He looked around for Jack Grimaldi, met the little pilot just returning from the general direction of the kitchen.

"Jesus, man, I missed them." The expression on Grimaldi's face was one of self-reproach.

"Forget it. I can see you had your hands full."

"The fact remains, I blew it."

"Did they leave the building?" Bolan asked.

"As far as I can tell, they split up in the service area," Grimaldi said. "Some ducked out back, most of them went upstairs."

"Find out who left," he said. "They can't have gotten far."

"Will do. I'm sorry, man."

"Forget it."

Bolan passed the bank of elevators, took the stairs instead. It was a judgment call, but short of sitting in the lobby, there was no way he could cover all the elevators. No matter which elevator he chose, there was a risk that his targets would be coming down in another. On the stairs, at least he had a chance to make some time.

Combing above the third floor, he heard voices overhead, a group of men descending, muttering. He reached the landing, waited, let them come to him.

Bolan counted voices, settled on a minimum of four. If some of them were keeping quiet, then his count went out the window. Any way you sliced it, it could only be a delegation from the Mob, attempting to slip out while there was time.

He had the mini-Uzi braced against the banister when feet and legs came into view, with torsos following, then heads. He recognized Ernesto Cavalcante from Chicago, and his underboss, a weasel named Plumeri. Two guns leading, four more stacked behind them, bringing up the rear.

The mini-Uzi's magazine held forty rounds, and Bolan let them have it all. The pointmen saw it coming, tried to get their weapons up, but there was no time left. A hail of parabellum shredders killed them where they stood and sent them tumbling headfirst down the stairs.

Don Cavalcante and his sidekick came next, both gaping at the fallen soldiers, trying to flee when the bullets found them, ripping fabric and flesh. Bolan let the muzzle climb, still firing, taking down the backup gunners in a snarl of arms and legs. One of them fired, then another, wasting bullets as they fell together, blasting one another with the final spasms of their dying trigger fingers.

He checked Ernesto for a pulse, made sure that it was finished, scrambling over corpses to continue on his way. The powerful Chicago Family was a headless serpent now. It would be someone else's job to finish off the body, follow up on Bolan's lead before another capo took control.

He climbed, reloading on the run, with battle echoes ringing in his ears. How many more to kill, before the game was done?

Hang on, he thought. I'm coming.

GUZMAN AND HIS SOLDIERS waited long enough to see which floor the elevator stopped on, then they piled into the second car, reloading weapons as it took them up to number eight. The car stopped first on six, a fortysomething couple gaping at the band of armed Colombians and taking to their heels before the door hissed shut again.

You had to laugh at fools like that, thought Pablo. They were living in a dream world where the Good Guys always won and money in the bank could buy a measure of security. The peasants always thought they had it made, until the roof caved in and buried them alive.

On eight, they heard a rush of voices as the door slid open, Pablo urging one of his young *pistoleros* to step out and have a look. The soldier took three steps before a shotgun blast ripped through his chest and dropped him squirming on his back.

"¡Soldados! Vamanos!"

They left the elevator in a rush, all firing, Pablo bringing up the rear. A few yards down the corridor, three mafiosi took the brunt of that incoming fire, their bodies jerking spastically, held upright by the bullets ripping into them and through them. When they fell, a momentary stillness settled on the killing ground. Then the second wave of armed defenders struck.

They fired from open doorways, ducking out and back again, like actors in some kind of slapstick comedy turned deadly. The elevator door had closed behind them, cutting off retreat, and they would never reach the staircase at the far end of the hall.

Their only viable alternative, the one hope of survival, was attack.

With sudden desperation, Guzman led the way, shouting for his soldiers to follow him, uncaring at the moment whether they obeyed or stood and died where they were. But they *did* follow, whooping like aboriginals from the Colombian jungle, blazing a path with their shotguns and automatic weapons, staggering the entrenched defenders with the sheer ferocity of their assault.

It did not matter if the bullets found them, ripping flesh and snapping bone. If one man staggered, fell, his comrades carried on the charge, still firing. Pablo Guzman took the point and breathed in gun smoke, plaster dust, screams. He passed the first door, firing into it, and veered toward the second. Saw a mafioso grappling with the jammed slide of an automatic pistol, shot him in the chest and leapt across the crumpling body as it fell.

Inside the suite, two men stood facing him, the color long gone from their faces. On his left, Carmine Tattaglia. On his right, the capo's underboss, a ferret by the name of Rossi.

"What the hell is this?" Carmine demanded, striving for bravado, not quite making it.

"You don't know who I am?" asked Guzman. The idea was both infuriating and hilarious.

"Why should I?" asked Tattaglia.

"He's Guzman," Rossi muttered, almost whispering.

"Say what?"

"He's Guzman, damn it!" Close to shouting now, as if his boss was hard of hearing.

"That's impossible," Tattaglia said.

"Because your men reported I was dead?" asked Pablo, smiling. "They were wrong."

"You think that shit was my idea?"

"I think it's time for you to die," said Guzman, index finger tightening around the trigger of his MAC-10 submachine gun.

The pistol seemed to come from nowhere, whipped out from behind Tattaglia's back. The capo squeezed off two quick rounds from fifteen feet away, and Pablo felt the hammer strokes of impact on his chest and shoulder. He was reeling, falling backward, but his finger clenched around the Ingram's trigger, spewing death at some 1,200 rounds per minute.

There was no way he could miss at that range, even as a third round struck him in the lower body. He was firing, falling, conscious of his targets going over backward, crimson splashing on the walls and furniture.

How much of it was his?

As Pablo Guzman hit the floor, he had a sudden revelation: this is how it feels to die.

THE LAST FOUR Rasta men, Jason Frost leading them, made it to the seventh floor of the hotel by pure dumb luck. Survivors of the clash outside the conference room, they were retreating from that massacre when they encountered one of the hotel employees, looking dazed and frightened. Jason grabbed him, held a pistol to his skull, demanding Roman Graffia's room number.

Even now, he thought, it might not be too late.

The trembling man babbled ignorance, but after Jason cocked the pistol, he agreed to check the registration files. They marched down to a lobby strewn with corpses, guests and Hilton staffers having fled the scene, and squandered precious moments while the clerk tapped keys on a computer, reading numbers off the screen.

Don Roman's suite was on the seventh floor, for all the good it did. Would he be fool enough to go back there, when several easy steps would take him out to the street, away from danger?

It was Jason's only chance, a gamble he would have to take, unless he chose to wallow in defeat.

He shot the whining clerk and led his four survivors to the nearest elevator, half expecting the police to burst in any moment. When the car arrived, an old man in a gaudy floral shirt stood blinking at them, terrified, and Jason shot him, too. They stood around his leaking corpse and rode the elevator up to seven, Jason cursing the delay and wishing he could smoke some ganja now, for courage.

He was braced for anything when they arrived on seven—anything, that is, except what happened. When the door hissed open, there stood Roman Graffia, with eight or nine grim bodyguards, all showing weapons.

"You!" The capo's face flushed brilliant red. "You fucking coconut!"

"Sicilian shit!"

The guns went off like thunder, deafening inside the steel box of the elevator car. Frost fired until the slide locked open on his pistol. One bullet struck him, then another and another. He was falling, clinging desperately to his empty pistol, crumpling to the floor beside the white-haired stranger he had executed moments earlier.

Men fell around him, Rastas and Sicilians, some collapsing silently, others cursing and shouting as they died. It took a moment for the wounded posse chief to realize that there was no more shooting in the smoky box where he lay tangled in a corner, pinned down by a dead man sprawled across his legs.

Frost shoved and kicked the body clear, pain radiating from his wounds with every halting movement. He was able to reload the automatic, even though his hands were going numb. A fallen Rasta brother had the elevator door jammed open, rocking as the door slid back and forth against his ribs.

Frost dragged himself across the fallen bodies, crawling on his belly, grimacing with pain. He reached the hallway, shoved a dead or dying mafioso to the side, and craned his neck to look for Roman Graffia.

The don was on his hands and knees, some twenty feet away. His progress was arrested for the moment, and it looked like he was on the verge of passing out, head dangling toward the floor. From where Frost lay, a spreading crimson stain was visible on Roman's jacket, seeping through one side. A flesh wound? Worse?

Frost rushed the first shot, missing altogether, but the second round struck Roman in the buttocks, knocked him forward, sprawling on his face. When Jason tried to finish it, he found the gun was jammed, somehow, and he did not possess the strength to clear it.

He threw the piece away and kept on crawling, fought the pain with everything he had. It seemed a little better now, in fact, or was he simply going numb?

"I'm coming for you, white meat!"

Underneath his hand, warm steel. His fingers closed around a Colt revolver, blood flecks on the barrel, praying it was loaded. Five or six feet distant, Roman Graffia was turning over, slowly, painfully, to face his enemy.

The capo had a shiny little automatic pistol in his hand.

"I'm all yours, coconut," he said, lips pulled back from his dentures in a ghastly smile.

I don't believe this, Jason thought. *I. Don't. Believe.*

The guns went off together, their reports merged into one.

As JOHNNY REACHED the corridor, he found Grimaldi waiting for him. "This way!" snapped the pilot. "We've got people on the move!"

They passed the kitchen, Johnny wondering about his brother but afraid to ask. He needed concentration now, above all else, the kind of focus that could save your life in killing situations, with a bit of luck thrown in.

Outside, the velvet shades of twilight had descended on Barbados, but the temperature was still mideighties, matching the humidity. The exit served a parking lot, half-filled with cars, and Johnny looked for any sign of movement that would signify a human presence, friend or foe.

A door slammed, somewhere on his right, immediately followed by the sound of a large engine turning over. Tires screeched on the pavement, and he spotted the sedan before its driver finished cranking through a three-point turn.

Thank God for smallish parking lots and inexperienced valets.

Grimaldi ran in one direction, Johnny in the other, trying for a kind of pincers movement. Two men could not technically surround a vehicle—or anything else, for that matter—but they could still try to stop it, take out the driver and passengers before they reached the highway and escaped.

Johnny launched himself across the hood of a Toyota compact, came down painfully and felt a bolt of pain lance through his ankle. Damn it! He refused to let the sprain retard his progress at the final moment, running on a mix of anger and frustration, thinking fast as he lined up the shot.

A local car, not flown in from the United States. The odds against an armored vehicle in Bridgetown would be astronomical. If he could find the range and make his first shots count...

He squeezed off one short burst and saw the windshield glaze, as if with sudden frost. The driver lost it, swerving, plowed into a Volvo with sufficient force to halt his progress. He would have to back up now and try again, if he was still alive. If Johnny gave him the chance.

A second burst ripped through the windshield, found its target at the wheel. The driver's head snapped back, blood spattering the men behind him. Who? The younger Bolan still had no idea, except that they were mafiosi and, as such, his chosen targets.

Doors sprang open, gunmen piling out, and Johnny met the first one with a short burst to the chest. The guy was dead before he toppled over backward, almost tripping a companion emerging from the back seat of the car.

Grimaldi took the second shooter with a burst that punched him forward, facedown on the asphalt. Johnny still had no idea whose men these were, but he was closing on the car regardless, braced for anything. A soldier piled out on the driver's side, unloading with a .45, and Johnny shot him in the face. Before the guy could fall, a second burst from Grimaldi set him spinning like a dervish, long legs tangled in a corkscrew as he hit the deck.

And that left one.

A smallish, gray-haired man was huddled in the back seat, staring at the face of Death as Johnny leaned in through his open door. The boss of Jersey, Joseph Graziano, had no weapon, and his hands were trembling as he raised them shoulder-high.

"You almost made it, Joseph."

"Quote a number," Graziano said. "You want a million dollars? Two?"

"Your money's no good here."

"Three million! Jesus, please!"

"Do you believe in Jesus, Joseph?"

There it was, a glimmer. Graziano took a gamble. "Yeah," he said. "I do."

"Good deal. You see him, where you're going, give him my regards."

The MP-5 stuttered, spewing brass around the inside of the car, Don Graziano twitching as the bullets drilled him, pinned him to his seat. When Johnny lifted off the trigger, Jersey's former capo seemed to melt, a sculpture made of sand, dissolving in the rain.

"We're done here," Johnny told Grimaldi, backing out of the sedan.

Together, they turned back toward the hotel.

ON NINE, Mack Bolan took a moment, caught his breath and peered out through the tiny window in the door that opened off the service stairs. No one was visible from that restricted vantage point, but Bolan knew the risks involved in going farther. If they had guards in the corridor beyond, it would be touch and go. If DiBiase and his men were gone...

The ticking doomsday numbers brought him out of it, and Bolan tried the handle, found the door unlocked. He eased it open, praying that the hinges would not squeal, rewarded by the barest whisper.

Speed. Audacity. The readiness to kill or be killed.

Now!

He lunged into the corridor and took the mafioso watchdogs by surprise. They had been staked out near the elevator, some yards to his left, as if unconscious of the stairway at their backs. One of them now heard him coming, swiveling to greet him, but the hardmen had already lost their chance.

Three of them, sporting guns, and Bolan took them down with one burst each, no more than ten rounds altogether. That left thirty in the mini-Uzi's magazine and one spare left, before he had to fall back on the 93-R for his sole defense.

Three down, and he was moving past their prostrate bodies when a door flew open on his left, beyond the elevators, and an agitated gunner barged into the hall.

"Hey, what the fu—"

A burst of parabellum slugs took his face off, punched him backward through the doorway, dropping with his pudgy legs across the threshold. Bolan pivoted in time to catch another mafioso stepping from a room across the hall, a shotgun braced against his hip. The Executioner plunged headlong to the carpet, firing as he fell, the blast of buckshot gouging out a two-foot pattern on the wall. Return fire from the mini-Uzi slammed the shooter back against the doorjamb, rubber legs collapsing as he died.

In front of Bolan, as he scrambled to his feet, a scared, familiar face. Don Julio ducked back and out of sight before the Uzi spoke again, but Bolan knew his hiding place. The hunter moved relentlessly, alert to any other ambush, stopping short on one side of the door. He crouched, aware that hotel walls were something less than solid in the finest of establishments, and not bulletproof.

Somehow he had to get inside.

A flash, and Bolan knew exactly what he had to do. He crept back to the fallen gunners near the elevator, chose a man about his size, and dragged the corpse upright. With one arm wedged behind the dead man's back, limp hand inside the waistband of his trousers, Bolan had a kind of handle to support his human shield. It wasn't much, but with a little luck, it might combine the elements of shock value and cover, long enough for him to penetrate the suite where Julio had tucked himself away.

He marched back to the door in lockstep with the zombie, forced to juggle his inanimate accomplice as he hit the latch with a resounding kick. The door sprang open, flying back to strike the wall, and Bolan let his front man lead across the threshold.

He caught a glimpse of DiBiase, Vince Scarpato, and an unknown man, gaping at him as he barged into the room. They seemed to recognize the dead man in his grasp, and hesitated firing long enough for Bolan to surprise the nameless gunner with a short burst from his SMG. The guy went over backward, sprawled across a chair that flattened underneath his weight, and that left two.

Scarpato had an automatic in his hand, but it was years since he had pulled a trigger for himself, and Bolan guessed that he had lost his nerve. The Uzi stitched a line of holes across his abdomen from hip to shoulder, slammed him back and out of frame.

And that left one.

Don Julio was firing for effect, his pistol slamming noise and lead at Bolan, scoring hits on Bolan's human shield. The dead man jerked and grunted with the impact of each bullet, almost seeming lifelike in his captor's grasp. One bullet took an ear off, almost grazing Bolan's face on the flyby, and then DiBiase was backing away, cursing as he retreated toward the balcony and tall glass sliding doors.

Bolan brought his mini-Uzi up beneath the dead man's arm and squeezed the trigger, nailing DiBiase with a burst that plucked him off his feet and hurled him through the plate-glass door, collapsing on the balcony outside.

The dead man folded when the Executioner released him, slumping to the floor, and Bolan stepped around the body, moving to the shattered door. The would-be Boss of Bosses was alive but fading fast, his weapon lost somewhere amid the shattered glass and shredded drapes. He stared at Bolan, eyes already glazing over as he tried to speak.

"You can't do this to me," he whispered.

Bolan stared right back at him and said, "It's done."

Below him, somewhere in the heart of Bridgetown, he could hear the sirens of police cars, ambulances, drawing closer by the moment.

They were playing his song.

"You won't believe it," Hal Brognola said. "It's like a Chinese fire drill."

"Don't get ethnic," Barbara Price, the Stony Man Farm mission controller, reminded him.

"Oh, yeah. I keep forgetting. Anyway, you had to be there."

Bolan frowned and said, "I was."

"The rest of it, I mean. You talk about a shock wave. When the word came back from Bridgetown, it was like a flock of headless chickens." Hal turned sideways in his seat to glance at Barbara. "Is a chicken reference politically correct?"

"So far," she said. "They haven't got a lobby yet."

"New York is in a shambles, losing all three capos off the top, along with underbosses. We expect some rumbles in the next few weeks, providing NYPD and the Bureau can't round up the heavy hitters."

"Someone else's problem," Bolan told him. "For the moment, anyway."

"That's what I figure. And New Jersey's not much better. Graziano had a fair successor waiting in the wings, but he's got trouble with the tax man coming up. Could take him off the streets for six or seven years, if he goes down behind it."

"What a shame."

"Miami, who knows what to say? They've got so many dealers in Dade County, I don't think they'll miss old Roman much. His number two went with him, there in Bridgetown, but the infrastructure's more or less intact in Florida. Right now, they're catching more heat from the Cali crowd than from the DEA."

"Those guys deserve each other," Barbara said.

"No argument. You want to hear about Chicago?"

Hal was beaming. Bolan didn't have the heart to let him down.

"Sure thing."

"They're planting Ernie day after tomorrow, a Capone-type funeral. The Windy City loves its rogues."

"Who's moving up?"

"There seems to be a difference of opinion, there," Brognola said. "A youngblood on the South Side has his eye on Cavalcante's chair, but there's a faction out in Cicero that doesn't trust him worth a damn. There could be trouble coming up. I wouldn't be surprised."

"And California?"

"Johnny is supposed to keep us current, but the boys are mourning over Danny Dick right now. Ironically, their pullout from the conference may have saved the Family. At least for now."

"Your people ought to have some angles they can work, before the whole thing gets reorganized."

"We're working," Hal replied. "Believe it. Funny thing about a shooting war, all kinds of weird things get uncovered when the smoke clears. We'll be picking up the pieces from Barbados for the next two months, at least. I wouldn't even want to guess about indictments, but I see no end of trouble for your playmates."

"What a shame."

"I knew you'd sympathize." Hal's smile was very nearly ear-to-ear.

"I think there must be rules against a man deriving this much pleasure from his work," said Bolan.

"Sue me," said Brognola. "It's a rare occasion when I get to crack a smile these days, much less break out champagne."

"Did Leo get that other business squared away?" asked Bolan. Meaning Sharon Pryor.

"Five by five," Brognola said. "The undercover operation was a washout, insofar as DiBiase and LaRocca were concerned, but nothing's wasted. You know that. We're sifting through it now and moving down the ladder. Half the heirs apparent in New York are on our hit list. Talk about your basic power vacuum, I can hear the sucking noise from here."

"I thought that was the pipes downstairs," said Barbara Price.

"Hey, everybody's a comedian. You ready for some dinner, people?"

Bolan considered it, shook his head. "I'll settle for some rest," he said.

Across the table, Barbara caught his eye and kept the smile from showing. "I'm a little tired myself," she told Brognola.

"Jeez, you shrinking violets. Guess I'll have to take that T-bone on all by myself."

"Bon appétit," said Bolan, rising from his chair.

"In case I didn't say it yet, good job." Brognola's face was almost somber now. "The Man is pleased, the Bureau's getting there. Sometimes you win one, eh?"

"Sometimes."

But as he left the situation room, Mack Bolan knew that it would only be a temporary victory, at best. No triumph in his everlasting war was permanent. He might destroy an enemy today, but somewhere, somehow, there would always be another. Waiting for him. Starting out from scratch.

Tomorrow, right.

But there was still tonight, and Barbara Price.

Tomorrow, Bolan thought, would take care of itself.

Gold Eagle presents a special three-book in-line continuity

THE
ARMS
TRILOGY
★   ★

Beginning in March 1995, Gold Eagle brings you another action-packed three-book in-line continuity, THE ARMS TRILOGY.

In THE ARMS TRILOGY, the men of Stony Man Farm target Hayden Thone, powerful head of an illicit weapons empire. Thone, CEO of Fortress Arms, is orchestrating illegal arms deals and secretly directing the worldwide activities of terrorist groups for his own purposes.

Be sure to catch all the action featuring the ever-popular THE EXECUTIONER starting in March, continuing through to May.

Available at your favorite retail outlet, or order your copy now:

Book I:	March	SELECT FIRE	$3.50 U.S.	☐
		(The Executioner #195)	$3.99 CAN.	☐
Book II:	April	TRIBURST	$3.50 U.S.	☐
		(The Executioner #196)	$3.99 CAN.	☐
Book III:	May	ARMED FORCE	$3.50 U.S.	☐
		(The Executioner #197)	$3.99 CAN.	☐

Total amount $_____
Plus 75¢ postage ($1.00 in Canada) $_____
Canadian residents add applicable
federal and provincial taxes
Total payable $_____

To order, please send this form, along with your name, address, zip or postal code, and a check or money order for the total above, payable to Gold Eagle Books, to:

In the U.S.
Gold Eagle Books
3010 Walden Avenue
P. O. Box 9077
Buffalo, NY 14269-9077

In Canada
Gold Eagle Books
P. O. Box 636
Fort Erie, Ontario
L2A 5X3

GOLD
EAGLE®

AT95-2

Nuclear terror strikes from the sea

STONY MAN™ 16
DEEP ALERT

Terrorists exact a high price from America in fear and
bloodshed, but the Stony Man action teams pay back
with interest. The technowarriors at the Virginia command
base provide state-of-the-art intelligence for the surgical
strike force in the field—to carry out Presidential orders
that are always brutal, dirty and dangerous.

Available in May at your favorite retail outlet. Or order your copy now by sending your
name, address, zip or postal code, along with a check or money order (please do not
send cash) for $4.99 for each book ordered ($5.50 in Canada), plus 75¢ postage and
handling ($1.00 in Canada), payable to Gold Eagle Books, to:

In the U.S.	In Canada
Gold Eagle Books	Gold Eagle Books
3010 Walden Avenue	P. O. Box 636
P. O. Box 9077	Fort Erie, Ontario
Buffalo, NY 14269-9077	L2A 5X3

Please specify book title with your order.
Canadian residents add applicable federal and provincial taxes.

SM16

**Adventure and suspense in the
midst of the new reality**

JAMES AXLER
DEATH LANDS®

Shadowfall

The nuclear conflagration that had nearly consumed the world
generations ago stripped away most of its bounty. Amid the ruins
of the Sunshine State, Ryan Cawdor comes to an agonizing
crossroads, torn by a debt to the past and loyalty to the present.

Hope died in the Deathlands, but the will to live goes on.

Available in May at your favorite retail outlet, or order your copy now by sending your
name, address, zip or postal code, along with a check or money order (please do not
send cash) for $4.99 for each book ordered ($5.50 in Canada), plus 75¢ postage and
handling ($1.00 in Canada), payable to Gold Eagle Books, to:

In the U.S.	In Canada
Gold Eagle Books	Gold Eagle Books
3010 Walden Ave.	P. O. Box 636
P. O. Box 9077	Fort Erie, Ontario
Buffalo, NY 14269-9077	L2A 5X3

Please specify book title with order.
Canadian residents add applicable federal and provincial taxes.

DL26

Remo and Chiun stay in the dark
to deflect an evil spectrum in

THE Destroyer

The Color of Fear
Created by
WARREN MURPHY
and RICHARD SAPIR

When a diabolical superscientist turned supercrook
creates a laser that uses color to control emotion, he puts
the world in a kaleidoscope of destruction. CURE goes on
red alert. And the DESTROYER is determined to catch the
enemy blindfolded!

Look for it in April, wherever Gold Eagle books are sold.

Or order your copy now by sending your name, address, zip or postal code, along
with a check or money order (please do not send cash) for $4.99 for each book
ordered ($5.50 in Canada), plus 75¢ postage and handling ($1.00 in Canada), payable
to Gold Eagle Books, to:

In the U.S.	In Canada
Gold Eagle Books	Gold Eagle Books
3010 Walden Ave.	P. O. Box 636
P. O. Box 9077	Fort Erie, Ontario
Buffalo, NY 14269-9077	L2A 5X3

Please specify book title with order.
Canadian residents add applicable federal and provincial taxes.

DEST99

In June, don't miss the second
fast-paced installment of

D. A. HODGMAN

STAKEOUT SQUAD

MIAMI HEAT

Miami's controversial crack police unit draws fire from all
directions—from city predators, local politicians and a
hostile media. In MIAMI HEAT, a gruesome wave of cult
murders has hit Miami, and Stakeout Squad is assigned
to guard potential victims. As panic grips the city, Stakeout
Squad is forced to go undercover…and dance with the
devil.

Don't miss MIAMI HEAT, the second installment of Gold
Eagle's newest action-packed series, STAKEOUT SQUAD!

Look for it in June, wherever Gold Eagle books are sold.

Or order your copy now by sending your name, address, zip or postal code, along
with a check or money order (please do not send cash) for $4.99 for each book
ordered ($5.50 in Canada), plus 75¢ postage and handling ($1.00 in Canada), payable
to Gold Eagle Books, to:

In the U.S.	In Canada
Gold Eagle Books	Gold Eagle Books
3010 Walden Ave.	P. O. Box 636
P. O. Box 9077	Fort Erie, Ontario
Buffalo, NY 14269-9077	L2A 5X3

Please specify book title with order.
Canadian residents add applicable federal and provincial taxes.   SS2

**Don't miss out on the action in these titles featuring
THE EXECUTIONER®, ABLE TEAM® and PHOENIX FORCE®!**

SuperBolan

#61436	**HELLGROUND** In this business, you get what you pay for. Iberra's tab is running high—and the Executioner has come to collect.	$4.99	☐
#61438	**AMBUSH** Bolan delivers his scorched-earth remedy—the only answer for those who deal in blood and terror.	$4.99 U.S. ☐ $5.50 CAN. ☐	

Stony Man™

#61894	**STONY MAN #10 SECRET ARSENAL** A biochemical weapons conspiracy puts America in the hot seat.	$4.99	☐
#61895	**STONY MAN #11 TARGET AMERICA** A terrorist strike calls America's top commandos to the firing line.	$4.99	☐

(limited quantities available on certain titles)

TOTAL AMOUNT	$
POSTAGE & HANDLING	$
($1.00 for one book, 50¢ for each additional)	
APPLICABLE TAXES*	$ _____
TOTAL PAYABLE	$ _____
(check or money order—please do not send cash)	

To order, complete this form and send it, along with a check or money order for the total above, payable to Gold Eagle Books, to: **In the U.S.:** 3010 Walden Avenue, P.O. Box 9077, Buffalo, NY 14269-9077; **In Canada:** P.O. Box 636, Fort Erie, Ontario, L2A 5X3.

Name:_____

Address:_____ City:_____

State/Prov.:_____ Zip/Postal Code: _____

*New York residents remit applicable sales taxes.
 Canadian residents remit applicable GST and provincial taxes.

GEBACK9A